FIC
CARL

HWLCFN

Chicago Public Library

R0400545119

Lucifer's crown

W9-CFA-407

LITERATURE AND LANGUAGE DIVISION
THE CHICAGO PUBLIC LIBRARY
400 SOUTH STATE STREET
CHICAGO, ILLINOIS 60605

LITERATURE AND LANGUAGE DIVISION
THE CHICAGO PUBLIC LIBRARY
400 SOUTH STATE STREET
CHICAGO, ILLINOIS 60605

MAR   2004

LITERATURE AND LANGUAGE
THE CHICAGO PUBLIC LIL
400 SOUTH STATE STREET
CHICAGO, ILLINOIS 60605

Lucifer's Crown

Lucifer's Crown

Lillian Stewart Carl

Five Star • Waterville, Maine

Copyright © 2003 by Lillian Stewart Carl

All rights reserved.

This novel is a work of fiction. Names, characters, places and incidents are either the product of the author's imagination, or, if real, used fictitiously.

First Edition
First Printing: September 2003

Published in 2003 in conjunction with
Tekno Books and Ed Gorman.

Set in 11 pt. Plantin by Al Chase.

Printed in the United States on permanent paper.

ISBN 0-7862-5348-7 (hc : alk. paper)

ßo 400545119
LITERATURE AND LANGUAGE DIVISION
THE CHICAGO PUBLIC LIBRARY
400 SOUTH STATE STREET
CHICAGO, ILLINOIS 60605

Dedication

This book is dedicated to the people who made it possible: Lois McMaster Bujold, Beth Fleisher, John Helfers, Patricia C. Wrede, and most especially to my husband, H. Paul Carl, who believes in me.

I also owe a debt of thanks to the spirit of J. R. R. Tolkien, whose Story has enriched my life.

Chapter One

The gate stood open beneath its ancient stone arch. Maggie Sinclair walked through it into the grounds of Glastonbury Abbey. Turning around, she began, "When you see Salisbury . . ."

Her tiny flock was no longer at her heels. Muttering, "I'm a teacher, not a border collie," she doubled back.

In the dank shadow of the archway two people passed close by her. "I'm telling you, Vivian," the middle-aged man said in a Scottish accent, "there's no good will come of it."

The woman laughed. "Leave it, Calum. No harm in having a bit of a giggle with the group tonight. I'll have a story for the paper."

"Ah, you and your stories for the paper," he retorted.

"I'm a journalist," the English woman said. "Writing stories is what I do."

What's going on tonight? But the couple went on into the Abbey, leaving Maggie's curiosity unsatisfied.

Emerging into the thin October sunlight, she looked right and left along Magdalene Street. *Yeah,* she thought, *there were a lot of things no good would come of.* This trip might be one of them. But it wasn't that she was running away. Teaching was what she did.

Her students were ranged around the corner into Silver Street, taking in the signs and the shops: the Rainbow's End Café, the King Arthur Public House, the National Federation of Spiritual Healers. The Brigit Healing Wing, Pendragon, The Goddess and the Green Man, and the Library of

Avalon. The butcher, the baker, the candlestick maker. The ten-foot-tall gateway of the medieval George and Pilgrim Inn looked like a mouth shaped in an O of astonishment, mirroring the expression on the faces of the three students. "Hello?" Maggie called.

Rose Kildare, the Botticelli angel, smiled. Beefy campus jock Sean MacArthur, Rose's shadow, looked casual. Senior citizen Anna Stern, who seemed fragile but had set the pace on their trek up Glastonbury Tor, said, "Look at the books in this window. The Holy Grail. Astrology. Standing stones and earth energy. Feminism. Ecology. Celtic Revival."

"That's Glastonbury," said Maggie. "It's surrounded by sacred sites dating back thousands of years. During the Middle Ages pilgrims came to see England's most famous collection of Christian relics. Now anything goes."

"The shop owners may sell crystals and aromatherapy candles along with the crucifixes," said Rose, "but the pilgrims are still coming."

Sean shook his head. "Pilgrims? Some of these people are weird."

"Most of us," Maggie began, then amended, "many people are looking for a capital-S Story that will transcend the limits of their own lives. This is why we're doing the legends of Arthur, right? Come on—here you take advantage of the sunshine, you don't hide from it like we do back home in Texas."

She herded the students into the vast expanse of the Abbey grounds. Broken walls and amputated arches sliced through the smooth green lawn. A sixteenth-century manor house rose from its far rim. Medieval slate roofs made a serrated edge beyond the encircling walls. The grassy bulk of Chalice Hill closed the horizon to the east, hiding all of the Tor except for the tower of St. Michael's church at its peak. Billows of white and gray cloud sailed overhead, trailing shadows across the ruins.

The last time Maggie had been here, during the summer, tour buses belching diesel had lined up outside the gate. Now the crows, strutting across the grass like smug prelates, outnumbered the people.

She spotted the couple she'd passed in the archway. Vivian was sitting cross-legged inside the chained-off rectangle where the high altar had once been, probably meditating. A typical Glastonbury moment, both innocent and presumptuous. Calum stood nearby, so still he might have been meditating, too, although in Maggie's experience, men were as likely to meditate as to read instruction manuals.

She said to the students, "When you see Salisbury and Canterbury cathedrals you'll get an idea of what Glastonbury once looked like. Towers, vaults, carvings, colored glass. So much wealth and power concentrated in the hands of a not-always-holy church helped motivate the Reformation."

Pointing, she went on, "Most medieval churches were built in the shape of a cross. Here's the nave in front of us, the long upright where the civilians hang out. There are the transepts, the two short horizontal arms. Beyond them, in the short upright, is the presbytery or chancel, which is priest territory. And the choir, where the monks sang the Office."

Anna and Rose looked toward the arches that had once supported the main tower, now tall stumps. Sean shrugged. "This was in the required reading."

"But we're here now," said Rose. "It's different when it's for real."

What isn't? Maggie called Sean's bluff. "Okay, so what was in the north transept there, and why?"

"The chapel of St. Thomas Becket," he returned with a smirk and a sweep of his camcorder. "These buildings went up right after he was killed at Canterbury."

"All right!" said Maggie. "Go sit down in the choir and we'll get beyond the required reading."

Jostling good-naturedly, Sean and Rose settled next to Anna against the north wall and produced paper notebooks from their backpacks. Maggie had banned individual computers, knowing the lure of chat rooms and games. They could use her laptop to check their e-mail, and their papers weren't due until after they got home in January.

Here in the choir she didn't hear any echo of plainchant, just the thump-thump of a boom box. The guilty party was a kid with spiked purple hair. He'd have a long wait if he was here for the yearly rock festival, known as much for mud as for music.

A man with red hair and a classy leather jacket sauntered across the shadow of the south transept arch. *Nice body,* Maggie thought, but his walk indicated self-absorption. Was he watching Vivian? No. From the angle of his head Maggie deduced he was looking at Rose. Like any male with enough testosterone to merit the definition would not look at Rose.

Two priests in black cassocks strolled along in deep discussion, of the nature of God, perhaps, or the nature of Sunday dinner. Beneath the russet-leaved trees across the way, three figures dressed in white robes raised their arms in prayer. Neo-Druids, guessed Maggie, modern Glastonbury being nothing if not ecumenical.

A wind scented with baking bread and either incense or cider blew her hair across her forehead and impatiently she scooped it away. "The Lady Chapel there was built over the oldest church in Britain. Legend says the Virgin Mary herself was buried here. So many other people had themselves planted nearby, Glastonbury came to be called the graveyard of the saints.

"The well in the crypt of the Lady Chapel may date from an ancient earth mother religion, with its stories of her dying and reviving son. Ditto Glastonbury Tor, and Chalice Well just below. Funny how this is the only spot for ten miles around that you can't see the Tor. Makes you think the first Christians built here to hide something."

"Or from something," said Anna.

Maggie nodded. "Exactly. Legend says the Tor is the gateway to Annwn, the Underworld. Tonight, Halloween, is the old Celtic holy day of Samhain, when the gate opens, the veil between the seen and the unseen thins, and spirits walk among us." She glanced at the couple by the altar. Was Vivian's "bit of a giggle" a Samhain ceremony staged by born-again pagans?

"The fire of 1184 destroyed buildings dating back to a seventh-century Saxon church or an even earlier Celtic one. By the twelfth century Glastonbury was Roman Catholic. There was bloodshed when the Normans moved in, but that's the Normans for you, settling arguments with swords—Becket's martyrdom being an example. You could make a case for him getting himself killed, seeing martyrdom as a good career move."

Anna's brows quirked. Rose grinned. Sean was looking at something behind Maggie's back.

"When the monks were rebuilding they found what they believed was the burial place of King Arthur." She gestured toward another chain-enclosed area. "The stories about him were originally pagan, but Glastonbury claimed them about the same time the stories of the Holy Grail were grafted onto them.

"During the sixteenth century Henry VIII threw the Roman church out of Britain. His troops looted the monasteries and sold the rubble. The eighty-year-old abbot of

11

Glastonbury and two of his monks were accused of hiding treasure and were executed up on the Tor. Religious principles in the service of avarice, or the other way around?"

The students listened, Rose mesmerized, Anna taking notes, Sean's eyes wandering away and then returning. The afternoon faded as the clouds clotted into gray lumps. The wind went from damp and cool to wet and cold. Finally Maggie emerged from the far side of the historical thicket. "Let's hit the museum. Then we'll find a pub and have supper. The local cider comes from that old Celtic cauldron of inspiration—it gives you an inspiring buzz."

With enthusiastic murmurs the students pulled themselves to their feet, Sean helping Anna as well as Rose. They shouldered their packs and headed off like a hip grandmother and her polite grandkids. *Good,* Maggie thought. She had enough to worry about without adding group dynamics to the list.

The grounds were deserted, leaves swirling across the turf. In the metallic light the ravaged walls gleamed like tarnished silver. The place still had its dignity—and its secrets, Maggie told herself.

She laid her hand against the north vault. At first the stone was warm. Then a cold deep as time kissed her palm and sent a shiver up her arm. Gazing up the trajectory of the arch, she imagined a current flowing through flesh and stone alike, connecting earth and sky.

Tonight was All Hallow's Eve, when the church sent its saints to sweep lingering pagan spirits under its rug. Tonight was Samhain, the pagan New Year's Eve. In two months another New Year's Eve would end the year 2000. For sixty days the past and the future would possess the same metaphysical space and time, just as the old and new millennia had done this entire year.

And then? Maggie thought of Dante's *Inferno*: "In the middle of the journey that is life, I came to myself in a dark wood where the straight way was lost." *And I have miles to go before I sleep,* she concluded with a grimace. Her hand wasn't cold anymore, just gritty, as though her morsel of flesh had warmed the ancient stone.

She tucked both hands into her pockets and hurried after the others, telling herself that the only ghosts haunting the twilit ruins were her own.

Rose felt like one of those air-headed kids who couldn't remember what socks were for. The third morning of her first trip overseas and she couldn't find her notebook. She must have left it at the Abbey. Unless Sean had taken it. But it wasn't her notebook he wanted.

Her steps thumped loudly in the mist. The buildings along Magdalene Street weren't indistinct enough to be illusion, but weren't solid enough to be real. Lighted windows made smears of pale yellow, like the haloes Rose used to paint around saints and angels. *The* George and Pilgrim *was five hundred years old,* she thought. The Abbey—the newest Abbey—was eight hundred. The oldest building in Dallas was a log cabin from the 1840s, set on a concrete plaza hot as a pancake griddle.

Here the sky seemed smaller and the horizon closer, even though the houses and shops were so little Rose felt like Gulliver in Lilliput. The air smelled different, soft, damp, hinting of smoke and mildew. Aged air, well-used. And cold. She couldn't remember the last time she'd been cold.

Beyond the Abbey wall, the truncated towers looked like the ghosts of huge cowled monks pacing toward the choir for Matins. Maybe they were going to turn and look down at her as if she were the Lilliputian. Rose had expected Glastonbury to be a place of mystery and romance. It wasn't disappointing her.

The screech of metal against stone echoed from the semicircle of darkness that was the Abbey gate. Good—the custodian was opening up. She plunged past him, saying, "I left something here yesterday, I'll be right back."

"Right you are, Miss," he returned, startled.

The window of the museum gleamed like obsidian to Rose's left. Beneath her feet the cobblestone walk gave way to grass, swallowing the sound of her steps.

Yesterday the ruins had seemed as romantic as a lyric poem. She'd sat against the sun-warmed choir wall, watching a woman do yoga poses on the site of the altar and wondering if that was eccentricity or sacrilege. She'd listened as Maggie's crisp voice softened until she was almost chanting the tales of Joseph of Arimathea and the precious blood of Christ, King Arthur and the Isle of Avalon, the mother goddess and the mother of God.

Now the ruined walls were illegible lines half-erased by the mist. Skeletal tree branches hung motionless overhead. Magdalene Street was quiet, but this shrouded expanse was deathly silent. The sun was rising above the fog, but this gloom was neither daylight or dark. By the calendar it was All Saints' Day, but here it was still Halloween. The cold filtered through Rose's shoes and up her legs, raising goose bumps on her denim-clad thighs. This wasn't the campus, was it, with spotlighted security phones every few steps.

Inhaling the smoke-flavored air, she looked toward the roofless shell of the Lady Chapel, its empty windows opening onto darkness. She imagined light, stained-glass windows, gold reliquaries, candles—and a choir dressed in blue robes, the Blessed Virgin's color, singing the *Stabat Mater* or the *Regina Caeli*. Or the *Magnificat*, her favorite.

She imagined Mary sitting in her bedroom—Rose saw her own room with its posters and books—when suddenly the archangel Gabriel appeared and announced she was going to give birth to the Son of God. Rose would've said, "Wait a minute, how's this going to work?"

But Mary said, "Be it unto me according to thy word." And, "My soul doth magnify the Lord, and my spirit doth rejoice in God my savior, for he hath regarded the low estate of his handmaiden; for behold, from henceforth all generations shall call me blessed."

Not that Rose had any aspirations to sainthood. Or to being anyone's handmaiden, either. It was that her Stories had a soundtrack. She began to sing beneath her breath, *"Magnificat anima mea Dominum . . ."* Then she stopped. Talk about whistling past a graveyard!

But who's watching, anyway? she asked herself. And with a sudden jerk of her heart answered, *he is.*

A human figure stood between the north transept and the site of Arthur's tomb, veiled by the mist. Except for two glints, eyes catching the light like a cat's, Rose saw only a blur for a face . . . It—he—turned toward the darkness, took two strides, and was gone. A cloak or loose coat billowed behind him, radiance shimmering along the floating cloth like the last fiery rim of a bonfire.

She blinked. She really had seen him. And he'd seen her. So she'd been standing there singing, that wasn't any weirder than doing yoga on the altar. Why was he out here so early?

She heard only the slow drip of water in the crypt. The steam of her own breath added to the mist. The back of her neck prickled, but she wasn't going to go back to the hostel and tell everyone she was too scared to get her book.

Up the nave she hurried, glancing warily toward the north transept beneath its broken vault. Of the church proper only

St. Thomas's chapel still had its original walls, making an alcove that this morning was deep in shadow. That's where the man had been standing, next to something . . . Rose peered into the dark chapel and stopped dead. A long white shape lay on the grass, a shape as still and silent as the stones around it.

Oh God. The prickle in Rose's neck merged with the goose bumps on her legs. She forced her feet to carry her forward.

The lines of the woman's naked body were as smooth as those of a marble effigy. She lay on her back, one hand at her side, the other on her breast, fingers curled as though holding an invisible object. Her chalky face and the dark hollows of her eyes looked up to where the sky should have been but wasn't.

It was the yoga woman. *I don't believe this. It isn't happening.* "Hello?" Rose croaked. But the woman's marble-like chest didn't move. From her body emanated not the odor of sanctity, the sweet scent of a saint's incorruptible body, but the stench of mortality and death.

Outside the chapel something moved. Rose spun around with a gasp. A shape and a quick flutter—it must be a bird, one of those big crows they'd seen yesterday. If it was the man he'd be trying to help the—the dead woman. Wouldn't he?

This was a nightmare, yes, but it wasn't a dream. Rose felt the blood drain from her face. Her head spun. All Saints' Day sacrilege pray for us sinners now and at the hour of our death *go for help* . . .

She sprinted toward the gate and the lighted windows of the custodian's lodge.

Chapter Two

Just as Mick walked into the office the phone went. He dropped his rucksack on the desk chair and lifted the receiver. "Dewar Woolen Mills, Mick Dewar speaking."

His father's voice said, "Thank God. I rang the flat, I didna ken where you'd gone."

Mick frowned. He was away to university in Glasgow, where else would he be going on a Monday morning? And he knew he'd given Calum the number of his mobile. "Where have *you* gone, Dad? You didna ring last night. I stopped in at the office to see if you'd left a message with Amy."

Calum's voice was thin and taut and his words stumbled. "I didna have time to ring—I came away from Glastonbury in the wee hours, used up my petrol and stopped outside Carlisle . . . The hounds of hell are after me, Mick."

"Eh? What?"

"There's something you're needing to know. I never told you before, I didna believe it myself, but it's true, it's true . . . My telling you will have them after you as well. God, damned if I do, damned if I dinna."

"What?" Mick's heart drummed in his chest like the drops of water drummed onto the asphalt of the car park outside the window.

His father's ragged exhalation sounded like fabric ripping. "Listen to me. The Bruce's relic, it was at Arbroath not so long since. Sinclair came to my father and me and we helped him shift it."

"Alex Sinclair, your chum from university?"

17

"His father. I met Alex later. I'd say that was a right co-incidence, but nothing's a coincidence, is it? Nothing at all."

Alex had died donkey's years ago, hadn't he? Mick remembered his father lifting his glass in a salute to the dead. Was Calum drunk? Whilst his father had a taste for the whiskey, Mick had never known him to take too much. But then, he hadn't seen overmuch of Calum of late. He had the university, the band, and the lasses.

Calum wasn't drunk. He was exhausted. He was ill. He was terrified. "Dad?" said Mick, his own voice shaking. "I— I'll hire a car, I'll . . ."

"It was our duty then. It's our duty now. Oh God, Mick, I should have told you this long since, but I didna believe it. No time now. Time's run out, it's come to an end. Protect it, Mick keep it from them. From him."

"Protect what? From who?" In the back of his mind Mick heard the voice of his literature lecturer correcting, "from whom."

"From himself. *Am Fear Dubh*. Take the A68 and the A7—the high road, eh?" Calum's voice cracked into a dry giggle. "Take the high rood—road—to Fairtichill, and then the wee road west . . ."

"Dad, you're not sensible."

"Then up you go, toward Schiehallion, the fairy mountain with its triple peak. My grandfather Malise used to tell about that road, and then he'd say each man has to bide his own weird. Meet his own fate."

Something wasn't right with his father's geography, but then, all of this was dead wrong.

"You'll take the high road," Calum crooned. "I'll take the low road past Ercildoune and into the gates of hell. They're coming. They're outside the door. Mick, I . . ." His voice

18

stretched thinner and thinner and then broke.

"Dad? Dad!"

The echoing emptiness of the open line made Mick's head feel hollow. He stared at the receiver. His hand was numb. Pins and needles danced along his arm. Cold sweat ran down his back. *Oh God.*

The office smelled as it had always done, of wool, paper, and old sausage sandwiches. Beyond the window the rain fell. Puddles on the pavement reflected the orange glow of the street lights. Above the sign reading "Dewar's Fine Woolens" rose the distant, gnarled outline of Edinburgh Castle, half-erased by the mist and the gloom.

"I dinna believe this," Mick said. "It's not happening."

It was happening. And he was sitting there like a gowk. He batted at the phone cradle. When he heard the ordinary electronic pips of British Telecom he punched "999."

"Emergency services."

"Mick Dewar here. My father rang from a petrol station outside Carlisle. He's ill, off his head . . . Aye, I'll wait."

He threw his rucksack on the floor. It hit with a solid thunk, spilling books and folders and the long case of his practice chanter. If he didn't get himself to his lecture and hand in his essay he'd be docked points. Right now he didn't give a damn for either the lecture or the essay.

He dropped onto the chair. On the desk stood the snap taken last spring, of him with his father in front of Dunnottar Castle. The stark ruins on their cliff above the sea looked like a studio backdrop behind the two smiling faces. Faces that were strikingly similar: square chins, keen gray eyes accented by supple eyebrows, high foreheads fringed by dark hair, Calum's silver at the temples, Mick's caught in a ponytail.

That day Calum went on about a braw lassie smuggling the crown of Scotland away from besieged Dunnottar. The crown was a relic, right enough, but it was safe in Edinburgh Castle.

That had been their only outing this year. Mick no longer had time for playing tourist. Now his dad was on his own, ill, hurt, far from home . . . Mick slammed his fist onto the top of the desk. The picture fell over.

He crammed the books back into his rucksack. On top lay *Idylls of the King and other Poems* by Tennyson. One passage leapt suddenly to his mind: "The curse has come upon me, cried the Lady of Shalott."

"Hello?" said the dispatcher in his ear. "Mr. Dewar?"

"He sounded as though his curse had come upon him," said Mick.

"Sorry?"

"His fate, his doom. His weird." Mick pulled a face. He was havering, daft as Calum. "My father rang me from a petrol station. He's off his head, he needs help. Carlisle. The car's a Ford Mondeo . . ."

His hand clenched round the phone. He was going to bloody well find out what had happened to his father. And then he'd sort it out.

Maggie added a spoonful of sugar and a dollop of milk to the mug, and pressed it into Rose's hands. The British regarded tea as a specific against anything from toothache to war. When in Britain do as the Brits do. There wasn't much else she could do.

It had been an hour since Rose ran into the youth hostel as though the hounds of hell were at her heels. Her hands were at last starting to warm up. Her color was better, too, if her features were still pinched. Although even in shock she was beautiful. With her fresh complexion and waves of golden hair Rose fulfilled the promise of her name, all the more lovely because she seemed artlessly unaware of her beauty.

Turning forty, Maggie informed herself, *isn't so bad you have to envy a twenty-year-old girl who looks her age.*

Sean buffed the far end of the dining table, adding the smell of polish to those of disinfectant and bacon, his face carefully neutral. He was a handsome young man, yes. His manner ranged just far enough between cocky and callow to be charming. But Maggie sensed something deliberate in both.

She told herself, *so you're down on men. You don't have to get your back up because a twenty-year-old boy acts his age.*

"Sorry I went off by myself. I should've asked Sean to go with me, but I didn't . . ." Rose glanced at the young man's broad back.

Maggie filled in the rest of the sentence, *want to encourage him,* and said aloud, ". . . think there would be any danger. Of course not. Small town, a civilized country—uh-oh. Here we go."

A man in a dark suit thrust open the doors of the vestibule and walked into the dining room. "Good morning. I'm Detective Inspector Jivan Gupta, Somerset Constabulary." Although he wasn't a large man, he carried himself like a king—or a maharajah. His mahogany complexion was cut horizontally by a splendid black moustache. Similarly black hair was trimmed in a military style.

Maggie started to run her fingers through her own short, thoroughly undisciplined auburn hair and caught herself. "Good morning."

Pulling out a chair, Gupta sat down. From his inside pocket he produced pen and notepad. "Miss Kildare? Do you mind answering a few questions?"

"Anything I can do to help." Rose shoved the mug away, set her chin, and sat up straight.

Maggie extended her hand. "I'm Maggie Sinclair. Instructor in British History, Southern Methodist University, Dallas, Texas. I'm leading the seminar group."

"Dr. Sinclair." Gupta's handshake was brisk and firm.

Maggie's jaw tightened. "No. Just 'Ms.' "

"How many students do you have, Ms. Sinclair?"

"Three."

Sean left the polishing cloth lumped on the table and leaned against the fireplace. "My name's Sean MacArthur."

"I'm Anna Stern." Anna stepped into the room, propped her broom against the wall, and sat down.

Anna's contained movements, her whip-thin body, her cap of silver hair made her resemble an ambulatory Ionic column. While Maggie insisted on "Ms.," Anna was unaffectedly "Mrs.," a widow pursuing her intellectual interests, not a political agenda. *You don't have to envy a sixty-five-year-old's composure, either,* Maggie instructed herself.

Gupta asked, "You're stopping here at the youth hostel, are you?"

"Just for two nights," Maggie replied. "Today we're moving to the B&B where we'll be staying until the end of the year. Temple Manor on Old Beckery Road, about a mile west of the Abbey."

"Ah, yes. The former owner is a great friend of mine."

"Thomas London, the historian?"

"Yes." Gupta nodded. "You'll be stopping in Somerset until the end of December?"

"We rejoin the other groups in London at Christmas, attend the New Year's Eve concert at Canterbury, and get home the first week of January."

Gupta wrote that down. "Now then, Miss Kildare. Soon after entering the Abbey this morning you found the body of a woman. You told P.C. Barnes you weren't in the grounds above five minutes. The custodian agrees."

"It seemed longer than five minutes," Rose said in a steady voice.

"No doubt. Why did you go into the Abbey before it opened?"

"I left my notebook there yesterday. At least, I think that's where my notebook is."

"But you didn't collect your book?"

"No."

"Our lads haven't turned one up. Can you describe it?"

"It's an ordinary spiral-bound notebook with a red cardboard cover. My name's inside."

"Did you see anyone in the Abbey grounds?"

"Yes," answered Rose. "A man—at least, he walked like a man—was standing next to the north transept, maybe thirty yards away from me. He made eye contact for just a second, then—well, he just melted away into the mist."

"Description?"

"Hard to say. He was wearing a loose coat or a cloak—you know, there was cloth fluttering behind him. A dim light shone around it, like he was carrying a flashlight."

"A torch."

"No, a flashlight."

"Same thing, here," murmured Maggie.

"An electric torch." Gupta's teeth flashed in a quick grin. "And?"

"His eyes were weird," Rose added. "Shiny, like a cat's."

"The custodian didn't see anyone enter or leave," Gupta went on, "but climbing the wall's no trouble. The Abbey attracts all sorts, toe-rags, travelers, layabouts. People looking out a place to kip."

And people looking for a Story, Maggie thought.

"We saw a couple of weirdoes in sleeping bags up on the

Tor yesterday morning," said Sean. "They must've been whacked out on something to spend the night in the cold."

"Perhaps they felt the holiness, not the cold," Gupta told him.

"Is holiness in the eye of the beholder?" asked Anna.

"Not necessarily," he answered. "Now, Miss Kildare, was the man standing just beside the dead woman?"

"No, but close enough he must've seen her."

"You saw only this one man?"

Rose shifted uneasily. "Right after I found the—I found her—I heard a noise. I thought the guy had come back, but it was just a bird. I think."

The cold shiver already tightening the back of Maggie's neck started to drip queasily into her stomach.

"We'll make inquiries," said Gupta. "The man might could come forward on his own. If nothing else, perhaps *he* saw something or someone."

"How long had she been dead?" Rose asked. "Do you know?"

"Our best guess just now is that she died between one and four this morning."

"You couldn't have helped her." Maggie patted the young woman's arm.

Rose sighed acceptance. "Do you at least know who she is?"

"Not yet," replied Gupta. "You told P.C. Barnes you thought you recognized her?"

"I think I saw her at the Abbey yesterday afternoon."

Gupta reached into his pocket, pulled out an instant photo, and laid it on the table. "Take your time."

Rose's clear blue eyes narrowed in something between thought and pain. She bit her lip and released it. "That's her. She was doing yoga exercises where the altar used to be."

"She was?" Maggie reached for the photo.

Her glasses were upstairs, but still she could see this picture altogether too well. A human body rendered every courtesy, painted and permed and displayed on satin cushions, still seemed cruelly empty. This woman's poor neglected flesh was obscene. Even so, Maggie recognized the woman's dark hair and eyes and heart-shaped face. "I saw her walking into the Abbey with a man. Later I saw her sitting on the site of the altar, but I missed the yoga poses. My back was turned. As usual."

Gupta drew himself to attention. "She was with a man?"

"A middle-aged man with a Scottish accent. He said something to her along the lines of, 'No good will come of this, Vivian.' And she answered, 'Nothing wrong with having a giggle with the group tonight, Calum. I'll get a story for the paper.' He came back, 'You and your stories,' and she came back, 'I'm a journalist. Writing stories is what I do.'"

"They were arguing?"

"Disagreeing. He seemed to be worried about this group gathering, while she wasn't. I would've thought he was her father except for the difference in accents."

"Hers was English, then?"

"Yes. I've been to the U.K. often enough I can pick up the regional accents," Maggie explained.

Gupta didn't quibble. "This is all very helpful. Thank you, Ms. Sinclair."

"You're welcome," Maggie said. Funny, people usually didn't think her curiosity was at all helpful.

"Did the man—Calum—have odd, shiny eyes at all?"

"I didn't notice." Maggie looked again at the photo. What had Vivian been holding in her hand that now curved so suggestively around thin air? Shaking her head, she handed the photo back to Sean.

25

He went a bit pale around the gills, then recovered himself with a grimace worthy of John Wayne. "Yeah, that's the woman from the altar. She was hard to miss, contorting herself like that. And she was wearing a tight sweater under her coat, she was really . . ."

Stacked. Maggie finished for him. Yes, Vivian had a voluptuous figure. She'd probably spent years dieting, and now look at her.

Sean passed the photo on to Anna and shrugged, a nonchalant gesture that Maggie, through long and often grim experience with the male species, had learned to interpret as embarrassment.

Handing the photo back to Gupta, Anna said solemnly, "Yes. She was exercising on the site of the altar."

"Did she seem despondent at all?" Gupta looked around the room.

"No," Maggie replied. "She seemed very pleased with herself."

"Yeah," said Sean. "She was kind of grinning up at a guy in an overcoat—I guess that was Calum—like she was coming on to him."

Rose shook her head. "No, not like that. Like she was showing off for him. But he just looked serious and kind of sad."

"Suicides," said Anna, "can be very cheerful once the decision is made, believing peace to be at hand. If that's why you asked, Inspector."

Maggie visualized the agonized ghosts of suicides in the *Inferno* and thought, *peace?*

"Yes," Gupta said, "that's why I asked."

"You think she lay down out there on purpose, so she would die of exposure?" Rose asked faintly.

"She could have done. Although now that you tell me she

was after going to a party, I'm thinking she could have been drunk or drugged, and didn't know what she was doing."

Samhain, Maggie thought. When the Unseen becomes visible. When the spirits of the dead walk the Earth. A night that in the twentieth century had become an excuse for role-playing and trick-or-treating. "She could have been killed somewhere else, and her body dragged into the Abbey."

Rose's eyes widened. Sean's brows rose. Anna tilted her head. A spark danced through the depths of Gupta's dark eyes and vanished. "No one's said anything about murder, Ms. Sinclair."

"No, of course not. I've got too good an imagination," Maggie said quickly, and wondered just what that spark signified.

"Did you find her clothes?" asked Sean.

"Yes, piled in the corner of the chapel. Ordinary undergarments, tights, a long white dress. No coat. No handbag. And the one curious item, the sheath of a small knife. But we didn't find a knife anywhere about."

Maggie asked herself, *why not?* And she didn't like her answer.

"But she wasn't stabbed?" asked Sean.

"Not a mark on her, so far as I could tell, but the pathologist will be drawing his own conclusions. I'll issue a bulletin for this Calum chap and ask Vivian's friends to come forward. Did you take particular notice of anyone else at the Abbey yesterday?" Gupta looked from face to face. Every pair of eyes looked back at him, but it seemed to Maggie that only hers showed apprehension. *Too good an imagination.*

She remembered the two priests. The Druids. The guy with the leather jacket and the kid with the boom box. Assorted tourists. She shook her head. No one else had anything to offer, either.

Gupta clicked his pen. "Right. If you would be so good as to call in at the station and give us statements before you relocate?"

"No problem," Maggie answered.

"I knew travel was broadening," Rose said, "but I'm going to have stretch marks on my brain."

"Believe me, this was not supposed to be part of the curriculum."

"One of my roommates found a body while he was playing paintball," said Sean. "The cops said he'd been shot in a drug deal. Probably deserved what he got."

"All life," said Anna, "deserves dignity."

Gupta knew a good exit line. Pocketing his note pad, he stood up and started for the door. "Thank you. I'll keep you informed."

The students murmured various courtesies. Maggie, too, stood up. "I'll see you out."

Gupta held the doors for her and they walked out into the morning. Even though the sky was still lidded with gray, the mist was thinning. Nearby buildings looked almost like solid structures. A sign on one read, "Moon Childe Shoppe. Candles, crystals, aromatherapy, aura soma readings, vegetarian meals. Credit cards accepted. Discounts for Bodhisattvas." The window was filled with bright, shiny baubles and beads. Just what a Bodhisattva, a being who turned away from nirvana to help humankind, would want with baubles and beads Maggie couldn't say.

Gupta folded his hands behind his back. His eyes, gleaming jet on mother of pearl, surveyed the Moon Childe Shoppe without the least spark of amusement or condescension. It was Maggie's suggestion of murder that had kindled a response.

Better to be thought a fool than to speak and remove all doubt, she reminded herself. But since when had looking like a fool ever stopped her? "Vivian could have intended to die. Maybe she saw herself as Ophelia or the Lady of Shalott, beautiful and pitiable. Still, I can't shake the feeling that Vivian was no suicide. Last night was Samhain, as I'm sure you know."

"Yes. The Wicca group held their bean-feast and bonfire out beyond Baltonsborough. Had a bit of a row with another group, I hear."

"Not so long ago your job would've been to make a bonfire of the Wiccans themselves, to the greater glory of God, of course."

"I believe in England witches were hanged," Gupta said equably.

Persisting, Maggie curled her fingers against the breast of her sweater, miming the dead woman's pose. "The sheath you found with Vivian's clothes. Was she holding in her hand the knife that went with it?"

"It's likely, yes."

"What if the man Rose saw this morning took it?"

There was that spark again, many sparks, a meteor shower flaring in Gupta's eyes. "You're thinking the man in the cloak is involved with Vivian's death and was trying to conceal evidence when he was interrupted by Miss Kildare?"

"He knows she saw him." Maggie exhaled through pursed lips. "Please tell me I'm just going overboard. That Rose isn't a witness. That she's not in danger from this guy."

"I can't tell you that. You may be right. Even though," Gupta cautioned, "this is all conjecture."

"Then here's another conjecture for you. Iron was once considered to be a talisman against evil spirits. It still is, in some circles. Maybe the same circles that believe spirits, good, bad, or indifferent, were out for a stroll last night. What if Vivian died as the result of a ritual? That would still be murder, wouldn't it?"

"It certainly would," he said. "If there are any local groups capable of murder, though, they're keeping themselves well hidden."

"They would, wouldn't they?"

"Most of the neo-pagans—and some others I could name—are harmless loonies. On occasion one group or another will overdose on psychologically potent symbols, yes, and create an unhealthy situation, but you can say that of any group searching for meaning."

"No kidding. Since the beginning of 2000 didn't bring anything but a few computer glitches, the apocalypse crew has gotten even louder."

"Most of the world believes in neither the millennium nor the apocalypse," Gupta pointed out.

"Like that Zen tree that's forever falling in the forest—if you don't believe in it, does it exist?"

"Mind over matter. Scientists tell us the Ganges River is teeming with lethal bacteria, but when the faithful bathe in its sacred waters, they come away purified."

And that is evidence of things unseen, thought Maggie. *Faith.*

A truck passed, changing gears as it struggled up the rising ground to the east. Up what had been the coastline of the Isle of Avalon—if you believed the Matter of Britain, the stories of Arthur, the quest for the Holy Grail. There were worse things to believe.

The wrinkled, green face of Glastonbury Tor loomed through the mist. Supposedly the terraces on its sides were the remains of an ancient ritual pathway, a labyrinth. The tower on its top did resemble a monolith marking a place of power. Or a tiny stone spear impaling the hump of a huge dragon. Churches dedicated to St. Michael the dragon slayer often occupied ancient high places considered gates to the

Underworld. The Otherworld.

"Christianity," Gupta said, "has a spot of bother excusing the existence of evil if God is wholly good, although Thomas London tells me that evil comes from within man, not from God. The great Hindu gods combine benevolence and malevolence, creation and destruction, in the same beings. Pagans think that supernatural forces are inherent in the earth itself, forces that are never impersonal, but are very much involved, intelligent, even ironic."

"And which have to be placated?"

"Acknowledged. The sort of thing that was going on last night." Gupta's smile was lopsided, angling his moustache upward. "Here, we could discuss the nature of faith all day if we'd no jobs to go to."

Shows where my mind is, Maggie thought.

"I'm a policeman, not a philosopher, certainly not a holy man. But I'm telling you this: I've lived here fifteen years. My wife's a native. Glastonbury is one of the world's great holy places. Odd things happen here, and no mistake."

Was Gupta, the Glastonburian, making fun of a gullible tourist-cum-pilgrim? No. He was dead serious. So was the woman Rose had found in the Abbey.

All Maggie had wanted in coming here was a chance to visit Britain again. To teach—and to remind herself—that intelligence wasn't something to be ashamed of. To make a start, however feeble, at the rest of her life. And now? "So I get to play bodyguard as well as teacher, chauffeur, and mother. Great."

"It's early days yet," Gupta said reassuringly. "We'll have it sorted soon as may be. As for Rose—well, you'd better be cautious is all."

"I'll try to contain myself. Thank you." Maggie managed a smile.

Touching his forefinger to his eyebrow, Gupta strode away up the street.

Her smile crumpling, Maggie started back into the hostel. She'd better call Bart Conway, the coordinator in charge of all the seminar groups, before he saw a newspaper using "SMU" and "mysterious death" in the same sentence. And they were expected not only at the police station but at Temple Manor. Plus Rose needed to get to St. Mary's for the All Saints' Day mass. At least she'd be safe there . . .

Maggie told herself not to worry about Rose or the Lady of Shalott, about pilgrimage and belief, about faith and credulity and what might crawl into the cracks in between. But she knew she would.

Chapter Three

Thomas London watched as the mist at last grew silvery, then transparent, and then in ephemeral strands was sucked into the blue afternoon sky like Dante's blessed souls ascending into heaven. He liked Dante, even though the Italian poet had made a more compelling story of the Inferno's torments than of Paradise with its unfolding rose of angels.

Gulls squawked overhead. A car sped past. To the west a quarter moon sank toward the horizon. To the east, beyond the lichened slate roof of the manor house, Glastonbury Tor gleamed in the sun. At this distance the tower looked little larger than a pin.

In the seventh century Pope Gregory had ordered his missionaries not to destroy the ancient temples of Britain, but to set up altars and relics and replace pagan sacrifices with church festivals. Some of the old gods had then been named demons. Some had been named saints. With a wry smile at God's sense of humor, Thomas ducked through the narrow doorway into the chapel. In the cold, musty shadows his breath resembled a wraith.

Today pilgrims were returning to the holy place of Glastonbury, reclaiming their roots. Today mankind stood in the center of the labyrinth and contemplated its path out again. Today, All Saints' Day, the new year overlapped the old as the new millennium overlapped the old. The End Time had come at last.

Switching on a light bulb, he gazed searchingly up at the rood. The crucifix, flanked by two carved figures, stood above the ancient screen dividing the tiny nave from an even smaller chancel. The faces of Our Lord, St. John, and St. Mary Magdalene were deeply shadowed, and revealed nothing of the future.

Very well then. He had his work. Below the desiccated wooden lace of the screen seven canopies—three on one side of the opening into the chancel, four on the other—marked niches for the portraits of saints. So far he had completed St. Joseph of Arimathea, St. Bridget, and St. Denis, the fresh colors of the new paintings glowing amongst the ghosts of the old. Now Thomas squeezed out a blotch of lapis lazuli and dabbled his brush in it. Kneeling, he touched the brush to the blue cloak of Mary, Queen of Heaven.

The sound of footsteps made him spin around. "Ah—Alf. Good afternoon."

"And to you, Thomas." Alf Puckle squeezed through the door. "Here's the mobile. Canon O'Connell wants a word."

Thomas wiped his hands and reached for the tiny device. "I never intended for you to play my secretary, Alf. These modern contrivances that are to be our servants make servants of us."

"Right you are," Alf said with a chuckle. "No rush bringing back the phone, Bess and I are laying on a high tea for the Americans. There's always an extra scone for you."

"Thank you." Thomas waited until Alf had paced away, then raised the telephone to his face. "Good afternoon, Ivan."

Ivan O'Connell's cultured voice said, "I'm afraid it's not that good an afternoon, Thomas. The relic has been stolen."

The relic. The Word as a work of Art. The book known as the Lindisfarne Gospels. Thomas sagged as though an assailant had just delivered a blow to his stomach. So it was happening, then, after all.

"The curators of the British Library moved the Book to the new building two years ago," O'Connell went on. "Or thought they had done. But Jane Buckley, their authority on medieval manuscripts, noticed that some details of the artwork were wrong. She made tests, and has pronounced their book a forgery."

"A forgery," Thomas repeated.

"The thief went to the trouble to use the appropriate parchment and ink, and to copy the drawings line for line and color for color. Save that the copy is perfect."

"Those details of the patterns the original artist left unfinished, to show his humility, are now complete."

"Yes, just that. Jane, knowing my keen interest in the Book, rang me this morning."

"Is the cover of the copy a forgery as well?"

"No, it's the 1853 metalwork cover. An ordinary thief would pry off the gems and melt down the silver, I suppose, but . . ."

". . . an ordinary thief would not have gone to such great lengths to duplicate the Book. Nor would he have the resources to do so." But then, Thomas told himself with grim certainty, Robin Fitzroy was no ordinary thief.

"Scotland Yard are interviewing everyone who had access to the Book during the move," O'Connell went on.

"The secular authorities do excellent work. Even though I doubt if the theft of the Book is totally within their sphere, I trust you'll keep in contact with them."

"Of course. Thomas, I must confess that when old Lionel Weston told me a canon of Canterbury has been the guardian of the Lindisfarne Gospels ever since the Book was brought south, and asked me to succeed him in that post, I thought the entire business was one of those English traditions preserved under glass, a quaint custom whose origins have been lost. Thanks to you, I'm no longer certain of that."

"Thanks to you," Thomas said, "for bringing me the news."

Outside, automobile doors slammed. Judging by the cries of "awesome" and "is this cool or what?" the Americans had arrived. Those young, unclouded voices made Thomas feel dreadfully old and tired.

"Well then," O'Connell said. "How are you getting on with the chapel?"

"I'm just now finishing the portraits on the rood screen."

"Lovely. I'll be there December twelfth for the re-conse-cration."

December twelfth. Six short weeks away, with the end of the year soon after. Judgment Day, perhaps. Perhaps the Apoca-lypse, that old Greek word meaning "revelation." Thomas had intended for this chapel to be his offering to a Glastonbury renewed in faith as well as to God. But now he wondered if his work would, at the end, be naught but mockery.

"I'll remember you and the Book in my prayers," O'Connell concluded. "May the blessings of All Saints' Day be with you."

"And with you, Ivan." Thomas switched off the phone and thrust it into the pocket of his coat. Odd, how close the air of the chapel had become. Like that of a tomb, dank and heavy with an acrid odor he knew to be that of paint but felt was that of his own dishonored soul.

He'd hoped to slip quietly through the End Time, passion spent, purpose fulfilled, redeemed at last. But that hope had always been presumption. Of course his nemesis would chal-lenge him, now, at the end. Of course he would take up that challenge. As he'd taken up the challenge long ago, and then, at the sword's point, allowed the consequences to fall upon a bystander? Thomas clenched his jaw so tightly the muscle cramped.

His relic was safe. But the Book, the relic he'd wishfully thought to be safe in plain sight, had been stolen. Would the secular authorities turn it up in time? He doubted it. And what of the others? It was long past time for him to stop assuming they were safe and ask. Ask most especially Alex Sinclair, who was not himself the guardian of a relic but a knight in its service. This secular world regarded many things as nothing more than quaint customs.

"I know what needs doing," Thomas said to the as-yet blank face of the Blessed Mother. "But now, more than ever, I am incapacitated by my guilt."

Laughter echoed outside. The light bulb flared and winked out. And in that moment, between light and darkness, the portrait of St. Bridget blinked her compassionate blue eyes. The statue of Mary Magdalene looked down at him, her brown eyes gleaming with irony. The cloak of the Blessed Virgin rippled blue and green, like the sea encircling a holy island—St. Cuthbert's stormy Lindisfarne, or the antediluvian stone of St. Columba's Iona.

Shadows gathered densely in the corners, but around Thomas himself they lay like gauze. An elusive odor of fresh flowers teased his nostrils. With a sharp inhalation of terror and gratitude mingled he dropped to his knees. "Blessed St. Mary, Blessed St. Bridget, Blessed Virgin Mother." He stared from face to face to face. Bridget's eyes were flat paint. Mary Magdalene's eyes were hollow carved wood. The Blessed Virgin's cloak was streaks of blue paint, incomplete. As the patterns of his life were incomplete.

"*Ave Maria gratia plena,*" Thomas began, and by the time he concluded, "*et in hora mortis nostrae,*" his hair was no longer prickling on his neck. "Thy will be done," he said, and groaning he stood.

How difficult it was to say "Thy will be done" and know it was indeed God's will and not his own. All he could do was be receptive to signs and portents. He had just been given three. Now what? He limped to the arrow-slit of a window. Crisp air curled through the opening. Outside this chapel, his cell, the garden bloomed in its fall reds and purples. An angelic voice said, "Hello there."

Startled, Thomas saw a young woman sit down on the bench beside the hedge.

"Come on, come here," she said. Dunstan, the resident cat, leaped up and settled onto her blue jeans, gazing adoringly into her face as she stroked his sleek fur.

As well he should. Thomas had noticed the same young woman at St. Mary's on Sunday, as well as at the All Saints' mass only hours ago. How could he not? She was beautiful, with hair like spun gold and cheeks like rose petals. But today the curves of her brows and lips were pinched. Even the fairest flower could feel the frost.

She turned her face to the sun, revealing eyes the same lucid blue as those he'd given St. Bridget. The ache in Thomas's heart eased. No wonder angels were often depicted as young women. A woman, Mary Magdalene, had been the first to recognize the risen Christ, the Word made flesh. A woman scholar had acknowledged the truth about the counterfeit Book . . .

Truth. The truth might make him free, hard as it would be to confess outside the seclusion of the confessional. But who would believe his story? Thomas had friends of the intellect, but no friend of the soul. He'd expected to pass through the End Time alone, as always, and to conclude his purpose whether healed or not. And yet, now, he saw that without truth there could be no healing. And without healing he could not fulfill his purpose.

Sunlight poured over the roof of Temple Manor. Glastonbury Tor and its tower reached heavenward. Tautly, Thomas smiled. Of all things, the Tor made him feel young and vigorous again. If never as young as the angelic maiden, brought to his doorstep by the hand of a merciful God—even though he didn't yet know why.

Telling himself that one must correct *Magnificat* before learning *Te Deum*, he stepped from the tomb into the garden.

"Ellen," said a silken voice. "Wakey, wakey."

Ellen Sparrow turned over and kicked at the blanket. The gray air stank of diesel and rubbish. From beneath the window came the mutter of engines, voices, and footsteps. Robin stood at the edge of the bed, staring down at her with those brilliant green eyes she found both compelling and uncanny. Even in the shadows his red hair gleamed. She hadn't heard him open the door.

"Why are you wearing Vivian's glad rags?" she asked.

"I thought I'd keep the cloak. It's Scottish wool, after all. It'll remind me of how easily women can be corrupted." He spread his arms wide, so that the green cloak opened out into a semi-circle like a Romish priest's robe. Gold stitching in elaborate snaky patterns edged the neck and the front opening. Beneath the cloak he was still wearing the posh suit and tie he'd worn last night. He deserved the best. Wearing the cloak, he'd purify it, and no mistake.

Last night he'd gone away with Vivian, not Ellen. For good reason, she reminded herself. "Did you settle with the cow?"

"Vivian? She'll not be troubling us any more."

"She was never one of us, was she?"

39

Robin's pink lips curved into a smile, but his eyes remained hard. "No. She served her purpose, though."

Last night Ellen had been one of the family. She'd waded into the fray alongside Reg, ahead of the others, breaking and kicking. She could still hear the cries of the unbelievers as they ran, and the satisfying smash of her cricket bat against their idols. For an hour, she'd been strong.

She sat up. Her mouth tasted of acid. "The cleansing went down a treat, right enough."

"Yes, it did. A pity the constabulary were so quick to respond, but then, they'll learn right from wrong soon enough." In a swirl of green and gold Robin turned to inspect the CDs stacked on a shelf. He picked up the Mozart *Requiem*. A spasm of his fingers cracked it like an egg and tossed the broken bits aside. "You don't need this."

"Calum gave it me."

"Did he give you these, too?" Robin's forefinger tapped the stack of paperback books piled next to Ellen's special-edition Bible.

"Yeh. He says I have a good mind."

Robin's eyes glinted. "Who is the truth, the path, and the light?"

"You are, Robin. You're the business."

"I'll tell you what you need to know. If there's anything in a book I haven't taught you, then it's blasphemy. If there's anything in a book I have taught you, then it's redundant. Calum should know better than to muddle his mind and yours with books."

"Yeh," Ellen agreed, adding, "Why did he bugger off so sudden-like last night?"

"He had to get back to his business." Robin stepped across to the basin. He upended a cup, dribbling brown water, and rapped it smartly against the tap. The cup shattered. His elegant fingertips chose a shard shaped like a leaf-bladed spear. "Ellen, I have work for you to do in Glastonbury."

"Yeh, anything." She clawed her hair away from her face. She'd used the last of her shampoo and hadn't the cash to buy more. To buy food, for that matter. Last night Reg had bought her a takeaway curry, all the while grumbling about sods too lazy to work. But she was working, for Robin.

She'd met him last year, when he saw her pinch that Yank tourist's pocketbook. He hadn't shopped her to the cops. He'd told her that soon money wouldn't matter. Soon the toffs in their posh cars and posh clubs, the skinny little birds who'd slagged her off for her clothes, the pillocks at school who teased her and then used her body—all of them would be consumed by the fires of Armageddon whilst she would be taken up to heaven alongside Robin himself, if only she believed.

Ellen crawled from the bed. Her bare feet slipped on the newspaper cuttings scattered across the linoleum—rallies, revivals, marches, pilgrimages—explosions, massacres, assassinations.

The green cloak billowed round Robin's body even though the room was close and still. She slipped beneath it and wrapped her arms around his ribs. Slender ribs, strong as stone.

He wrapped her in the cloak. His body was cold as death and she shivered. But she held on. His beard tickled her ear. His icy lips traced a path along her jaw until they found hers. His tongue, tasting of wine and flowers, slipped inside her mouth like a snake, probing, pushing, pursuing until she was bent backward against the basin. His right hand moved up her body beneath the T-shirt and his left pressed the crockery spear against her temple. It pricked, and she felt the blood run down into her hair. "Are you baptized in the one true faith?" he murmured.

"Yes."

His thumb smeared the warm blood across her forehead. "Are you bathed in the blood of the ram?"

"Yes, oh yes. Please, Robin, love me."

His eyes glinted green as gemstones. In one movement he spun her about, threw her down on the bed, and fell on her. Ellen clutched at him, cloak and all. She didn't like this part, but then, she wasn't any good at it, or so the sods at school told her. It didn't matter. Robin had chosen her, alone of all her sex.

She gasped in pain and ecstasy both as he drove himself into her. He was cold, and hard, like iron. But when he was inside her she wasn't empty any more. Better cold than nothingness. Better pain now, and in the future the ultimate reward.

From the corners of her eyes she saw the posters covering the stains on the wallpaper whirling like confetti, film actors and rock stars and prints of works by old foreigners Calum had given her—Nativity, Crucifixion, Rolling Stones. Robin's voice was soft and subtle in her ear, "I am the way and the life. Who believes in me shall never die."

Outside a bus bleated. The sunlight faded. Robin's body crushed her against the bed, again and again. "Love me," she whimpered.

The gold stitches on the green cloak shone like a bonfire. In the glory of gold and green the room disappeared and Ellen Sparrow glimpsed the light eternal. But as yet it was beyond her grasp. "Love me. Please, love me."

Robin laughed. In spite of her clenched jaw she smiled. She'd made him happy. That was worth any pain.

Chapter Four

Mick was sure three days had passed since he'd talked to his dad. But it was only Monday afternoon. The clouds had thinned and a smeary quarter moon slid down the western sky into the murk of the city. A whiff of peat smoke filtered into the office.

At first the telephone had gone and gone again—the local police, the English police, a dispatcher in Carlisle asking questions but giving no answers. Calum and his car had vanished into thin air.

Now the telephone huddled sullenly, the shoulders of its receiver hunched. When Mick switched on the desk lamp he felt like a copper having a go at a prisoner. He'd already had a go at everyone at the mill. Calum's secretary, Amy, rang everyone he'd ever done business with. No one had seen him since his meeting in Birmingham on the Friday.

Nothing vanishes into thin air, Mick told himself.

In the filing cabinet he found a map of Scotland. Spreading it across the desk, he scanned every inch of the A68 and the A7. The roads ran south from Edinburgh, past Lauder and Stow, until they joined at Melrose. From there the A7 went on past Jedburgh and over Carter Bar into England, following the old Roman road to Hadrian's Wall. The Wall met the western sea at Carlisle. Perhaps . . . Perhaps what?

Calum had taken Mick on a tour of the Borders some years back, stopping at ruined castles and ruined abbeys and ruined forts until he begged for mercy, a Coke, and a fry-up. *Now that same holiday would be a treat,* Mick thought, grinding

43

his teeth. As soon as he found his dad he'd organize it.

Not one town in the map index was named Fairtichill. The black triangle labeled *Schiehallion 1083 metres*—one black triangle, not three—lay between Loch Tay and Loch Rannoch, in the Highlands. Mick didn't think that, fairy mountain or not, it had moved house to the Borders. Folding the map, he jammed it back into the cabinet. It caught on something, so that he couldn't shut the drawer.

He spread the files apart to see what was lying beneath them, and picked up his great-grandfather Malise's *sgian dubh*. The knife was sheathed in black leather trimmed with whorls of silver. Its bone handle was smoothed by years of use. At its top nested a flat chipping of what looked to be black marble, even though every other *sgian dubh* Mick had seen displayed a semi-precious gem. When he drew the steel blade it glinted bright and sharp. For such a small knife, extending from his wrist to his fingertips, it was surprisingly heavy. Its cold kiss sent a shiver up his arm. Why had Calum hidden it here? The last Mick had seen of it, it had been tucked away below the blankets in his mother's kist.

Replacing the knife in the drawer, he picked up Calum's check book. Amongst the amounts written to Jenner's Department Store and Safeway's were five checks for fifty pounds each made over to "Ellen Sparrow." His dad had been on his own for three years now. Nothing wrong with him having a lady friend. But Mick didn't know sod-all about his father's life, did he?

The phone went. His heart lurched. He fumbled the receiver, then slammed it to his ear. "Mick Dewar."

"Mr. Dewar," said a male voice with a clipped English accent. "Detective Inspector Gupta of the Somerset constabulary here. We've just received a missing person report on your father. He was seen at Glastonbury Abbey yesterday afternoon with a woman, a journalist named Vivian. Do you know her?"

"No." *Another woman?* "Does she know where he is?"

"She was found dead this morning."

Mick slid spinelessly down the chair, cradling his head on the bar at its back. "Dead? How?"

"We don't know yet. Why do you ask?"

"When my father phoned this morning he was ranting something terrible, saying someone was chasing him, saying there was something he'd never told me. He was off his head. Maybe he . . ."

". . . witnessed a death?" Gupta asked carefully.

Mick's nod was more of a shudder. "Who saw Dad with this Vivian?"

"Several Americans on a study course. The lecturer overheard Calum warning Vivian off an event scheduled for last night. Do you know his plans for last night?"

"No. He was doing business in the south of England, and had an appointment this morning at Glastonbury, to view a line of sheepskins, but he never showed. Mind you, he planned his trip round the weekend, so he could have a tour of Stonehenge and Salisbury and the like."

"Do you have a photograph of your father and a copy of his itinerary? It could be the man at the Abbey was another Calum, but that would be too much of a coincidence, I expect."

Mick heard his father's ragged voice saying, *Nothing's a coincidence.* "Oh aye, I'll put you onto the secretary."

"Thank you. We'd also like a statement from you detailing what he said in his phone call. We'll arrange for someone . . ."

"No." Mick sat up straight as a ramrod. He had something to be going on with at last. "I mean, aye, I'll do anything to help. But if something in Glastonbury drove my dad round the bend that's where I'm needing to be."

"Very good, then. If you'd call round the station when you arrive."

"That I will. Amy?" Mick shouted toward the door. It opened so quickly she must have been listening outside. "The Inspector here needs a bit help."

"Half a tic," Amy replied. The door shut.

Mick replaced the receiver and heaved himself from the chair. He gathered up the map and the checkbook and put them in his rucksack. *A hire car,* he thought, *not the train, so he could stop in at Carlisle . . . A woman in Glastonbury is dead. Dad's in danger.* Beyond that his usually fertile imagination withered.

He retrieved the *sgian dubh* from the drawer. Traditionally a man thrust the small knife into the top of his sock when he wore the kilt. But this was one was round, not flattened to lie against the leg. No matter. Mick wasn't going about his work in fancy dress. He slipped the knife into the inside pocket of his jacket. If this business concerned relics, then he had one to reckon with.

In two long strides he was out the door.

A purring cat just had to repel evil, Rose thought. This one even had a patch of white fur just below his chin, like a priest's collar.

A cool, crisp breeze rustled the glossy needles of the yew hedge at her back. A dove cooed . . . There it was, perched on the sagging, green-etched roof of the old church. Very old, judging by its narrow round-headed windows and massive walls of weathered stone.

Sean's voice came from the front of the house. If his arm on the back of Rose's seat in the mini-van was any indication, he intended to take being the only guy in the group as far as it would go. Not that he was just a pretty face. He had a brain. The problem was, he knew he was a pretty face with a brain. He'd breathed, "And would a rose by any other name smell as sweet?" into her ear five minutes after the plane took off. What? Didn't it occur to him she'd been hearing that one all her life?

He'd made a big deal about his interview at the police station. He'd made a big deal about his knee operation while they were climbing the Tor, like they all hadn't had to stop and rest. If he didn't take the hint soon she'd tell him to his face. The group didn't need to be tiptoeing around anybody's libido.

Although she'd rather have a romance than a mystery. A murder mystery. Finding the dead woman might be a story, but it wasn't at all entertaining. She still felt cold and queasy. Maybe she should start wearing her mother's miraculous medal of Mary instead of just keeping it in her billfold.

But it wasn't murder. Was it?

An older man dressed in a sweater and jeans walked around the corner of the church. The wind ruffled his short dark hair, picking glints of silver from it. He called, "Good afternoon. I'm Thomas London. May I join you?"

"Oh, hi! Please, sit down."

Sitting down, he offered his hand to the cat, who acknowledged him with a dignified sniff and a blink of his golden eyes.

None of London's books included his picture. Rose wondered just what she'd expected him to look like—the stereotypical professor, withered and wittering? This man was tall and broad-shouldered, with a strong, deep voice. His face was scholar-pale, though. And his smile was lean and angular, as though he'd gone so long without smiling he wasn't sure how to do it.

"I'm Rose Kildare," she told him.

47

"Rose Kildare," he repeated, staring at her so intently she could see herself reflected not only in his glasses but in the ash-brown eyes beneath.

Some days she hated the way people looked at her. Some days she was secretly pleased. Then there was today, when she knew her looks were only happenstance. "Rose is an old-fashioned name," she told him, "but I like it. People don't say 'huh' when they hear it, and you don't hear it every five minutes."

"Rose is a lovely name."

"My sisters are named Faith and Grace, with our Irish Catholic heritage and everything."

London nodded. "St. Bridget of Kildare lived here at Beckery. In fact, the name might be from 'Bec-Eriu,' little Ireland. Or it may mean 'Beekeeper's Island,' but, bees having been associated with virgin priestesses since time immemorial, that returns us to Bridget."

"I didn't know that. But that's why I'm here, flagrant curiosity. Is this your cat?"

"He lives here, yes, but he possesses himself. His name is Dunstan."

"After St. Dunstan?" Rose counted down the points with her forefinger. "He was abbot of Glastonbury, archbishop of Canterbury, patron saint of goldsmiths, and drove the Devil away by pinching his nose."

"You've been swotting up, I see."

"I came on this seminar because I love history."

"How are you getting on, then, with your seminar?"

"It's going great. But I found a dead woman in the Abbey this morning." She shook her head, but the image was caught like a thorn in her mind.

"What?"

Rose rushed through her summary, ending, "I feel like I

48

should apologize to her, for seeing her like that."

His brows drew down. "Finding her was very difficult for you."

"Not as difficult as dying was for her. Unless she wanted to die. But we saw her in the ruins yesterday, alive and well. Maggie even heard her talking about having a good time. That's how we know her name, Vivian. And now she's gone."

"In what part of the ruins did you find her?" asked London.

"The north transept. St. Thomas's chapel."

"Ah." He winced, although Rose couldn't imagine why that part of the story was any worse than the rest. "Who's been assigned to the case? Jivan Gupta?"

"Yes. He's good, isn't he?"

"The best. I'm sure he's already asked you if you saw anyone else at the Abbey this morning."

"I caught a glimpse of a man with the strangest eyes, like a cat's when the lights hits them just right. Contacts, I guess."

"Did the man see you?"

"Oh yeah, he saw me." She couldn't keep the edge out of her voice.

London asked quietly, "And did you find your notebook?"

"No. But it's hardly important with somebody dead."

"We don't always know what's important, do we?" His voice had a rasp beneath it, like velvet lined with sandpaper. He was looking at her, but he was also seeing something a long way beyond her. "An innocent bystander could well find—herself—at risk."

"Maggie, our teacher, told me to watch my back."

"By all means. Choose your friends cautiously. Though I say it as shouldn't, I suppose."

"That's okay, you come with references."

His quick laugh had more irony in it than humor.

"I came here to, well, witness everything I can," Rose went on, "but I never intended to be a witness."

"One can most unexpectedly find oneself answering a call to witness truth," said London.

"I'd like to know the truth, and not just about Vivian. About everything. Theological. Intellectual. Romantic, in every possible sense. Beauty and magic and . . . But it's like searching for the Holy Grail, you know? You look and you look but you don't know if you're good enough to find it. Not that I'd recognize it if I did." She laughed, too, at her own pretensions.

"The Holy Grail? Don't be so sure you wouldn't recognize it."

"Yo, Rose!" called Sean's voice. "Food's on the table!" He burst around the corner of the hedge and stopped.

"This is Mr. London," Rose explained, and gently dumped the cat, who sat down and began washing his face. "You know, Maggie told us about him."

"Oh." Sean extended his hand. "Sean MacArthur."

Standing up, London returned the handshake. "There's nothing older but the hills, MacArthur, and the Devil."

"Huh?" asked Sean.

"An old Scottish saying. Indicating the antiquity of your family, I daresay."

"Oh. We're from Plano, Texas, actually."

"It was nice meeting you," Rose told London.

"My pleasure," he returned gravely.

Rose loped off beside Sean, telling herself that London was a gentleman and a scholar in the truest sense of the expression. She'd heard his words, but she hadn't necessarily heard what he meant by them. He was going to be as demanding a teacher as Maggie. Still, between the purring cat and the cultivated academic, Rose felt a lot better about life going on and everything.

Sean opened the massive wooden door of the house, releasing the scents of baking bread and frying bacon. *Food for the body,* Rose thought as she stepped inside. One appetite at a time.

Chapter Five

Only in the U.K., Maggie reflected, would you *eat* your tea. But here, "tea" was more than beverage and national restorative, it was a meal she and the students badly needed. Fat insulated the body from shocks.

Bess Puckle's soft round face appeared in the dining room door. "More chips? Scones? Freshen the pot?"

"Oh no, thank you," replied Maggie.

"Righty-ho." Bess vanished back into the kitchen.

Maggie wiped the clotted cream and jam from her lips. "It's going to go straight to my hips," she told Anna, "but it sure is satisfying."

Anna had nibbled while the others chowed down. She shook her head apologetically. "I haven't been able to eat rich food since I was a child in Warsaw. With the war, we were on very short rations."

A Jewish child in Warsaw during the war, Maggie repeated silently. Short rations didn't describe it. But Anna's composure rejected sympathy.

"There's evidence for that belief," Maggie told her.

This time it was Alf Puckle who appeared in the doorway. "Nothing else? Then let's have us a shufti round the house." He led his guests into the corridor, saying, "Sorry we couldn't accommodate you last night, but we're always full up October thirty-first, what with the loonies and their fires and their dancing. Some even walk along those farm plots on the Tor, thinking they're a labyrinth." Alf shrugged. "No harm in it, but no purpose in it either. No need for supernatural moonshine, the real world's enough for anyone."

Not necessarily. But then, "not necessarily" was probably what Vivian, the Lady of Shalott, had felt. Maggie glanced at Rose. The young woman seemed less grim now, thank goodness and Temple Manor.

Rose looked askance at their host. "Do you go to church, Mr. Puckle?"

"Easter and Christmas, when Bess gets stroppy." Chuckling, Alf raised the latch of a door. It opened with a screech along a rut worn in the stone floor of a medieval hall. The interlaced beams of the high ceiling made patterns of light and shadow above a fireplace large enough to roast SMU's mascot pony.

Sean's head hit the lintel with a thud. "Shi—oot!" he exclaimed, censoring himself in mid-word.

Maggie flinched, but knew better than to try and check him over.

"Some say folk were smaller back then," Alf said consolingly, and opened his arms to the room. "Bess and me always wanted to own a property with some history. It was a right bit of luck when her vicar recommended us to Thomas. He offered us a hire-purchase plan—we manage the place as a B&B and make repairs and such, and in time we've bought it. Bess's daughter wasn't too keen on living here. But she's an adult now, making her own way." A shadow touched Alf's face, then passed so quickly Maggie wondered whether she'd noticed it.

"Very generous," she said. "But he couldn't keep it up by himself, could he?"

"No. Last of his line, he is. Just goes to show you, one man's misfortune is another's good luck. This here's the Great Hall, the oldest part of the house. Fourteenth century. The rest of the place was added on a piece at a time. Windows, chimneys, stonework—it's a right jumble and more than a bit drafty, but personable."

"How much renovation did you have to do?" Anna asked.

"Not so much as you'd expect. The Londons made a good fist of the upkeep over the years—no rising damp, no woodworm. Place just needed some life in it, is all."

Smiling contentedly, Alf guided them through a maze of rooms, staircases, windows, and fireplaces. Timber floors creaked. Doorways sagged. Stone and brick exuded that earthy, musty odor Maggie always found so appealing, the scent of the past. The furnishings of the house ranged from antique to junk, sprinkled with twentieth-century fundamentals such as flush toilets and electric lights. By the time Alf waved them through the front door with its wrought-iron knocker, Sean had forgotten to act blasé, Rose was openly enchanted, and Anna's sharp eyes hadn't missed so much as a nail.

An archway led from the courtyard to a lawn. Beyond the weathered stone wall encircling the grounds, ravens cawed, adding ambience, and a car honked, subtracting it. Still, the car was heading down to the bridge over the River Brue, where Sir Bedivere had returned Excalibur to the Lady of the Lake.

Alf gestured toward the house. "That wing there's the latest, early eighteenth century."

Silvery half-timbering abutted gray stonework which abutted off-white plasterwork laced by flaming Virginia creeper. The red bricks of the Tudor chimneys looked as though they'd been knotted and woven. *Magic,* Maggie thought. Temple Manor was a quilt sewn by the hands of time and man, and like a quilt it was both shelter and allegory. Its gravity made her frame house look like the Little Pig's house of straw.

"This way, Thomas will be in the chapel. That and the cottage is all he kept for himself." Alf led them around a corner and past a yew hedge. Beyond it lay a formal garden, overlooked by the many-paned windows of the gallery. "He tells some good historical tales, he does, not all dates and acts of Parliament and such."

"I've been reading his books for years," Maggie said. "I assigned a couple to the group."

"Very well-written," Anna added.

"I liked the one about monastic life," said Rose, "how the monotonal notes of the chants reverberated against the stone."

Sean shook his head. "The books are okay. Heavy on people's feelings but light on the battles."

"People in battles have plenty of feelings," Rose told him.

"Here we are," announced Alf. "Oldest building on the property. Twelfth century, on seventh-century foundations."

The church stood aloof on an expanse of lawn, its ancient stone blushing in the sunshine. A dove peered down from a corner of the roof. "Supposedly St. Bridget left a bell here," Maggie lectured. "She began her story as Brighid, a Celtic goddess with similar attributes. Bridget's nuns tended Brighid's sacred fire in Kildare, Ireland, until the Reformation. The newer chapel here at Beckery was dedicated to Mary Magdalene, a saint whose origins are all too human. This is as ancient a site as Glastonbury, and just as much on the pilgrim circuit."

"Like the monks finding Arthur's grave in the Abbey, pilgrims being right good business and all." Alf winked conspiratorially.

"Arthur saw a vision of the Holy Grail here at Beckery," Maggie went on with a smile, appreciating his honesty. "Lancelot retired to a hermit's cell by Chalice Well. Guinevere was kidnapped and held on the Tor." Ravens exploded from the trees beyond the wall and skeined into the distance. "And according to some stories Arthur lived on in the form of a raven, a pagan borrowing if ever there was one."

"The Arthurian legends," Anna said, "are Western Europe's equivalent to the Dreamtime of the Australian aborigines. Myths of origin and identity."

"Stories," said Alf dismissively.

But, Maggie thought in silent protest, *stories were honest, too.* "With the name 'Temple' I assume the manor was originally a Templar preceptory."

"The Knights of the Temple of Solomon," said Sean, pumping his fist in the air. "They were tough."

"This was once a preceptory, right enough," Alf said. "After the Reformation, the Londons fitted out a chapel in the house, still being Catholic and all, and the chapel here became a barn. But our Thomas's seen to its restoration right and proper. Go on ins . . ."

A screech tore the sky. A reddish-brown missile shot by the edge of the roof. Everyone jumped. The dove disappeared. "A falcon!" Alf exclaimed.

The bird of prey landed atop the roof tree, its hooked beak turning right and left, its bright eyes scanning its domain. Then it launched itself toward the north and dwindled into the distance. One white feather drifted down to Rose's feet. "No, it didn't get—oh, there she is."

The dove's small white head peeped out of a crevice between two stones, no doubt counting its blessings.

Maggie exhaled. Rose, a dove . . . She had to stop looking for signs and portents.

"I'll leave you to it, shall I?" Alf glided away across the lawn.

"Thank you," Maggie called. "Onwards," she said to her

charges, and stepped over the deeply-furrowed stone threshold.

The tiny chapel was dark and still, redolent of mildew and paint. Dust motes eddied in swords of sunlight that glanced through the narrow western windows. Below the eastern window sat an altar holding a crucifix and a vase of crimson flowers. To one side stood a small wooden cabinet.

The light drew gleams of color from the niches of a rood screen so old the wood looked moth-eaten. Above it loomed the obviously new crucifix. The figure of the man hanging from its crosspiece curved downward, as though his poor, torn palms ached to embrace every soul standing below and turn misery into triumph. Sunlight danced across the thorns in his crown, making it a crown of stars. *Such artistry!* Maggie thought.

Anna stood a bit apart, respectful but unmoved. Rose looked upward with eyes as bright as votive candles. Sean shuffled his feet, playing the bored sophisticate again.

Maggie did a bit of foot-shuffling herself. It'd been years since she'd attended a church service. Her wedding had been in her mother's Episcopal church. Later, the rite had—no, it was she and Danny who had failed. It was she who had disillusioned herself. The sacraments were valid if you believed in them. What had Gupta implied? That you could choose to believe? But she wasn't sure she believed that, much as she wanted to.

A man ducked through a second doorway. "Ah, here you are."

Norman, Maggie thought. Except for his arch of a nose, his body was all straight lines. His eyes were the faded brown of the Bayeux tapestry and the angle of his chin implied aristocratic hauteur. Only a sprinkling of gray in his hair and a few lines and sags in his face conceded age. Maggie had expected

Thomas London to be old and frail. This man was no older than fifty. He must have been publishing when he was fifteen.

He reached up to a dangling socket and inserted a light bulb. Light flooded the niches in the rood screen. Turning around, London said, "Rose, Sean, it's good to see you again. And you must be Ms. Sin . . ." He stopped abruptly, clearing his throat. "Your name is Sinclair, isn't it?"

"Maggie Sinclair." What? Had he seen a wanted poster hanging in the post office? "It's an old Scottish-Norman name."

"So it is." His handshake was cool and considered. "Have you by any chance relatives in Scotland?"

"Not that I know of."

"But surely the 'Maggie' is for Margaret, as in Scotland's St. Margaret."

"No, it's for Magdalena, I'm afraid." With the light reflecting off his glasses Maggie couldn't see London's eyes. Still, she took a step back from what she sensed was a very intense gaze. So her name wasn't a common one. She didn't owe him a character sketch of her single-before-it-was-cool-to-be-single mother.

Anna stepped forward. "My name is Anna Stern, Mr. London."

"Ah," he said, and unbent so far as to turn to her and return her handshake. "How do you do, Mrs. Stern. And it's Thomas, please."

"Then I'm Anna," she told him.

"Where did you find such an awesome rood?" asked Rose.

"I must confess to carving and painting it and the other figures," Thomas replied.

"Are you restoring the pictures or making new ones?" Anna asked.

"Restoring, as best I can."

58

Feeling more and more like a one-trick pony, Maggie stepped closer to the screen. A partially completed painting of the Virgin Mary filled the niche beside the doorway. Of the others only three were finished. "The saints associated with Glastonbury, right? Joseph of Arimathea, Bridget, David of Wales, Dunstan, either St. Paulinus of York or St. Neot of Cornwall . . ."

"St. Dubricius," said Thomas, "also known as Merlin."

"Who's the guy carrying his own head?" asked Sean.

"St. Denis."

Maggie protested, "But he's affiliated with Paris."

"I lived for a time in France, in my youth." Thomas's strong but graceful hands chose a brush from a tray of art supplies.

"You show Bridget with her cow and everything," said Rose, "but you don't show Joseph holding the Holy Grail."

Thomas smiled gently down on her. "The story of the Holy Grail begins in the mists of pagan antiquity. Now we identify it as the vessel of the Last Supper and Passion of Our Lord. In some stories, though, it is not a vessel at all, but a plate, a reliquary, or even the emerald that fell from the crown of Lucifer when he was cast out of heaven. Some say the Grail was brought to France by Mary Magdalene, or here to Glastonbury by St. Joseph. Churches in Italy and Spain claim to hold the Grail, and it is also reputed to be in a private home in Wales. Some even say it is the philosopher's stone."

"Indiana Jones lost it down a crevasse," said Sean with a grin.

"Even the Nazis exploited the story," Anna said.

"Like all demagogues, they perverted the true story to serve their greed for power." Thomas squeezed tubes of blue and green and mixed the colors. Crouching, he painted a streak of teal below Mary's tranquil face.

The color of a peacock's tail, Maggie thought. The peacock, symbol of Roman Juno, like Mary Queen of Heaven. But Thomas would know that already. No need to point it out.

"Funny," Rose said, "that Mr. Puckle caters to pilgrims and what he calls loonies when he himself doesn't believe in the supernatural."

"The supernatural? Vampires, witches, demons?" demanded Sean.

" 'Supernature' is a very recent concept," Maggie said in her best professorial voice. "Most people throughout history have regarded magic as a natural phenomenon. Even if most of us go our entire lives without encountering any magic, mystery, whatever."

Thomas asked, "Would you recognize mystery if you did encounter it?"

The hair rose on the back of Maggie's neck. It was chilly in here, she rationalized. Both physically and psychically. Was he jealous of his academic turf? She sure wasn't a threat to him. "Off we go, y'all. We're looking forward to your lectures, Thomas."

"Maggie. Rose, Sean, Anna." He bowed slightly, in regal dismissal.

Shooing everyone outside, Maggie reminded herself that she was going to have to work with Thomas London. He would set very high standards for her, let alone the students. His lectures would be delivered in a resonant voice with rounded vowels that made her own American accent sound like a quack . . . *Don't let him make you feel inferior.*

She wondered again if she'd bitten off more than she could chew by taking this trip, and not just because one of her students was already involved in a—murder, she articulated. None of Gupta's assurances were going to change her leap of faith—or her leap of fear—that that's what it was.

Maggie dawdled outside the garden gate, letting the others go on ahead, and told herself that her academic paranoia wasn't important. Especially in the face of murder.

Chapter Six

The sun poured a reddish-gold radiance over ancient house and modern town. The cold air scoured Maggie's lungs of the odors of paint and mildew and something else—the odor of sanctity, maybe, in this saint-haunted place.

A car turned into the parking area, stopping next to the Puckles' Range Rover and Maggie's leased mini-van. It was so small it was almost a toy, the sort of transportation you bought for the second family car. Inspector Gupta emerged from it like a hermit crab from its shell. "Good evening!" he called to Maggie. "Are you settling in, then?"

Think of the Devil and he appears. "Yes, thank you. How's the investigation going?"

"We're making progress. I've a photo to show you, but first I'll have a word with Thomas. You've met him, have you?"

"Yeah. He's in there." She fluttered her hand over her shoulder.

"Right." Gupta strode on across the grass and into the bloodshot eye of the sun.

Maggie trudged into the house and gathered her charges in the lounge, a long low room overlooking the courtyard. The cat, Dunstan, was already ensconced on the sill of the bay window. Rose sat down next to him. Anna dealt herself a hand of Solitaire. Sean turned on the television. "Hey, we're on the news!"

The screen filled with quick images, fluorescent orange mesh draped over ruined stone walls, a police car next to the

Abbey gate, Gupta intoning a noncommittal statement that did not, thank goodness, mention Rose.

"Also in Glastonbury last night," the newscaster went on, "on a farm outside Baltonsborough, a group celebrating a pagan holiday got into a row with several Christian missionaries. This is Reginald Soulis of the Freedom of Faith Foundation." A heavy-jowled individual, hair slicked back and lips pursed in disapproval, said, "We were sharing the word of God with the Devil-worshippers when they attacked us."

Maggie had read about the Foundation in the *Times*. It sounded like yet another in-your-face holier-than-thou group that was more political than religious. She'd never figured out why believing in one version of God meant you had to stamp out all the other versions. Were believers that insecure in their faith?

"Whoa," said Sean. "Devil-worshippers."

"Technically," Rose said, "you have to believe in the Bible to believe in the Devil."

"Although 'Devil' with a small 'd' includes a variety of beings, depending on which Dreamtime you're evoking," added Anna.

Without getting the other side of the story, the news announcer segued into a commercial. A hyperthyroid actress chirped, "Mood Crisps! Crisps dusted with St. John's Wort satisfy your mind as well as your body! The new snack food for 2001!"

Maggie had paused in her pacing long enough to mutter, "Bah humbug," when the sepulchral thud of the iron knocker made everyone jump. A moment later Alf ushered Gupta, live and in person, though the door.

"Alf, Bess, if you'd join us?" the detective asked. "Could you switch off the telly, lad? Thank you. Sorry to be in a bit of

63

a rush, but I need to get myself back to the station as soon as may be."

So much for the dog and the slippers in front of the family hearth, Maggie told herself. But other than a loosened tie and the whisker-shadow on his cheeks, Gupta didn't seem too much the worse for wear. He pulled two photographs from his jacket, one the all-too-familiar instant, the other an image on a sheet of fax paper, and handed them to Bess.

"Oooh-er," she said. "What a pity, that."

Gupta said, "We've identified the dead woman as Vivian Morgan, an investigative reporter for the Oxfordshire *Observer.*"

A murmur ran around the room "Who's this other, then?" asked Bess.

"Calum Dewar, a wool-merchant from Edinburgh. He's gone missing, and this time there's suspicion of foul play." Gupta handed Maggie the paper, his dark eyes not shying away from her silent *why am I not surprised?* "Is this the man you saw?"

Maggie held the black and white photo far enough away she could focus on it. She recognized the man's dark hair gone gray at the temples and his forehead creased by worry. What she hadn't noticed yesterday were the upturned lines at the corners of his eyes and mouth which implied humor, even imagination, although in the photo they emphasized the dour respectability of his expression. His eyes were light-colored—they might reflect oddly. Passing the photo on to the students, she said, "Yes, that's him. Why do you suspect foul play?"

"Calum rang his son from Carlisle this morning, cutting up rough, saying someone was chasing him. I thought Thomas might recognize him or Vivian from some conference or other, but he doesn't." With a thoughtful frown,

Gupta collected the photos and tucked them inside his jacket.

A telephone chirped and Bess hurried off to answer it. "And?" Maggie prompted.

"We traced Vivian to the Shambhala Guest House. She left late last night, wearing a green cloak with gold embroidery, away to the Samhain ceremony at Baltonsborough, or so she told the proprietor."

"A cloak," repeated Rose.

"The ceremony that turned into a riot?" Maggie asked.

"The very same."

Sean asked, "Did you find a knife to go with that sheath?"

"No."

"And you don't know how Vivian died?" asked Anna.

"Not as yet."

Alf clucked his tongue. "Nice young lady like that. And the Scotsman—well, he'll turn up right as rain, just you see."

"I hope so," said Gupta. "We're expecting his son here tomorrow. Don't you have a single room empty yet, Alf?"

"That we do. The lad's welcome to it."

Maggie opened her mouth, then shut it. The Dewar boy didn't have an infectious disease. They owed him some sympathy, already.

"I don't suppose we can tell him anything more about his father and Vivian," said Anna "but he might feel better if he tells us about them."

"Perhaps," returned Gupta. "Save the lad's never heard of Vivian."

"Oh . . ." Rose's voice trailed away, as she no doubt visualized half a dozen possible scenarios.

Maggie didn't need to visualize any scenarios at all. Her stomach felt hollow, as though she were riding a rapidly dropping elevator. But taking the kids and running back to London wasn't an option. They'd signed up for a course in

Arthurian legend and history and that's what they were going to get, even if the syllabus included footnotes in crime and weirdness. It would all blow over soon . . . *Yeah, right* said the part of her mind which was like a pebble in her shoe.

"I'm off, then. Thank you," Gupta said to everyone, without quite looking at anyone, and turned toward the door.

"I'll see you out." Maggie grabbed her coat and followed him out the door and across the cobbles of the courtyard. When they were past the deep shadow of the archway she asked, "So Rose is still on the hook?"

"If I say 'no,' will you stop worrying yourself about it?"

"But I'm living proof worry is effective. Ninety per cent of everything I worry about never happens."

Gupta smiled at that. "Lovely evening," he commented, and climbed into his car.

That he hadn't answered her question was answer enough. Maggie stood with her arms crossed as he drove away. A scent of smoke teased the frosty wind. The lingering glow of the sunset made the sky a translucent Prussian blue. One bright light hung above the horizon, a planet or maybe even a UFO. Funny, people used to see angels and demons and now they saw UFOs. *Signs and portents, oh my.*

She heard a bell ring, and again, and then again. The pure notes spread outward like ripples in a pond, seeming to still the wind and quiet the noises of the town. Was that St. Bridget's bell tolling the end of All Saints' Day, the eve of All Souls'? That was pre-Reformation practice, but then, a lot of early rituals and symbols had been revived, to illustrate transcendence for a material and secular age.

Maggie's shoulders loosened. The stars blossomed, one by one, as the clear peal of the bell filled the night. When it stopped the silence echoed. And then from the depths of that silence came a reply, distant music played on some subtle

66

wind instrument. The slow lilting melody was a lament. It was a lullaby. It was unearthly and otherworldly and fingered her spine like a flute. And yet a laughing ripple of harp strings ran through it as well, and she laughed in delight.

Then the music was gone, leaving only a resonance in her mind. A car drove by. The wind gusted so fiercely her hair blew back from her scalp and her nose tingled. Shaking her head—was it Glastonbury's reality that had lost its edge, or her own?—she walked back toward the house and the task in hand.

Chapter Seven

Thomas shut the door of the manor house behind him, making the knocker creak. Despite glints of sunshine the wind was chill, scented with sea-spray and the tang of cold iron.

The Puckles were doing right by Temple Manor, bless them. They had been only briefly his employees. Now they were friends, eager to feed him sumptuous meals and lend him their electronic equipment. This morning, though, Thomas had purchased his own cellular telephone. He strode off across the courtyard, once again berating himself for believing that he could go through the End Time without incident.

The phone number in his address book for Alex Sinclair had connected him with a fish and chips shop. Alf's Internet terminal had listed several Alex Sinclairs, none of them the right one. Finally, hope failing, Thomas checked the archives of the Edinburgh records office and there found Alex's name. He had died in an automobile crash fifteen years ago.

A series of telephone calls had determined that his other fellow guardians were well, their relics safe. It was Ivan who, through no fault of his own, had lost the Book. And Alex, too, had died without fault, but also without issue, so that the location of the Stone died with him. Although Alex had never been the relic's actual caretaker. Thomas himself only now suspected who was. For a man named *Dewar*, an old Gaelic word meaning "guardian," to go missing, leaving behind a woman dead in a significant place, was no coincidence. It was deliberate challenge.

Robin Fitzroy. His enemy's name sliced his mind like a sword.

Just outside the archway a rubber ball flew by his face and bounced off the wall behind him. "Sorry!" exclaimed the MacArthur lad. "I was going in for a lay-up, with that bracket up there as the goal, you know?"

"Hey, Sean!" Maggie's voice came from inside the courtyard. "I'm on the five-yard line!"

"Hail Mary!" Sean returned, and threw the ball toward her.

The American dialect had certainly produced some arresting idioms. "Maggie," Thomas called, "would you care for a cup of tea? We should discuss your students' curriculum."

"Oh," she said. "Sure. I'll get my laptop."

"My cottage is just off the chancel of the church." As he had feared, Maggie had interpreted his reaction to her name yesterday as dislike, perhaps even professional jealousy. He mustn't become so distracted by his age-old task that he neglected contemporary courtesies.

Rose sat on the bench by the garden gate, writing in a blue copybook. Her cheeks were pink, her hair tousled, her eyes shining like a glimpse of heaven. It might have been autumn on the calendar, not to mention in Thomas's soul, but this vision of spring made his heart leap with joy. He would have knelt at her feet, but Dunstan was already there, grooming his sleek black flank as though visions were an everyday occurrence.

And yet Rose was no angel. She would come down from her pedestal, sooner rather than later—a pedestal provided very little room to move, after all, and the mud beneath was the source of life. But how and when she descended had to be her own choice. He could only pray that she'd taken his veiled warning about Robin to heart, for it was Robin, he felt sure, who'd seen her with his eyes of adamant in the Abbey yesterday morning.

"Hi," she said.

"Hello, Rose. You're hard at it, I see."

"I'm trying to recreate the notes I took and then lost. Maggie says she free-associates when she lectures, but between us we'll get most of it."

"Maggie's a good teacher, is she?"

"Oh yes. She even knew why there was a bell ringing last night."

Did she now? "And why was that?"

"Ringing a church bell on the night of All Saints' Day wards off evil spirits. Like throwing salt over your shoulder, except that's superstition."

"One man's sacrament is another's superstition."

Rose grinned agreement. "Were you ringing a bell in the chapel?"

"Yes. A replica of St. Bridget's bell."

"Once a priest, always a priest, I guess."

"Yes. Even so, I've been—inactive—for many years now."

"Did you leave the church," asked Maggie's voice, "or did the church leave you?"

Thomas looked round.

"Sorry," Maggie went on, "I was eavesdropping."

"My faith is no secret," Thomas replied. "Would you care for a cup of tea, Rose?"

"I promised Sean I'd play basketball," she answered. "Thanks anyway."

"Please don't break anything," Maggie told her. "I'd like to get y'all back to your parents intact."

"No, ma'am," said Rose with her brightest smile. Dazzled, Thomas managed to escort Maggie toward the outside door of his cottage without tripping over his own feet.

"That smile is like a flash bulb going off in your face," she said.

"Breathtaking," Thomas replied. "What a shame there are—shall we say vandals?—who would spoil such beauty. But I would assume from your Freudian slip you know that."

"Freudian slip . . . Oh no." Maggie's face went, appropriately enough, the magenta of a *Rosa gallica*. "Return her to her parents intact. Like a girl that age is going to be a virgin. Sorry."

"Your concern does you credit. Jivan—D.I. Gupta—expressed concern as well." Opening the door, Thomas ushered Maggie into the house that had once belonged to the chapel's priest, two minuscule rooms up and down.

The staircase to the bedroom was little more than a ladder. A medieval hooded fireplace contained soot-blackened andirons and a pile of ashes. Bits of shabby furniture stood upon a threadbare carpet. A computer and an audiotape player were conspicuously anachronistic. Lancet windows in the massive stone wall admitted a modicum of afternoon light.

Maggie set her laptop computer on the table. "Yeah, I feel responsible for the kids. I don't have kids of my own. I'm—ah—I'm divorced." She turned toward the nearest bookcase, presenting Thomas with her knotted shoulders. Choosing a book, she ran her fingertips down its spine as though she were stroking a lover's body.

Her windblown hair made an auburn halo that softened her angular features. A steadiness in her gaze testified to an exacting intellect, and a tightness at the corners of her mouth suggested unresolved regrets. Her rounded body carried itself with the nervy poise of a thoroughbred horse. Thomas filled the kettle and set it on the electric ring. "You must find

71

the students stimulating as well as worrying."

"The campus in the fall is downright intoxicating. The changing leaves. The smell of new books. All those bright young faces." She replaced the book and combed her hair with her fingers. "I like the way you write, putting the religious and social aspects into context. Most historians use past events to beat their own ideological horses."

"St. Bernard said, 'Every word one writes smites the Devil.' Mind you, it's fashionable nowadays to consider religious faith either a psychological idiosyncrasy or a deficiency in character. We rationalize away evil and medicate away visions."

Maggie glanced back at him. "I wondered if religion was your horse."

"One to ride, not to beat."

"Do you ever question your faith?"

"Frequently. And it always answers. To paraphrase Plato, the unexamined faith is not worth believing."

"Your faith answers? Not the church? Is that why you left it?"

"As with any event, there were many reasons." The evasion came smoothly to his lips, but this time left a bitter aftertaste. Again he felt strong as any physical appetite the need to speak the entire truth. And yet how, when the truth would appear the most bare-faced of lies?

"Not that I know anything about it," Maggie told him. "I was brought up Episcopalian, and would probably be a Unitarian, except . . ."

That would require belief, Thomas concluded for her.

She considered two stitchery samplers hanging above the books. One was in Latin, the other in Greek, both illuminating St. John 1:1: "In the beginning was the Word, and the Word was with God, and the Word was God." Below them stood a lead cross covered with misshapen capital letters. *"Hic jacet sepultus inclitus rex arturius in insula avalonia,* Here lies buried the famous King Arthur in the island of Avalon. This is a copy of the cross which turned up in 1191 in Arthur's grave in the Abbey, isn't it? Not that the grave really was Arthur's, but if you can't prove it was you can't prove it wasn't, either. The cross was probably a twelfth-century forgery . . ." Maggie spun round. "This can't be the original!"

"Can there be an original of a forgery?"

"Sure. If this cross was made in 1191 it would be an important antiquity. It would be a truth, just not the truth you expect."

"The cross was given to me. I couldn't say whether it's the original or not, to tell you the . . ." Thomas busied himself with the tin of tea. "You shall know the truth, and the truth shall set you free."

"To thine own self be true," she replied, "thou canst not then be false to any man."

Speaking with this woman was like speaking a litany. "Sometimes the truth depends upon your point of view."

"From the Bible and Shakespeare to *Star Wars*?"

"Every age re-writes the old myths, but they remain valid."

"Yes," Maggie said, but her brittle tone said, *maybe.* Stiff as a crab, she sidled past the fireplace to another bookcase, where she stared into a flat box. She groped in her pocket for her glasses. "Good Lord, you've got a set of his seals."

The kettle whistled. It took Thomas a moment to realize what the shrill noise was. He rinsed the pot with boiling water, then added a spoonful of tea leaves and more water. Steam wavered upward and caressed his cheeks, but his face was already warm.

"Beautifully preserved," Maggie went on, her nose almost touching the two oblongs of gold. "In the official one you can see each wrinkle in the robe and the ribbons on the miter. And each little letter is perfect: *Sigillum Tome dei gratia archiepiscopi cantuariensis*. The seal of Thomas by the grace of God archbishop of Canterbury."

Odd, his hand was trembling. Still, Thomas managed to pour milk into a pitcher without spilling it.

"And the second one here, with the Roman figure in the middle—Mercury?"

Mercury, thought Thomas. The patron of alchemists. And liars.

"This one says *sigillum Tome Lund* big as anything. 'Lund' being short for 'Londoniensis.' Thomas of London, which he was before he became a V.I.P. I bet there have been lots of Thomas Londons over the years, not just the ones in your family."

There's only ever been one Thomas Maudit. He placed cups and saucers on the table.

"But we know him as Thomas Becket. Becket was his father's name, a place name, 'Le Bec' in Normandy maybe. Or a nickname, 'Beaky,' like a prominent nose, you know?"

Thomas knew.

"I always liked the Norman 'fitz,' son of, from the Latin *filius*. Often the bastard son, although you have Henry FitzEmpress, who was thoroughly legit. Good old Henry II. Or, in this context, bad old Henry II. Have you seen the movie *Becket*? The one based on Anouilh's play? Terrible history, but a good story, even though Becket himself is played way too detached. The real man had to have had ambition and the guts to match to rise from merchant's son to Chancellor of England. You have to feel sorry for Henry, he thought if he put his buddy the Chancellor into the Archbishopric he could manipulate the church. But Becket turned against him, whether out of a higher loyalty or an excess of pride is hard to say."

Yes, Thomas thought, *that is hard to say.* The pride that was self-respect all too easily became the pride that was arrogance.

Again she spun round, her enthusiasm loosening the defensive set of her shoulders. "I doubt if Henry meant for his knights to kill Becket, let alone inside Canterbury Cathedral, he was just so frustrated he went into one of his rages—the story was he was descended from the Devil—and off they went, swords drawn, thinking they'd make points. No pun intended," Maggie added. "There's only one imprint of Becket's personal seal known, no one's ever found an official one, and you've got both. These are genuine, right? As the kids would say, that's too absolutely cool for words."

Any moment now Maggie would notice that she was performing a monologue. Clearing his throat, Thomas said, "One of the joys of owning an old house is that the most amazing objects turn up in the lumber rooms."

Maggie tucked her eyeglasses away. With a positively post-coital sigh she collapsed into a chair. "So what else do you have? The Holy Grail?"

Thomas's face relaxed into a most unaccustomed grin. With a flourish he set the teapot on the table. *Yes, by all things holy and a few that are not.*

Maggie's body was tautening, again taking offense at his manner. "Nothing like telling a scholar what he already knows. Less than he knows—I don't have a doctorate."

"Nor do I." He sat down, poured the tea, strong and fragrant, into her cup, and pushed the sugar bowl toward her. "You're the first person to recognize those seals for what they are. *Memento mori*—souvenirs of death."

"My Ph.D. dissertation was on the tangle of politics and religion in twelfth-century England. I never finished it, though. I got married. You wouldn't think those would be mutually exclusive, but they were." She spooned sugar into her cup. "In Mexico today is *El Dia de los Muertos,* the Day of the Dead."

"All Souls' Day," Thomas said. "A time to remember that death is not in and of itself evil."

"The bell-ringing last night was—evocative. So was the music you played."

"Music? I rang St. Bridget's bell is all."

"Oh. I thought I heard a flute or . . . Never mind."

Yes. He chose his words carefully. "Perhaps the ringing of the bell serves less to drive away evil spirits than to attract good ones."

Maggie looked up. Her brown eyes were the color of bittersweet chocolate. He was reminded of what Rose had said about wanting romance and magic. But what in the girl was an exciting itch of possibility had in the woman become the ache of needs unfulfilled. What in the girl was a desire for knowledge was in the woman a desire for truth. Did she, too, have need of a new friend? Even when he bent his head over his own cup he could feel her gaze probing him. She thought he was a bit cracked. Yet her bearing was more bemused than critical, and her posture was almost relaxed, like a sentry setting his sword to the side but still close at hand.

The tea filled Thomas's mouth with hints of new-mown hay, blackberry jam, caramel. "Yes, Anouilh's Becket was too cool, never revealing the passion and the pride searing the man's soul. I prefer Eliot's version."

"*Murder in the Cathedral,* yes. How does it go? The last temptation is the worst treason, to do the right thing for the wrong reason."

Closing his eyes, Thomas felt his heart swell painfully, like a long dried fruit at last blessed with moisture. Patterns of coincidence and harmony. Rose, faith, and grace. Thanks be to the merciful hand of God, and to the quick tongue of Magdalena Sinclair.

He opened his eyes. She was watching him, demanding the truth. He inhaled . . . And was interrupted by a smart rap at the door. Thomas exhaled. "Come in!"

"Ms. Sinclair," said Jivan Gupta, closing the door behind him. "Thomas."

"It's Maggie," she told him, and added sugar to the cup she'd already sweetened.

Thomas said, "Good afternoon, Jivan. Sit down. Have a cuppa."

"Thank you." Jivan sank into the third chair at the table. His moustache drooped, and a faint gray tint to his complexion hinted of too many meals eaten from takeaway containers and too little sleep anywhere, let alone in his own bed. He accepted the cup of tea and drank deeply. When he spoke, his consonants were tightly clipped. "A preliminary toxicology report shows no drugs and only a trace of alcohol in Vivian Morgan's body. There are, however, petechia, broken blood vessels, in her eyes, and very faint bruising about her mouth and nose."

"She was suffocated?" asked Maggie.

"It seems likely." Jivan cradled the warm cup between his hands. "The pathologist also found signs of sexual activity, whilst the forensics chaps turned up three sets of footprints entering the Abbey grounds from Chilkwell Street."

"Three sets?" Thomas asked.

"One set matching Morgan's slippers crossed a muddy patch in the choir. That was overlaid by the prints of a shoe or boot in a larger size, which was overlaid in turn by the prints of a man's heavy shoes. They—he—stood there for a time."

"So even if the man Rose saw was Calum Dewar," said Maggie, "someone else was there, too. A voyeur? Maybe a jealous one?"

Thomas bit his lip. Even though he was quite sure who Rose had seen, offering that intelligence would change the topic of conversation from "who did it?" to "how do you know?" Neither would it explain Dewar's role, about which he had only implications of guesses.

"Morgan was seen at Baltonsborough Sunday night," Jivan went on. "The Willow Band, a neo-pagan group that meets here to celebrate the old Celtic holidays—law-abiding citizens one and all—were interrupted by a dozen or so members of the Freedom of Faith Foundation. A respectable organization, Maggie. You have similar ones in America."

"Oh yeah," she said dryly. "We do."

"Neither side will admit to starting off the violence. Some of the Foundations were carrying cricket bats and the like, but only to defend themselves from the 'unbelievers,' as they say."

"Blessed are the peacemakers, for they shall be called the children of God," Thomas murmured, and caught Maggie's caustic glance. "Was anyone injured?"

"Bumps and bruises. The Willows say the Foundations were after bashing their vases of flowers and such like. The Foundations say the row wouldn't have happened at all if the Willows had listened to reason." Jivan drained his cup. "Vivian Morgan was there at the start of the Willow ceremony but no one remembers seeing her after the row began. Two people have tentatively identified Calum Dewar amongst the Foundations, but no one remembers seeing him during the row, either."

"I overheard him trying to talk her out of going," said

Maggie. "Maybe he took her away before things went down-hill, to protect her."

Thomas refilled Jivan's cup. "Speaking of protection, have you considered the implications of Vivian's knife, Jivan? Assuming she had one, of course."

"Maggie said something about iron protecting one from evil spirits."

"The iron-working Celtic invaders," she replied, "called the indigenous bronze-working population of Britain the little people, the ancient ones. They were conquered by iron, so iron fended off their magic. The tradition survived Roman, Saxon, Dane, and Norman invasions well into Christian times."

Jivan nodded. "Some of those old Celtic stories are similar to the ancient Sanskrit texts of India."

"Both being survivors of the original Indo-European culture," Thomas added. "You're thinking Vivian tried to defend herself with the missing knife, either literally or symbolically."

"There's no way of knowing. Not yet."

"Not yet," Thomas repeated, and went on, "Alf tells me the Dewar lad is coming here. Good—I'd like to speak with him."

"The Salisbury force wants to take his statement, as well. Calum and Morgan were there Saturday, touring the area. Calum booked his hotel room for Sunday as well, but never turned up. We found a guidebook from Old Sarum amongst Morgan's possessions, with a brochure for the Foundation tucked inside. The tour guide says several Foundation members were there warning the tourists off pagan festivals."

"Old Sarum," said Maggie. "That's one of the places I'll be taking the kids. But it's only open on the weekends this time of year, so we're just going into Salisbury tomorrow, to the cathedral library."

Oh good, Thomas thought. "May I come with you? The cathedral librarian is an old friend. Perhaps we could offer the Dewar lad a ride as well."

Maggie threw up her hands. "Sure, why not? The more the merrier."

Jivan got to his feet. "We'll have the matter sorted soon."

"You say that like an incantation," Maggie told him. "Repeat it long enough and it'll come true."

"Our expectations affect the world around us." Thomas ducked her exasperated look by standing up. "Let me see Jivan to the door, Maggie. Then we can discuss a lecture on the history of Salisbury."

"See you later, Inspector," said Maggie.

"Cheers," Jivan said, although his expression said otherwise.

Thomas opened the door to reveal Sean, his face burnished by the wind and cold, poised on the doorstep. "Oh, hi. Is Rose in there? We were going to play basketball but she hasn't shown."

"Rose?" Maggie materialized at Thomas's shoulder. "She was sitting on that bench."

"Her notebook's there," Sean said.

"She wasn't there when I walked past," said Jivan.

"Okay," Maggie said, "so I'm paranoid. Let's find her."

Paranoia, thought Thomas, *is not inappropriate.* Setting his jaw, he said, "I'll help you search."

They walked out into the ragged remnants of daylight. The clouds had thickened into billows and bulges of shadow, muting the brilliant colors of the countryside like a painting coated with layers of varnish and time. The blue copybook lay on the bench, pages flapping in the wind.

"Yo, Rose!" called Sean.

Maggie walked briskly toward the garden gate. "Rose?"

The wind snatched the name away and shredded it to nothingness.

Chapter Eight

It was only when Rose penciled two dots above the word "pilgrimage" and closed her notebook that she realized how cold she was. She stood up and stretched.

Clouds flocked across the sun, tarnishing the bright colors of the landscape. The frosty wind fanned Rose's cheeks. She smelled smoke and something sweet, like flowers. She heard . . . A bus drove by, the yew hedge rustled, and a faint but clear voice called her name.

Rose. If the wind itself had a voice, this would be it, soft and silvery but neither male nor female, making her name less of a word than a sensual sigh. She peered into the garden.

Bushes with golden leaves and red berries lined the stone walls, bees careening from leaf to leaf. Below the diamond-paned windows of the gallery lay thick banks of purple foliage. Brick paths defined plots holding flowers and plants with neat labels—leek, columbine, hyssop, mullein, yarrow. In the center a low hedge coiled around the statue of a woman. She stood with one hand pressed to her breast, the other outstretched. The pose reminded Rose of Vivian in the Abbey.

The voice reminded her of nothing on Earth. *Rose,* it called. *Come into the garden, Rose.*

She walked into the garden. A warm breeze stroked the back of her neck and her nostrils flared with the heady scent of May. A smooth, undeniably masculine voice said, "Rose."

A man was standing inside the far gate, next to a bed labeled "wormwood" and "angelica." His casual pose showed off chino pants, boots, and a leather bomber jacket. His red hair was trimmed in a hip buzz cut and a red beard drew a sinuous line along his jaw and chin. A ray of sun spilled through the clouds, striking copper highlights from his hair and a glint from an earring. Neither shone as brightly as his eyes, emeralds gleaming beneath lids chiseled as deep and cold as those of a Roman statue.

Rose stared. This guy couldn't be for real—those green eyes had to be fashion contacts . . . He was the man from the Abbey. Taking a giant step backward she demanded, "How do you know my name?"

"Thomas London told me about you."

"He did? Who are you?"

"My name is Robin Fitzroy. I worked with Vivian Morgan. You found her body, I hear. Do you know what happened to her?"

Rose almost retorted, *don't you?* "I don't know anything. You'll have to talk to Inspector Gupta."

"Gupta is probably of these tiresome policeman who makes the evidence fit his solution instead of the other way round. Where would that leave me? A suspect, I should think. When the obvious suspect legged it."

"Excuse me?" Rose asked.

"The Scotsman. I told Vivian she deserved better, but she had to have her giggle. Calum's a bad lot. When he took her away I went after. I couldn't bear to watch, though. I might could have helped her, if I'd stayed." Robin's voice was the same as the wind's and yet different, darker and heavier, not chiffon but damask. It poured words into Rose's senses. "Not properly respectful of the Abbey, were they? And really, a quick and dirty shag on the cold grass when a firelit room with a canopied bed is much better suited to the slow friction of flesh against flesh."

Firelight, a canopied bed—that was one of her favorite scenarios. But the right guy with the right attitude hadn't come along yet. Rose was beginning to wonder if he ever would.

"I can guess what happened to Vivian," Robin went on. "I know what happened to you. You thought you were safe in the Abbey. You've been told all your life that a holy place is a safe one. But you weren't safe, were you? Something ugly and frightening got in. No wonder you feel betrayed."

She hadn't thought about it in those terms, and yet . . .

Robin took several steps toward her. He raised his hand. His fingers were long and elegant, his nails the pale gleam of mother-of-pearl. He gestured as though spilling flower petals from his palm.

The scented air caressed Rose's face and lifted her hair. *Magic* . . . The word tripped and fell over the edge of her mind. She wanted magic, but this wasn't it. This wasn't real. And yet magic wasn't real. Was it?

The bush at Robin's feet stirred. Purple shoots spread into leaves the same glistening green as his eyes. Buds swelled and opened into deep pink roses. He bent, plucked one perfect blossom, and held it out to her. "A rose for a rose. To show you that you can still trust your own beauty."

That wasn't right—beauty faded quicker than flowers. And yet the amazing eyes compelled her forward. Her stomach was melting down into her abdomen. She wondered what she'd do if he touched her.

The rosy petals swirled tightly into the heart of the flower. There among the golden stamens quivered a scarlet globule like a drop of blood. Reflected in its surface Rose saw Sleeping Beauty pricked by a thorn, Snow White biting an apple, Eve greedily stuffing the fruit of the tree of knowledge between her lips so that the juice ran down her chin and dripped onto her naked breasts. She clenched her hands, planted her feet, and looked back at the green eyes. "Who are you really?"

"Your friend. You'll be needing one. Thomas London defiles everyone and everything he touches. He seems so polite, so wise, but it's all a fraud."

The scent of flowers gathered thickly around her. His voice, the airy wind-voice, the solid man-voice, filled her head. The sensation was so exquisite it was nauseating. She shut her eyes.

"He'll speak against me," said the voice. "He'll tell you lies. But you can't trust him. He'll use you like he's used so many others, and then he'll betray you the way your faith betrayed you yesterday."

You're confusing me. Stop it. Go away. And something popped like a bubble, inside her senses rather than outside her body.

Rose opened her eyes. Robin was gone. The bush was an ordinary bush. Dunstan sat next to the garden gate, paws set primly together. The wind was cold. An icy raindrop plunked onto her head and ran down her temple.

Dunstan trotted away as Sean looked through the gateway. "Here she is, she's okay!"

"Why shouldn't I be okay?" demanded Rose.

"Hello? You witnessed a murder?"

"No I didn't . . ." Maggie, Thomas, and Inspector Gupta hurried into the garden. Rose said, "The man I saw in the Abbey was here. He knew my name. It's like he knew me."

Thomas's scowl edged Maggie's for fierceness, but only because Maggie looked scared as well as mad. "I don't believe this," she said.

"Believe it," Thomas told her.

His moustache flaring, Gupta whipped out his notebook the way an American cop would whip out his gun. "What did he say to you, Rose?"

She shook her head, trying to make sentences out of sensation. "His name is Robin Fitzroy. He said you told him about me, Thomas."

"He's a friend of yours?" Maggie's head jerked up toward Thomas's.

Thomas hesitated a moment before replying. "I know him, but he's no friend. I most certainly did not tell him about you, Rose. He seemed to know you, I should think, because he reads people like you or I read books."

Rose made a face. "That's it! He found my notebook! There were some poems in the back, personal stuff, and my name and this address inside the cover."

"Great." Maggie knotted her arms across her chest.

Anna peered around the gate. "Bess sent me to tell you it's tea time."

"The man Rose saw in the Abbey yesterday morning was just here," Maggie told her.

Anna joined the group. The accident scene, except Rose wasn't sure whether she'd just had an accident or not. "He said he worked with Vivian."

"There's no one in her office by that name," said Gupta.

"He said he was worried when Vivian went off with Calum and so he followed them. They were having sex so he left. He doesn't know what happened. He said Calum is your obvious suspect."

"His use of the word 'suspect' implies that he knows there was foul play," murmured Thomas.

Rose edited out Robin's sexual innuendo—her sexuality was no one's business but her own. She wasn't going to analyze her faith in front of everyone, either. "He warned me against you, Thomas. He said you use people. You're right, he's not your friend." *Even though he said he was mine.*

"I only hope," said Thomas, "I can set a good enough example . . ."

"I didn't believe him," Rose said quickly. "Well, his version of what happened is believable, I guess. He could've come back to the Abbey in the morning because he was worried about Vivian."

Gupta kept on writing. Thomas kept on scowling. Maggie said, "Good trick, getting in and out of the garden without anyone seeing him."

"That's it," said Rose. "It all seemed like a trick. First I smelled flowers, then he picked a flower from that bush and tried to give it to me. A flower with a drop of blood in it. I closed my eyes because I was dizzy. Then I heard you calling me and he was gone."

Gupta's dark brows arched. "Describe him, this Fitzroy chap."

"Shiny green eyes. Red hair and beard. Hip clothes. Earring, some sort of jewel. About thirty or thirty-five. Handsome. Almost too handsome."

"Oh boy," said Maggie. "I saw a man like that in the Abbey Sunday afternoon. He wasn't with Vivian and Calum, though."

"Probably casing the joint." Sean scuffed at the path.

Gupta asked Thomas, "Do you know where we can find him?"

"No, I don't know where you can find him."

"Even though you know him?" Maggie demanded.

"No," Thomas answered, the word round and hard as a hailstone.

"I'll make inquiries," said Gupta.

Sean eyed the little bush, its yellowed stalks obviously past their prime. "A flower. Blood. Yeah, right."

"I didn't make it up," Rose told him. "I didn't imagine it, either. It's like I was drunk, only I wasn't."

"No, you weren't," Thomas said. "To use an old and much debased Scots word, you were 'beglamoured.' A glamour is both magic spell and hypnosis."

"A trick," said Sean. "An illusion."

"The world is nothing but illusion to begin with," Gupta commented.

Maggie returned, "That's not a particularly helpful philosophy for a policeman."

"I compartmentalize." Gupta turned to Rose. "If you meet this man again, let me know. He may or may not be telling you the truth of what happened, but he does seem to be trying to gain your sympathy. Perhaps he intends to lure you away."

"If he wanted to eliminate me, he could've hit me over the head when I walked into the garden."

"True enough." Gupta clicked his pen thoughtfully, then tucked it and the notebook back into his jacket.

"I'm sure Bess wouldn't mind if you joined us for tea," Anna told him.

"Thank you, but we're expecting the Dewar lad at the station."

Rose compressed her lips. Robin had told her Calum was a bad lot, but he hadn't said anything about Calum's son. Maggie was looking up at Thomas, chin jutting, eyes narrowed. He looked down at her, sad and pale and very still. Just because he knew Robin didn't mean anything was his fault. Did it?

Sean sidled toward the gate. "Tea?"

Everyone turned to follow. Anna asked, "Thomas, is the statue in the knot garden another of your works?"

"Yes, it is," he replied. "Mary Magdalene, the Beautiful Sinner, beloved of Christ."

"Ah." Anna, too, tilted her head to look up at Thomas, except her expression was more quizzical than belligerent.

Maggie shot a look at the statue that avoided its maker, and made an about face. "Come on, Rose, let's get you inside."

Let Maggie have a maternal moment, it didn't hurt. *Especially,* Rose thought, *since I seem to have picked up a really off-the-wall stalker.* She glanced back to see Thomas standing stiff and still next to the statue.

Maggie retrieved her laptop from his cottage and Rose rescued her notebook from the bench. Gupta caught up with them as they trailed Sean and Anna toward the courtyard. "I've known Thomas since the year dot," he said. "He's the elder statesman hereabouts. Quite the chess player. His openings are subtle, but his end games can be right devastating."

"In other words," Maggie said, "you don't care that he seems to have some sort of prior relationship with this Robin Fitzroy character?"

"Thomas has a wide circle of acquaintances. And whilst he'd be the first to tell you he is his brother's keeper, I don't believe he actually is. Good night." Gupta went on toward the parking area. Maggie patted her laptop against her hip but said nothing.

More raindrops plopped onto Rose's head. Her hands were so cold she could hardly clasp her book. She was starving. She'd eat tea, scones, a horse, anything. Sexual sublimation, probably, along with all the other sublimated emotions, like confusion. And fear.

She could still hear Robin's voice. *All your prayers, all your beautiful music, they couldn't protect you.* And, *He'll betray you the way your faith betrayed you.*

No, she thought. Faith wasn't supposed to keep things from happening to you. Faith helped you deal with what did. And something was happening to her.

Believe it.

Ellen's shoes splashed into a puddle amongst the cobblestones. Rain sheeted off the roof onto the hood of her coat. She hunched her shoulders.

The scene inside the lounge was broken to bits by the small panes of glass in the window. The two young Yanks were dancing about to "First Rites," the single from Nevermas's new album. Naff name, that, and the words were blasphemous.

The Yanks looked to be toffee-nosed ponces like the ones at school. The blond bird was air and grace and other lies. The lad was a bit of all right, if not a patch on Robin. The woman working at a laptop must be the teacher, a sharp-faced trout who held herself like she'd just stepped in dog shit. An old woman sat in the corner reading a book. Alf Puckle stood smiling in the door. A stench in the nose of God, he was, like Glastonbury itself.

Where Vivian died. Ellen had always thought the woman was a gormless cow and that proved it, falling asleep in the ruins. She'd been shagging Calum, Robin said. Ellen thought Calum had better taste.

The cat leaped onto the windowsill. Its shining golden eyes stared at her standing in the rain and cold, shut out. She trudged across the yard, climbed the stoop in front of the kitchen door, and knocked.

It opened. Bess's round face peered out. "Ellen?"

"Here, Mum."

"Come through, love, come through."

Ellen ducked inside and stood dripping on the slate floor. The corridor was a white-painted tunnel, the only light caught in the rectangle of the dining room doorway at its end. The beat of the music reverberated in Ellen's stomach. "How are you keeping, Mum? Are you sleeping any better?"

"No I'm not, but the doctor gave me some tablets." Somewhere in the house the telephone went. Bess pulled a face. "Another reporter, I reckon. They've been at us since the American lass found the body."

"Don't talk to reporters, Mum. The media are part of the secular, Satanic conspiracy. Visit one of the Foundation-approved web sites, there's the truth for you."

"You've gone over the top with this Foundation business, Ellen."

"I'm better off now than I've ever been, Mum!"

"Squatting in that filthy loft?"

"Robin says you have to reject the world and its evil if you're to be saved in the End Times."

"Live here with us," Bess insisted. "I know you don't always get on with Alf, but he looked after me and you both after your dad left us."

"It's Robin who looks after me. Who'll look after you, too, if only you'll let him into your heart."

"Robin's a fine inspirational speaker, I'll give him that, but I joined St. John's church here in Glastonbury . . ."

"The Anglicans aren't true Christians. They've been corrupted like the Romans and the others." Ellen lowered her voice. "That's why Robin sent me here, to warn you."

"Warn me?" Bess asked.

Ellen whispered the name. "Thomas London. He's an evil man. He betrayed God. He hasn't even given you his true name. It's Thomas Maudit. That's 'cursed' in French. Thomas the Cursed."

"No," protested Bess. "He's a proper gentleman, he is."

"He's lying. He'll use anyone he can to prevent God's son from coming into his kingdom . . ."

"Nice," said Alf's voice. His bulk blocked the light in the door of the dining room. "Here she is with that religious codswallop."

Ellen stood her ground. Robin would be proud of her for standing her ground. "I'm telling you, Thomas Maudit will drag you down with him. You have to hate the sin and punish the sinner to be saved at the end."

"Saved from what? End of what?" Alf demanded.

"Saved from Hell at the end of the world. Less than two months now."

"Tripe and onions!"

"Alf," said Bess, "please."

He sighed. His chins softened. "Ellen, I only ever want what's best for you. Just like any dad wants for his daughter."

"You're never my dad."

"Please, Ellen," Bess said.

"Ah, leave it." Alf pulled several bank notes from his pocket. "Here, lass. This'll tide you over till you find work. You're welcome here, mind you, we can always use another pair of hands."

"Me? Washing up and scrubbing toilets for Yanks?"

"They're nice, well-spoken folk," protested Bess.

Ellen saw her opening. "Touring the naff old places, are they?"

"Yes, they're off to Salisbury tomorrow."

"But you have one room empty, don't you? My old room?"

"That's for the lad from Scotland, Mick Dewar. His dad's gone missing and he's helping the police. He'll be here to-night." Bess opened her hands. "They're all off tomorrow.

No one'll be here but us. I'll cook a lunch for you, and we'll have a nice chin-wag just like old times."

For a moment Ellen wanted to sit down with her mother so badly she felt sick. But it was too late for that. It was hard, knowing what was right whilst others went wrong, knowing that her own mum might have to be sacrificed . . . No. She wouldn't let it come to that. Her faith would save them both. "Thanks, Mum. Some other time. I have to go."

She opened the door. The rain was teeming down, reflecting the lights of the house in shimmering waves. The drumming of the water was almost loud enough to drown out the music.

"Here you are." Alf pulled an umbrella from a stand behind the door. With a swoosh its black fabric leaped outward into bat's wings.

"Oh. Ta," Ellen said. *Now why did he do that?*

"God bless," said Bess's voice behind her.

He has. The door snicked shut. The rain beat on the umbrella. Her feet were wet, the night was dark, but *he* was waiting. Ellen plunged into the shadow beneath the archway and collided with the wall. Pain streaked hot across her left hand. Ripped it on a nail, most like. Damn and blast!

She ran, slipping and stumbling, down the road toward Pomparles Bridge. A dark green Jaguar waited there, the glint of passing headlamps trickling like liquid fire down its windscreen. Chucking the umbrella away, Ellen scrambled into the cool leather-scented interior of the car. There. *They* were shut out.

Robin's eyes flashed green in the gloom. "Well?"

"Mum says the Americans are off to Salisbury tomorrow. Calum's son's coming here tonight."

"And?" he asked.

She was his favorite, wasn't she? He listened to her even

though he already knew all the answers. To him all hearts were open, all desires known. "The traitor's off to Salisbury as well. Good job, that, we can turn over his chapel and find the artifact."

"He'll not be keeping it in his chapel, although it's close to hand, I expect. Not that it will serve his purposes without the other two."

"We have the Book. Calum's after bringing us the Stone."

"Well now," Robin said, his voice a low growl, "Calum's not working with us any longer. Vivian corrupted him and turned him away from us. She paid the price for her treason, struck down by the hand of God."

Ellen went even colder. "You told me Calum was a special friend."

"He's gone wrong, hasn't he? See how strong our enemies are, how watchful we have to be? But God is on our side."

"Yes, he is." A car came along the road from Glastonbury. It stopped, headlamps spotlighting the sign "Temple Manor B&B," then turned into the car park. The twin red eyes of its tail lamps disappeared behind the wall. Was that him, then, Calum's son? Calum set great store by him. "Mick will be corrupted by the traitor as well!"

"I'll sort him out."

"That's good of you, Robin." Ellen held her throbbing hand in front of her face. In the dim light she could see blood red against her skin.

"Hurt yourself, have you?" Robin took her cold hand in his and lifted it to his lips. Just the slightest breath, tingling across her palm, and the pain ebbed. "There you are."

Her palm was whole again. "Robin, you're the business!"

"Yes," he replied. He started the car. It purred up the

road. The lights of Glastonbury smeared and ran down the windows, as though the town was drowning and she and Robin alone were saved. Ellen nestled into the seat, safe at the left hand of God.

Chapter Nine

Mick raised the knocker and let it fall. He was minded of the sanctuary knocker at Durham cathedral. Sanctuary. The word had a good sound to it, solid, like the reverberating thud of iron upon iron.

The door opened. His bleary eyes focused on the man who stood in the opening. "Mr. Puckle, is it?"

"Puckle it is, lad. Come through." And, over Mick's shoulder as he stepped across the threshold, "Thomas. Filthy night, isn't it?"

"And yet without rain nothing would grow." The second man was tall, with a stern pale face like the stone effigy of a Crusader. He closed his umbrella and shut the door. "Good evening. Mick Dewar, I presume?"

"Aye, that I am."

"Thomas London." His handclasp was firm if cool.

"The missus has already gone up to bed—headache—but I can lay on some sandwiches and a cuppa," said Puckle.

Mick flexed his icy fingers. "Thank you kindly."

The distant beat of Nevermas's newest hit reverberated not in his ears but in his entire body. The lads had done themselves proud—brilliant bit of work, "First Rites." It had played on the car radio so often the words furrowed Mick's mind: *From the world, the flesh, and the Devil deliver me. From the world, the flesh, and the Devil make me anew.*

"I'll show him to his room," said London.

"Righty-ho." Puckle walked toward the rear of the house.

Mick followed London to the staircase. The long triangular treads spiraling upward were bowed deeply on the wider side. Each one groaned in turn beneath his feet. Shadowy corridors led from the landing. London opened the door of a small, spotlessly tidy room close by the stairs. "Thank you kindly," Mick said again. "And the loo?"

"Just there, across the hall. I'll leave you to it. The dining room's downstairs on the left." London's footsteps receded down the steps.

Mick dropped his rucksack on the bed. The weight inside his jacket as he draped it over a peg was the *sgian dubh*. All this time it had rested heavy as a bad conscience against his heart.

The face reflected in the mirror above the washbasin wasn't his own—bloodshot gray eyes were cushioned by black bags, stubbled cheeks were creased by hours of gritted teeth. His hair was a mare's nest. He yanked the elastic band from his ponytail and combed the dark waves smooth. He splashed his face with warm water and gargled with cold. *A hot bath,* he thought. Clean clothes. The starched white pillowcase on the bed beckoned him to sleep.

No. Waking or sleeping all he'd hear was his father's voice, begging for help he couldn't give. All he'd see was the road ahead, empty.

Mick hirpled back down the stairs, his feet clumsy on the misshapen treads, and stopped. The lass climbing the stairs also stopped, two steps below him. Her face turned toward him like a daffodil toward the sun. He'd once read an essay saying that flowers proved the grace of God. He must have died and gone to heaven, then, and here was an angel come to welcome him.

But she was staring as though she were the one peeking through the Pearly Gates, her eyes blue as wee bits of sky or sea. Her lips parted. "Hi."

She was one of the Americans Gupta had mentioned. "Hello yourself."

"I'm Rose Kildare."

"Mick Dewar."

"Oh, you're Calum's son. I found—uh—I'm sure you'll find him real soon now. Sorry, I'm in your way." Without taking her eyes from his she edged toward the narrower side of the staircase and lost her balance.

He grasped her hand to steady her.

"Thank you," she said.

"No problem." Even after he released her hand its warm shape nestled in his. Her fragrance teased his nostrils. He inched past, until he was one step below her and they stood nose to nose. "I'll be seeing you later, then."

"Oh yes." She smiled.

Blinded, Mick managed to walk himself down the stairs and into the dining room without falling.

Thomas London sat at the table, stirring a cup of tea. The man's expression was that grim he might as well have been digging a grave with his spoon. Gupta had told him about this chap London as well. He might help sort this business about relics. Mick had already sorted Gupta—no, his dad wasn't jealous and possessive of women.

A plate of roast beef sandwiches and crisps waited. So did a black and white cat, sitting beside his chair. Mick tore a wee bittie of beef and held it out. "There you are." The cat nipped it from his fingers.

He sat down, bit into the sandwich, and chewed. His jaw felt heavy.

London pushed a steaming cup toward him. "Do you mind if I join you?"

"Not at all," Mick returned thickly.

"I believe I'm a friend of your family. That is, I am if the most recent Malise Dewar of Glendochart was your—great-grandfather, I suppose?"

"That was my great-grandad's name right enough. And his grandad's. But my dad's the family genealogist."

"There's no news of him, I take it?"

"No." Mick forced the wad of beef, bread, and mustard down his throat and gulped tea, burning his tongue.

A woman stepped through the doorway. She was dressed in jeans and a sweatshirt depicting a cartoon armadillo, tire tracks a grid across its body. Her auburn hair swept back from a high, clear forehead. She frowned at London, not in anger, Mick thought, but in puzzlement. Her dark eyes suggested that she was frequently puzzled, and the tilt of her chin that she made a habit of asking questions.

"Maggie," London said, "this is Mick Dewar, Calum's son. Mick, Maggie Sinclair. She's here with a group of students."

"I'm sorry," Maggie said, and for a moment Mick thought she was apologizing for being there. "I saw your father and Vivian Morgan Sunday afternoon. My student, Rose, found Vivian's body Monday morning."

"Rose? I met her on the staircase. Thought I was hallucinating."

With a short laugh, Maggie pulled out a chair and sat down.

"Gupta asked me if I knew Vivian Morgan, But I dinna ken her from Adam. From Eve." Mick forced down another bite of sandwich.

"Your father's an amateur historian?" London prodded.

"Aye, like old Malise, right keen on history and tradition."

"Could you tell me what he said when he rang you?"

Mick had repeated the words so many times they played counterpoint to "First Rites" in his gut: *From the world, the flesh, and the hounds of hell* . . . "He was havering about not believing something and then finding it was true. He said the hounds of hell were after him, and they'd be after me if he told me. Then he was going on about a relic."

"A relic?" Distant lightning flickered in London's eyes.

"He didna give it a name. It was the Bruce's, he said, at Arbroath Abbey. His friend Sinclair's father came to his—dad's—father and they shifted it."

"Sinclair," repeated Maggie, with another pucker at London.

He said, "King Robert the Bruce. And Alexander Sinclair of Stow, near Melrose, am I right?"

"Oh aye, same name for father and son both."

"Was the son killed in an automobile accident fifteen years ago?"

"Aye. He's gone, and his dad, and my grandad and his dad—they're all gone." Mick's breath caught in his throat. He washed it down with tea. "Dad said that it's our duty to protect it—the relic, I reckon. From, he said—if I understood the Gaelic—*Am Fear Dubh*. 'Dubh' is 'black,' but—ah, he was off his head, going on about time coming to an end."

"Not a bit of it." London's eyes were growing brighter, shot with light. "Calum was, to use the old Scots word, fey. Facing his doom or his destiny. He'd just seen the old family stories in a new light. As for *Am Fear Dubh*, it means 'the Black Man.' The Devil."

That's daft, Mick thought. But still a chill oozed down his back.

"Did your father tell you where they hid this relic?"

"Not so's you'd understand. Take the A68 and the A7, he said, to Fairtichill and Schiehallion, the fairy mountain—'sidhe' means 'fairy' in the Gaelic, so that's sensible, at least. But he said 'the mountain with the triple peak,' which is dead wrong. And both the A7 and the A68 run south from Edinburgh, not northwest. There's no Fairtichill at all. He started singing, 'you take the high road and I'll take the low road, past Ercildoune and into the gates of hell.' Then the line went dead."

"The A7 and the A68," repeated London. "Ercildoune."

"He was confusing some of old Malise's tales, I'm thinking." Light footsteps came down the staircase. Rose, a vision in denim, walked past the doorway. She sent Mick another smile. His rigid lips softened in a reply. Then she was gone, her steps absorbed by the distant beat of the music. Or else by the beat of his own heart . . . Now wasn't the time to be eyeing the lasses. "My dad's in trouble."

"I'm afraid he is," said London. "And so are you."

"Why? He didna tell me anything." Mick shoved his empty plate away.

"Oh yes he did. Several things, amongst them that your grandfather and Alex's father relocated a relic that was associated with Arbroath Abbey. He also mentioned 'Fairtichill,' the old Gaelic name of the village of Fortingall, which lies at the mouth of Glenlyon as Schiehallion lies along its course."

"Fortingall, is it? Dad and I always stopped there on our way to see his folk in Killin. We'd view the old yew tree in the churchyard and have a piece at the hotel."

"That's supposed to be the birthplace of Pontius Pilate," said Maggie. "Wrong time period, but a good story."

London nodded. "Robert Campbell, who directed the massacre at Glencoe, was indubitably born in the area. The story is a morality play, I should think, of the hazards of simply following orders."

"From fairies to Pilate," Mick said, "there's a leap for you."

"It's not so vast a leap as all that. A little alchemy at work, you might say." London's smile almost reached his ash-brown eyes. "Do you know the etymology of your own name?"

"A Gaelic word meaning 'guardian' or 'keeper,' my dad says."

"Yes. Like 'Baker' or 'Fisher,' *deoradh* is an occupation used as a surname. You may have heard of the relics of St. Fillan of Glendochart. The caretakers were named Dewar."

"And Killin's at the head of Glendochart, aye, but how, but why . . ." Mick's brain ached. London's words ebbed and flowed like the tide. "My dad and I've been on our own for three years now, since my mum died, you'd think I could help him when he was wanting help."

"You may yet be able to help him, Mick. So might we all."

"We?" asked Maggie.

"Sinclair," said London. "The etymology is French, 'Saint Clair,' holy light. The St. Clairs have long been knights in service of holy relics in France and in Scotland both. There's no such thing as coincidence, Maggie."

Her brows arched. So did Mick's. "My dad said that."

"Did he now? He'd realized, I expect, that he—and you—are chapters in a long and very old story. Just yesterday my friend Ivan O'Connell told me that the relic he's been guarding has gone missing. I should think that relic you guard is threatened as well."

"We're no guardians of anything."

"Your family has reduced your knowledge to rumor and quaint custom is all. And your alliance with the Sinclairs has confused the issue. Do you by any chance have a *sgian dubh*? One with a black stone chipping in the hilt?"

"Oh aye, that I do. It's upstairs."

"Yes!" London smiled again, this time a fierce, bright

smile that swept from his mouth to his eyes and flashed like a brandished blade.

Mick stared. "The knife's the relic, is it?"

"It's a memento of the relic. I should keep a keen eye on it, Mick. Keep it with you."

"Let me guess," said Maggie. "This has something to do with the sheath for a little knife that Gupta found in Vivian Morgan's things."

"He showed it me. It might could be one of the souvenirs we sell in the mill slop. Shop." He burped mustard. "I've never heard tell of this Morgan woman. And there's another one—Dad's been making checks over to an Ellen Sparrow."

"Has he now?" London laid his hands on the table, as though contemplating a chess game. He had the long fingers of an artist on the strong hands of a warrior. "I feel certain your relic has something to do with Vivian's death, which in turn is part of a larger pattern."

"How?" Maggie persisted. "I know people all over the world worship relics . . ."

"We Catholics do not worship relics. We revere the saint they represent. A relic is a bridge between the seen and the unseen, between the flesh and the spirit. A metaphor made tangible."

"Eh?" said Mick.

"Our reverence for relics connects our faith to the much older beliefs from which it sprang, beliefs that revered the natural world."

"Eh?" Mick said again.

"That doesn't answer my question," said Maggie.

"Suffice it to say that relics—and three relics in particular—give us the chance, allow us to choose, to bring good into this world. But there are those who prefer to bring evil." London set his hand on Mick's forearm. "Lift up your heart,

Mick. You were brought here for a purpose. We were all brought here for a purpose. We're off to Salisbury tomorrow, and you're booked to ride along. I suggest you have a rest."

"Oh aye, Dad was on a tour from Salisbury, but . . ." At his feet sat the cat, his paws tucked beneath his breast, his golden eyes half closed, radiating sleep. Mick's eyelids felt like sandbags. He was tempted to ask London, *who are you,* but he suspected he'd get no better answer. Yawning, he pulled himself to his feet and turned toward the door. "Good night, Mr. London. Ms. Sinclair."

"Peace be with you," London said quietly.

The stairs seemed the height of Ben Nevis. Mick stopped halfway to catch his breath. From down the corridor soared a glorious soprano voice, ". . . the word made flesh, in the world made true . . ." *Rose.* If he and his mates had a singer like her their band would be as brilliant as Nevermas . . . The band didn't matter now.

Maggie's voice said, "What's that supposed to mean? We were brought here for a purpose?"

"You want answers, do you?"

Yes, I do, thought Mick.

"Yes, I do," Maggie replied. "You got any?"

"A few. And it's time I acted upon them. Come with me tomorrow to Old Sarum, a place of many meetings and many partings, and I'll share my answers with you."

The house creaked. Maggie said, "Yeah. Sure. Why not? Which is one question I'll answer myself, thank you." A chair scraped. Footsteps paced toward the back of the house.

Mick had no answers at all. He stumbled into his room, collapsed onto the bed, and landed hard in a pool of nightmare.

Chapter Ten

Maggie stood in the garden, trying to corral her wits. The morning sky shone a flawless blue, washed clean. Sunlight played across the gallery windows with their tiny panes of glass like fingers playing across a harp.

The gentle flute and harp music she'd heard after the All Souls' bell was echoed, oddly enough, by the lilt of "First Rites," the song the kids played over and over again last night. The insistent beat of electric guitars, drums, and bagpipes was not soothing, though, but energizing, throbbing in her gut like a second heart. *No wonder the Scots marched into battle behind a piper,* Maggie thought.

The eyes of the statue of Mary Magdalene, the penitent, were filled with both regret and hope. One hand rejected the past, the other reached toward the future. Was the work sensitive or manipulative? Which was Thomas? What did he want from her? *We were brought here for a purpose,* he'd said, which meant his motive was between pretentious and profound. Something Miltonian, along the lines of justifying God to man? As much as Maggie wanted to respond, *yeah, right,* that old pebble in her mind and that new pulse in her gut whispered, *if only.*

Outside the garden gate, she found Mick just closing his cell phone. He was clean-shaven and neatly ponytailed, but his eyes were haunted and hunted both. "Still no news?" she asked.

"Not one bloody word." Mick tucked his phone into his jacket. "London's a wee bit daft, is he?"

"He's either crazy or he's saner than anyone I've ever met."

"Oh aye, Inspector Gupta said something like that."

Maggie wondered about Gupta, too, but held her tongue. Together she and Mick walked to the car park, where Rose and Sean waited beside the mini-van. Anna had already claimed a middle seat. Thomas stood with his hands in the pockets of a heavy tweed coat, exuding a warm scent of wool and soap.

His smile was affable, even though something in his eyes reminded Maggie of dark clouds massed on the horizon. "Good morning. I'll sit beside you, shall I, so I can offer the appropriate remark every so often?"

"Please," Maggie said with a wave of her hand. In some people Thomas's old-fashioned speech would be ludicrous, but it fit him, every inch—and he had a good many inches—the scholar.

"Did you sleep well?" Thomas asked Mick.

"I kept dreaming my dad was standing over me, all pale and woeful."

Maybe he was, Maggie thought with a shudder.

Rose touched Mick's sleeve. "I'm sorry."

"Thank you," he said, and ten years slipped off his face.

Disgruntled, Sean clambered into the back seat. Maggie rolled her eyes. With his sense of entitlement and his truculent need to prove something—anything—Sean reminded her of her former husband, Danny. Whatever Thomas needed to prove was nothing so straightforward as his manhood.

Rose settled on the far side of the same seat, leaving the center vacant. Mick sat down next to Anna. Maggie settled herself behind the wheel. "Seat belts on? Good. Off we go."

By the time they reached the main road she was ordering herself to relax. She'd driven on the left before, and chauffeured people talking about less interesting topics than Alfred the Great and Arthur—who, Thomas said, fought against the Angles but became the hero of English—the red dragon of Wales, the cross of Christ, the cauldron of the Great Goddess—the earth principle, said Thomas, and the male and the female. Not only his patrician accent but Mick's Scottish lilt made the American voices sound flat as the whine of a power saw.

The names on the road signs—"Charlton Mackrell," "Compton Pauncefoot"—elicited outrageous puns even from Anna. The world, the flesh, and the Devil swelled inside Maggie's stomach until she felt ready to explode. The original prayer, she thought, went, "From the *deceits* of the world . . ." That was the issue, wasn't it? Deceit and trust. And yet the world was not deceitful. People were.

Soon they were driving through the narrow streets of Salisbury, making circles around the silvery spire of the cathedral. At last Maggie found a car park and turned everyone loose. Rose, Sean, and Mick moved off in a clump. "Maybe Sean's accepted him," said Anna. "Nothing like comparing stories of pub-crawling and bar-hopping to forge a brotherhood."

Thomas ushered the group through an ancient archway and into the vast enclosure of the Cathedral Close. Sean aimed his camcorder toward the spire. "Church towers and spires are today's standing stones," Maggie lectured. "Both cosmic pillars and phallic symbols."

"Raised not only to the greater glory of God but to the arrogance of man," murmured Thomas.

"You know you've created God in your own image, when you think your enemies are His enemies," Maggie returned.

"Quite." Thomas's eyes glinted with something more than sunlight.

Fey, she thought. Maybe that described her mood, too, goaded by fate into—into what? Demanding answers?

They entered the cathedral through the north porch, passing a bulletin board lined with notices. Inside, ash-gray Gothic arches sprang one upon the other higher and higher, until the vault of the nave ceiling was the vault of heaven itself. Shape and shadow met in an austere harmony, plainchant in stone. The air was cool and damp, scented with mildew, flowers, and candle wax. The throb in Maggie's stomach beat like a drum, *dust in your hands, wet by blood, knotwork in flesh willing when the spirit is weak . . .*

Delivering commentary, Thomas led them past another chapel of St. Thomas Becket to the far end of the building. "Here we have the Prisoners of Conscience window, created only twenty years ago."

Beyond a grove of slender marble pillars glowed a stained glass window, multiple faces and forms on a blue background. The Virgin's tranquil blue, Maggie noted, not Mary Magdalene's red, despite—or because of—the blood shed by centuries of martyrs. "Martyr" meant "witness," after all—a conscious witness, not an innocent bystander. *Wet with blood, feet of clay . . .*

Mick, Rose, and Sean threaded the blue-gray pillars to the far side of the chapel. Behind her, Maggie heard Anna's hushed voice, each word carefully measured. "The faces in the window look like the faces on the train platform as the soldiers loaded the boxcars going to Auschwitz. Most of my family died at Auschwitz."

"I'm very sorry to hear that," Thomas said.

"The one redeeming feature of the Holocaust was that so many people risked their lives to save others. You remind me of one of them, a Catholic priest who carried many Jewish children to safety. I was one of those children. I've often wondered what happened to that man, whether he paid for his faith with his life."

"I should imagine," Thomas said, his quiet voice resonating among the pillars, "he lived on to continue his search for redemption."

Maggie glanced around to see Anna cast one last look at Thomas, part baffled, part calculating, and then walk quickly after the others. What was that all about? Redemption? Was that something you found, like buried treasure? Was it something you earned by building a cathedral? By risking your life for another? Simply by believing? You didn't find it by persecuting other people, Maggie knew that much.

The students, Mick, and Thomas were moving down the far aisle. She hurried after them. At the crossing of the nave and the transepts Thomas told them to sight upward along a column. It was perceptibly bent, the stone sagging beneath the weight of the great spire. In the south transept he announced, "The chapels of St. Margaret of Scotland, who reconciled the Celtic and Roman churches. St. Lawrence, a Grail-saint. St. Michael, dragon-slayer and weigher of souls, who was an angel long before the life of Our Lord. And," Thomas added, "here's Mrs. Howard, the librarian. Edith!"

The woman who emerged from a door in the corner of the transept could have been anywhere between fifty and seventy, with short gray hair and a stylish purple sweater and skirt. "Good to see you again, Thomas. And this must be the student group from America."

Maggie introduced herself and the others, concluding, "Thank you so much for letting the students use the library, Mrs. Howard. They all know their topics. If you could just show them the references, they can take care of themselves." She punctuated her sentence with a severe look. "Right?"

"Don't leave the cathedral," Thomas directed.

All three faces, Anna, Rose, and Sean, nodded agreement.

"I'll sure we'll get on famously." Mrs. Howard led them toward the door. Rose shot one last smile at Mick and was gone.

"I'll be having a wee dauner down to the police station." Mick swayed back and forth, like a magnet caught between positive and negative poles, then fell into a brisk walk that carried him around the corner.

Maggie saw that a stringy-haired girl was watching them from the ranks of wooden chairs. Well, Mick and Sean were almost as eye-catching as Rose, in a more terrestrial way. Taking a deep breath, she turned to Thomas. "You said you'd answer some questions."

"Yes, I did. Although the answers may be more than you want to hear."

The word made flesh, in the world made true, and the Devil take his due from your hands. The words, the images crowded together in Maggie's head, beating out time, beating time itself. She was caught between medieval fantasy, soap opera, and the Twilight Zone. She was caught in Thomas London's eyes, their embers flaring into a fire so hot and strong she felt sure she was casting a shadow on the gray stone of the floor.

The issue, she thought, was not only what he wanted from her, but what she wanted from him. Maggie reached for her keys. "Try me."

Chapter Eleven

"Park in the farmyard," Thomas told Maggie.

She had driven the three miles from Salisbury without speaking, but not, he thought with a glance at the sun-dappled highlights in her dark eyes, without thinking. Now she parked in the farmyard and leaned over the steering wheel to look as skeptically up at the vast mound of Old Sarum as she looked at him.

What were the children singing last night? *From the deceits of the Devil deliver me?* An appropriate motto for the day's work—assuming the day's work went as it should. As, please God, it must. This time he would not betray his own decision.

The slams of their doors echoed from the looming earthen ramparts. Thomas climbed the gate across the path and offered Maggie his hand. She took it. Her flesh sent a wave of warmth up his arm, as though the same swift palpitation of hope and dread pulsed in her body as in his.

They walked toward the mound of the Norman stronghold that rose above the hub of the Iron Age hill fort, past the ruined gatehouse and up to a track atop the highest earthen battlements. There they stood, braced against the rush of wind, not quite side-by-side, not quite back-to-back. A landscape sculpted by time and man rolled away before them, the cathedral city of Salisbury looking like a child's model in the valley below. Catching his breath, Thomas smelled not only smoke but a teasing odor of incense. The Otherworld, then, did indeed interlace itself with this one, here and now.

Maggie's nostrils flared. Her expression of skepticism deepened into suspicion, but all she said was, "Okay, we're here. How about those answers—you know, who, what, when, where. Why."

"Today is the feast day of St. Winifred of Wales. The story of her martyrdom is yet another echo of an old Celtic tale. Her shrine, Holywell, draws pilgrims to this day."

"That's the when. And the where?"

"Celt, Roman, Anglo-Saxon, Dane—the many peoples of Britain have all been familiar with this place. Sarum was once the site of a great Norman castle and a greater cathedral. But by 1164 secular and spiritual rivalries had driven Sarum into decline. King Henry II preferred his hunting lodge at Clarendon, just beyond that hill."

"The Constitutions of Clarendon," Maggie said obligingly, "were a compromise in the power struggle between church and state. Becket as Archbishop of Canterbury signed, but the next day retracted his signature. His allies mocked him, saying, 'Only our leader fled the field.' "

Thomas's jaw tightened, sending a ripple of tension down his spine. Waves of grass rose and fell like sea-swells around the massive earthworks. Hares gamboled up and down the slopes.

"Going beyond history to legend," prompted Maggie, "Sarum is one of the places that might be Camlann, where Arthur was defeated."

"Like Glastonbury, Sarum is older than the legions, older than the Celts. Look there, beyond the spire of the cathedral—can you see the mound of another hill fort, Clearbury Ring?"

She squinted toward the southern horizon. "Oh—yes."

"Stand atop Clearbury and sight north, and the line will pass through the cathedral, across Sarum, and into the circle of Stonehenge. Close by Amesbury, where Guinevere did penance after Camlann."

"Ley lines are more wishful thinking than real."

"Mostly, yes. Not this one. Nor the line through Glastonbury, which begins at St. Michael's Mount off Cornwall, passes through other high places devoted to St. Michael, and ends at Avebury stone circle."

"Those lines must cross somewhere, like x marks the spot."

"They cross at Liddington Castle, another ancient hill fort, reputed to be the site of the battle of Mount Badon, Arthur's greatest victory."

"Where he won a generation of peace . . ." Maggie's brows cramped. "By the time the Saxons reached Glastonbury they'd become Christians, and didn't destroy it. Are you trying to tell me that Glastonbury is so important that supernatural forces, God, whatever—arranged history around it?"

"All I can tell you is that Sarum is a place of conflict and exclusion," Thomas answered. "The Waste Land of Arthurian myth. Whilst Glastonbury is a place of inclusion, growth, and renewal. Avalon."

"So inclusion is your answer to life, the universe, and everything?" For a long moment she considered his words, her expression indicating an emotion between incredulity and impatience. "That's great. I like it. But where do Vivian and Calum come in?"

"They are but the tip of the iceberg. Its body is a pattern which was laid down in deepest antiquity by those supernatural forces we call faith. But I can't play my role in that pattern, or lead anyone else into his—hers—without confronting Robin Fitzroy."

Maggie's gaze raked him like a cannon salvo. "I wondered

when we were going to get to him. Have you arranged to meet him here?"

"I hope to attract his attention." Thomas set off along the path which followed the top of the battlement.

Below lay the foundations of the cathedral, its crossed arms diagrammed in concrete, the arc of the ancient earthworks making of it a Celtic cross. Another symbol almost filled the square of the cloister, the whorls of an immense fingerprint drawn upon the green grass. Across it cut black bars, as though canceling it out.

"A labyrinth," Maggie said, catching him up. "A Cretan spiral. Another pre-Christian survival."

"Yes," said Thomas, as much to himself as to her. His senses itched like skin wearing a hair shirt. *The word made flesh, feet of clay* . . . Here and now, it had to be here and now. He led the way down a flight of muddy steps so quickly Maggie had to run. In moments they stood inside the cloister.

She brushed her fingertips across the stiffened grass. "The labyrinth is paint, but the bars are burned. Did the Foundation people try to break up a labyrinth ceremony here? If all this is about freedom of religion, then you can count on me."

"Thank you." Thomas considered her intelligent and demanding face, her cheeks burnished to the crimson of a ripe apple by the cold wind. She was more than a pawn if not quite a queen—a knight, perhaps, leaping at unexpected angles. The queen waited at the center of the labyrinth, whether Mary the Holy Mother or Ariadne the Great Mother didn't matter. The journey mattered, and the defeat of the beast who blocked the way.

Maggie stood up, brushing off her hands. "Have I passed the historical trivia test? Are you going to tell me what's really going on here?"

His smile was taut as a bowstring. "It's not your test, but

mine. Until I tell the truth about who and what I am, I cannot move freely against Robin."

"Is he blackmailing you?"

"In a way. You see . . ." Thomas's ear caught the step behind them. He turned. Maggie stared.

Robin stood just outside the cloister walls, his hands on his hips, his head cocked to the side, the sunlight gleaming on his red hair but not touching the cold depths of his eyes. As usual, he was fashionably dressed, thick shoes, denim trousers and jacket, a heather-green pullover.

So then, as he had gambled, Robin could not resist the chance to crow. Thomas pretended indifference, even as his heart pounded loud as a snare drum beating a call to arms. "Maggie, may I introduce Robin Fitzroy?"

Robin looked her up and down. He smiled, his eyeteeth glinting between his pink lips. "Ah yes. You were lecturing your students in Glastonbury Abbey Sunday afternoon. I was tempted to join the group, you were expressing yourself so beautifully."

Maggie's chin went up. "You did join the group, didn't you? But not because of me. You were harassing Rose."

"Now, now, did she say 'harass'? I think not. I was merely offering her my help and protection against Thomas here, a well-known liar and seducer. It's not too late for you, is it? What lies has he been telling you?"

Maggie looked sharply from Robin to Thomas and back.

"If *you* were an honest man," Thomas told him, "you would speak with Inspector Gupta about Vivian Morgan's death."

"I'd be happy to talk to him," Robin returned, voice like silk. "I have no reason to protect Calum Dewar."

"I very much suspect Calum is an innocent man. So innocent he almost fell into your trap. But he's thwarted you, hasn't he? You may have the Book, but you don't have the Stone."

"The Book?" Maggie repeated. "The Stone?"

Robin's smile faltered. His eyes flicked toward Maggie. Thomas dared to interpret his expression as doubt. And yet the silky voice went smoothly on, "My people have the Book, yes. We'll soon have the Stone. And we'll have your artifact as well, for I have long held you as my vassal."

"You have never been my lord, only my jailor. But I cannot defend the honor of God when my own honor is in doubt. Therefore I shall confess publicly—to a woman, Robin. To a woman."

"That's what you're playing at, is it?" Robin demanded. "She'll not believe you if you do tell her, you fool."

"Perhaps. Perhaps not."

"In all these years you've never had the bollocks to tell anyone the truth. Balls, to our American friend here. Or has she already discovered their absence for herself?" Robin's voice frayed.

Maggie's face was a study in bewilderment, but for once she held her tongue. It took an exceptional person to realize when she was out of her depth, and silently Thomas saluted her.

"To believe you is to despise you!" Robin hissed.

"Maybe so. Still, I hereby reject you and all your deceits." Stiffly Thomas unfurled his full height. He raised his hand, fore and middle fingers pointed upward. *"Pax domini sit semper vobiscum,"* he said, and traced up and down, left and right.

"How dare you wish me the peace of God!" Robin's face contorted, and suddenly he was no longer handsome. "If you want so badly to suffer, then do so, and the both of you be damned!"

Thomas had only a moment to brace himself. To throw a quick apology toward Maggie. To pray, *Blessed St. Winifred, let her witness!*

Robin gestured, two fingers down, in mockery of Thomas's blessing. The movement drew darkness from the bright sky, darkness split with lightning and the screams of tormented souls.

Unless it was his own scream, of pain far worse than any physical agony. Falling, Thomas landed hard inside the all-too-familiar memory, inside the all-too-familiar illusion that illustrated the memory, not on grass but on stone flags covered with rushes. Darkness encompassed him—no, there was light, guttering torchlight, and the face above him wasn't Robin's but Henry's. Henry, who had been the friend of his soul, until, in their pride, they betrayed each other . . .

The parchment lay before him. His gold seal touched the wax. The watching eyes gloated. He knew then that to compromise was to put aside pride. And yet pride was knit into every sinew of his body. Pride sustained him from Clarendon to Northampton across the Channel and so to exile in France. There eyes looked at him with respect, even love, love he did not deserve. For seven years he endured those eyes, and at last made his decision.

The towers of Canterbury cathedral were gray against gray December skies. His clerk's sober voice told him that for once he should unbend far enough to take advice. But it was too late, he'd pushed Henry too far. And now their quarrel would end at the sword's point, with him assuming a martyr's crown, with Henry at last on his knees in penitence.

It was night in the cathedral. The monk's voices quavered as they sang Vespers, and the words—*magnificat anima meum Dominum*—resonated eerily amongst the columns. He turned as the knights rushed clattering through the cloister door, and went down to meet them. Edward, go, David, go with him. But in their love the monks stayed beside him, even as swords glinted in quick red reflections of the altar lamp.

Outside the lamp's feeble gleam the shadows thronged thick and black, concealing everyone and everything—except for Maggie in her jumper and jeans, her fist pressed to her mouth, her eyes huge, amazed, horrified, *seeing* . . .

David stood blocking the crypt staircase, his arms raised like a priest welcoming his congregation. Thomas stood behind a pillar in the musty chill air of the crypt. It was David's voice that called upon St. Denis, one of Thomas's patrons. It was David's voice that was stilled suddenly by blows of metal first upon bone and then upon stone.

The mailed footsteps fled into silence. He stood in the darkness, cold sweat streaming down his back, as above him the monks crept forward. The Archbishop's face was shattered, they said, and the bony crown of his skull lay like a chalice on the bloody pavement. His face—David's face—was shrouded with blood, holy blood, the blood of the martyr.

Thomas's pride dissolved in that blood. The greatest courage, he realized, wasn't pride but humility. Darkness spiraled past his eyes, dark and flame, blood and sweat swirling in a vortex, not sucking him down but pushing him up, as the mouth of Hell spat him out.

Tears burned his cheeks and stone cut into his shoulders. The light was so bright he turned away—they'd found him, hiding in his shame . . . No. Clear blue sky arched overhead. The wind sang cold and clean. This was Sarum. The ruined cathedral lay behind him, its stone patterned in the body of Christ, its cloister anointed with the ancient spiral path.

Always before he'd waked from the memory-illusion to find himself lying unmanned at Robin's feet, Robin's laughter acid in his ears. But not this time. This time Maggie's dumbfounded face peered down at him, her eyes small labyrinths. This time Maggie's voice stammered, "Are you—you all right?"

That, Thomas told himself, *is the question.*

Chapter Twelve

Every fiber of Thomas's body ached fiercely and his stomach churned. That was nothing new. What was new was the sudden hope that he was no longer alone in his agony. He set his hand on Maggie's cheek and lightly brushed her lips with his own. *"Pax domini sit semper tecum."*

"Yeah, sure, peace be with you too." She sat back with a thump. "I've stopped wondering if you're crazy. Now I'm wondering if I'm crazy."

"You're quite sane, I assure you."

"Yeah. Right. So what was all that—that—I could see the stone and the grass and you right through it but you were in it, too." Maggie took a shuddering breath. Her eyes darted up, down, to the side and back to his face, wild surmise beating against the borders of rationality. "Okay, I don't see any projectors or whatever, and if I did, I'd still want to know why you were playing tricks on me."

"What you saw was no trick. It was the memory of my guilt. In the words of St. Bernard of Clairvaux: "This is the worm that dieth not, the memory of things past.""

"Oh yes," she said emphatically. "But—but—why did you goad Robin into—into doing that? So I could see? Was that your truth? If I know the truth does it set you free?"

"We'll find out soon enough, I expect." Thomas sat up. He fumbled through the grass, found his eyeglasses, and put them on.

Maggie's features resumed their angularities, each sharp enough to pare away doubt. Her front teeth sank into her bottom lip. Her eyes remained fixed on his face. "You're not trying to tell me you're Thomas Becket, England's greatest saint."

"No, I'm Thomas Becket, England's greatest fraud. Thomas Maudit, Thomas the Cursed."

"Other than the small detail that all that was eight hundred years ago, the knights sure as heck killed somebody!"

"They murdered David, a monk of Glastonbury Abbey who'd come to me only the day before with a message from his abbot. My clerk mentioned how much he looked like me, tall, fair of face and dark of hair. And so did my spiritual son David play Galahad to my Lancelot."

"Succeeding where you failed, you mean?"

"I'd spent years making my decision, but at the last second turned tail and ran, betraying every principle I so loudly declared I believed. In that same second David made his decision and stepped into my place. My sin of omission murdered him as surely as if my hand wielded the sword."

"Weren't you wearing your archbishop's robes?"

"No. I was cold, and wore an ordinary black cloak and monk's cowl. In the darkness and confusion, our—ex-change—went unnoticed."

"No one wondered what happened to David?"

"Many men ran away from the scene. His abbot may have inquired after him. I don't know. I do know that I compounded my sin by concealing the truth. For although I made a good confession and was absolved, and tried to put things right by showing forth David's example, I have never admitted publicly that I stole the name of martyr, his name, until now."

"You didn't mean for it all to happen like that . . ." Maggie stopped dead, apparently realizing she'd just expressed belief. But whilst her brow was furrowed, her shoulders weren't stiff and square but rounded, and her hands lay open in her lap.

Thomas felt as though he were bleeding into those cupped hands. "Soon after David's murder I walked barefooted to Jerusalem and joined the Knights of the Temple. But my guilt followed me. I took no major wounds, and the minor scrapes and burns to which flesh is heir healed cleanly. I grew no older, and in time realized that by God's judgment I was made immortal."

"That would be a curse, all right." Maggie's wide brown eyes were the eyes of the Magdalene in his vision, bright with irony.

"In my first life I was a proud and often violent man, sharp-tongued, stiff-necked, narrow-minded. I not only wielded great power in both secular and spiritual worlds, I cast ambitious eyes upon heaven itself. It is not surprising that the pattern of my life has been left incomplete until I truly learn humility. And until I complete that supernal pattern which has been taking shape here, in Britain, since well before I was born."

"Which brings us back to the relics and Robin and all that." She waved her hands as though forcing her way through a thicket. "I know one thing, when he left here he was royally pissed."

"Realizing that no protestation on my part could have convinced you of the truth nearly as effectively as his demonstration. You drove him away, I take it?"

"Me? Well, yeah, I guess so. He was standing there with that smug smile—smug people just infuriate me—Danny, my ex, he was like that, so superior . . ." Maggie shrugged, a gesture meant to be casual and yet was anything but. "I told Robin it was all a trick. I told him to leave you alone. Then he sneered something about 'As for you!', which scared me bad enough I yelled, 'For God's sake go away!' He sort of reeled back, then stomped off. I looked down at you, and when I looked back up he was gone, like the earth swallowed him up. Which isn't a bad idea, come to think of it." She smiled weakly. "Must be your influence, I don't usually go around calling on God."

"Well played," said Thomas, and his lips, too, managed a pinched smile. With a faint purr of engines a solitary airplane passed overhead. The wind smelled of many things, smoke, animals, but no longer of incense.

Maggie raised her hand toward him but took it back without touching him. He was sorry—very rarely did anyone touch him. "Why me? I'm honored and everything, but two days ago we were total strangers."

" 'Be not forgetful to entertain strangers,' " he told her, " 'for thereby some have entertained angels unawares.' "

She laughed bitterly. "I'm no angel. I don't even have any faith."

"Don't you? You're making a leap of faith in believing me."

"That's because I don't want to believe I'm nuts."

His smiled softened. "We've never met before, so the truth shan't betray a friendship built on my false pretenses."

"Okay," she said warily.

"You're a scholar, a truth-seeker. You already know the pattern not only of my life, but of my work. You recognized the seals in the cottage, for example. You appreciate the significance of mythology and legend."

"I was joking about a historical test."

"You're a woman. The most profound of alchemical signs is the union of male and female . . ." She stiffened. "On a metaphysical level. Wisdom is personified as female. It's for good reason Robin abhors women."

She nodded. "Right."

"I was given a sign the day you arrived at Temple Manor. My carving of Mary Magdalene looked at me with your eyes. As, by the by, my painting of St. Bridget looked at me with Rose's."

"And my name turns out to be Magdalena—not to mention Sinclair—and hers Kildare. Okay, I can see why you'd say we were brought here for a purpose. But as far am I'm concerned, I came here because I wanted to."

"So you did. Every free choice of your life has brought you here, for the connection between choice and destiny is as subtle as an alchemical reaction. You can just as freely choose to go—perhaps you have served your purpose here today." He leaned toward her. "I should, however, like you to be my friend. I should like to have you beside me in the End Times."

"The End Times. Oh, brother." She ran her fingers through her hair, as though brushing away cobwebs. Again her eyes cast around, found nothing but earth, wind, and sky, and returned to Thomas's face. "No, I don't want to go. Even though I don't know what to believe, Thomas, except that you're true."

True Thomas? He looked across the sun-bronzed grass of the great mound, and thought of other mounds opening into the timeless earth, the deep heart's core. *Ercildoune.*

"I mean, you believe you're telling me the truth, and it's hurting you like hell."

"So now, with the truth in your grasp, do you despise me?"

She did touch him then, setting her fingertips against the arch of his cheekbone. "I'm not in the absolution business. I can't make it all right for you."

"No, that struggle I still face. But you have strengthened me to make it."

Her hand fell away and clasped its mate in her lap. After a long moment they loosened, releasing, perhaps, some measure of doubt. "You've got some nerve. At least Calum didn't realize what he was dragging Mick into. You knew exactly what you were doing with me."

"Yes, I did. I apologize most profoundly for my presumption."

She snorted. "I was asking for it. Maybe it doesn't matter whether I believe your crazy tale—and that, that vision—just as long as I go along with it. Maybe I'll get around to believing it. I've always been a sucker for a good story."

Her empathy was cool rain on a parched land. The pain and the weariness drained from his limbs. His voice trembled. "Thank you."

"You're welcome," she returned. "But you realize I've barely started asking questions. I mean, who the hell is Robin? Was it really you who saved Anna when she was a child? What's all this about relics?"

"I should imagine Anna has re-appeared in my life to recall me to my task . . ." He had to keep himself from babbling like a river undammed. "Your answers will come, and in quantity, although they will no doubt spark further questions. However, since Robin's favorite tactic is to divide and conquer, I suggest that just now we return to Salisbury for a bit of connecting."

"Only connect. Sounds good to me." Maggie stood up and brushed herself off, brisk and resolute.

The wind was cold, but for the first time in years Thomas wasn't. He cast one last glance back at the labyrinth—at last, his path lay before him, difficult though it was. Perhaps, in time, he could share the blessing of his faith with Maggie. But whilst she was accepting of his guilt, bless her, she was at yet wary of his affection.

With a long exhalation of relief and gratitude, Thomas struggled to his feet, and together with his new friend walked down the path away from the wasteland.

125

Chapter Thirteen

Mick closed the door of the police station behind him and blinked, blinded by the light.

Calum had been in Salisbury on the Saturday, the officer in charge said. He'd had a tour of the ancient sites with Vivian Morgan. The coach driver knew sod-all, as did the receptionist at Calum's hotel. No, Vivian hadn't stayed there as well. Mick wasn't sure what he thought of that—he would have liked his dad to have a girlfriend, though not one who turned up dead in peculiar circumstances.

No one in Salisbury had seen Calum since the Sunday. He'd even left his things at the hotel. Mick had looked through the familiar old suitcase, its contents smelling so strongly of his dad tears came to his eyes, and found sweet eff-all. At last he'd asked for it to be sent on to Edinburgh.

Back to the cathedral, then. Back to waiting about. Mick trudged down the steps, his shoes as heavy as his heart. Outside a small grocery a rack of newspapers displayed a mixtie-maxtie of headlines: a missionary imprisoned in China, a massacre in Rwanda, ethnic cleansing campaigns in the Balkans, orthodox Jews attacking secular Jews in Jerusalem. The photos of his father were inside, Mick suspected, one missing man insignificant amidst such madness.

The pavement was crowded. It had gone noon. Rose might fancy a lunch. Mick felt better when he was with Rose, lighter, almost hopeful . . . "Michael Dewar?" asked a male voice.

Mick stopped dead and looked round. "Aye?"

The man's dark suit, regimental striped tie, and overcoat testified to his line of work before he held up a warrant card. It read not "Wiltshire Constabulary" but "Scotland Yard," and identified its bearer as Robert Prince, Detective Superintendent.

Mick came to attention. "Oh, aye!"

"Let's stop here, shall we?" Prince waved Mick into a tea shop and settled him at a table in an alcove decorated with one of the William Morris prints his mum had liked, an image of the Lady of Shalott. "Tea and scones," Prince told the waitress. Then he leaned confidingly across the table. "There are things we can't tell the local plods. Things that are a bit too sophisticated for them."

"Aye?"

"Your father, Calum Dewar. He's working for us at present."

Mick's nervous system went like a fireworks display. "He's okay?"

"Yes, quite. If you'd stayed in Edinburgh we'd have contacted you by now, to let you know. It took a bit of doing to track you here."

"But he sounded so ill and scairt when he rang me, and he'd been seen in Glastonbury . . ." *I canna do anything right,* Mick told himself.

The waitress clattered tea things and a dish of weary-looking scones onto the table. Prince reached into his jacket and pulled out a bit of paper and a snap, a school photo of Mick himself.

Mick had never liked that snap. At fifteen he'd looked a proper gowk, bad haircut, eyeglasses, no chin. But now he seized it. "My dad kept this in his pocketbook."

"He asked me to give it to you as a reference. And this letter."

The blue-lined paper had a serrated edge, as though torn from a spiral-bound notebook. A small flower was drawn in pencil at the bottom. Calum's handwriting filled the top half: "Mick, Sorry to put the wind up you, but I had a bit of a turn. Do you mind Housesteads, the Roman site, we visited there a wee while? Come quickly, I need your help. DON'T TELL ANYONE! Have a care for a man named Thomas London—he's a nasty piece of work. There's a good lad. Dad."

His hands trembling, Mick folded the snap inside the paper and tucked both into his pocket. His fingertips brushed against the *sgian dubh*. It tingled against his skin, sending pins and needles up his arm. *Steady on.* He took the hot cup in both hands and gulped, burning his tongue. "So what's all this in aid of?" he lisped.

"The international trade in illegal antiquities."

"You dinna mean Dad and his relic . . ." A flash of Prince's green eyes made Mick lower his voice. "Dad's helping Scotland Yard to guard an antiquity?"

"Very good!" said Prince with a smile. "Got it in one!"

"Dad was havering about protecting a relic. From *Am Fear Dubh,* he said, the Black Man, the Devil, but that's not sensible, is it? Unless that's the name of a gang of thieves, like the Mafia's Black Hand."

"London's organization is like the Mafia. They're responsible for museum robberies, antiquities smuggling, raids on excavations, the lot. Calum will tell you everything you need to know at Housesteads. When can you leave?"

"This evening, I reckon." *Rose. Thomas London. A nasty piece of work.* "London seems a decent enough chap. He's with a group of Americans . . ."

"I should think they will be safe so long as they don't interfere with his activities." Prince smeared strawberry jam on his scone, jam as red as his hair and tidily trimmed beard.

"Safe?" repeated Mick. "They might be in danger?"

"The woman found dead at Glastonbury Abbey was a journalist. Perhaps she grew a bit too inquisitive about London and his gang." Prince's white teeth closed expressively on the bit of scone.

The back of Mick's neck squirmed. "Gupta told me I could trust London. He must be bent himself."

"Gupta, eh? There's your black man, I expect."

"But Dad never made racial . . ."

"No fear," Prince went on, "we'll pull the students out if need be. Unless they've been corrupted. The teacher, Maggie Sinclair—well, as they say, crime makes strange bedfellows. And she and London are certainly bedfellows."

Mick hadn't had that notion of them at all. But they'd been planning to go away together this morning, hadn't they?

"Just now, though," Prince went on, "we can't let London know we're onto him, or we'll lose him and the artifact as well. If we picked it up ourselves, however, your father would be out of danger. Do you know where it is?"

"No, my dad said something about Fortingall, by Loch Tay, and Schiehallion, the mountain further up the glen, save he said it had three peaks, and you could reach it by the A68 . . . No, I dinna ken where it is. I dinna ken *what* it is, to tell you the truth."

Again the green eyes flared. "London asked you to repeat what Calum told you, did he?"

"Oh aye, that he did. He seemed to know more about . . ." Mick stopped dead, only now realizing how easily London had drawn him out. "Oh no."

"We all run afoul of smooth-tongued rogues," Prince said consolingly. "Calum was clever enough to be cautious with you, and now that you know about London, you'll be cautious, too. Your father's life may depend upon it."

"Oh aye, now I know," Mick said, even though he felt he knew less now than ten minutes ago.

"I must be off. No rest for the righteous, eh? I'll meet you in Northumbria, and then you and Calum and I will fetch the artifact." Prince laid several coins on table, slipped on his overcoat, edged gracefully through the now crowded shop, and disappeared out the door before Mick could so much as thank him, let alone ask more questions.

He should be making somersaults of joy. Instead he was sitting there all cold and shilpit, the ashes of the fireworks drifting greasy gray across his mind. He swallowed the last of the tea. Odd, how fast it had chilled.

My telling you will have them after you, too, Calum had said. So why was he bidding Mick into danger after all? The relic? Mick knew about relics. The Honors of Scotland in Edinburgh Castle had been hidden and recovered again and again. He'd seen the crown, the sword, and the scepter when he and Calum viewed the Stone of Scone, newly returned from London, where for seven hundred years it had sat in the coronation chair in Westminster Abbey.

Well, not quite. In the early fifties a group of Scots Nationalists had pinched it and left it at the altar of Arbroath Abbey in Scotland. The Abbey dedicated to Thomas Becket by King William the Lion. The Abbey where King Robert the Bruce and his followers signed the Declaration of Scottish Independence. *It was at Arbroath Abbey,* Calum had said. *Sinclair came to my father and me and we helped him shift it.*

That afternoon at the Castle he'd stood by the display case and laughed beneath his breath. The Sassenach had stolen a common building block, he'd said. Robert the Bruce hid the true Stone. Mick could still see his father's face reflected in the glass, floating ghost-like above the ordinary red sandstone lump. "Bugger," Mick whispered. London wanted the

Stone, the real Stone, the ancient inauguration Stone, the hereditary symbol of Scottish unity.

Several inches of hereditary steel lay heavy along Mick's ribs. London knew about the *sgian dubh*. Did he want it as well? Why tell Mick to keep it with him, then, when he could've nicked it from his room?

He'd believed London, even when he'd said nothing was a coincidence. Calum had said that, too. A few days ago Mick would've thought that daft. But now the familiar patterns dissolved, and daft might well be sensible.

The waitress cleared away the dishes. Mick pulled himself to his feet and toddled unsteadily out the door. *It's our duty,* Calum had said. Was this mysterious duty more important than the both of them? Was it more important than Rose? She wasn't part of the puzzle, Prince had owned as much. He'd also told Mick to trust no one.

Despite the hurrying pedestrians, Mick had never felt so alone. He lifted his eyes toward the spire of the cathedral. Thin streamers of cloud flowed past it, so that it seemed to be leaning into the wind. Gritting his teeth, Mick walked toward it.

Gingerly Rose turned a page in the book that lay before her. It was an actual original source, a 1529 copy of Thomas Malory's **Morte d'Arthur**. "It befell in the days of y noble Utherpendragon whn he was kynge of Englande and so regned there was a myghty and a noble duke in Cornwayle . . ."

Yeah right, Rose thought. Like Arthur's mother Igraine hadn't known it was Uther crawling into her bed. All that about Merlin disguising him as her husband was just a convenient cover-up. What had Igraine felt when she found out she was a pregnant widow? Probably not much like Mary.

Through her lashes Rose glanced at Anna, who was writing busily, and Sean, who sat with his chin propped on his fist. His face had settled into soft curves that made him look young and vulnerable. No wonder he tried so hard to be macho.

Mick wasn't trying to be anything except himself, confused and hurting. Rose was pretty confused herself, not to mention tender around the emotional edges, but while she may have lost some innocence the last few days, she hadn't lost any family members.

She glanced at her watch. Almost noon. She picked up her bag, tiptoed across the creaking floor—it'd be hard to sneak up on anyone in England—and asked Mrs. Howard, "Where's the rest room, please?"

The librarian looked puzzled.

"The loo," translated Rose.

"Oh! It's downstairs, just off the cloister."

"Thank you." Rose sensed Sean's eyes follow her out the door.

She paused on her way back from the bathroom to admire the way the sun shone through the arcades of the cloister, drawing parabolas of light and shadow on the flagstone walk. Inside the nave of the cathedral she pondered the interlaced stone vaults. This beauty was long lasting, as long as it was cared for. She slotted a pound coin into the collection box.

The blue and silver miraculous medal on its chain was tucked in her billfold. Although her mother hadn't worn it for years, she'd insisted Rose take it with her. "For luck," she'd said, but Rose knew better. She'd behaved herself so far, hadn't she, although more for lack of serious temptation than through any particular virtue.

She strolled through the north porch and looked out over the Close. No Mick. No Thomas, no Maggie. Several decrepit vans painted with dragons and crescent moons edged the lawn. Two long-haired figures were raising a red canopy fringed with tassels. A bearded man holding the disc of a bodhran, an Irish skin drum, sat down on a stool. Next to him settled a woman with a keyboard. They broke into a lively Celtic-flavored tune that reminded Rose of "First Rites."

She realized she was walking along with everyone else in the area toward the makeshift stage. Okay, she told herself, Thomas said to stay inside, but she could find her way back.

A young man with thin, sharp features emerged from a purple van and struck a pose beneath the canopy, his white robe and gilded paper wings fluttering in the wind. "Christ!" he shouted, and Rose thought for a moment he was swearing. But he went on, "Jesus Christ, son of God! Lawful Lord of heaven! Your trust we violated, and so Adam fell. We repented, and so are received again into your favor. But there is one, not man but angel, who profaned your trust and would not repent."

A medieval mystery play! *Sweet!* Formal theology tended to be dry and distant, while the popular religious stories pressed emotional buttons. *Which*, Rose thought, *is why they are popular.*

"Lucifer!" proclaimed the actor. "Prince among angels, who in his pride refused to render homage to his lawful Lord, and so was cast out, throne overturned, crown broken, gates of heaven shut behind him."

"Eh?" said a voice. "What's that, then?"

Rose glanced around. The woman standing next to her was about her age. Half-hidden behind a curtain of lank brown hair, her face was pursed into puzzlement and resentment mingled. Her oversized coat smelled of stale sweat.

"In medieval times," Rose explained, "the punishment for denying one's Lord was to be cut off from the community.

Makes you sympathize with the Devil, but then, he made his choice."

The girl shot Rose a hostile glance and turned her back. Oops, that had been a rhetorical question.

The actor extended his arms. A couple of red-suited demons sprang from the van, wearing scowling Halloween masks and tails made out of wire coat hangers. They whisked away his robe to reveal a red body suit. Over his shoulders they hooked a new set of paper wings, black this time, charred along the edges. *Nice touch*, Rose thought.

The young man twisted his features into a sneer. "I stood before God and told Him I need not serve Him nor worship His son. I have myself to worship, my own image to bow before!"

The demons draped linked-paper chains over his arms. "My Lord, you can never defeat God," said the first one.

"He has called Men to take your place at his side," said the second.

"Then I shall deprive Him of them!" Lucifer declaimed. "I shall turn Men against Him, and bring their souls to serve me in Hell! How much more comfortable will I rest in these my chains, knowing that Men, too, have been denied the Kingdom of God! I shall send my demons to the Garden, to Adam and to Eve, and I shall tempt them, in their pride, to eat of the Tree of Knowledge. So shall they be separated from God's grace, and fall into my hands."

"That's what they want, isn't it?" said the girl at Rose's elbow, getting in to the spirit of the play. "They want to bring us all down with them."

She was answered by a silky murmur, "We shan't let it happen, Ellen. Be strong." And with a quiet laugh, "Cut along now. You have work to do."

Wait a minute. Rose spun around.

Robin Fitzroy stood just behind her, his green eyes polished with—anger? Or with exhilaration? Great, this was all she needed.

Ellen hiked away, her hands deep in her pockets. The music started up again, the beat of the bodhran echoing the leap of Rose's heart. "Hello," Robin said. "You're looking lovely today."

"Thanks." She stopped herself from adding, *so are you.* The denim jacket, the sweater, the jeans fit his body perfectly. His short red hair embellished his flawless features. The gold hoop in his ear was the finishing touch, as much a costume as the paper wings of the actor.

On the stage the red and black figure exulted over a couple with green construction paper leaves pinned to their T-shirts and jeans. Then a man in a modest brown bathrobe and a tinsel halo stepped between them. "I am the light of the world. Come with me, and be saved." He lifted a flashlight—the light of forgiveness breaking through the gates of Hell, Rose supposed.

"No!" protested Lucifer. "Leave them to me, and all the riches of this world will be yours!"

"True riches are stored in Heaven," Christ replied. "You have made Hell for your world, and it will be your dominion forever."

"So be it!" howled the red-suited actor. "Better to reign in Hell than serve in Heaven!"

Rose recognized that last as Milton, not medieval, but it made a good closing. The music reached a crescendo and trailed away into silence even as its tempo remained, a resonance in wind and stone and flesh—*of one substance with the word, of one mind with the flesh, begotten not made by grace out of blood* . . . The players took their bows. The audience applauded. So did Rose.

135

Robin didn't. "What a fearfully amateur effort. I thought your poem on the harrowing of Hell was better written, Rose."

She scowled. "So you did take my notebook."

"I was charmed by it. Do you mind?" His megawatt smile was brighter than the actor's flashlight.

"Yes, I do."

"I shall apologize then. Although I take it from your tone of voice that Thomas is already poisoning your mind against me. I have nothing to offer you but my word. Can you take that on faith, do you think, even though faith can be a very slender reed indeed."

Rose cocked her head skeptically.

"I should have a care for your teacher. She's just the sort Thomas likes to corrupt, a woman of a certain age and, shall we say, desperation? I saw them a few minutes ago, hanging on each other in a most embarrassing fashion. It's hard to believe Thomas is a priest. Do you think Maggie feels that her desires are more important than his vow? Does he?"

Rose shook her head. Again Robin was confusing her, telling her things she didn't want to believe but couldn't disprove.

"Let's have a bite of lunch, shall we?"

His voice was the melody of the keyboard, his words the rhythm of the bodhran, tingling in her nerves, drawing saliva into her mouth . . . Robin was three paces closer to her and she hadn't seen him move. His forefinger touched her chin and traced a line part fire and part ice to the hollow in her throat. A rich odor, like incense but probably cologne, clung to his hand.

One of the long-haired figures cut through the dispersing crowd, shaking a plastic bucket hung with bells. Wrenching herself away from Robin's way too intimate touch, Rose tossed several coins into the bucket. It was only fair, the troupe had put on a good show.

"Yeh, thanks, luv. Look for us in Glastonbury Saturday." The deep voice and glance up and down Rose's figure revealed the young man's gender.

Waving away the bucket, Robin said, "Act the man, Sunshine. Get a job."

With a shrug, the boy jingled on. Rose stepped further away from Robin. "There's a lot of unemployment here, isn't there?"

"Layabouts, the lot of them. Lazy ignorant sods beyond redemption."

"No one's beyond redemption," Rose said. "Maybe not even Lucifer."

Robin's green eyes blazed. For one quick moment Rose thought he was furious. But no, he laughed so hard he choked. "Oh Rose, your wit is truly exceptional. Come along, cider and a sandwich, is it?"

"I've got to get back inside, thanks anyway." She started toward the cathedral.

Robin fell into an easy stride at her side. "Would you like me to chase down that pillock and give him a couple of quid?"

"Just because street theater isn't as respectable as journalism, or whatever it is you do, doesn't mean he's not working."

Robin stopped, his hand on her arm pulling her around to face him. "When I told you I worked with Vivian Morgan I was telling you the truth, Rose. I was her spiritual advisor. I save souls."

"Excuse me?" She pulled her arm away, but she could still feel his fingers pressing through her sweater, against her skin.

"How do you ever know anything? You have to be told, by trustworthy people who know. I know. And I'd like to save you from the bad company you're keeping, and from the errors in your belief."

"In my belief?"

"Is what you believe the truth, Rose? Or have you let yourself be taken in by propaganda? You should decide for yourself."

"I've decided I need to get back. Bye." She walked as fast as she could without running to the huge doorway and ducked into its shadowed stillness. Emptied of the wind, the music, and the satiny voice, her ears rang. Her throat ached where Robin had touched it. When she turned to look, he was gone. *How does he do that?*

Rose stood in the porch telling herself that while Adam and Eve ate of the tree of knowledge, knowledge itself wasn't the sin. The sin was thinking that they knew everything. And right now, she didn't feel as though she knew anything—except that Robin had more than a physical agenda.

Chapter Fourteen

Whoa! There was Mick trudging across the lawn, looking like a lost soul turned belly-up in the harrowing of hell. And Maggie and Thomas rounded the corner of the building, he paler and finer-drawn than ever, she pink-cheeked and tight-lipped. *So something is going on with them,* Rose thought in surprise.

"Rose!" exclaimed Maggie. "Why aren't you in the library?"

"I went to the rest room, and then I watched the play." She gestured toward the collection of vans. "A mystery play. Robin Fitzroy was there."

Both Maggie and Thomas recoiled. "What did he say?" Thomas demanded.

"The usual. Messing with my mind." Rose waved her hand, brushing aside the awkward details.

Mick joined the group. His gray eyes looked blankly from face to face until they found Rose. There they clung.

She summoned up her sweetest smile for him. "They didn't know anything at the police station, did they?"

"No," he said. "Nothing."

"I'm sorry," Maggie said. She glanced from Mick to Thomas, her eyebrows lopsided. Thomas looked at Maggie, his forehead furrowed. Mick's stare was getting a bit unnerving, like he was afraid Rose would vanish if he blinked. She had the distinct impression each of them knew something she didn't.

Decisively, Maggie turned to Rose and shooed her into the cathedral. "We need to be getting back to Glastonbury."

"We're coming back here, aren't we?" Rose asked over her shoulder. "I've just barely scratched the surface with Igraine—I have a lot more of Arthur's women to go. Elaine, Morgan le Fay, Guinevere."

"Yeah, sure, no problem," Maggie said. Behind her Thomas did a double-take at the bulletin board in the porch. Tearing off a notice, he folded it into his pocket.

Rose collected her notebook while Maggie collected Anna and Sean and made another appointment with Mrs. Howard. Back in the van, Sean asked, "It's way past lunchtime, aren't we going to eat?"

"Oh," said Maggie. "Sorry. We'll ask Bess to fix another high tea."

"Whatever," replied Sean, rolling his eyes toward her back.

Maggie drove with her shoulders up around her ears and eyes strictly front. Thomas sat very still, gazing out the window, the reflection of his face looking like Hamlet's father's ghost. Mick's ponytail bobbed as he shifted restlessly. With so much tension crackling like frost in the air, Rose was actually glad Sean went rambling on about Arthur's twelve battles while Anna got in a few words about the non-Christian elements in the *Conte du Graal* and *Perlesvaus*.

By the time they reached Temple Manor the sun was dipping toward the southwest. Dunstan sat on the doorstep, licking the sunlight into his fur. Grudgingly he moved aside so Maggie could open the door. Sean went into the dining room. Anna headed upstairs, Mick just behind her. "Are you all right?" Rose called after him, but his only answer was the slam of his door. No, he wasn't all right, duh.

"I'll ring Jivan from my cottage," Thomas said with a look at Maggie that obviously carried a sub-text. His eyes were banked embers in his ashen face, his usually inscrutable expression positively opaque.

"Call me for tea," Rose told Maggie, and ran up the stairs just as Anna came back down.

She went into the room they shared and sat down beside the window. Crows called. Shadows lengthened. Her thoughts hopped from the silver stone spire to Mick's voice to Robin's eyes to Adam and Eve with their paper fig leaves. *From the world, the flesh, and the Devil make me anew . . .*

Priests fell in love and left the priesthood all the time. But Thomas and Maggie barely knew each other. How could they be in love? And neither of them seemed the type to just leap into bed without love, let alone without getting Thomas released from his vows.

For a religion based on the Word made flesh, Christianity was sure squeamish about sex. About any sort of appetite, really. A shame that all those high voltage signs the church staked out around sexuality came across as "it's dirty," not as "it's dangerous." Even without ever having had sex Rose understood that. It was a matter of honesty. Maybe, in 20-20 hindsight, Igraine justified her adultery because it had given the world Arthur. But she'd still been unfaithful . . . *If Robin is right about Thomas and Maggie,* Rose thought with a shudder, *what else is he right about?*

"Rose?" said Anna's voice behind her. "Time for tea."

"Oh! Thanks." In the dining room she sat down between Maggie and Sean. Mick's place was empty.

"I knocked on his door," Anna said.

"I'll try again." Rose leaped up.

"Leave him alone," Maggie told her. "He's going through a rough time."

Who isn't, Rose thought, but like a well-trained little girl, she sat back down. She nibbled on a scone but it tasted like sawdust. She was tired of sublimating. What she wanted wasn't food. It wasn't necessarily even physical, although the physical was there, like a rash.

Maggie, too, picked at her food. "Excuse me," said Sean at last, tossing down his napkin. "I'm going to see what videos they've got."

"I'll get my tatting." Anna went upstairs.

Rose and Maggie got up from the table and walked in opposite directions. From the door of the lounge, Rose watched Sean watch guns, cars, and women in skimpy dresses. Even when Anna sat down with the little spider's web of her tatting, Rose still hesitated, wanting neither car chases nor crafts but having no where else to go . . .

Another sound filtered through the mayhem, like a strangled oboe playing a lament or a lullaby. The tune was unearthly and otherworldly, fingering her spine like a flute. *Now what?* Rose walked into the hall. The music was coming from upstairs. It shimmered in her senses, calling her. Mick.

Maggie came slowly down the steps, pulling on her coat. When she opened the door a russet gleam of sunset flooded inside, making her look dazed and feverish. She went out the door and shut it behind her.

Rose couldn't help Maggie. She couldn't help Thomas. Maybe she could help Mick. She headed down the hall to the kitchen door. From inside came Alf's voice. "I know, luv, it's frustrating."

"If we could only do something to help her," said Bess.

"She's not thinking she needs help, that's just the problem."

Putting on an apologetic face, Rose knocked. "Come in," called Alf. He sat at the table with a newspaper and a glass of beer. His jowls drooped despondently but still he managed a smile for Rose.

Bess was loading the dishwasher. A glass of what was

probably sherry waited on the counter top. "Yes, luv?"

"I'm sorry to barge in, I wondered if I could take Mick a sandwich or something since he missed tea—I'll fix it if you'll show me . . ."

"It's no trouble."

Rose wondered who they'd been talking about. Even Bess's plump and rosy face sagged like bread dough that had risen and fallen again. Maybe it was the way the stars were aligned or something, but there was enough angst around here for month of soap operas. She stood making small talk while Bess assembled a sandwich, microwaved some leftover chips, poured a cup of tea, and put it all on a tray. "Here you are."

"Thank you. I'm sure he'll be very grateful."

"That he will," said Alf with a knowing smile.

Okay. She liked Mick. He seemed to like her. That, at least, was no secret. Rose balanced the tray down the hall and up the stairs. She tapped on the door with her toe. The music stopped. The door flew open. "Aye?" Mick's gray eyes, bright and sharp as steel, softened.

"It's an X-chromosome thing," she explained. "When a woman is worried about someone, she feeds him."

"Thank you." She could swear Mick sighed in relief as he took the tray and set it on the chair. "Come in, sit yourself down. I'd just made up my mind to talk to you after all."

After what? Rose pushed the door almost shut but not quite, in case the miraculous medal was peeking, and sat down at the head of the bed. Mick sat at its foot and pulled the chair closer.

Rose watched him eat, feeding her eyes while he fed his stomach. He was frayed around the edges. Even his voice was a burr. But frayed was more appealing than silky smooth. It was probably more honest, too.

She looked down at the bed, where a wooden instrument resembling a small clarinet lay like a bundling board between them. "Is that a bagpipe chanter? Were you playing it?"

"Aye, to both questions."

"I've never heard that tune before. Is it traditional?"

"I dinna ken. I heard it years ago, near Melrose, on holiday with my mum and dad. Never heard it since, but it stayed with me."

"I'd like to hear you play the pipes." Rose knotted her hands in her lap. "I'm sorry you missed the play outside the cathedral. I enjoyed it, even when Robin Fitzroy made fun of it."

"Who's this Fitzroy chap, then?"

"Good question. He keeps warning me about Thomas and Thomas keeps warning me about him. I don't know who to believe. Robin was here yesterday, but I first saw him in the Abbey Monday morning, just before I found Vivian. He has the strangest green eyes."

Mick set his teacup down with a crash. "Green eyes?"

"Oh yeah. He looks like a model, almost too handsome, you know? Perfect hair, perfect beard, sort of a coppery red color."

"He—he," Mick swallowed and began again. "He's watching out for you."

"Who? Robin?"

"He's scairt for your safety, if you must know."

"I don't know anything that's going on around here," wailed Rose, "and I'd lot rather have knowledge than safety!"

"It's a matter of life and death," Mick insisted. "I can only be telling you if you'll promise not to go telling Thomas or Maggie."

Rose would have thought he was being melodramatic, but she'd already discovered the death part. She gulped down her protest. "I won't tell them."

He leaned forward. "I met with a copper in Salisbury. Robert Prince, Scotland Yard. Red hair, green eyes. I reckon he's gone undercover as Fitzroy. Robin's a nickname for Robert and Fitzroy means 'son of the king.' Prince."

"An undercover cop?" Rose repeated incredulously.

"He was telling me that Thomas is a criminal, after stealing an antiquity. Prince is working with my dad to protect it. It fits what my dad told me afore he went missing. Prince said Thomas has seduced Maggie—in both meanings of the word. You canna trust her, either."

"I can't believe it—Thomas is a priest . . ." Rose's mind flashed like a strobe light, dark to light to dark again. Robin a policeman? Thomas a criminal? "Something sure happened between him and Maggie this morning."

"Thomas is a priest?" Mick shook his head. "That makes it worse, eh?"

"If it's true, it does," Rose told him. "What about your father?"

"He's okay. He gave Prince a letter for me. Here." From his jacket Mick took a sheet of paper.

She snatched it from his hand. "This came from the notebook I lost Sunday! See, in the corner, a doodle I did. Robin told me he took it, yeah—but, but—if Robin's a policeman, why is he avoiding Gupta?"

"Because Gupta's bent, or so he hinted."

"Gupta's the one who seems like a real cop, kind of tired and worn. Not Robin, he's so slick, he's like an actor playing a cop. No soul."

"Aye," Mick conceded with a grimace.

"And he told you just exactly what you wanted to hear about your dad, didn't he? That he's okay. That he's doing important work."

"Oh aye."

What am I trying to do? Rose asked herself. Convince Mick his father wasn't all right? But she had to say it. "If Robin's the bad guy then he'd want us to distrust Thomas, wouldn't he? And he's picked a damn funny way of protecting me, coming onto me and everything."

Recorded explosions sounded faintly from downstairs. Mick said, "Oh Rose, how can a man with any blood in him at all not come on to you?"

Funny, she'd never realized how the prolonged "o" of "Rose" shaped your lips into a kiss. She held out the letter, murmuring, "You're not so hard on the senses yourself, you know."

Mick took the paper, his fingertips lingering against hers. A tingle spread up her arm and filled her body. The sag of the mattress tilted them together, so that she sensed the warmth of his body and rich scent of cheese on his breath. The room went soft focus around the edges.

"What are you going to do, M . . ." The "m" of his name also made a kiss. She managed to say, "Mick?"

He smiled, a radiance in his eyes, a flash of teeth, and crescents cut into his cheeks. Suddenly she realized why people always seemed to be stunned when she smiled.

Then the gloom fell over him again. "I'm away to Housesteads to meet with my dad. My mum's dead, I've no brother or sisters. He's all I have."

"You'll be in danger," Rose said with a frown.

"I'm already in danger. So are you. I couldna go without warning you."

"I'm in danger from Thomas? Or from Robin?"

"I dinna ken. I only know what needs doing. Having an early night, and making a start tomorrow morning."

The front of Rose's body, facing Mick, was still warm. Her back was cold. Last week she'd known who she could trust.

146

Now she didn't. Well, she could probably trust Sean, but what could he do? And Anna was a nice lady, but ditto. As for the Puckles . . . She didn't know the Puckles.

She'd known Maggie for several months. Maggie had never told her wrong. And like Gupta, Thomas seemed more real than Robin. The question was whether she could trust her own perceptions.

Mick. She didn't know him, either, but if she had to make a leap of faith and trust someone, then it was going to be him. "Be careful, okay?"

"Okay." A glitter in his eyes made Rose think of the old word "fey," fairy-ridden, enspelled, doomed. "You as well, Rose. Have a care."

She stood up. "I will. Good night."

"Good night." Mick shut the door.

That sounded like "goodbye." Rose looked down each separate corridor and up and down the stairs, but it was night, and the different paths were dark. Sirens wailed like banshees in the lounge. *No way.* She went into her and Anna's bedroom, leaving the door half-open and flopping down on the bed without turning on the lights. Mick wanted answers. She wanted answers. That gave them the same goal.

A door opened. Stealthy footsteps pressed a creaking floorboard. In one bound Rose was at the door. Mick stood at the top of stairs, his backpack flung over one shoulder. It was like a freeze-frame in a movie, Mick balanced on one foot and the sirens' wail drawing itself out thinner and thinner. He was going into the dark, now, alone. Something in his face, the shadowed eyes, the parted lips, reminded Rose of Vivian Morgan. Who'd been left alone, in the dark, to die.

She was standing on the edge of a precipice, looking down, holding her breath. The melody Mick had been playing twined through her mind. Then Nevermas's guitars and drums and pipes flooded in, *The flesh is willing when the spirit is weak, the last shall be first and the proud shall be meek, on earth as it is in heaven.*

The music stopped. Time plummeted. Sirens howled, punctuated by the gunshots of Mick's feet on the stairs. Rose seized her backpack and shoveled some things into it. She tore a page from her new notebook, scribbled a message, and left it on Anna's pillow. Grabbing her coat, she sprinted out of the room, down the stairs, through the door, and across the courtyard.

Lights glowed in the windows of Thomas's cottage. Maggie must be there. Rose couldn't deal with them, not now.

The headlights of Mick's car came on, striking her across the face. They went out again and he shot out of the door. "Rose!"

She grasped his arms. "Didn't you think my promise was any good, telling me you weren't leaving until tomorrow?"

He grasped her back again, so that they braced each other. "No, lass, it's not that, I dinna want you to be in danger."

"I'm in danger here—you said so yourself. I'll be better off coming with you. Don't worry, once we're at Housesteads I'll call and let everyone know I'm okay."

He stared at her. The wind moaned. Trees flailed. Cars passed. *And just which one of us is fey?* Rose asked herself.

"We were brought here for a purpose, were we now?" Mick asked.

She knew just what he meant. "Looks like it."

"Let's get to it, then." He released her arms, leaving warm handprints on her sleeves, and opened the passenger side door. "In you go."

Rose stopped dead. Two small dots of light hovered close to the ground at the edge of the gravel parking area. Oh, it was Dunstan, almost invisible in the night except for the gleam of his eyes and his white fur collar. *Tell them I'm all right.* She climbed into the icy interior of the car and fastened her seat belt for what she fully expected to be one hell of a bumpy ride.

Ellen cursed her high heels. They weren't fit for anything, let alone for walking across the bleeding cobblestones of the courtyard. Trust Alf to keep the cobbles instead of putting down a proper pavement.

The tights cut into her waist, and even though the bra made her breasts jut out, its strap creased her back. But the discomfort was worth it. She had work to do. Pressing her lips together on their coating of lipstick she opened the door to the back hall. "Mum?"

The corridor was empty save for the cat, who gave Ellen a sarkey look and vanished round the corner. From the lounge came the sound of squealing tires and gunshots. The Yanks were watching a video. May *she* have joy from it, the one named Rose.

Robin would never fancy such a gormless little bird as Rose. She was working with *them,* was all. He had to seduce her to their side. Everything he told her would be a lie, he assured Ellen. Lying in defense of the faith was no sin.

Ellen pushed through the door to the kitchen. Alf sat at the table, a newspaper crumpled in his lap as he sagged forward, snoring. Prat, she thought. "Mum?"

Bess looked round the pantry door. "Ellen!"

Alf woke up with a snort. "What's all this . . . Blimey!"

Ellen tried a demure smile. "Here I am, just as you wanted."

"Thank God." Bess's face broke into a relieved smile.

Ellen looked away, pushing down a spurt of shame. *Poor Mum, not a clue.*

"Welcome home, Ellen." Alf's grin was almost frightening.

Bess pulled her daughter into a hug. She smelled of sherry. Ellen had no stomach for sherry. Robin now, he liked single malt whiskey. She turned sideways in the embrace. "Can I have me old room?"

"Oh, no dear, the Scots lad's in it. We'll put you on the z-bed in the lumber room for now. My, don't you look a treat!"

"I'll go on up then, shall I?" She picked up her carrier bag, full of new clothes and cosmetics. Robin had given her a handful of tenners, more cash than she'd seen in a year, and sent her off to Salisbury High Street. The shop assistants had been right shirty at first, until Ellen showed them the wodge of notes. They'd get theirs, soon enough now.

"Have you had your tea?" asked Bess. "There's a plaster on your hand, did you hurt yourself?"

Odd, how the cut had opened up again. She was too clumsy by half. "Don't fuss, Mum," she said, and escaped out the door and up the stairs to a crash of theme music from the video.

Chucking her bag into the lumber room, she tiptoed—easy to do in the bloody heels—to the door of her old room and set her ear to it. Nothing. She turned the knob. The room was dark and empty. The bed was made, if rumpled. On the chair sat a tray of dirty dishes.

So then, the Scots git was doing as he was told. Robin was brilliant, dead brilliant. And she'd already seen the trout—the teacher—and the traitor London, the degenerate priest, together in the cottage. They weren't having it off as she'd expected, though. Past it, most likely.

Footsteps bounded up the main staircase. The dishy American lad. Better and better. She knew what to do to turn the unbeliever to the truth. Ellen thrust one leg forward, shortening her skirt, and looked up through her stiffened lashes.

The lad came to an abrupt halt on the top step. "Oh, hi."

"I'm Ellen Sparrow, Bess's daughter. Haven't seen you before, have I?"

"Er—no. Sean MacArthur. I'm with the seminar group from Texas."

"Aren't you the clever one, then? Which is your room?"

"There, with the slanting ceiling."

Ellen linked her arm through his. "Let's have a dekko, shall we?"

"Yeah, sure." Flushing, he let her maneuver him down the hallway. When she stumbled over her shoes—no accident, that—he caught her. She nestled against his side. Thought he'd struck lucky, did he? Not bloody likely. A bit of snogging, that was all, to keep him hungry.

Ellen remembered Bess's joyful smile. Then she remembered Robin's voice, and Robin's eyes, and Robin's hands. The end justified the means, didn't it? She'd do Robin proud, and no mistake.

Sean opened the door, walked her inside, and shut it behind them.

Chapter Fifteen

Maggie stepped out into the twilight and shut the door. Its solid thunk was reassuring. She could believe in the reality of the wooden door and the cobblestones beneath her feet. Whether she was actually hearing the music dwindling behind her was another matter.

When she'd heard that melody the night of the All Souls' Bell, the instrument had been a flute, and the music so high and clear that even in memory she ached with longing. Mick was playing a chanter. Its tendency to squawk only made the music more compelling, transforming it from ethereal to physical, deepening the ache to ravenous hunger.

Stopping on the doorstep of Thomas's cottage, she knocked. He didn't answer. She walked around to the door of the chapel and looked into its dim interior.

Thomas lay before the altar, forehead to the cold stone floor, arms extended, glasses folded to one side. His hands were splayed as though embracing the earth itself.

He lay in the pose of penitent. Maggie made a swift about-face. Surprising someone at prayer seemed more disconcerting than surprising someone naked. Emotion revealed the soul—not the cheap and easy soul used to peddle self-help books, but that kernel of the Unseen lurking in every human body, making it more than a piece of meat. The soul that she wanted to believe in.

Maggie turned her face toward the west. The land fell away into a ruddy golden haze, as though El Dorado gleamed just beyond the horizon. But she lived beyond that horizon.

She knew El Dorado was nothing but illusion. As was Camelot and other human—dreams? mirages? aspirations?

To the south, inside Temple Manor's boundary wall, a tangle of bushes marked the site of St. Bridget's well. With St. Joseph's well in the crypt of the Lady Chapel at the Abbey and Chalice Well in its modern garden below the Tor, St. Bridget's well made a triad of ancient holy places. A Celtic triple spiral as well as the Christian Trinity. Was holiness inspiration or illusion? Maggie wondered. Could holiness really bring healing?

Darkness rolled across land and sky alike. Orange vapor lights sprang up like tiny campfires, tracing roads and parking lots. The cold wind hinted of car exhaust, dinners cooking, and farm animals safe in their barns. The Tor stood up hard and black against the deep indigo of the eastern sky, marking the entrance to the Underworld. No wonder St. Michael's church had been planted on top of it, the archangel's spear transfixing the pagan dragon—a depressingly male image.

But then, Arthur, devotee of the Virgin, was also identified with the red dragon of Wales. *Faith as metaphor,* Maggie told herself, *literally false but symbolically true.* Was it both literal and symbolic truth that Thomas was really Thomas Becket, born in 1120, died—more or less—in 1170? Could she afford to believe him? Could she afford not to? The melody of flute and chanter swelled inside her mind—*the words made flesh in the world made true.*

Stars appeared, one by one, in the vault of heaven. A Sunday school teacher once told the child Maggie that stars were God's lighted windows, telling us He was home. And if He was at home anywhere, it was here, in this place, where the past welled upward through the weight of time. Where pilgrims drank deep of belief, and healed.

Maggie's sigh was a frosty cloud that blended light with

dark. She could no longer feel her feet, and she suspected her ears were going to break off her head. Either she had to go inside or . . . The door of Thomas's cottage opened, emitting a soft ray of light. A small four-footed shape slipped inside. The door closed.

All right, then. She blundered toward the cottage. The majestic peals of Mozart's *Requiem* filtered through the door as she knocked. Thomas opened the door so quickly she hadn't time to lower her hand. She waggled her fingers in a wave. "Ah—you may be sick of me by now . . ."

"I was expecting you," he said. "Come in."

She went in. A fire leaped in the fireplace, spilling a warm radiance into the room. Dunstan reposed on the hearth in the feline version of prostration before an altar. The taped choir sang the *Dies Irae*, the day of wrath. The End Times. Judgment Day.

Thomas's face seemed freshly scoured, less deeply lined. His eyes, which this morning had been the scorched brown of fields burned before an advancing enemy, were now warm and calm. *There is something to be said for the power of prayer*, Maggie thought. Of confession. And of the courage to make both.

He took her coat. "Whiskey?"

"Oh yes, please."

"Lovely evening, isn't it? One understands why many ancient peoples saw the natural world as God."

"Yeah, we've lost touch with Creation." She stretched her hands to the dancing flames. "Mick was playing the same melody I heard outside, here, when you rang the All Souls' bell."

"Was he now? We must ask him where he heard it."

"All part of the historical, mythological pattern, right?"

"Myth is the history of the soul."

Maggie shook her head. "I feel like one of the characters in *The Lord of the Rings*. The one who asks if he's walking around in the old tales or on the earth beneath the sun."

"And he's told he can do both at once." Thomas handed her a glass of liquid that glinted like amber. He clinked his own against it. "Wi' usquebaugh we'll face the Devil. Robert Burns."

"L'hayim. No attribution." Maggie sipped. Smoke and fire exploded in her mouth, sending a wave of heat up into her sinuses and down into her throat. "Last week I was washing my socks, paying the mortgage, and assuring my mother that they have toilet paper in England. And I was assuring myself that coming here wasn't running away from my own angst. Not that angst is something you can run from."

"At times, confrontation is necessary."

Again Maggie ducked Thomas's scrutiny by turning to the bookcase. She ran her fingertip along the spines of novels from Chaucer and Malory to Austen, Hemingway, Tolkien, and Clarke. Between the novels sat studies of myth, history, and the ambiguous shore between. The texts, approved and apocryphal, of every religion of mankind. The handbooks of philosophers and nuts alike. Scientific primers from astronomy to zoology. And a copy of the *Malleus Maleficarum*, the fifteenth-century tract which authorized centuries of witch-hunting—a cautionary tale, if ever there was one.

Along one shelf stood a row of corn-dollies, figurines twisted out of wheat strands—a Celtic cross, a woman, a horse. "Harvest fetishes?"

"Christianity is deeply rooted in such ancient images and rituals," said Thomas. "That's why it's such a strong and vital belief."

"That's not an orthodox perspective."

"Faith is a continuum, not a dead end. We refine it like precious metal."

"Well, yeah . . ." Maggie sidled back into the fire's warm aura. "Tennyson wrote **Idylls of the King** to express the reality of the Unseen. I guess what I saw today did just that, didn't it? I mean, I'd like to suspend my disbelief. It takes a lot of work to be cynical about everything."

"Then sit here with me, Magdalena, and I'll show you how." Smiling, Thomas offered her the large wing-back chair facing the hearth. Instead she folded herself down beside Dunstan, leaving the chair to Thomas.

The choir sang the *Agnus Dei*, "Lamb of God which takest away the sins of the world, have mercy upon us, grant us peace." The cat's fur was warm and soft beneath Maggie's hand. He started to purr. Purring had to be a form of meditation. *This isn't happening*, she thought. Except that it was. *Believe it.* "So where do we start?"

"In the Grail stories, the Fisher King is healed by the asking of questions."

"Are you the Fisher King? Or Arthur, the folk hero who never really died? Or Lancelot, who lived out his life as a hermit in Glastonbury?"

"I'm Thomas, the poor clerk, who became a folk hero because David did die."

"Did you come to Glastonbury because of him?"

"Yes." The *Requiem* ended with a stirring *Lux aeterna*, Eternal Light. In the ensuing silence Dunstan's head shot up, his eyes flashing, his ears pricking. Maggie looked toward the window but saw nothing. Outside the wind muttered, inside the fire crackled.

Dunstan trotted purposefully to the outer door. Getting up, Thomas let him out. Then he returned to the shelf and slotted a new tape into the player. "Recorded music is one of the modern era's finest inventions—when you listen by choice, that is. Would you care for a cushion?" Thomas handed Maggie a floppy chintz pillow and sat down to the soaring violin solo of Vaughan Williams's *The Lark Ascending.*

"We have only a few ways to bridge the gap between the Seen and the Unseen," he went on, "between real time and the Dreamtime. Mathematics. Music. Poetry. Religion, myth, and the consolation of metaphor."

"The consolation of metaphor. I like it." Maggie settled onto the cushion. The music built, measure upon measure, the melody swelling higher and clearer until it gained the threshold of heaven and hung there quivering with both joy and heartbreak . . . The violin slipped back to earth on the satiated sigh of the full orchestra.

She realized she was leaning her head against Thomas's knee. His hand grasped her shoulder, warm and firm. "Lord," he murmured, "lift up the light of thy countenance upon us."

She floated, the hot, sinuous flames dazzling her eyes, the silence pealing in her head, the whiskey blessing her mouth. Then, suddenly, she jerked away from his hand.

"Not every caress expresses lust," Thomas said quietly.

"Sorry. Count me as one more victim of the sexual revolution."

"My generation exploited the flesh just as heedlessly. I did do myself, once."

"Sex is the original sin, isn't it? All Eve's fault."

"Not a bit of it. The original sin is pride, thinking that our own definitions of good and evil are God's. The flesh demonstrates the power and mystery of the physical world. Sexuality is only sinful when it is misused."

"And let me count the ways." Maggie emptied her glass,

holding the whiskey in her mouth for a long moment before letting it sear its way down her throat. Setting the glass aside, she wrapped her arms around her knees. "What's the Book Robin was talking about, a Bible?"

"The Lindisfarne Gospels. It was worked by the saintly hands of first Aidan and then Cuthbert, who in their humility never claimed authorship."

"Even an atheist could appreciate that, it's a work of art. But I thought it had been moved to the new British Library."

"Ivan O'Connell, the canon of Canterbury who is the Book's guardian, thinks it was switched with a forgery at that time. He rang just this morning to tell me that the removal men passed a security screening before they were hired on. And yet one of them, a Stanley Felton, gave in his notice the day after he handled the Book. Scotland Yard interviewed him, but he says he knows nothing."

"Great," said Maggie. "And the Stone?"

"The Stone of Scone, an ancient altar, a relic of St. Columba of Iona."

"It's on display in Edinburgh. Or was there another switch?"

"Yes, save this switch took place in 1296. The stone on display is a simple block of masonry. Like Arthur's lead cross, it expresses its own truth. Unlike Arthur's cross, we know that it's not the original Stone."

"So Mick's family has the real one?"

"I suspect it's still hidden, and that no one, not even the Dewars, knows where it is. Much to Robin's frustration." Thomas shifted uneasily.

No, Maggie thought, *Robin frustrated is not a pretty sight.* "He's some kind of demon, isn't he? The flip side of a saint?"

"Yes." The sibilant lingered on Thomas's tongue.

Maggie thought of those brilliant green eyes, like gem

stones, beautiful, cold, sterile. But Robin's identity was a little more than she wanted to tackle right now . . . A scraping noise came from the window, as though one of the shutters had moved. She glanced around—was the wind rising? Or was it the cat, wanting in again?

Thomas, too, looked toward the window. Backed by darkness, the glass reflected the glow of firelight from inside but revealed nothing from the outside. "I think we're a bit nervy," he said.

"You think?" Maggie let herself lean backward just far enough to touch the edge of the chair. Thomas's body was warm beside her, but he made no move to touch her again. Rats. His hand had been reassuring. "So why is it better for Calum and Mick to be in danger than for the Stone to be stolen? Why is it and the Book so important? Other than being valuable objects of art and antiquity."

"Because," Thomas said, "through relics God allows the supernatural to enter the natural world, thereby leading us toward the divine light."

"Illuminating the faith," interpreted Maggie.

"Three relics in particular strengthen each other."

"Three? Oh, that's right, you've got one yourself."

"Yes. I keep the Cup from which Our Lord drank at the Last Supper."

Maggie's hair rose on end. She twisted around to look up at him. "You mean you really do have the Holy Grail?"

"An element of it, yes." His face was a sketch by da Vinci, strong lights, stronger shadows. His glasses reflected the flames.

He is who he says he is, Maggie told herself, although whether that was thought or feeling or wishful thinking she didn't know. And didn't care. She looked back into the heart of the fire. "Okay. If I swallow who you are, then I might as well swallow that—that a symbol can be real."

"Symbols are real." Thomas's gentle laugh sounded like Dunstan's purr. "The Grail is the Celtic cauldron of rebirth and inspiration, the emerald that broke off Lucifer's crown when he fell from heaven, the philosopher's stone beloved of alchemists. It was Robert de Boron in the twelfth century who wrote that the Grail is the chalice or cup of the Last Supper. That the Cup was brought here to Glastonbury has been implied by many writers, but no one said so explicitly before Tennyson."

"You're the one who brought it here?"

"Yes. When I found the Cup, I found the purpose of my immortal life, as well as the means of my penance."

"To guard the Grail and all its symbolic baggage, is that it? Because we need it—them, whatever—to get us through the End Times? But 1999, 2000, 2001—they're all arbitrary dates."

"Dates that were fixed long before my birth. Although three significant stories did originate in my own twelfth century, amongst them the intermingling of the Grail stories with the stories of Arthur, bringing human emotions to the former, and providing motivation to the latter."

Maggie's brain was starting to twitch. But she felt as though she were reading a good book, and couldn't put it down. "So what's going to happen at the beginning of the third millennium? Armageddon?"

"I don't know what will happen. I know what I'd like to happen."

What? Oh . . . He hoped he would die. God knew she felt alone. How much more alone had he felt, year after year after year? She bent her head again to his denim-clad thigh. He didn't smell old at all, not sour or mildewy, but fresh and clean as a spring garden. *Touch me.*

He touched her, his hand stroking her hair and settling

lightly on her sweater-clad shoulder. *And there was consolation,* she thought, *in flesh against flesh.* Well, in flesh against wool against flesh.

"I fear," he said quietly, "that the end of the millennium—the actual end, the beginning of 2001—will indeed be the end of our world. That it will be an Endarkenment, if you will."

"If you lose the relics then you're no longer illuminating the faith, proving that there's an Unseen and that the gap between it and the Seen can be bridged. I get it. I think."

"Demonstrating that mankind was created with the opportunity to choose good over evil. Making sure that there is always someone who sets the example of embracing love and forgiveness over hate and vindictiveness. Of choosing inclusion over exclusion."

"Like you?"

"I am but the instrument of God's grace. As is the Grail."

"So Armageddon isn't a matter of armies clashing by night. It's a matter of individual choices. Why am I not surprised?"

"Because you are not afraid of asking questions," Thomas answered.

He intended that as a compliment. "You're part of some secret society guarding various relics?"

"No. Secret societies and hermetic traditions are elitist games. No true conspiracy can be sustained for long. Look at Mick's family, muddling through in the usual human fashion until their identity faded into legend. I'm one of a circle of friends. The existence of the relics is no secret, and their stories, their patterns, are common knowledge."

"True, yeah. But why are the Book and the Stone so important?"

"Because with the Cup they form a triad, an echo of the Trinity—three in one, one in three. The complete Grail. The

161

Stone, an ancient artifact of the Jewish people, is the father. The Cup, a relic of Our Lord himself, is the son. The Book, the Word decorated with images of the natural world, in a style that includes Celt, Anglo-Saxon, and Roman, is the all-encompassing Holy Spirit. Together they have what Jivan would call *prana,* the energy of the universe. Breath."

"Okay . . ." What had Thomas said to Rose about beglamoured? Maggie asked herself. And here she was, enchanted by his words, by his ideas, by his metaphors. Although she wasn't about to deny his physicality. Not his sexuality, but his physicality, the abstract made concrete, like a relic. But then, while he might be almost nine hundred years old, he was no relic. "The relics sound like Tolkien's rings of power."

"Without stretching the comparison too far, yes. Tolkien was a guardian in his own way, of the power of language and of the natural world. His father," added Thomas, "was even named Arthur."

Maggie couldn't help but laugh. "This is like calculus and poetry. I have to take them on faith, too." His reply was the clasp of his hand. No teasing movement of his fingers, no inquisitive probing of his thumb, just the steady clasp. "You've never told anyone all of this because you never wanted help before, right?"

"Quite right. It is for that perception, that glimpse into my pridefulness, that I need you, Maggie. I can only hope that somewhere in your heart you need me."

She didn't ask herself just what she was getting herself into here. She surrendered to the caress. "I think so, yes."

The last incantatory phrases of Mozart, of Vaughan Williams, even of "First Rites" ebbed into silence. In her mouth lingered the aroma of sun-warmed grain, the smell of the corn dollies, the tang of water from a deep well—didn't the Gaelic word for "whiskey" mean "water of life" . . . She closed her eyes. The glow of the fire was a sunrise through her lids. In just a moment more she'd sense that peace of God which passed all understanding, and grasp the state of grace.

The knock on the door was as harsh as the sudden thrust of a battering ram. Maggie's heart shattered and bits lodged throbbing in her throat and stomach. Thomas jerked. His voice strangled, he called, "Come in."

Anna opened the door. "I'm so sorry to intrude, but I just went up to the room I share with Rose, and this note was on my pillow."

Maggie lurched to her feet and grabbed the sheet of notebook paper. In a hurried scrawl Rose had written, "I've gone with Mick to Housesteads, Robin told him his father is there okay. R."

Thomas loomed over her shoulder. "Housesteads. The Scottish Borders. Anna, I'd be much obliged if you would ring Inspector Gupta. Ask him to come straightaway. And do you know where Sean is?"

"I'll find him." Anna vanished out the doorway.

Maggie stood reading the note over and over again, as though she could wring more than words from it. "Shit! Robin was so mad there at Sarum, I should have known he'd strike back as fast and as hard as he could."

Thomas's eyes were a landscape drifted by the ashes of pride. "No. It is I who have struggled with him for long, weary, years. I should have known. But the damage is done. We shall deal with it." He set the hot dry strength of his left hand against her cheek. With his right he made the sign of the Cross. "Magdalena, *dulcis amica dei.*" Then he seized his coat, handed her hers, and ran into the night.

Dulcis amica dei, sweet friend of God. *Yeah, right.* "Wait for me," Maggie called, and stumbled into the darkness.

Chapter Sixteen

The icy night air slapped Thomas's face. Beside him Maggie stumbled. He grasped her arm, guiding her into the courtyard, and threw open the door of the house.

In the light her face was white and cold, her eyes hard. A few moments ago she'd glowed in the firelight. Sulfur filled his mouth, overwhelming the last tang of sun-warmed grain. Damn Robin! But that was redundant, he was already damned.

Dunstan crouched halfway up the staircase, tail twitching, eyes watchful and wise at once. "That's why the cat ran off so suddenly. He heard Mick and Rose leaving." Maggie reclaimed her arm and rubbed at it.

I've hurt her, Thomas thought. *Probably not for the last time.*

Anna walked down the staircase. "Inspector Gupta's on his way. Sean's coming down. I'll get the Puckles." She went on toward the kitchen.

Thomas strode into the lounge and set about the fire. A vigorous bashing of the logs sent his resentment hissing like a shower of sparks up the chimney. God had given him anger to fight evil, yes, but he could not allow anger to misdirect his actions now.

"Divide and conquer," said Maggie behind him. "You warned me."

"Rose knew that Anna would come directly to you with her note. Trusting you—and by extension, me—must have been a very difficult decision for her. Just as trusting Rose must have been difficult for Mick."

"How did Robin get through to him so fast?"

"By playing on his vulnerability, I expect, his guilt about not being able to help his father."

"And now Robin has Rose, too!"

Thomas replaced the poker in the rack. "Robin will not have Mick or Rose alone, any more than he had you or me alone at Old Sarum."

Feet clattered down the staircase and Alf's voice echoed in the hall. "What's all this then?"

Several people burst into the room, Anna almost obscured behind Bess and Alf, the lad Sean mussed and red in the face, a girl lagging behind him . . . With weary resignation, Thomas recognized Ellen Sparrow. "Well hello, Ellen."

"This here's Bess's daughter," Alf explained to the others.

"Yeh." Ellen crossed her arms across her chest, concealing the bloodstained bandage on her right palm.

Maggie looked from Ellen to Sean and his slightly shame-faced expression. She swore beneath her breath.

"Anna," said Thomas, "would you hand round Rose's note, please?"

"Blimey," Alf said when he read it. "Housesteads. That's one of those old Roman forts along Hadrian's Wall. A long way from here."

"Rose ran off with Mick?" Sean's expression slipped off balance, incredulity warring with indignation. "Jeez."

"Ellen?" Thomas asked. "Do you know Robin Fitzroy at all?"

The girl sent an apathetic glance toward the note. "I'm a member of the Freedom of Faith Foundation, aren't I?"

As he feared, then. Robin had found himself yet another group of damaged souls who would be susceptible to his poison. "And Calum Dewar?"

She stiffened. "Yeh. He's a member as well, isn't he?"

The knocker on the front door thudded home, but before anyone could answer Jivan let himself in. The knot of people unraveled before him. "What's this about Miss Kildare?" he demanded.

Alf handed him the note. Jivan's features darkened as he read it. "Robin Fitzroy, eh? He's lying—we've heard sod-all about Calum Dewar, haven't even turned up his car." His eye fell upon Ellen. "I don't believe we've met."

"She's my daughter, Ellen Sparrow," said Bess.

"Been going about with this Fitzroy chap," Alf added.

Jivan whipped out his notebook. "Do you know where he is?"

"Nah," Ellen replied with a yawn.

"Could you show me the lad's room?" Jivan asked Alf. They went up the stairs. Doors opened and footsteps walked overhead whilst the faces in the lounge turned this way and that, not connecting. Then Jivan was back. "Nothing. Did anyone take notice of his car?"

"A Fiesta," said Sean. "Kind of a dirty red. A rental."

Ellen edged away. "Here, it's been a long day, I'm off."

"Do you need . . ." Bess began, but Ellen didn't stop.

Sean watched her plod up the stairs, his confusion almost palpable. Having a word with the lad wouldn't help, not when he was at the mercy of that hormonal imperative which could so often lead men into blind folly.

"I'll notify the authorities in Northumbria." Jivan shut his notebook. "Thomas . . ."

Thomas led Jivan outside, Maggie close upon their heels, and was halfway across the courtyard before he realized Anna was hurrying to catch them up. "I hope you don't mind," she said, "but I'd like to help, if I may."

"Yes you may, with thanks." Thomas ushered everyone into his cottage and narrowly avoided shutting the door on

Dunstan. With infinite dignity, the cat settled down on the hearth to wash his face.

The embers of the fire filled the room with a liquid orange glow. Thomas switched on the electric light and pulled out a chair for Anna. *She is less fragile than she seems,* he thought. She refused to trust the evidence of her senses and accept that they'd met in her childhood, for doing so would conflict with her understanding of natural law. Her refusal was her choice. He could not—he should not—go about ripping the veil of reality for everyone.

Jivan sat heavily down. "Miss Sparrow knows Fitzroy, does she?"

"I remember her as a fearful and embittered child, just the sort Robin easily exploits," Thomas said. "He's using her as a spy, I expect. Mick told me Calum was writing checks to her."

Swearing more audibly, Maggie took the fourth chair. "I saw her in Salisbury cathedral. She wasn't wearing the hooker outfit then."

Jivan's notebook reappeared like a rabbit from a hat. "I'll lay you odds that Fitzroy's lured Mick away because of this relic business. But where does the Foundation come into it? Morgan was a member, we've learned. Dewar as well. Fitzroy is a consultant."

"Consultant!" Maggie laughed sarcastically.

From his coat Thomas produced the paper he'd pulled from the cathedral notice board. "I've kept an eye on the Freedom of Faith Foundation for some time now, wondering if Robin were at work behind the scenes."

Jivan took the notice and read it aloud. " 'Are you concerned about the erosion of family values in Britain? Then attend the Freedom of Faith Foundation lecture at the Assembly Rooms, Glastonbury, Friday November 5.' "

"With the Guy Fawkes Carnival beginning on the Saturday," said Thomas, "the Foundation will find a wider audience here than they might normally do."

Jivan tucked the notice into his notebook. "A Foundation candidate just won a by-election in Leeds. My old chum Abdullah isn't best pleased. He thought he was simply voting for a conservative candidate, but now the Foundation is forcing through a measure to have the schools teach non-Christian children that their own faiths are wrong."

" 'Family values,' " Maggie said, "is one of those loaded phrases, isn't it? If you disagree with the candidate who uses it, then you're automatically against mom and apple pie."

"I'll attend the meeting on Friday," Anna said. "An educational experience would be an appropriate way to begin the Sabbath."

"I'd greatly appreciate your report," Thomas told her. "We may not be back by then."

"Back?" asked Jivan. "We?"

"I intend to go after Mick and Rose. Will you come with me, Maggie?"

"I think I should, yes," she replied with a frustrated gesture.

Jivan's dark eyes held depths of thought. "You know more about Fitzroy's motives than you've let on, Thomas."

"No use crying wolf until the beast enters the sheepfold," Thomas replied, adding silently, *Please, Jivan, trust me.*

Jivan's moustache curled upward. His fringe of dark lashes fell over his eyes. He nodded, almost imperceptibly.

Thank you. Thomas glanced at his watch. "Have you any news about Vivian Morgan?"

"Yes. The cause of death was suffocation. Not only did the pathologist find broken blood vessels in her eyes, but also microscopic green wool threads in her nose, throat, and windpipe. The bruising on her face is very faint, but if she'd been caught unaware . . ." He let the implication dangle.

Maggie didn't. "There's a nightmare for you. Smothered during sex. In medieval times they'd say she was taken by an incubus."

And so she was. Thomas could visualize the scene—the compliant woman, Robin's embrace, the cloak. "She wore a green cloak to the ceremony, didn't she? When Rose first saw Robin she thought he was wearing a cloak."

"That does make Robin out to be the man who was with Morgan, rather than Dewar. Still, we have no evidence he killed her."

"Why would either man kill her?" asked Anna.

"We are lacking a motive," Jivan admitted. "Perhaps Morgan was planning to expose Fitzroy in her newspaper for, well, for something. As for Dewar, we've very little evidence as yet, save that he wore shoes the same sizes as the prints in the mud. I've left messages at Foundation headquarters, but Fitzroy hasn't returned a one. I can have him brought in, I expect. Even if we find Calum alive and well, though, it would be the one word against the other." Shutting his notebook, Jivan massaged his eyes with his fingertips. "What was that ghost ship, the Flying Scotsman?"

"Flying Dutchman," Thomas told him. "Nothing so apt, I'm afraid."

"Right." Jivan stood up. "I'll walk you back to the house, shall I, Mrs. Stern?"

Anna scooted back her chair and rose. "Good night Thomas, Maggie. Don't worry, I'll keep an eye on Sean. And Ellen."

"Thanks," said Maggie. "It's not your responsibility, but . . ."

"Strangers took responsibility for me when I was young,"

Anna said, her eye straying to Thomas. "I can't pay them back, but I can pay forward."

"So should we all," Thomas told her approvingly. He opened the door for Jivan and Anna. "May God, in every name you know him, bless you both."

Shutting the door, he stood for a moment with his hand on the knob. This morning he'd been swept by the Holy Spirit, washed by the Blood of the Lamb, cleansed. And now? He was tired, yes, and paradoxically stronger than ever. His path lay before him. He had only to make one step at a time—and pray that each one went aright.

Maggie was gazing into the fireplace. Either her face had regained its color or the pink of her cheeks was only an illusion of the dying fire. "Gupta's sure cutting you a lot of slack," she said.

"We've had many compare-and-contrast conversations. I daresay he has no problem accepting the implications of the Unseen in this case."

"It's the Seen that worries me." Maggie turned to him, spread her hands on his chest, and tilted her face back to look into his.

Even in distress her eyes were a warm brown. *If Rose is air,* Thomas thought, *then Maggie is earth, the deep heart of the world.* He took her arms. His breath, his spirit, stirred her hair, which emitted a fresh herbal odor at odds with her often caustic words. The beat of his heart echoed in her palms so that her body quivered like a tuning fork. How many times had his heart beat over the years? More times than there were stars in the sky, probably. "Have faith," he told her. "This is all . . ."

". . . happening for a reason." Maggie's face relaxed into a wry smile.

"A garage in Glastonbury provides me with a vehicle from

time to time if you don't want to drive your mini-bus."

"Why not? In for a penny, in for a pound."

"Very good then. Let's get on with it."

"Give me five minutes." With a double thump on his chest Maggie turned away. "God for Harry, England, and St. George! Banzai! Remember the Alamo! Beauseant!" The door shut behind her.

Beauseant, both the battle cry and the battle standard of the Knights Templar. He hadn't heard that one for a long time. With a wry smile of his own, Thomas got on with it.

Chapter Seventeen

Mick turned into the car park, behind the sign reading "Housesteads Roman Fort. English Heritage." The Information Center was shuttered and the car park deserted except for a police car, its diagonal orange stripe shining fitfully as the sun played dodg'em with the clouds.

"Prince must be here," Mick said. "My dad rode with him, I reckon." Rose looked down at the bittie medal on a chain she'd been holding since they left the motorway café. "What's that?"

"A good luck piece my mother gave me."

"You're expecting bad luck, then?"

"Yes."

"But you came away with me even so?"

"Yes."

"You're not sensible, lass."

"That makes two of us." She draped the chain over her head and dropped the medal inside her jumper. "I ought to call Temple Manor now."

"Oh aye." The mobile lay on the floor of the back seat. He switched it on for her, then parked the car beside one of the exits. Odd, he'd thought having a late night whilst swotting for an exam was tiring. The exhaustion he felt now welled up from the depths of his soul, dreich and dull.

Rose groped in her pocket, pulled out an index card, and punched the buttons. "Hello, Mrs. Puckle? This is Rose Kildare. Yes, I'm fine. Can I speak to Maggie, please? Thanks."

Mick climbed out of the car, forcing his aching body to straighten. The police car was empty. Prince and Calum must be waiting at the ruins.

He and Rose had debated half the night just who Robin Fitzroy/Robert Prince was, what his motives were, and whose side he was on. The rest of the time they talked about relics, reviewed their life stories, and sang along with "First Rites" on the radio . . . *from alpha to omega, from word to blood, set a circled cross by the singing stones, here, at the end.*

It had gone midnight when they pulled into a layby. Mick's sleep had been ripped by passing headlamps and the roar of motors. When he jerked himself awake he didn't know where he was, save cold and alone. But the bonniest lass he'd ever seen lay asleep in the back seat, the light of dawn gleaming pink and soft on her face.

"Hello, Maggie?" Rose said into the mobile. "Oh, Anna. Hi. I'm fine. Yes, he's right here." She shot Mick a quick cautious glance.

He hadn't laid a finger on her, although the thought of touching her floated in the back of his mind like a vision of the Grail wafting just beyond the reach of unworthy knights.

"I see. Don't worry, we'll be okay. Thanks. Bye." She switched off, frowning.

"Maggie's not there?"

"She's out looking for us." Rose handed back the mobile. "Now what?"

"We climb." Feeling even guiltier than he had done already, Mick chucked the mobile into the bin and slammed the door.

White and gray clouds scudded overhead, pierced by shafts of sunlight. The countryside to the south was vast, drab, and empty. To the north rose a low hill thatched by brown bracken and heather, cut by a path. A few scattered sheep looked like dirty bundles of cotton wool. One bleated mournfully.

Rose turned up her collar, jammed her hands into her pockets, and followed Mick around the Information Center and onto the muddy path. Up they went, to the top of the hill. There, on the next hill, lay the fort, low, pinkish-gray walls cutting right angles across the hillside.

They walked down and then up the long slope to the fort. Of several buildings to the left the smallest was the museum. Mick had thought the model fort inside was brilliant. Calum had had to drag him away to view the ruins of the real thing.

"You know," said Rose, out of breath, "this area has as many stories of Arthur as Somerset. Guinevere was a Pictish Queen. Camlann was at Camboglanna just west of here. Mount Badon was Dumbarton, outside Glasgow."

"My dad says Dumbarton was called *Castrum Arthurii* up into the Middle Ages." Mick shouted through the south gate, "Dad? Are you here?"

Ravens flew upward, their harsh cries his only answer. With a sigh, Mick led Rose between walls that still stood to head height—one Roman, Calum had pointed out, and one medieval—and up several broad steps. Past the foundations of several ruined buildings, they came at last to the Wall itself, poised above a steep embankment. Here, at the peak of the hill, the wind came down like a fresh, cold mountain torrent. Mick's dark hair and Rose's blonde streamed away behind them like battle standards.

East and west Hadrian's Wall snaked along the rim of the hills. Traditionally, this was the border between Roman and Caledonii, between Saxon and Pict, between English and Scot. Between civilization and barbarism, as the southrons told it. But these harsh lands had known barbarians from both sides of the Wall.

To the north, the craggy hills fell and rose, fell and rose again in shadings of blue and gray, like ocean waves dashing themselves against the border of Scotland. The icy air crackled. Blue-black clouds massed on the horizon. "Can you imagine some poor Roman soldier getting transferred here from Glastonbury?" Rose asked with a shiver. "I bet the first thing he did was write home for socks."

Usually Mick loved the wilderness, the free expanse of land and sky, but now he felt the hills and the scrubby trees and the stones themselves were watching, not in disinterest, but in some sort of ironic intelligence.

"There's a horse," said Rose, "next to that stream."

Mick's eye followed her pointing finger. A gray horse stood beside the burn, its hooves sunk in the water-plants and mud. "My great-grandfather Malise had a tale about the *each uisge,* the water horse. If you climb onto its back, it will carry you away." He shook his head, but the gesture was more of a shudder. "I was but a wee lad then, I believed such things."

I didna believe it, but it's true. Calum's voice was so clear in his mind he spun around. And the voice went on—save it wasn't the same voice, it was tighter, hoarser. "Mick! Mick!" A human figure rose from a cellar-hole and waved.

Mick's heart somersaulted. "Dad!" He raced across the turf to the center of the fort, Rose running like an antelope beside him.

None too steadily, Calum climbed from the hole and stood, his tie and jacket fluttering. Hadn't he a coat? Had he been sleeping rough? "Dad! You're all right then, I wasn't half worried about you!"

"Then you took your sweet time getting here!"

"Hello, Mr. Dewar," Rose said. "I'm Rose Kildare."

Calum stared at her, his face pasty white, his lips crusted, his eyes red-rimmed and not quite right. Grizzled whiskers roughened the angle of his chin. Despite the cataract of wind Mick could smell his father's sour odor, as though he'd been sick. No, more than that. He smelled like the compost heap in the back garden after the neighbor's cats had been at it. "Dad, we need to be getting you to hospital."

"I told you not to tell anyone." Calum's hostile gaze turned from Rose to Mick. "What're you playing at?"

"Dad, it's okay, Rose is . . ." The man wasn't sensible. "Come along, Dad, can you walk to the car park?"

Calum evaded Mick's outstretched hand. "God himself has done me over, why not you as well? Redeem yourself. Help me remember when my friend Sinclair came to me. Do you mind what he said about the relic?"

"What? No, I dinna mind, I was wee then. What relic?"

"The Stone, of course. What else would I be talking about?"

The Stone of Scone? Mick's thoughts went spinning like leaves in the wind—a relic, an artifact, a ring of thieves, Scotland Yard . . . *The Stone.*

"Where is it, Mick?" Calum's feverish eyes darted up, down, right, left, and fixed on a spot behind Mick's back.

Mick's flesh crawled. He looked around, but saw nothing but ruined walls, grass, and a sky jostling with clouds. Rose seemed to have subtracted herself into her coat. He'd no business bringing her here, he had to see her safely away. He had to see his father safely away . . .

Calum seized Mick's forearms, his grasp like the talons of hunting bird, his voice so rough and hoarse it was unrecognizable. "Help me, Mick! Where's the Stone, not the new copy nor the old one, but the true Stone?"

Mick's eyes watered at the stench. "If you're telling me that Grand-dad and old Sinclair were in on the taking of the Stone of Scone in '50, fine, but they returned that one, we saw it in the Castle—if there's another, an original, I haven't the foggiest . . ."

"Tell me!" Calum shrieked, shaking Mick back and forth. His eyes darkened from gray to black, opening into some infernal pit.

Rose pulled at Calum's arm. "Mr. Dewar, you're hurting him!"

"Jesus Christ, Dad!" Mick wrenched himself away so abruptly Calum staggered, fell back onto the wall, and rolled into the cellar-hole. "Dad!"

Mick leaped forward, barking his shins on the stone rim. Below him, in the dark, muddy trench, lay Calum, curled on his side, his face turned away. His shirt was mottled with brown and green stains. His tie encircled his throat just beneath his jaw, his clean-shaven jaw, its swollen flesh a pasty purplish white where it hadn't been torn by the beaks of ravens. Beneath his head lay a block of red sandstone, its grainy surface almost camouflaging several smears of brownish red.

The sweetish-sick stench rising from the trench filled Mick's nose and mouth, choking him. He threw himself away, onto the grass, gasping for breath, watching his mind shatter into a thousand bloody fragments.

From a great distance came Rose's voice, leaping upward an octave and then breaking, "Oh no. Oh God, no. Oh Mick!" Her hand grasped his arm. "Mick, I think he's been—been gone—for a couple of days. Who were we talking to? What were we talking to?"

She wasn't screaming. A fine braw lass she was. Sunlight glanced out between the thick gray mounds of cloud, struck him across the face, and swept on.

Calum had said the hounds of hell were after him. They'd caught him. Mick would smell the stench of his father's decaying flesh the rest of his life. It seeped into his own flesh, into the very marrow of his bones. The hot tears slicing his face would never wash it away. "I should have known. My dad would never talk to me like that. Never."

"Of course not," Rose's heavenly blue eyes overflowed and a tear sparkled on the pink curve of her cheek. "Mick, we need to call for help."

"Oh aye." Mick let her lever him to his feet. He closed his eyes for a moment, but the sight, too, was burned forever on his brain—the chalky skin, the red stone smeared like an ancient sacrificial altar. A red stone like the one in the case in Edinburgh. A fake? The original? He didn't care, not now.

Cutting through the lament of the wind came the clip clop of a horse's hooves. The gray horse was picking its way down the steps, mane and tail fluttering. On its back sat a shape sketched in light and shadow, a skeletal form that was human and yet wasn't human at all. A gleam of sun struck cold flame from its brow, as though it wore a fiery crown. And yet it had no face, no eyes, no mouth, only a space above the bony shoulders through which the distant hills made blue shadows.

"Blessed St. Bridget," gasped Rose.

Calum's real voice in Mick's mind said, *Behold a pale horse, and his name that sat on him was Death, and Hell followed with him.* "I didna believe it, but it's true."

The figure raised the chill gleam that was its hand. From wall and trench rose shadowy shapes, wavering like reflections in glass. A low cry swelled up from the ground, a wail of agony and anger mingled. Ghosts, Mick realized. He hadn't believed in them, either.

Seizing Rose's hand, he pulled her into a run, away from the pale horse and its pale rider, across the grass toward the west. But from those walls more shapes arose. Eyes flickered, spidery hands grasped, dim shapes flocked forward. Surrounded, Mick and Rose shrank together, trembling body pressed against trembling body. "This isn't happening," said Rose.

It is. Mick couldn't breathe. The ground itself was sucking him down . . . The *sgian dubh.* He whipped it from his pocket and pulled away the sheath. Despite the shadow of the clouds, the tiny blade flashed.

"Blessed St. Bridget," Rose panted. "Blessed St. Patrick. Holy Mother of God." The shapes hesitated.

Once again Mick heard Calum's voice, and behind it Malise's voice, telling the quaint old tales. Well then, if he'd fallen into those tales, best he act accordingly. With the point of the knife he cut a circle in the turf about both him and Rose, and shouted toward horse and rider and shadows, "The Cross of Christ be upon me!"

The shapes quailed, rippling like phosphorescent rags.

Half behind him, still clutching his free hand, Rose dragged the medal from inside her jumper. "Mary, conceived without sin, pray for us who have recourse to thee. Mary, blessed among women, help us."

Another sunbeam raked the hilltop, almost extinguishing the threatening shapes. Then the light winked out, shadow fell, and the shapes condensed into twisted bodies, groping hands, leering faces. But they pressed no closer. The horse whinnied. The figure on its back sat deathly still.

Mick grimaced, straining after the words: "I gird myself today with the might of heaven, the rays of the sun, the beams of the moon, the glory of fire, the speed of wind, the depth of sea, the stability of earth, the hardness of rock. I gird myself today with the power of God."

Rose's voice joined in, like the peal of a bell. "God's angels to save me, from the snares of the Devil, from all who wish me ill . . ."

The low moan increased, so that the hilltop shuddered with grief and pain and jealousy.

Mick's and Rose's voices made one voice, "I arise today through the power of the Trinity, through faith in the threeness, through trust in the oneness, of the Maker of earth, of the Maker of heaven."

The moan rose to a shriek. The shapes threw themselves on the ground like men wrapped in flames, rolling and slapping. Then the sunlight glanced out and they were gone. The figure on horseback bowed, once, its wasted shoulders lowering and raising, and then it too was gone, horse and all.

Rose turned to Mick and threw herself into his arms. He held her as tightly as he could, the *sgian dubh* upright against her back. He didn't know how long they stood exchanging breath for breath. Long enough for his limbs to solidify, his stomach to firm, and his thoughts to spiral down to one bright point and hang there, balanced unsteadily, but still balanced. "Rose," he sighed against her warm scented flesh. If anything could take away the taste of decay that coated his mouth and nose, her fresh scent could do.

She tilted her head. "What was that with the knife?"

"Something I remembered. Like the prayer, St. Patrick's Breastplate, I dinna ken why that came to me. To us."

"Divine inspiration," she stated. "Same reason I actually remembered the prayer for the miraculous medal." Her arms locked around his chest, like a proper breastplate.

Mick looked around the fort, from the heights of the walls to the dark trench where Calum lay. Where his body lay, discarded. The mind, the spirit, the soul who had been his father was gone. With a long, ragged sigh he released Rose. He retrieved the sheath and replaced the knife. Respectfully he tucked it in his pocket. "Well then . . ."

"Hello there!" A man wearing a dark overcoat and tidy

suit was strolling toward them. His red hair shone in the sun. "There you are, Mick. And Rose. Good of you to come as well."

"Oh," she said. "It's you. Why didn't you tell me you're a policeman?"

"There's more than one way to save souls, isn't there?"

Fat lot of good Prince had done for his dad. Mick shot Rose a quick glance—no need to tell about the ghosts, he'll think we're bonkers. Nodding, she dropped the medal back inside her jumper.

Prince stopped an arm's length away, outside the turf circle. His smile was tight, not reflected in his ice-bright eyes, and his cheeks above his beard were livid. Mick didn't envy whichever poor sod Prince had just been tearing strips off of. He said, "My dad's dead."

"What? Where?"

"In yon cellar pit."

Still scowling, Prince strode across to the pit, looked inside, turned back. "I'll send for a forensics team. You shouldn't stop here. I know a safe house, Holystone, where you can rest until we've time for an interview. That's your Fiesta in the car park, is it? You can follow me."

"What about the policeman from that car?" Rose asked.

"Hm? Oh, the stupid clot was taken ill, they'll send someone after the car. Don't worry about him."

"But my dad, we shouldn't be leaving him here," Mick protested.

"The team will care for your father. Cut along now." Prince headed purposefully toward the gate.

"I don't trust him," Rose whispered.

"I dinna trust anyone save you. But I have to know what he's playing at . . ." Mick stopped to steady his voice. "Wherever he's taking us, you'd best nip off to the rail station and get yourself back to Glastonbury."

"I'm not leaving you, Mick. Not now."

"Rose . . ." But he didn't want her to leave him.

"It's getting on for one," Prince insisted. "The days are short this time of year." The green gleam beneath his heavy lids seemed miles-deep.

Mick met his stare with one of his own. Taking Rose's hand, he made sure his own body was between her and Prince as they stepped from the circle and walked together through the ancient gate.

Chapter Eighteen

Maggie gazed up at the walls of Housesteads. They were Roman rectitude imposed upon the Celtic interlace of the hills—or so Thomas would have said, if he hadn't been inspecting the footprints crossing a muddy patch in the path.

"Mick and Rose have been and gone, it appears," he said. "So has someone else. Come along."

"Yes, Kemo Sabe," Maggie muttered, but Thomas's long legs were already carrying him up the slope to the fort. He went through the south gate and headed toward the north, ravens flapping away before him. Reminding herself she was, after all, younger than he was, Maggie panted after him.

Rose and Mick had had more than two hours' head start. Even so, Maggie had hoped she and Thomas would catch up with them. She'd leaned forward eagerly, fixated on the vapor-lighted roundabouts which marked each passing city, while Thomas's voice spoke of the Romans who were as much before his time as his birth was before hers. They'd been the first but not the last to make a wasteland in Scotland and call it peace. Now Hadrian's Wall was more symbol than structure, like Old Sarum a wasteland.

They had slept a few hours, then stopped to shovel down a breakfast of eggs, beans, and strong tea that now sat like lead in Maggie's gut. She only caught up with Thomas at the peak of the fort.

His hawk-like profile turned west and then east. "There is Heavenfield, where St. Oswald won a battle against two pagan kings who wished to stamp out Christianity in

Northumbria. Oswald was a friend of Aidan, who was sent by Columba from Iona to Lindisfarne, as his predecessor Edwin was a friend of Paulinus of Canterbury. The Roman and Celtic myths intersect here, the story of the Stone intersecting the story of the Book." His eye fixed on the north. His silver-streaked hair blew back from his forehead.

All Maggie saw were the hills receding in ever more tender tints of blue until they faded from sight. Scotland. The wind wailed like bagpipes over the drumbeat of her own blood. The sun cut shafts like searchlights through the massed white and gray clouds. The air held a frosty crackle. Sheep looked like giant caterpillars huddling close to the ground.

Thomas turned back to the fort. "Look."

Muddy semi-circles made a path down a series of broad steps. "Are those hoofprints?" Maggie asked.

"I should think so, yes." He followed the trail, murmuring, "The horse stopped here at the intersection of the Via Principalis and the Via Praetoria. But no prints lead away."

"An illusion?"

"That evil smell is no illusion."

Maggie sniffed, detecting a pungency that seemed heavier than the air. "Oh no . . ."

"I am sorry to say I recognize that smell." Thomas paced across the turf to the ruins of what had once been a substantial building, and leaned over the wall. Every line in his body stiffened. His right hand moved up and down, left and right, making the sign of the Cross. Maggie didn't have to see his face to know what he'd found. The question was, who had he found? Fists clenched, she walked to his side and looked down into a trench.

The body was Calum's. At first she felt a rush of relief, and then shame to feel relief at all. The sweet sickly stench of death filled her nose and throat and she jerked herself away, doubly sorry she'd eaten breakfast. She retreated upwind and let the icy gale scour her lungs. Poor Mick, she wailed silently. Poor Rose. Had they found him? Was Robin here?

Thomas murmured in Latin cadences. Calum had probably been Presbyterian, but surely his soul wouldn't be offended by Thomas's efforts on its behalf. When he at last turned away from the pit his skin was almost gray, the circles below his eyes the deep plum of day-old bruises. "Just as . . ." he began, and coughed. "Just as I feared. Calum died probably on the Monday, soon after he disappeared. He's lying on a counterfeit stone. Whether he tried to convince Robin it was the real one, or whether he himself thought it was, we may never know. I'll take the east, you take the west. We must learn what happened to Mick and Rose here."

Dumbly, numbly, Maggie moved off. She scouted the other ruins, cringing at every hole, and came at last to a stretch of grass leading to the west wall. "Thomas! Come look!"

He sprinted toward her. The center of the circle gouged in the turf may have been trampled flat, but Maggie could've sworn it was greener and fresher than the dead, dry grass outside.

Thomas said, "They were attacked."

"What?"

"One cuts a protective circle around oneself when attacked by evil beings. And Mick's *sgian dubh* would cut a very strong circle."

Maggie shut her eyes and opened them again. But she'd long since suspended her disbelief. "Beings? Plural? Not just Robin?"

"He could well have raised some very threatening ghosts. I wonder, however . . ." Thomas glanced back at the horse's hoofprints. "I'd very much like to find the constable who has so carelessly abandoned his car in the car park beside the Information Center."

"Oh, boy." Again Maggie took the west, poking around the overgrown foundations of the gate and leaning over the Wall proper. To the north the clouds were thickening with snow. To the east the Wall angled past a boggy area and what looked like a small gate. Thomas had dropped into the earth—no, there he was, rising from a crouch. He beckoned. She raced down the slope.

He stood in the foundation of a guard house, a stone rectangle just the size to hold a human body. Maggie skidded to a stop. *Oh no, not another . . .* This body was alive. The constable's upturned face was chalk-white. Sandy hair fringed his forehead and blood smeared his temple. The yellow windbreaker he wore over his navy blue uniform was almost too bright for Maggie's dark-adapted eyes.

Thomas patted the young man's face. He moaned. His eyelids opened, revealing eyes the blue-gray of the Border hills. He tried to sit up. Maggie stepped discreetly aside while the boy—he had to be well into his twenties, but right now he looked all of sixteen—reeled and retched and at last sagged bonelessly against the wall.

"My name is Thomas London," Thomas told him. "This is Maggie Sinclair. You are police constable . . . ?"

"Willie Armstrong." He ran his tongue around his lips and made a face. "Bugger it. Sorry, madam."

"You're entitled to a little profanity," Maggie said.

"Armstrong, there's a good Borders name," said Thomas. "Are you stationed at Hexham?"

"Aye, the Chief Inspector had a call from somewheres south, sent me to look out a man and a woman in a red Fiesta."

"How did you come to be here, so far from the car park?"

"No one was there, so I had a walk along the walls, and I— I don't know, that part's all muzzy. I reckon I stepped on a loose rock and fell." His eyes rolled independently of each other and he shut them.

One side of his head was swollen and discolored, partly bruised, partly cut. The trickle of blood on his temple lengthened. A few red drops plopped onto his jacket. Thomas pulled a crisp white handkerchief from his pocket and pressed it against the wound.

"I bet there's a first aid kit in his car," Maggie said.

"I'd rather get the lad himself away." Thomas handed her the handkerchief, fished inside his coat for his cell phone, and walked several paces away.

Maggie sat down beside the constable. His thin body, all bone and sinew, trembled. She patted his head with the handkerchief. He peered blearily up at her while Thomas explained the situation in full outline form, concluding, "Very good then."

A jerk of his head summoned Maggie to a private conference. "Far from falling," he told her, "it appears as though P.C. Armstrong was bashed with a stout stick or a rock and his body concealed here."

"Robin? Disposing of a witness?"

"As you or I would swat an insect."

"But Robin meant to kill Calum, didn't he?"

"It's hard to say. If Calum withstood bribes, tricks, and threats, then yes, Robin or a confederate could well have struck him down. Or Calum could have attempted to escape, and fell." Thomas looked back toward the top of the hill, his face hard and stern as the countryside.

"So Robin dumped his body in that hole and told Mick to come here. Is that sadistic or what?" Maggie scowled. "Does

187

anger just play into his hands? Because I am really pissed."

"Fear is Robin's weapon, too. Don't fear your anger. Faith cannot exist without passion."

"Glad to hear it." She looked back at Willie. He was retching again. So that's where the word "wretched" came from. Something in his posture, knees and elbows like a pile of pick-up sticks, reminded her of Sean. Of who Sean was beneath his sophisticated mask. She had to get back to Glastonbury for him. She had to find poor orphaned Mick. Rose, she had to find Rose . . . It wasn't that she was afraid of her anger. It's that she was afraid, period.

A wobbling wail, like a nauseated banshee, cut through the wind. "Is that a siren? That was fast."

"The secular authorities do very well when confronted with secular circumstances. Stay with him." Thomas started toward the road.

Maggie sat down beside Willie and applied the handkerchief. A snowflake whirled into her face, then another and another, leaving quick icy kisses on her cheeks. No more rays of sun penetrated the low, pewter-gray clouds. The wind was raw, the stone beneath her clammy, Willie's hand cold. He was slipping back into unconsciousness. She began to babble to him, "This time last week I was in my back yard pruning my roses, wearing shorts and a T-shirt—I hadn't worn a sweater since half-past March . . ."

By the time Thomas returned with the paramedics, the snow was falling thick and fast, driven sideways by the wind. Willie's mates wrapped him in blankets and carried him away on a stretcher. Several other figures moved through the ruins of the fort, among them another stretcher team, this one in considerably less of a hurry.

Cars sat skewed across the parking lot. Flashing blue lights cast eerie reflections through the snow. Directing operations from a van was a business-suited man who introduced himself as Detective Chief Inspector Mungie. Maggie guessed the name was spelled Mountjoy, even though the man had nothing joyous about him. His saturnine face and short-cropped hair made her think of Julius Caesar confronting the Ides of March.

Thanks to police bulletins, Mountjoy already knew the basics—Vivian Morgan dead, Calum Dewar missing, Mick Dewar and Rose Kildare at large and possibly in danger. It took him only a few moments to take Thomas's and Maggie's statements. He didn't mention the hoof marks and the turf-cut circle disappearing beneath the snow. Neither did Thomas, no doubt reasoning that they fell beyond the domain of the secular authorities.

"Robin Fitzroy," Mountjoy said at last. "I've heard the name."

"He works with a religious group," Thomas answered carefully. "The Freedom of Faith Foundation."

"Ah, that's it. I attended their rally in Newcastle—Clive Bland, the footballer, made a grand speech about how we Christians are under siege by the secular humanist conspiracy. You're not telling me Foundation members are after doing criminal activity, are you? They're good moral folk."

"Bashing your constable is criminal activity. And Calum Dewar's lying dead . . ."

"We've no evidence as yet, have we? Not till we lay young Mr. Dewar by the heels. You're sure your Miss Kildare went with him willingly?"

"Yes." Maggie bit off the word.

"If you'll excuse us." Thomas's hand urged her out of the van, not that she needed urging. "We'll be stopping at the Hotspur Arms, Otterburn."

"Very good then," Mountjoy told them, with a raking

glance that, judging by his inscrutable expression, Thomas didn't miss.

"Shit," said Maggie as soon as they were out of earshot.

"He may have attended a Foundation rally, but so have many other people. Calum went so far as to join up. We must keep our minds open."

"Sure, just as long as Mountjoy does, too." Thomas opened the door of the mini-van and Maggie climbed inside. Her refrigerator wasn't this cold. "Otterburn?"

"The hotel is a safe place on our way north."

"North?" He shut the door. Her teeth chattering, she watched one of the flashing lights move onto the road. Its siren dwindled and died beneath the fury of the wind. Constable Willie seemed like a nice kid.

Mick and Rose were nice kids. *Oh God, if only we knew where they went from here!*

Something flew against the window and hung there shivering. For a moment Maggie thought it was a small white bird. But it was rectangular. An index card. In another second it would sail away and be in France by suppertime. Carefully she rolled down the window and grasped the card. It was one of the ones she'd given to the students when they arrived at Temple Manor, with its address and phone number. A flower sketched in the corner was as good as a signature. *Rose.*

On the back of the card, in the same hurried scrawl as her other note, Rose had written, "Robin take us safe house, Holyscone. Rose."

Two days ago, Maggie thought, *I'd have bleated about coincidence.* Now she recognized an answered prayer when she saw one, even if seeing one sent her stomach into free-fall.

The driver's door opened. Thomas piled inside, snowflakes thick on his hair. "What's that?"

"A note from Rose. It blew up against the window, otherwise we'd never have seen it. A mini-miracle, I guess." She handed over the note. "Holy Scone? Do you think she heard him right?"

"Not at all, no. I should think he's taking them to Holystone Priory, north of Newcastle. Almost within sight of Lindisfarne, but a very different sort of place. I'll inform Mountjoy, shall I? Although he'll not be sending anyone there alone, not after Constable Armstrong's misadventure. We'll get there first." Thomas darted out into the snow.

Maggie was trying to picture herself as the U.S. cavalry riding to the rescue when Thomas slid back into the car and asked her, "Are you all right?"

"Cold. Nauseated. Mad as a wet hen. Scared spitless. I'm just fine, thanks. And you?"

"Likewise." Solemnly he looked at her, into her, through her, all at once.

The light in his scalded brown eyes was the only warmth in this God-forsaken place. Maggie wanted to lean across the seat and kiss him. But he was already spoken for, and she didn't want to embarrass him, and she didn't believe in romance anyway, not any more.

Starting the car, Thomas turned on the headlights and drove into the whitecaps of snow.

Chapter Nineteen

The tail lamps of the green Jaguar brightened as it turned onto a smaller road. Mick guided the Fiesta into the same turn and switched on the windscreen wipers. Frozen hard, they bounced across the glass but still scraped semicircles in the thickening snow. "I learned St. Patrick's Breastplate from my great-grandfather, he being a bit ecumenical for his generation. The *sgian dubh* was his, too. He was always saying it was magic. I thought he was having me on."

"Was it magic that drove away the evil spirits?" Rose asked. "Or was it the prayer? I mean, if you believe in evil spirits then you have to believe in good ones like saints and angels."

"I dinna ken what's real, lass, let alone magic."

The gray and brown fields were fast turning white, the rare tree bent double in the wind. Mick couldn't see a single roof or lighted window. This wasn't country to be lost in, not in a storm, with darkness coming on fast. Last month he'd turned twenty-one years old. Now he felt eighty.

"Is he taking us into Scotland?" asked Rose.

Well, perhaps only sixty. "No, we're going east. That glow on the clouds, that's Newcastle, I reckon."

"Robin may be on some sort of secret mission, yeah, but we don't have to follow him."

"I owe it to my dad to follow him."

"You've seen too many movies where the good guy walks into a trap because the script says he can fight his way out."

"A trap? Is that what you're thinking?"

"I don't know what the hell I'm thinking," she admitted, her voice suddenly very small.

He'd brought her here, he owed her as well . . . His thought defaulted yet again to one horrible image. "My dad. He shouldna be lying there all cold and alone."

"They're going to find him real soon, Mick."

"Eh?"

"I promised you I wouldn't tell Thomas and Maggie, so I left a note for Anna. She told them we were going to Housesteads. When I talked to her she said they were on their way."

"You didna trust me?" he demanded.

"I trusted you," she retorted. "I didn't trust Robin. Besides, I've known Maggie almost a year now, and she and Thomas—well, they just feel trustworthy, okay?"

"Sorry." Mick's sigh was almost a groan. "We might as well listen to your heart, lass. Look where my head's brought us."

"I left another note in the door of the Information Center back at Housesteads. I bet it's blown away by now." Rose put her hand on her jumper, probably touching the medal. "Mick, where's the cell phone?"

"In the bin."

"No it's not." She scrabbled along the back seat, across the floor, in the glove box. "Great. He took the phone and the map both. He wouldn't have done that if he was telling us the full story, would he?"

Mick swore. "We're on our own then, lass. And I'm no so sure where we are. Or who we're with, for that matter."

"You're with me." She set her hand comfortingly on his thigh. A pity he was too distracted to appreciate her touch.

The hills on either side grew less harsh. The snow slowed and stopped. A dour gray twilight fell over land and sky alike.

The Jaguar cut ruts into the white trough between stone walls which was the road, until at last it turned through a stone gateway.

At the end of an alley of huge, black, leafless trees stood a mansion from a nightmare, a monumental block of masonry with turrets, dormers, and gables all capped with snow. Two lighted windows looked like eyes on either side of the gaping maw of a *porte-cochere*. "Lovely," Mick said.

"If you put up some Christmas lights," said Rose, "it might look a little more cheerful."

Mick parked beside the Jaguar and pried his fingers from the steering wheel. He felt like he was outside his body looking back at himself, every reaction dulled . . . Despite the dim light, Rose's eyes shone. Anything he could say would be either daft or stupid. Strengthened, he lifted her hands to his lips and kissed each one.

Her smile poured over him. She opened the car door. "Is that the wind? Or is it the ocean?"

The wind was souching and moaning amidst the branches of the trees. But yes, Mick heard a rhythmic undertone. He thought of Dunnottar, and Iona, and Orkney, all the seashores he'd visited with his dad.

Prince stepped out of his car. "Filthy weather."

Rose's smile soured. Mick tossed her her rucksack and retrieved his own. Snow sifted over the tops of his shoes on the way to the *porte-cochere*. The plaque by the massive door read, "Holystone Priory."

"Oh," Rose said under her breath.

The door was opened not by a gargoyle but by a white-haired granny wearing a flowery dress that would look a treat on the Queen Mum. "Come in, come in, the kettle's on, you must be perishing from the cold."

"Mrs. Jeremy Soulis," said Prince with an elegant gesture.

"May I present Mick Dewar and Rose Kildare? They're helping me with my inquiries and are need of food and shelter."

"Friends of Robin's are always welcome here," said the wee woman, smiling and bobbing.

Sharing a wary glance, Mick and Rose stepped through a vestibule into a hall bright with gold-trimmed wallpaper. Mrs. Soulis guided them on up a grand staircase and along a hallway. "Here you are, a nice bedroom for each of you. Tea in half an hour, back down the stairs, through the gallery, and into the dining room." Rose murmured a thank-you and walked into the first room.

Mick stepped into the second, wended his way past carved and gilded furniture, and gazed out through the brocade-covered window. Below lay an expanse of white broken by blots of shrubbery. At the edge of the snow-blanket the North Sea rolled outward in parallel steely glints, merging so subtly with the ash-gray sky the horizon heaved. He pulled a face. He was wobbling badly enough, thank you.

The tortured profile of the house ended at an ell whose stern stone walls, narrow windows, and slate roof were obviously medieval. Was that the priory, then? Had there really been a holy stone in these airts? His dad might have known. His dad wouldn't be telling him, though.

In the cold marble bathroom Mick brushed his teeth. But no toothpaste could clear away the sick-sweet reek in his nose and mouth. Only time could do that, and at present he wasn't taking the long view. He tucked the *sgian dubh* into his waistband, beneath his jumper, locked his door, and chapped at the next. Rose opened it straightaway. "Your door locks," he told her.

"Yeah, but I bet this place has secret passageways." She closed up her room and fell into step beside him, her freshly-brushed hair gleaming in the light of elaborate wall sconces.

Beside her he felt puggled and travel-worn. "Did you see the old building at the end of the house? Like Thomas's chapel . . ." A shape whisked through a darkened alcove. "Is that a cat?"

"Looks like one," answered Rose. "The food smells good—good for the soul as well as the body, right?"

"Oh, aye." She was doing her best to take him in hand after his bereavement, food being the equal of affection and all.

They walked through the gallery, gawping at the moldings, arches, and cornices. Every space that could hold an ornament held two—Mick had never seen such conspicuous consumption in all his life. Along the walls hung portraits of people in period clothing, their eyes reptile-cold.

The dining room seemed chilly as well, despite the fire blazing in an alabaster fireplace and a crystal chandelier glittering above a table fitted out with linen and silver. Soulis keeked in from the kitchen, her dress now protected by a ruffled pinnie. "Here you are then. Sit down."

They sat down. She brought out lukewarm plates laden with eggs, bacon, and sausage. The food wouldn't do to fill the hollow beneath Mick's ribs that was his heart, but it would do his stomach. He began scoffing the lot.

Prince came poncing in and sat himself down at the head of the table. Soulis handed him a plate, then sat down with the teapot. "Kildare, is it, dear?"

"Yes'm," said Rose, her mouth full.

"You're Irish, then."

"American. My ancestors went there during the potato famine."

"Well then," said Soulis, "if they wouldn't shift for themselves it was just as well they emigrated, isn't it?"

196

"The crops died so they couldn't eat and they couldn't pay their rent," Rose returned. "The landlords wouldn't help."

"No need to encourage idleness in the lower classes. Oh no, dear, much better your family unburdened respectable people and made their way elsewhere. Although America's quite the peculiar place, isn't it? Those dreadful Hollywood films . . ." She clucked her tongue. ". . . what they force us to watch these days! But of course the producers and studio owners are after undermining our culture, aren't they?"

Rose stared up at her. "Excuse me?"

Prince buttered a scone.

"I'm from Scotland, myself," Mick offered cautiously.

"Are you then? I'd never have known, you seem a well-mannered young man." Soulis passed the jam. "I suppose you're looking for work? Better you stay at home, we already have foreigners taking the work from our own lads. I understand why you'd want to leave a frightful wilderness, but no fear, you'll find work guiding shooting or fishing parties."

"Have you ever visited Scotland?" Mick asked, between a laugh and groan.

Rose added, her brows atilt, "Or America?"

"Oh no, why should I want to visit God-forsaken places like that? Although, to be fair, we aren't half having our own problems here. My sister lives in Bradford, she says the blacks had the cheek to build one of those heathen temples there. Can you imagine, in the midst of a country built on good Christian principles?"

And on neolithic stones, Druids, Mithras, and Woden, Mick thought.

"My next-door neighbors back home are from Lebanon," said Rose. "They're of the Ba'hai faith."

"Are they now? What a shame the authorities cater to Satanists and cultists. In the old days they would have been

moved on, and right smartly, too. Good job we have the
Freedom of Faith Foundation to protect us. Politicians natter
on about pluralism and multi-culturalism, moderation and
tolerance, but we know the truth, don't we? That God-
fearing folk like us are under siege." Smiling affably, Soulis
added hot water to the teapot.

Calum had attended Foundation meetings. Mick looked
sharply at Robin. His lips were curved in a satisfied smile.
Across the table Rose stopped eating and stared at her plate.

Soulis leaned across to refill Mick's cup. "My neighbors
up the road, now, are proper moral folk. Their family goes
back to the Conquest. Would you care for another scone?
Milk? It's the European Union, you see. Do you know that its
bureaucrats will not allow our teachers to tell our children
England is the best of the best? Why, I hear that now the
Channel Tunnel's open the road signs in Kent are printed in
French and German as well as English! There's a shocking
erosion of values for you."

Prince leaned back in his chair. From his pocket he produced a long cigar. Leaping to her feet, Soulis offered him a
lighted match. He puffed away like a dragon, the tiny flame of
the match reflected in his uncanny green eyes. Swirls of pun-
gent smoke rose upward.

"God decreed that man have dominion over the Earth,"
Soulis said, sitting herself down again. "The EU would have
us save plants and animals that God has doomed to extinc-
tion, destroying our businesses and forcing us to live in pov-
erty! Imagine that!" She turned to Rose. "You're in England
to learn proper ways, I expect."

Shriveling, as though she were trying to disappear, Rose
murmured something about the study course and her university . . .

"Now why," interrupted Soulis with a puzzled look,

"should a nice girl like you waste her time at university, reading books that would be better off for a burning, like as not. You'd best take care you're not infected by these feminist sorts. Equal rights, they say, when everyone knows their true goal is to reject the authority of their husbands, kill their children, practice witchcraft, destroy capitalism, and become lesbians. Another egg, dear? Fresh tea?"

"No, thank you," Rose said, half-strangled.

"And for you, lad?"

Mick laid his knife and fork across his plate and scooted back his chair. "Thank you, Mrs. Soulis. The food was right tasty." It was the company that made his gorge rise. "I think I'll have a rest now."

"Good idea." Rose said. "Thank you."

Prince gestured with the cigar, leaving a blue vapor trail. "I'll come and fetch you presently. Lydia, may we use the library?"

"Of course. I'll take away the dust covers, shall I?"

Mick pulled the door shut behind them. Coughing, Rose wrapped her arms around her torso. "Robin agrees with all that crap Mrs. S. was spouting, doesn't he?"

"He hinted my dad was warning me off Gupta when he said *Am Fear Dubh,* the Black Man. Have you seen a telephone?"

"No. No books, either, although I guess they're in the library. Sounds like she never goes there—and I don't mean because of the dust covers. Look, there's the cat."

This time Mick saw the beastie clearly, a gray and white cat gliding on silent paws through the shadows at the end of the hall. It watched from a safe distance as they stopped outside Rose's door.

She turned her bonny face up to his. "Now what?"

Instead of being merely clapped out, now Mick was

clapped out and nervy. "Let me steady myself a bit. Then we'll decide what to do."

"See you in a few minutes, then, and we'll plot." With a quick kiss on his cheek, she unlocked her door and went inside.

Mick waited long enough to hear her turn the key behind her, but not long enough for his cheek to stop tingling. He went into his own room, stripped off his jumper and his shirt, and had a quick wash in the basin. The room was so cold he broke out in gooseflesh.

Next door water splashed as well, then stopped. In the sudden silence he heard the faint pulse of the sea. This place might just as well be a desert island. What the hell was he doing here? Helping his dad? No, getting himself and Rose into deeper trouble. It depended on who Robert-Robin-Fitzroy-bloody-Prince really was, and what he was about.

Had Prince bashed Calum over the head? Hard as it was to think of Calum murdered, somehow it was worse to think of him falling, crawling into that muddy pit, and dying slow and all alone. And why? For a rock? For a legend?

Mick remembered his mother dying, all tucked up tidy in a hospital bed. Leaving the Royal Infirmary that night he'd looked at the streets of Edinburgh as though they were Martian valleys. Now even Mars would've seemed more familiar than this bewildering landscape. Who, what, where—*why?* That was it, wasn't it? He was here because he had to know why, and when he knew why, he wouldn't feel so bloody helpless.

Faintly Mick heard Rose singing *No Man's Land*, a lament for a dead soldier. "I hope you died bravely, I hope you died well . . ."

Her brilliant voice ripped Mick's grief open. A sob caught his throat, and tears gushed in hot streams down his face.

"God," he moaned. He didn't know whether he was calling his father's God, or Rose's, or Thomas London's, or whether there was a God actually there, listening to him—it didn't matter, the word came spontaneously from his soul. "God help us."

Rose's voice stopped but the words hung on, invisible clouds of melancholy. For a moment Mick wallowed in it. Then he groped after his senses, this being a very bad time to lose them.

His bedroom door opened. *Gowk*. He'd seen that Rose's door was locked but forgot his own.

"Mick?" her voice called.

He wiped his face, even though he had nothing to be ashamed of. She wouldn't be laughing at him, not Rose.

She stood just inside the door, her blue eyes filled with warmth and compassion. She raised her arms toward him. From the hall beyond came a faint scraping noise.

Mick went dizzy. He shut his eyes. When he opened them Rose's arms were snaking around his chest, her red lips parted invitingly. She was no longer wearing a jumper, only a T-shirt, and her small, firm breasts pressed against his naked chest. Static flooded his mind. He swept her into an embrace so fierce it startled him, kissing those red lips and tasting every corner of her mouth until dark spots swam before his eyes.

She wasn't even breathing hard. "Mick," she whispered, "I know what we need to do. We need to get the Stone ourselves. We owe it to your father."

"Eh?" he said, his mouth full of her flesh—cold flesh, that was strange—what soap had she used—its odor was sweet and thick as caramel.

She was pushing him toward the bed. "Where's your knife, Mick? Here, in your jacket? Show me your knife, why don't you?"

That was a double meaning . . . She pushed him down on the duvet, straddled his hips, and pulled the *sgian dubh* from his waistband. "Let's get the Stone ourselves. Tell me where it is."

He saw her delicate hand holding the knife. He saw her eyes as dark a blue as a midsummer gloaming when the sun never quite set. He saw the canopy of the bed arching behind her and the gray cat sitting in the open doorway, its head tilted as though watching its favorite pantomime.

"Mick, where is the Stone?" Her lips smiled, but her eyes narrowed. Her voice grated oddly and her accent had changed into a parody. "Don't you want to help your father? After you let him get hurt?"

A chill slithered up Mick's spine and sunk sharp teeth into his mind. No time to be losing his senses? Hah! "Get away!" He threw her—it—aside and seized the knife. Ripping it from its sheath he swept it across the duvet. Feathers exploded into the air. "The Cross of Christ be with me!"

The image vanished. It was there and then it wasn't. Like magic. The bed curtains fluttered and fell still. The cat's tail twitched.

If Mick had had the Stone he'd have given it to Prince right enough, between the eyes. The man had made that image, somehow. More than image. Mick had felt it, his body had responded to it, he'd seized it like an animal. *Nothing personal,* he thought toward the cat, but Rose deserved better of him.

Rose! Mick leaped up, ran into the hall, and rained blows on her door. "Rose!" No answer. He tried his own key. It turned. Inside, her things lay on the bed but she was gone. She wouldn't have gone with Prince alone, Mick told himself. If he'd forced her she'd have struggled and shouted out. Unless he'd used an illusion on her, too.

Mick raced back into his own room. He threw on his clothes, packed his rucksack, then ran into Rose's room and packed hers. They were leaving this place, now, Prince and Soulis and his own muddled head be damned.

Clutching their belongings in his left arm, he took the *sgian dubh* in his right hand and walked down the hall as though he knew where he was going. The cat was waiting for him at the top of the stairs, and led him into the darkness.

Chapter Twenty

Rose had washed her face and hands when they first arrived. Now she washed them again, and brushed her teeth clean. The food had tasted good at the time, but now the lingering flavor of the cloyingly sweet jam reminded her of the stench of death.

Her fantasies had never included a dead body. A dead body that walked and talked. But that hadn't been Calum. That had been an illusion, like the ghosts and the figure on horseback.

Her fantasies seemed weak and thin compared to the real thing. The real thing was *glamorous*. Magic. Not rabbit out of a hat magic, but something both dangerous and seductive. Robin was seductive. But even if he didn't have anything to do with Calum's death, let alone the illusions—and Rose wasn't betting the farm on either—he was sure dangerous. It was Mick who was alluring, beguiling, charming . . . Rose suddenly realized she was singing "No Man's Land." Good God, he could probably hear her. Nothing like total insensitivity.

Making sure the miraculous medal was still hanging like a warm tear drop next to her skin, she unlocked her door. The hall was darker, puddled with shadow. Some of lights had gone out. She knocked on the next door. "Mick?" The push of her hand opened it. Go figure, he was all protective of her and forgot about himself. "Mick?"

He was wearing only his jeans. The corners of his mouth were soft and the light sparkled on his cheeks. He'd been crying.

Rose's heart melted. She opened her arms, wanting to comfort him, to feel his skin beneath her hands . . . A noise echoed from the far end of the hall. Robin was coming to get them. He'd laugh at Mick for crying. She had to protect him. Putting her fingertip to her lips, partly gesturing silence, partly blowing a kiss, Rose turned away from the door.

No one was there. Playing games? she asked herself. Okay, she could do that, too. She'd try a little eavesdropping while Mick pulled himself together, then go back and get him.

Rose tiptoed down the stairs. The entry hall was empty. So was the gallery. In the dining room ashes littered the hearth and crumbs the tablecloth. Except for the gleam of a couple of digital displays, the kitchen was dark. The library? She didn't know where that was.

A slight draft tickled the back of her neck. She spun around. Mick was standing just behind her. "You scared the hell out of me!" she wheezed.

"Sorry, lass. I didna want you going about by yourself."

"Yeah, Robin could be lurking anywhere."

"Oh aye." Mick's lips were tight, his eyes shadowed. Taking her elbow, he steered her into a dim back hallway. "Let's have us a recce, eh?" They stopped in front of a carved wooden door, its top not a Gothic pointed arch but a Norman round one. Mick pushed it open. It protested with a long, atmospheric squeal.

Oh, this is the old priory, Rose told herself. *Cool!*

Very cool. Once across the hollowed stone sill she was engulfed by a cold that made the rest of the house seem toasty. The air smelled like wet dog—mold, probably. An anemic white light gleamed beyond a double row of massive pillars. Ignoring the creeping sensation between her shoulder blades—it was okay, Mick was with her—she walked toward the light.

A hurricane lamp, holding a colorless candle, sat on a small table to one side of the chancel. In the center stood a massive altar, a slab of rosy gray rock with rough-cut sides. The cross on its top seemed sad and lonely, and cast no shadow on the wall. In front of the altar—oh no! Shards of the same rock lay across the floor. Some of the pieces were large enough Rose could make out the incised shapes of horsemen and dragons. Ancient pre-Christian carvings, she guessed, and maybe newer ones, a devout medieval mason adding his own stories to a sculptured rock. A megalith. A holy stone.

A vandal had hacked away all the carved pictures. Rose looked at Mick. "How could anyone do this?"

"If it was like one of those Pictish stones it was all heathen images."

"No, look there—you can just see the top of a crucifix."

"Popish pictures, then. Not the sort of things for a proper church."

Rose's brows tightened. Mick had admitted he wasn't a churchgoer. But he'd spoken so feelingly of his great-grandfather's stories. He'd known "St. Patrick's Breastplate." How could he shrug away meaningless destruction?

Lydia Soulis and some other Foundation members had had themselves a sledgehammer party. They hadn't made the chapel holier. They'd profaned it. Destroying a work of art and history went right along with Lydia's hateful words, perverting faith into something ugly. That wasn't as bad as killing people in the name of faith, Rose supposed, but still it outraged her. "Like cutting off your nose to spite your face," she said.

"Eh?" asked Mick.

Shaking her head in disgust, Rose turned toward the door and stepped on what had once been a white tile labyrinth. She could make out the paths, inky black gouges in the gray stone of the floor. Bits of tile lay scattered like broken teeth. The vandals hadn't even bothered to pick up after themselves, leaving the broken bits lying around like trophies. "Mick, what if Robin wants to destroy the Stone? Maybe he thinks it's sacrilegious."

Mick smiled. It wasn't the smile she remembered—his mouth curved but his eyes stayed cool. His fingertips brushed the hair away from her temple, sending a tremor through her body. "All this disna matter, does it? Just scraps of rock. Just a filthy old room, not near as nice as our rooms upstairs. Mine has a fireplace and a canopied bed. Has yours?"

Yes, it did, although the fireplace was cold and empty. But while Mick was the best candidate for the right guy with the right attitude she'd ever met, this was absolutely the wrong time and the wrong place.

"Let's go upstairs, lass. No one's about, no need to be timid. Or are you timid for another reason? I dinna mind that you've no experience. I've enough for the both of us." Beneath the Scottish burr his voice was soft as silk. Seductive didn't begin to describe it.

Maybe Mick isn't the right guy after all, Rose told herself with a stab of disappointment . . . They'd talked about a lot of things last night, but she'd never told him about her bed and fireplace fantasy. And she'd sure never told him she was a virgin.

His smile grew into a grin so wide his teeth gleamed moistly, as though he was going to go for her throat. *Oh, shit!* This wasn't Mick. She should have realized that five minutes ago.

In one sinuous movement he reached behind her neck, opened the clasp of her necklace, and pulled it from beneath her sweater. "Hey!" Her voice echoed harshly from the vaulted ceiling.

He held the medal before his face, the gold and blue winking in the sickly light. "You dinna believe in this foolishness, do you? It's only cheap metal and paint, not even decent artwork."

"I believe in what it symbolizes." She grabbed for the necklace.

"And you so intelligent, too." He tossed it toward the dank crater at the center of the broken labyrinth.

"I'm intelligent enough to recognize that you're not Mick!" She turned to get the necklace and smacked face-first into an invisible barrier, a sheet of vapor so cold goose bumps broke out on her arms.

The smooth voice behind her, no longer burred, said, "Well done, Rose. You've caught me out, haven't you?"

Double shit. She turned slowly back around.

Robin was no longer dressed in his dark suit and striped tie. He was wearing tall boots, snug leather pants, a white silk shirt and a green cloak embroidered with gold thread in serpentine Celtic interlace. His smile was sardonic. His eyes glittered green in the pale light.

"Who are you really?" Rose asked, trying to be mad rather than scared.

"I told you the truth. My name is Robert. Affectionately nicknamed Robin. And I am a prince."

"Yeah, right." She tried to back away, but the cold held her immobile, as though she were locked in a stone sarcophagus. Cold oozed from the floor, deadening her legs, her back, the nape of her neck. She glanced toward her medal, a tiny glint of gold and blue beside the jagged black hole.

When she looked back Robin was wearing a brass crown rimmed with green stones. One setting, the one above his forehead, was empty. "My father's crown. From time to time I try it on for size." He took a step closer. Rose's nostrils filled with a musky, moldy odor, rotting roses and gardenia with a bitter afterglow of sulfur. "You want adventure, don't you? You want romance. But you'll never have either until you break free of that faith which has failed you."

"My faith drove away the ghosts at Housesteads."

Robin laughed. "No, I sent them away, to show you that I care for you. A lovely young woman like you deserves better than a naive boy like Mick."

"No." Her lips and tongue were so cold she could hardly speak. She pressed against the barrier. It didn't yield.

"Why do you cling to your so-called purity? Because of a worthless old story? Don't you realize how far behind you are? All your friends are enjoying life and you're sitting alone. I can be your adventure, Rose."

Some of her friends were pretty darn sorry they'd rushed into "enjoying life." But yes, she did feel left out. Just last summer she'd broken it off with a guy she liked, but who thought waiting was dumb . . . Her thoughts whirled away like snowflakes. "M-Mick's upstairs."

"I'm not selfish. I sent him someone to amuse him. Did he think of you? No. He leapt on her as soon as she walked in the door, no questions, no discussions, just that friction of flesh against flesh that is the natural inclination of human beings. The birthright of us all."

Rose shook her head. *Not Mick. No.* She grasped at another snowflake. "Thomas and Maggie are coming after us."

"You led them straight to the Stone, didn't you? I warned you they were up to no good, Rose. And now you've helped them."

She writhed. That wasn't quite right, but it wasn't wrong, either.

"I am the man of your dreams, Rose. Lancelot to your Guinevere. Uther to your Igraine. The spirit who fathered

Merlin on a princess of Wales. The Holy Ghost to your Mary." His hands cupped her upper arms, his thumbs teasing the roots of her breasts. "You want me, Rose. You want to learn what I can teach you. You don't want to cling to a faith that demands sacrifice and shame when what you deserve is pleasure."

Chills trickled down her back, teasing, caressing, even though his fingers felt like icicles. She wondered if his other body parts were icy as well—that's what the old witches said when they were bullied into confessing they'd slept with the . . . Suddenly she heard Thomas's voice: . . . *the emerald that fell from the crown of Lucifer when he was cast out of heaven.*

Every fiber of her body trembled with more than cold. With terrifying knowledge. With soul-deep horror. With desire so strong her spirit melted and ran like candle wax, blistering her senses and then congealing.

His hands kept her from sagging to the floor. His odor seeped into her chest. His cold breath stirred her hair and the frosty aura of his body radiated through her clothes. She saw the vaults beyond his head and a light moving across the windows and the tiny cross insignificant against the dishonored stone. The warm vapor of her breath rose before her eyes and then dissipated, as though it had frozen, too.

Robin's lips on her cheek were so cold they were hot. His tongue probed the corner of her mouth. Prickles of electricity raced through her body and she shuddered. But it wasn't a shudder of cold or of revulsion. It was a shudder of delight. Somewhere deep in her gut a small flame, like a pilot light, licked toward him. That flame was capable of warming even him. That's what he wanted. He wanted her to want him.

She did want him. And if she took him, then every belief she held would be a lie.

Rose couldn't move her body, but she could turn her face

210

away from those lips and that sharp-edged tongue. "No," she whispered. "It doesn't matter whether I want you. It matters whether I want my integrity. Whether I choose my faith."

He stopped.

"Blessed Virgin Mary, conceived without sin, pray for us who have recourse to thee." Something popped like a soap bubble. Robin released her. The barrier behind her broke open. She lurched back, and leaped toward the center of the shattered labyrinth. "My soul doth magnify the Lord," she said, her voice gaining strength, "and my spirit rejoices in God my Savior."

Robin stared at her, eyes blazing and fists clenched.

"For He that is mighty hath magnified me, and holy is His name and His mercy is upon them who fear Him." Something moved in the darkness at the end of the nave. Rose grabbed up her medal and spun around.

Mick, the real Mick, walked slowly up the aisle holding his knife in front of him. Its tiny blade reflected the feeble light. So did his eyes as they looked from her to Robin and back. How long had he been standing there? Not that she'd done anything . . . She'd stood there not doing anything, that was the problem.

Mick was beside her. His knife scraped along the tiles. His shoulder braced hers. His voice spoke: "I gird myself today with the power of the Trinity . . ." A warm breeze wafted up from the encircling furrows. The tiles shifted like blowing leaves.

"Don't be stupid," said Robin, but still he retreated a step. "Take what I offer you. Choose the easy way. Or else I'll have to . . ."

"No," said another voice, a strong, clear voice that rang through the chapel. The bright beam of a flashlight sent the shadows reeling.

211

Thomas came walking down the aisle, Maggie at his side. No, Maggie was in front of him and he was holding her back. That's what the light in the windows had been, the headlights of a car coming along the driveway. They'd found her note. Thank God and the Blessed Mother and all the saints in heaven, they'd found her note.

Robin sneered, "Give over, Thomas. You're not strong enough to confront me."

"I am now," Thomas said.

With a vicious curse, Robin made a slashing gesture.

Sparks swirled around Thomas and then winked out. He stopped, shook himself, and smiled. Rose had never seen such a brilliant smile, joy radiating so brightly from his face that it repelled the darkness.

Maggie looked up at him with a grin of her own. "All right! Yes!"

"Always the vandal, aren't you, Robin?" Thomas started walking again. "You can't create, so in your jealousy you destroy. But some stories are too strong for you."

Robin's face was stark white with rage. He lifted his hands. Cold flames licked upward from his palms and shredded into nothingness. "Stories? My people reject stories, and take pride in their ignorance. A fine jest, isn't it, that their pride leads them to me."

"Not a jest," Thomas said, "but a tragedy."

Sarcastically Robin bowed, accepting the compliment.

"Stories illuminate the dark corner in which you hide. For the ancient language, the ancient images of our Stories, are the most powerful relic of all." Thomas's hand traced the sign of the Cross. "*In nomine patris et filii et spiritu sancti, ite.* Depart, begone!"

The last word fell as heavily as a stone over a tomb. Tiny lights like corpse-candles played in the folds of the green cloak. It swirled, and man and cloak vanished, leaving random sparklings that slowly, one by one, winked out. The scent of rotting flowers welled outward and disappeared on a gust of cold air. For a long moment the chapel was filled with a profound silence. Then, distantly, Rose heard again the murmur of the sea.

"What?" Maggie asked Thomas, "Does it work better in Latin?"

"Force of habit," he told her.

She turned to Mick and Rose. "Are you all right?"

Mick managed a stunned nod. So did Rose.

"I knew you could withstand him," said Thomas, lifting and pressing each of their hands in his own warm grasp. "But you've taken damage, I fear."

After Housesteads, Rose had thought she and Mick had fused together, one mind, one heart. Now they turned away from each other. The last hour was like getting kicked in the stomach—it didn't hurt now, but it was going to.

Frowning, Maggie looked around. "Look at that sculptured stone. And the labyrinth, ruined."

"He knows that a tree without roots is weakened," said Thomas.

"Who is he, then?" Mick asked, his voice husky.

"My nemesis. Our nemesis. Both enemy and fate."

"That crown," said Rose. "He said it was his father's."

"Robin finds it useful to evoke Lucifer's name. But he claims other antecedents as well, ancient principles of darkness and evil."

Maggie shoved Rose and Mick down the nave. "Let's get out of here."

"What about Mrs. Soulis?" Rose asked.

"Soulis, is it? I'm not surprised." Thomas turned the flashlight so that it lit up several stone plaques set into the walls beyond the pillars. Each was carved with a name and two dates: "James Soulis, 1742–1791. Francis Soulis, 1765–1837. Emeline Soulis Dashwood . . ."

Mick asked, "They were all his?"

"No. Some of them chose to reject him, as you did." Murmuring, *"Dona eis requiem,"* Thomas shut the door.

The gray cat sat in the hall, beside two coats and backpacks. "We walked right in the front door," said Maggie, "but the cat led us to the chapel."

"Me, too." Mick gathered up the packs and handed Rose her coat.

Thomas extended his hand toward the cat, who blinked gravely and then faded into the shadows. "Well, then," he said, and set a brisk pace through the house.

A line of pale light leaked from a doorway off the entry hall. Inside, Lydia Soulis sat in front of a TV. A voice was declaiming, "These people are woodworms gnawing away at the institutions built by good Christians like us! It's time for a godly extermination!" She nodded eagerly, eyes glittering in the cold blue light of the screen.

Rose's stomach squirmed. "We ate her food."

"Food is the gift of God," answered Thomas, "to sustain that flesh which binds us to God's creation. Appetite isn't shameful."

She got the message, but she wasn't sure she agreed.

Maggie opened the outside door. The wind swept past them and into the depths of the house. Rose heard things falling and breaking even as Mick's hand propelled her toward Maggie's mini-van. "Go with her, Rose."

She wasn't surprised he didn't want her with him any more. She went with Maggie, letting Thomas drive Mick in the Fiesta.

The cars accelerated up the drive. The bulk of Holystone

Priory receded into the darkness until it became darkness itself. Rose slumped against the seat, no longer thinking, no longer feeling. The last thing she saw before falling asleep was the clouds thinning and stars throwing a faint gleam across the silent face of the snow.

Chapter Twenty-one

The newsreader was a flash git with a fruity public-school accent, the sort that thought he was better than the likes of her . . . Ellen realized what he'd just said. "Edinburgh businessman Calum Dewar was found dead at Housesteads Roman Fort this afternoon."

So Calum was dead, too. That's what happened when you betrayed Robin, which was the same as betraying God. No reason for the words on the telly to make her stomach turn over.

She remembered Calum's doubtful half-smile lit by the nutter's bonfire, and Vivian laughing. Robin had said to humor Vivian, she wrote for a newspaper, she could help spread the message. They'd gone off together, Vivian in her stupid cloak and Robin elegant in his posh suit. He told Ellen he was giving Vivian a special interview. She knew what that meant. The thought of him bonking Vivian made her sick.

Calum went off into the dark after them. He'd always been too curious by half. Is that how he betrayed God? No matter. She didn't need to know. Robin told her what she needed to know, didn't he?

That night Ellen had joined in the cleansing with a will, picturing Vivian dead. What she'd never pictured was Calum dead. He'd been good to her. She'd trusted him. But she'd been wrong. She didn't like being wrong. It made her feel small and weak.

"That's Mick's dad," said Sean from the settee beside her. "Sh—oot."

Anna Stern looked up. She was sitting in a chair by the fireplace, the moggie curled on her lap. Ellen wasn't keen on cats, they were too bleeding sure of themselves.

"Dewar was a member of several service clubs and the Church of Scotland as well as the Freedom of Faith Foundation. He's survived by a son, Michael. Now this word." An advert came on, all bright lights and thumping music, "Time is running out to buy your year 2000 T-shirts . . ."

"Shoot," said Sean again. "I bet Calum was carrying a lot of money around with him. They love to get guys like that alone and rip them off."

"Who is 'they?' " Stern asked him.

"Huh? Oh, criminals. The police ought to just dump them in jail and throw away the keys."

"It's easier to punish after the crime than to prevent it happening," said Stern.

A woman reporter, hair just so, cosmetics just so, began to natter on about refugees from Eastern Europe forced into prostitution, and the trade in little girls in Thailand. *That's just the way it is,* Ellen thought. Some people were strong, and some people were weak. The scab on her hand itched. She picked at it.

Robin hadn't been wrong about Calum. Calum was simply a good liar. He'd never been a believer at all. He never changed his mind. How could he change his mind? Robin was the truth and the path, he was. If you believed in him and his word, you'd never die. Calum didn't believe, so he died. All his kindness to her had been a lie. Robin hadn't protected her from Calum's lie . . . Her hand was bleeding again.

". . . just human nature," Sean was saying. "Everybody's got the Devil in them."

"Everyone has God in him or her as well," replied Stern. "We shouldn't blame a Devil for our own bad choices."

Sean's face went wrinkly, as if he were thinking that one through.

Stern went on, "We experience God's presence in other people. He is never absent from a truly good act, and never present in a truly evil one."

"Like the Holocaust?" Sean asked. "That was evil."

"Yes. A great evil that grew from many little ones."

"The Holocaust is Zionist propaganda," Ellen said. "It never happened."

The moggie stretched, flexing its claws. Stern's cool blue gaze made Ellen shrink against Sean's side. "It did happen, Ellen. I was there."

Robin said it, I believe it, and that's that. The woman was daft. Or a liar, most like.

"Gee," said Sean. "I'm sorry."

"Thank you. Still, many of us experienced good as well as evil during those times. I learned the meaning of an old Hebrew saying . . ." Again Stern's eyes targeted Ellen, bright, clear eyes that made her feel like a bit of rubbish. "Always look for the truth, but God help those who think they've found it."

Tripe and onions, Ellen retorted silently.

Sean put his arm around her. He was a prat, but the circle of his arm wasn't half bad when she was feeling so sick and small.

". . . in the Borders," said the news reader, "clearing skies will bring sunshine and an end to the unseasonably early snowfall."

Chapter Twenty-two

Thomas gestured a farewell to the black car as it turned onto the road. Beyond the driveway the snow-covered fields were cut by walls into segments like those of a stained-glass window, tinted delicate shades of rose and gold by a glorious dawn.

The gray stone of the hotel blushed in the light. In an upper window a curtain twitched. Maggie? Thomas went back inside, thinking that the Hotspur Arms' scent of coffee and old books was positively inspiring. No wonder the place had long been a sanctuary in the burnt and bloody Borderlands.

Caterina Shaw came through the kitchen door, a loaded tray held before her. A blond Labrador was making its best effort to retrieve any crumbs. "Breakfast, Thomas?"

"Bless you," he told her.

"Here, use the sitting room, have you and your friends some privacy." She set the tray on a low table before a chintz-covered settee and pulled forward a couple of chairs. "There you are. Shall I light a fire?"

"No need. We shan't be stopping much longer. Thank you." He stroked the dog's sleek head. It was that warm and smooth, he wondered how anyone could choose fur dead, stitched, and buttoned.

"Cheers." Caterina hastened into the dining room, where plates and cutlery rang like chimes amid the sweet voices of children. Thomas poured himself a coffee and picked up a bacon roll. *One benefit of immortality,* he thought, *was the opportunity to enjoy many breakfasts.*

"Coffee, yes!" Maggie strode into the room, sat down on the end of the settee, and poured a cup for herself. "Was that Mountjoy in the black car? Why didn't he just call?"

"Like Jivan, he realizes there's more going here than two mysterious deaths. Unlike Jivan, he's suspicious of the role we're playing."

"You said he's not necessarily one of Robin's minions."

"No. But it worries me that he made do with my version of Mick's and Rose's adventures instead of waiting to speak to them."

"Don't bother me with the facts, my mind's made up?"

"Yes." The coffee, at least, was dark, rich, and honest.

"What about Holystone?" asked Maggie.

"Mountjoy says they interviewed Lydia Soulis, who was very helpful."

"That's it? What if she told Mountjoy the same story Robin told Mick, about you being an antiquities smuggler?"

"That is quite possible, even likely."

"Great." Maggie took a bite of a bacon roll, chewed, and swallowed. "Meanwhile, back at the ranch, Anna says she, Ellen, and Sean are going to the Foundation rally this evening."

"Good." Thomas bit into his own roll.

"Not necessarily," Maggie said, and then, "Robin tried to zap you last night and couldn't do it, could he?"

"If by 'zap' you mean enspell me in my own memories, no, thank God."

"So I guess if a demon can't get you, you don't have to worry about all the fat in that bacon." Her grin was broad, and for one blessed moment, unguarded.

Thomas laughed, and reveled in laughter until a haggard Mick walked in, followed a few moments later by Rose, who appeared if not haggard at least unfortunately wilted.

Maggie vacated the settee for them. They sat several feet apart and ate their breakfasts with fair appetite. Thomas read Maggie's thoughts in the angle of her chin and mouth: Mick and Rose made a handsome couple, worthy of each other in flesh, in mind, in spirit, and yet the same circumstances that had brought them together could well, in the end, drive them apart. "Chief Inspector Mountjoy was here this morning," he said. "P.C. Armstrong is expected to make a full recovery, thank God."

"Amen," said Rose. "I can't believe he was lying down there . . ."

". . . when we could have helped him," Mick concluded.

"You had other concerns," Thomas assured them. And, as gently as he could, "Your father's body will be sent home tomorrow, Mick. It appears as though he died on the Monday, of a blow to the head. Mountjoy has alerted a Superintendent Mackenzie in Edinburgh, who would like to interview you."

"Oh aye, I'd best be getting myself home . . ." He didn't look at Rose. She didn't look at him.

"Did you know your father was a member of the Freedom of Faith Foundation?"

"I suppose so, aye. He was lonely after Mum died and did work for charities and such. But he said nothing about Vivian Morgan or Ellen Sparrow."

"You know, Robin was talking to a woman named Ellen at Salisbury. Hard to believe anyone would . . ." Rose bit her lip. Mick shot her a swift glance.

"He is a compelling figure," Thomas told the young woman. "Deliberately so. But you are not the innocent he took you to be. The dark side of innocence is gullibility."

"Yes—no," Rose said, and went quickly on, "I can't

imagine Mick's dad saying hateful stuff like Mrs. Soulis did."

"Psychic poisons are the more deadly for being subtle," said Thomas. "Calum, I expect, never fully comprehended just what Robin was about until it was almost too late."

Maggie leaned forward. "Vivian's death opened his eyes?"

"I should imagine so, yes."

"Robin killed her," Mick said rather than asked.

"She was suffocated by the same cloak Robin was wearing yesterday, but which was hers to begin with." Thomas paused, looking from face to face. "Vivian's death had a purpose, to awaken Calum from his evil dream and warn you, Mick. And to bring us all together."

Rose shot Mick a sharp glance of her own. Maggie rolled her eyes, but said only, "Robin might have thought Vivian's *sgian dubh* was your family heirloom, Mick."

"Why's that so important, then?"

"The knife," Thomas said, "is a clue to the whereabouts of the Stone of Scone, also known as the Stone of Destiny."

"Our ancestors may have kept the Stone, but Dad didna ken where it was," Mick protested. "All he ever told me is that the Edinburgh stone is a fake, that Edward the First didna steal the true Stone in 1296."

"The Edinburgh stone might well be a double fake, if the one left by the thieves-cum-patriots at Arbroath Abbey in 1951 was not the stone stolen from Westminster Abbey in 1950. What Calum believed, I expect, is that the Arbroath stone was a second, similar, red sandstone building block. The Westminster stone remained hidden in a mason's yard until Calum's father and Alex Sinclair the elder carried it elsewhere in 1959." Thomas emptied his cup and set it down. "Calum's car was found amongst the farm buildings at Housesteads. Have you any idea why he'd go there?"

"He said once it would make a grand defensive site," said

Mick. "And he was right keen on all the building stones scattered about."

Thomas pictured the desperate man brought to bay in such a cold and lonely place, and winced. "I suspect that your grandfather and Alex hid their stone there, in plain sight, so to speak. With its history, Housesteads was not an inappropriate hiding place."

"That stone has a important history," Rose said, "but still . . ."

". . . Robin wasn't fooled." A spasm of pain contorted Mick's face. Rose raised her hand toward him, then let it fall again. Silently Thomas repeated a prayer for Calum's bloodied but ultimately unbowed soul. "I have notified friends, who will find another place for the Housesteads stone."

Maggie tilted her head quizzically. "And the genuine Stone?"

"The genuine Stone is a black marble altar, perhaps of meteoric origin like Islam's sacred Kaaba. Supposedly it was Jacob's pillow, making it older even than Moses's tablets. It served for many years as King Solomon's altar, encased in metal latticework decorated with emeralds, and was kept with the Ark of the Covenant in the temple in Jerusalem. The Ark itself disappeared many years before Christ, popular films to the contrary."

Everyone smiled, if wanly.

"When the temple in Jerusalem was looted by Roman troops, the emeralds disappeared into the imperial treasury. The Stone was in turn looted from Rome and kept for many years in Merovingian France. Thence it was carried to Ireland, and by St. Columba to Iona, where it served as his altar. After his death it became the inauguration stone of the earliest Scots. In time it was brought east, first to Dunkeld and then to Scone, as a symbol of the inclusion of Scot and Pict, of Briton, Northman, and Norman, in the British story."

"So far so good," said Maggie. "What about Robert the Bruce?"

"Bruce was crowned upon the genuine Stone at Scone on Annunciation Day of 1306."

"Lady Day," said Rose. "March twenty-fifth. The day Gabriel appeared to Mary."

"Bruce carried the Stone with him when he fled west after his defeat at Methven soon after. With the English and their Scots allies hot upon his heels, he gave it into the keeping of Malise, the *deoradh* of St. Fillan in Glendochart. The name Malise, Mick, comes from the Gaelic *Maol Iosa,* 'servant of Jesus.' In Bruce's haste the Stone was accidentally chipped. Malise affixed the chipping to a *sgian dubh.*"

Mick jerked as though he'd been stung and put his hand to his waist.

"Does anybody know where the Stone is?" asked Rose.

"I don't believe so, no," Thomas replied. "Indeed, that question should remain unanswered, as Robin manifestly does not know either."

"Let sleeping stones lie," said Maggie.

"But Robin will not be letting us lie, will he now?" Mick demanded.

"No. Robin traced Calum through the story of the Stone, hoping he would reveal its location—although Robin might have settled for the *sgian dubh,* which can guide him to it. Now that his deceits have failed to win him either, well . . ." Thomas paused.

Outside a horn honked. Footsteps raced out the front door, "Bye Mum, Dad, after school, then!" Voices speaking in different accents echoed from the dining room. Through them all ran George Shaw's affable, "Good morning to you, a grand day, isn't it? Are you having a good holiday? Kippers, is it? Miso soup and rice? Right you are."

Mick's clear gray eyes demanded and accused at once. "So who's Robin, then?"

"He was once Robert, Duke of Normandy, father of William the Conqueror. In his arrogance and greed he murdered his older brother and took the dukedom for himself. Some years later, in 1035, he ostensibly made a penitential pilgrimage to Jerusalem and died on his way back. In actuality he lusted for even greater power, and so sold his soul to principles of evil. Now he moves from Dreamtime to real time and back as it serves his will."

"Whoa," Maggie said, sitting up. "Robin is Robert the Devil? An old Norman legend says he's doomed to wander the Earth until Judgment Day."

"So legends often reflect a reality beyond history." Thomas leaned back in his chair, tired, knowing he had no time to be tired. Judgment Day was upon them all.

"He said he was Lucifer's son," Rose said. "That makes sense—Lucifer is the symbol of pride."

"So Robin proudly asserts himself the equal of Our Lord, God's son."

"That's where he gets 'Fitzroy,' " said Maggie. "And Robin may be a nickname for Robert, but it's such an innocuous Camp Fire Girl name."

"An effective *nom de mal* for one so deceptive. 'Robin' is old French for both 'Devil' and 'ram.' You've seen, surely, the images of Robin Goodfellow, the spirit of the woods—horns, cloven hooves, caricatured sexual organs. Robin claims to be 'ram of God,' as Our Lord is 'lamb of God.' "

Rose was looking downright queasy.

"Robin sent the ghosts after us at Housesteads," said Mick.

"When he failed to trick you with Calum's image, he proceeded to frighten you, so that you would turn to him for rescue. But you drove away his illusions on your own. Save for the figure on horseback, that is, which was a manifestation beyond his control."

"Death," Rose murmured. "You're right, that one actually bowed to us."

"Not to you, I should think, but to the name you invoked in St. Patrick's Breastplate, he who conquered Death."

"Why would the name of Christ drive away pagan ghosts?" asked Maggie.

"Firstly, because the Celtic church was well aware its roots run very deep into pagan thought and imagery. Saints Patrick and Columba were even regarded as Druids of a sort. And secondly, because the particular spirits Robin evoked were those who in life would have been welcomed by the Cross, but who chose instead to dash themselves to death against it."

Rose pulled her Mary medal from inside her sweater. "I called Her, too, and she helped."

She helped. "Well done!" Thomas told her.

Mick shook his head so briskly his tail of hair made a fluid figure eight. "Sorry, but I'm not so keen on religion. Look at Scotland's history, fanatics persecuting and murdering in the name of God."

"As have done many of Robin's finest followers," said Thomas. " 'Men never do evil so completely and cheerfully as when they do it from religious conviction.' "

"Blaise Pascal," said Maggie. "He should have included convictions like Communism, Nazism, or even Robespierre's 'liberty.' "

"Even though every faith has adherents who drive apart rather than bind together, that doesn't mean faith itself is evil," Thomas counseled. "Coerced faith isn't true faith. True faith is lucid, not blind. It can only be taught by example, and freely chosen with knowledge, intent, and consent."

"Lucid faith," murmured Maggie.

"I suppose I'm agnostic," Mick said. "Needing evidence, like."

"If what we saw yesterday wasn't evidence," asked Rose, "what is?"

Maggie raised a professorial forefinger. "Evidence is material we choose to admit, and facts are evidence we choose to accept."

"Faith is the substance of things hoped for, the evidence of things not seen," Thomas concluded. Sunlight struck the far wall of the room, illuminating row after row of well-used books. *Thy Word is a lamp unto my feet, and a light unto my path.*

Mick shut his eyes. Rose gazed somberly at him. Maggie was eyeing Thomas. "If God can't stop evil," she said, "then He's powerless. If He could but He won't, then He's malevolent."

"God gave us free will so that we can choose between Good and Evil," Thomas answered.

"Wiggled out of that one," Maggie returned.

Mick looked up, his face taut as a drumhead. "If Robin sent ordinary yobs after us, or told his followers they'd be doing a good deed by murdering us, would a prayer see them off?"

Rose slipped her medal back into her sweater, awaiting an answer.

The only one Thomas had was, "Perhaps. In prayer as in magic, motive is everything."

"But my dad . . ."

"Chose death over dishonor. There are worse things than death, Mick."

This time Rose did touch the young man's arm. He glanced at her gratefully.

Stubborn lot, the Dewars, Thomas thought. *Thank God.* He extended his hand. "May I see your knife?"

"Oh aye. Odd sort of thing, that. It—it tickles." Mick hiked up his jumper, plucked the *sgian dubh* from his waistband, and handed it over.

The leather sheath was recent—Thomas didn't recognize it. But the bone handle of the knife itself, and the black stone chipping lodged securely at its end, he knew. "A long time it's been since I've seen this," he murmured, and drew the knife from its sheath.

The blade was heavy, smooth and sharp enough to leave a shallow groove in his thumbnail. A sliver of his face reflected from the shining metal. Memory cascaded over him, sweeping him into reverie . . .

He smelled unwashed men, horses, and smoke. A cleaner smoke than that of the pyre that had burned sullenly before the cathedral of Our Lady in Paris. There the last Grand Master of the Temple and the preceptor of Normandy had died under the self-righteous gaze of King Philippe, as a red-headed advisor murmured in his ear, "They worship the Devil. Kill them all, take their wealth, and they will never again dispute your power." So were the Templars brought down not only by Philippe's pride and greed but by their own.

Thomas's chain mail jangled. Except for similar janglings, and the quiet ripple of the Bannock Burn at the foot of the hill, the camp was quiet, as were all camps the night before battle. He'd had a stomach full of battle in Syria and southern France. And yet he'd come here, to Scotland, a land whose misty greens and blues soothed his eyes so long dazzled by sunstruck yellow. The remaining Templars needed a refuge. The Bruce needed help in his quest for Scottish independence.

A man came through the darkness, white robe gleaming, staff striking the ground. Thomas rose to his feet. "Who goes there?"

"Malise, the *deoradh* of St. Fillan. I've brought the relics for his majesty." The white-bearded man held out three parcels, two large, one small. His clear gray eyes shone with a light of their own, reflecting no scarlet from the fire.

"Very well," said Thomas, and turned toward the tent behind him.

Its flap opened. William Sinclair, Bishop of Dunkeld, peered out into the night. The wind fluttered his robes, revealing the glint of steel beneath. "Malise," said Sinclair. "Come in."

The *deoradh* entered the tent. The flap fell behind him. Male voices rose and a bell rang. The Bruce was praying tonight to his favored saints, not only Fillan, but Andrew, Cuthbert, and Thomas of Canterbury, who had also defied an English king. The smoke blew into Thomas's face and he coughed. On the far side of the burn, the English were praying, too.

Yesterday Bruce had bested an English knight in single combat. The soldiers said this was a sign that God was on the side of the Scots. Thomas suspected it was a sign of Bruce's strong arm, that God had already averted his face from the coming slaughter. Such suspicions had destroyed not Thomas's faith in prayer but his faith in battle. And yet here he was, for the Bruce spoke words that stirred his soul . . . *it is freedom alone that we fight for, that no man will lose but with his life.*

Eighteen years before, Thomas thought, *King Edward not*

only stole the crown of Scotland and with infernal presumption gave it to—David's—shrine at Canterbury, he forced Bruce to swear on Thomas's own sword to remain loyal to England. Whether that oath was binding was a fine moral point indeed.

The tent flap opened. Starting down the hill, Malise stumbled. Thomas caught first his arm and then the bundles as they slipped from his grasp. Beneath the wrappings of the largest, silver filigree winked. The second clanged gently. "St. Fillan's staff? His bell?"

"Yes." Malise took back the relics and swaddled them securely. "Would you like to see this one as well?"

Thomas unwrapped the smallest parcel, revealing a knife. Its bone handle felt warm. Curiously he drew it from its sheath. Was it the steel blade that flashed, or its guardian's eyes?

The knife was heavy, smooth, sharp. Thomas felt rather than heard the black stone chipping in its handle ring against his fingertip. The hairs rose on the back of his neck. "What trick . . ." But he knew what it was he held. Once already he'd sensed that part sound, part touch, like the sting of a bowstring snapping raw flesh—when he'd accepted a plain wooden box from the hands of Esclarmonde de Perelha.

"The Stone was meant to break," said Malise, "so this morsel could echo the whole."

The chipping chimed, beyond hearing, resonating in Thomas's heart, thrilling his soul. It was but one note, clear and strong, of a three-part chord. In time, he told himself, he'd hear that third note. For the myth demanded evidence, exacted revelation, showed itself so that the people of the north and west would know faith. *"Magnificat anima meum dominum,"* he murmured, and with a genuflection returned the knife to its keeper.

Malise made the sign of the Cross over him and kissed his

face. "*Pax domini sit semper tecum,* Thomas." The old man faded into the shadows before Thomas realized he'd never told him his name . . .

"Thomas!" said Maggie's acerbic alto. "Hello!"

He was in a homely room filled with light. His chest felt hollow as the cold fireplace, and yet amidst the ashes and cinders his heart still burned.

"You spaced for a minute," said Rose's sweet soprano.

Mick enunciated, repeating the question Thomas no doubt hadn't heard, "My great-grandfather showed you the *sgian dubh,* then?"

"I've seen it before, yes." Thomas touched the marble again, wondering whether its chime came from within it or himself, and handed the knife back.

Mick weighed it in his hand. "You're telling me, then, the Stone is important enough to die for?"

"Yes," said Thomas. "I am. It is a vitally important relic, one of three. Robin already has one of the examples of inclusion, the Book, the Lindisfarne Gospels. The Stone is the second. I keep the third."

"Robin says 'artifact,' " Maggie put in, "not 'relic.' "

"Because a relic—particularly these relics—reveal the presence of God, which Robin himself has rejected and would therefore deny us all. He cannot even touch the relics himself."

"Like matter and anti-matter?" Maggie turned to Rose's and Mick's blank faces, "Robin wants to destroy the relics. At the stroke of midnight, Greenwich Mean Time, New Year's Eve. And if he does, we turn into pumpkins."

"Eh?" Mick asked.

"As you saw at Holystone," said Thomas, "Robin wants us to renounce our shared beliefs, the roots of our faith, thereby leading us to choose evil over good. If his followers destroy all three relics, he would be immeasurably strengthened."

Mick and Rose stared at Thomas. *Two days ago,* he thought, *they would not have believed a word of it.* But what was one more leap of faith when they'd already bridged perceptual crevasses?

In the hall the dog's collar jingled merrily. An infant laughed. The different accents in the dining room made an intricate composition, a canon, perhaps. Mick said, "Just who are you, then, Thomas?"

His gray eyes, Rose's blue eyes, Maggie's brown eyes, each bright and sharp as Excalibur, turned upon him. He faced them squarely. "In my earliest life I was Thomas Becket. I was not killed in 1170. I let someone else take my place, and it was he who died."

Neither Mick nor Rose so much as blinked.

"I am like Robin, in a way. But he exists beyond the veil through which I can only peek. He evokes the powers inherent in the dark places of the world and of the human mind, and uses them to corrupt and control. I have no powers, save those I can invoke through prayer."

"You were called to oppose him?" Rose asked.

"Yes. For my greatest sin, like his, was pride. We first met during the Crusades, a time of pride gone mad."

Maggie looked at Rose. "At Old Sarum Thomas told me—showed me—who he is. It shook me up. I can imagine what Robin said happened there."

"Don't," Rose told her.

"Supposing," asked Mick, "Thomas is one of Robin's illusions?"

"Would one of Robin's illusions drive him away with the sign of the Cross?" Rose retorted.

"Well, no." Shaking his head, Mick started to laugh. A

thin, painful laugh, but a laugh nonetheless. "No offense," he said to Thomas.

"None taken," Thomas returned with a smile.

Mick slipped the *sgian dubh* into his waistband. "If we're accepting everything else you've told us, why not who you are as well? In for a lamb, in for a sheep, or whatever the saying is."

Maggie waved her hand. "I'm not sure whether you really need to believe him or not, Mick. Just go with the flow. Works for me."

"As for our going . . ." Thomas glanced at his watch, "I want to ask advice of an old—friend—near Melrose."

Maggie grinned. "You? Ask advice?"

"I have learned a modicum of humility over the years, thank you. Mick, I assume you and your father visited Melrose?"

"When my mum was alive we'd go every year—she loved the Eildon Hills above the town."

"Is that where you heard the music you were playing the night you and Rose left so abruptly?"

"Oh aye, just there. My mum said it was fairy music."

Yes. "Melrose is like Glastonbury, a place where worlds intersect." Thomas leaned forward, intent. "Mick, Rose, remember that Robin's favorite tactic is to divide and conquer."

The young people glanced awkwardly at each other.

Maggie added, " 'If we don't hang together, we will most assuredly hang separately.' "

"Benjamin Franklin," Thomas said. And that sentiment made a fine conclusion. Standing up, he stretched, every fiber creaking.

"We get the message," Rose said, and with a lopsided smile at Mick, "Come on, let's get our stuff. Looks like we ain't seen nothing yet."

"Oh aye," Mick said, eyes wide. Side by side, if not quite together, they walked out of the room.

They will never again be the children they once were, Thomas thought, just as tempered steel blades could never again be chunks of iron.

Maggie got to her feet. "Good going. You're up to three allies. Ready to take on the armies of darkness?"

"We have many more allies than that, even if they don't all know it." Setting his hand on her warm back, Thomas guided her through the doorway.

Chapter Twenty-three

Mick's Fiesta was still following the mini-van. Although he and Rose weren't sitting close together they weren't on opposite sides of the car, either. But as much as Maggie wanted to put the bloom back in Rose's cheeks, she couldn't. Rose's relationship with Mick was her own.

With a long exhalation, Maggie looked over at Thomas's austere profile. "You pulled your punches a bit with the kids, didn't you?"

"By not naming the Grail? Yes. But only a bit. They will be hearing that word quite soon enough, I think, and feel the weight of it."

Okay, Maggie thought, but she let that go. Along with the two hundred other issues she was trying to let go.

There were the Eildons, bumps on the Scottish horizon rapidly becoming three high hills. A sign indicated the miles to Earlston, AKA Ercildoune, home of Thomas the Rhymer—who, among other things, had disposed of an evil nobleman named de Soulis.

Thomas London, Thomas Maudit, slowed and turned off the slush-gray A68 onto a smaller road signposted, "Melrose." The Fiesta followed, and followed again onto a narrow lane, tires crunching through a pristine blanket of snow. When a fence blocked the lane, Thomas stopped the mini-van and Mick pulled in behind.

The slams of four car doors were swallowed by an uncanny silence. Even the wind was still, as though the hills were holding their breath. Beyond a stitchery of fences Maggie could see the rooftops of Melrose smeared by smoke. The elegant limbs of several Scots pines wrote Gaelic haiku on the sky. A bird floated high above.

"Hill North," Thomas said, his gloved hand gesturing toward the steep hillside above them. "Topped by an Iron Age fort and a Roman signal post. Their camp at Trimontium lay beside Melrose."

"Trimontium," translated Rose. "Three peaks."

"My dad," Mick said, "was going on about a mountain with three peaks off the A68."

Thomas knocked the snow from the steps of a stile topping the fence. "I believe in his distress Calum combined two different sites with similar legends—the Eildons and Schiehallion—perhaps because the Sinclairs' home is at Stow, a few miles beyond Melrose. Our Lady's shrine there once had its own holy stone, but it was broken up to pave a road. Over we go."

Maggie scrambled over the stile after Mick, muttering "Pave paradise and put up a parking lot." Louder, she said, "Arthur is buried at Glastonbury, in Avalon. He and his knights are also sleeping here, waiting to be called."

"Evidence exists that a historical Arthur lived in southwestern England, in Brittany, in Wales, and here in the Scottish Borders." Thomas offered Rose his hand. "In his story myth and history intersect."

"Which is why we're here," concluded Rose, leaping lightly onto the snow.

Maggie squinted up the hillside, a patchwork of white snow, pinkish-gray rock, and brown heather, and saw something move. A white horse. She looked sharply around at Thomas. So did Rose and Mick. He smiled. "Your mother, Mick, was not far wrong when she told you that you heard fairy music here."

"This is where Thomas the Rhymer met the Queen of Elfland," said Mick, "a lady fair riding a milk-white steed."

Rose said, "You're Thomas the Rhymer? True Thomas? The tongue that cannot lie?"

"Not a bit of it, no," Thomas said quickly. "Thomas Learmonth lived in the thirteenth century, whilst I was fighting in Palestine and the Pyrenees. But I heard of him and of this place. For many reasons I had grown curious about the Celtic view of creation, nature as evidence of God's grace. Therefore, when I found myself in Scotland in 1314, I came here."

"This isn't the Celtic area of Scotland," Maggie pointed out.

"And yet I met the Lady here," he returned, "because it was here that I at last searched for her."

"The Lady?" Rose repeated, just as Maggie asked, "The Faerie Queen?"

"Yes." Thomas took off along a path that ran up the southern flank of the hill, toward the horse. Sharing a dubious look, Mick and Rose scurried to catch up. Maggie labored behind wearing her own expression, skepticism ebbing into resignation.

A brownish-white rabbit hopped across an open space like a bouncing snowball. Maggie expected it to pull out a pocket watch and mutter about being late . . . With a hiss like the fall of a blade, a brown blur shot right past her face. She jerked back and bounced off Thomas's chest.

The bird of prey seized the rabbit and in a mighty beat of wings carried it away, leaving behind only a pitiful squeal and a patch of churned snow sprinkled by blood.

"Whoa," said Rose, releasing Mick's arm. "What was that? A warning? Big brother is watching?"

"Bugger," Mick said with a groan. "If you knew Dad was talking about the Eildons, then Robin did do as well. Because I told him."

Thomas laid a soothing hand on his shoulder. "Perhaps it was only a bird securing his lunch. Perhaps it was Robin, intending to intimidate us. But this place is a *geassa* or *locus terribilis,* hallowed by the steps of the Lady, and as long as the relics are safe, evil cannot enter here. Come along."

The horse was waiting in a hollow on the hillside. It gazed at them with dark blue eyes, its mane and tail pennons of silver silk. Thomas let it nuzzle his hand and then stroked its neck.

Chin up, mouth firm, Mick surveyed the land, his land, spread out below the hill. The snowy landscape glistened beneath a blue sky. White and blue. The Scottish flag was a white St. Andrews cross on a blue field. The symbol had appeared to some early king in a vision, Maggie remembered. If Thomas force-marched her up one more hill, she'd start having visions all right. Maybe that's why so many holy places were high places.

Thomas wasn't even breathing hard. Behind his glasses his eyes gleamed. "This world is described by scientists and ensouled by poets and priests, who recognize that in some places it meets the Otherworld—islands, hills, wells." He pointed toward a hollow in the snow, in the shadow of a thorny bush.

It was the mouth of a well, the snow mounded on its stone rim and clinging to the grillwork blocking its mouth. Maggie was tempted to lean over and yell, "Anybody home?"

She didn't have to. "We come into her presence with a psalm," Thomas said. Backing away from the horse, he began to chant, "I will lift up mine eyes unto the hills, from whence cometh my help."

The faint tang of peat smoke in the air became the scent of—frankincense and myrrh? The hair rose on the back of Maggie's neck. *But the psalms are Hebrew,* some part of her mind thought. And another part answered, *only one of the Lady's titles is Queen of Faerie.*

Thomas's textured voice sent the incantation into a hush so deep surely the people in Melrose must be able to hear. "The Lord shall preserve thee from evil, he shall preserve thy soul. The Lord shall preserve thy going out and thy coming in."

A ripple of harp strings didn't so much break the hush as fill it. Suddenly the horse was draped with dozens of tiny silver bells that sent a trill down the hillside. Rose gasped. Mick swore beneath his breath.

"For the Lord is a great God. In His hands are the deep places of the earth, the strength of the hills is His also."

The sunlight sparked, smeared, and ran. Maggie smelled damp earth, flowers, herbs and spices. Dizzy, she shut her eyes. The ground beneath her feet fell away. A strong hand seized hers and held it. No, she wasn't falling. She was standing on a cool, dry surface.

"The Lord be with you," Thomas said.

A low, vibrant woman's voice answered, "And also with you."

Maggie peered out through her lashes. The sun shone. Banks of spring, summer, and fall flowers all bloomed at once. Vegetables lay ripe and full among green leaves. Apple and pear trees groaned with both blossoms and fruit. A stream ran between glistening rocks, beneath a rainbow, harp and bells echoing in its voice. Birds sang and insects hummed. This was the melody she'd heard twice before.

She was clutching Thomas's hand. She dropped it. On her other side Mick and Rose stood close together, each face turned up in awe and bewilderment.

The horse still stood before them. On its back sat a woman. Her form was soft-edged, made of light rather than illuminated by it. Red hair spilled down her back and across a green cloak embroidered with gold Celtic interlace. Hair and cloak alike lifted and fell gently in the scented air.

"Salve Regina," Thomas, his voice trembling. *"Gloria in excelsis Dea."*

Regina. Dea. Latin for Queen and for goddess. Maggie glanced at him.

His face was that of a youth, taut and untried—no, it was his usual face, world-worn and world-weary. But his eyes shone. "Diana, Venus, Minerva. Artemis, Aphrodite, Athena. Hecate, Leto, Kybele. Gaia, Demeter, Hera."

The Lady's face, as much as Maggie could see of her face, changed and changed again, from young girl to mature woman to ancient crone. Her hair faded to white, darkened to black, brightened to flaxen yellow.

"Ishtar, Astarte, Asherah. Tiamat, Inanna. Hathor, Maat, Isis. Lakshmi, Kali, Parvati. Shakti. Shekhinah. Sophia."

She was thin, she was buxom. She was tall and then small. Her features coarsened and refined in turn. Through it all she smiled, serenely, knowingly, sternly.

"Freya, Iduna. Macha, Epona, Danu. Cerridwen, Rhiannon, Maeve. Morrigan. Brighid."

Her pale skin became olive, then a rich mahogany brown. Her eyes went from green to blue to brown to bottomless black. Then she was white again, red-haired and green-eyed, in what Maggie assumed was her Celtic avatar.

"Lilith."

Much-maligned Lilith, the first woman, whose sin was in refusing to bow down to Adam, in choosing instead to be his equal.

Thomas's voice faded and died. The Lady gestured, her hands spreading stardust. Maggie wanted, insanely, to add, "Tinkerbelle." But Barrie's sprite was no doubt yet another version of the Lady, if degenerated from her true beauty and majesty . . . Insanity and mysticism had a lot in common.

The Lady spoke, and the music was in her voice. "You are presumptuous, Thomas, not only to bring these mortals, your friends, into my presence, but to include them in your task."

"Presumptuous, yes. But when does the humility I seek become the cowardice I once displayed? No man can stand alone, least of all I. I need these friends, as they need to see you now, because I am asking them to do more, to risk more, than other mortals."

"And have they chosen freely to come here? Have they chosen freely to commit themselves to your task?"

Thomas looked at the others. His eyes didn't plead, they didn't command, they asked. *Have you?*

The Lady turned to Mick. For just a moment her face solidified into features that resembled his—something in the shape of the chin, the angle of the cheekbones, the coloring. Mick's mouth fell open. *His mother,* Maggie thought. The Lady had taken the image of his mother.

"She is with me always, Michael. As is your father, resting in my eternal embrace."

Mick's voice caught and burred. "I dinna suppose you slipped some sort of drug into our coffee, Thomas?"

"We're all seeing the same thing," Rose told him in an urgent whisper.

"Believe in me as you will," said the Lady. "I am inside your belief, I am beyond it, I am above it. I am within you and without you, whether you believe in me or not."

Mick stared at her, fists clenched at his sides. Then, slowly, his hands opened and raised, so that he offered her his defenseless palms. "Oh aye," he whispered. "Aye."

The Lady's smile turned to Rose's thoroughly disconcerted face.

The Lady's cloak became a brilliant blue. "I heard you calling me."

"As Bridget?" asked Rose. "Because Mary was a human being . . ."

"Through Mary I hear your prayers. Through Mary I intercede in the world." The horse disappeared. The Lady stood before them, her belly swelling beneath the cloak. Then she held an infant in her arms. She lifted him upward and opened her hands, and he vanished into a glory of light. "The Lord is with me. The Lord is in me. The Lord is of me. And of Mary."

Rose frowned slightly, then her expression eased. "Yes."

It was at Beckery, thought Maggie, that Arthur had a vision of Mary celebrating the Eucharist with the body of her son. And yet Mary was human, the ultimate saint. She shut her eyes, dizzy again. Seeing visions was hard work.

When Maggie opened them the Lady was looking at her. Her cloak flushed red. "I have worked through Mary of Bethany. Mary of Egypt. Mary Magdalene, the beloved of Christ, the sinner redeemed. For man does not live by bread alone but by the word of God, and by my blood and that of Mary's son."

The words fell past Maggie's mind into a deeper part of her being. That frantic little pulse that beat in her viscera slowed and evened into the cadence of waves upon a shore: *In the name of the Mother, the daughter, and the holy spirit . . .* Beyond the Word, beyond the Blood, lay silence. *Be still,* went the psalm, *and know that I am God.* Maggie opened her mouth, but found only one word inside it. "Yes."

The clear morning light became the gilded glow of evening. The fruit trees thinned, and beyond them rose the great trees of the wild wood, the eyes of birds and animals peering unblinking from their shadow. The Lady was sitting on a seat of living roots, branches, and tendrils. A crown of roses rested on her head. Her voice was wind and water, leaping like flame and steady as the earth itself. "Thomas."

"Many years ago," he said, "I sat with my head against your knee, and you opened my eyes. You told me that my task is to guard the Cup, and to assist the guarding of the Book and the Stone, and to attend the other relics in my prayers. But Robin has stolen the Book. He threatens the Stone."

"Robin profanes my green cloak. He leads my people to deny my presence and that of my saints." A long green serpent coiled at the Lady's right hand, head swaying, scales glinting like jewels. It grew clawed feet and wings the colors of a peacock's tail. As a dragon it flew away into the forest and vanished with a rustle of leaves.

The leaves became red, orange, yellow in the honeyed light of sunset. Clouds thickened, darkness rolled down the sky, and a flicker of lightning illuminated the Lady's demanding face. At her feet, the stream turned to blood.

Snow fell across Maggie's upturned face, the flakes so cold they burned. Beside her Mick and Rose stood like statues.

"Lucifer went to mankind after his fall," said the Lady, "and by mankind was made strong again. You have called Robin from the darkness. Only you can defeat him." The clouds parted. Stars shone out, jewels spread across the indigo of heaven. "But I shall strengthen you in your battle, as I have done since long before Arthur rode to Mount Badon with Mary's image upon his shield."

"Should I offer battle?" Thomas asked. "How do I know whether I choose Badon or Camlann?"

"You must offer battle at the cusp of time, not with your sword but with the Grail. For at your Badon, those who believe in peace may choose a peace lasting not for a generation but for a millennium."

A radiant full moon rose from behind a distant mountain. In its light Maggie saw Thomas's face, stark white and stern.

"Mankind stands now at the Apocalypse, the time of revelation. If you raise the Grail, one in three, three in one, at the beginning of the new millennium, it will draw the veil aside. Only then may I lift my lamp beside your path into the future. Only then can your wounds be healed."

Thomas's eyes filled with radiance and terror both. "I am not worthy to reveal the three relics."

"When does your humility become cowardice, Thomas? When does it reveal your lingering pridefulness? The Grail is a moment of eternity become time. You alone amongst men are a moment of time become eternal. If you don't reveal the Grail, then who will?"

"But if I remove the relics from their hiding places," Thomas protested, "Robin might take them for himself and destroy them. Then your portal will be closed, and men will no longer know that light is theirs to choose."

"You will guard the relics, Thomas, you and your friends. Through you the proud will be scattered and the greedy put down from their seat."

Thomas blinked. His lips tightened and then parted. And he said, on a long sigh, "Thy will be done."

Maggie laid her hand on his arm. His body vibrated like a plucked harp string. But when the night paled and flushed in a delicate pink sunrise, she saw that his face was as tranquil as an effigy on a tomb.

Thomas went on, his voice steady, "My help cometh from the Lady who made heaven and earth. In her hands are the deep places of the earth, the strength of the hills is hers also."

The Lady smiled, slowly and sensuously, as Mary might have smiled to hear the archangel Gabriel's sweet somethings in her ear. Sunlight washed over the garden and flowers bloomed. She raised her hand. "I bless and keep you. The light of my face shines upon you and brings you peace."

Maggie felt her consciousness being pulled out through her toes. She winced. Sunlight streamed from a blue sky. Snowy fields glistened. She was clutching Thomas's arm in both hands. Mick and Rose looked around, stunned. A cold wind bent the pines into genuflections.

For a long time no one moved, no one spoke. Beneath Maggie's hands Thomas's arm stopped trembling. When she at last let him go and looked at his face, he was either grimacing or grinning. Shaken, probably, and stirred as well, after his little magical mystery tour through time and space.

"The Grail?" asked Rose in a very small voice.

"Yes," Thomas answered.

"Some saint you are," said Mick, "worshiping the mother goddess."

"I do not worship her. I render her due reverence as the female aspect of God."

"Shows you the limits of pronouns," Maggie said. "We sure got our marching orders, didn't we?"

"It is not enough merely to keep the faith," said Thomas. "We must show it forth."

The wind freshened, growing warmer and softer. Mick's ponytail and Rose's scarf waved like flags. Maggie could hear water dripping. It was probably the snow melting, not her brain leaking. It wasn't that she didn't know what she was getting herself into. It was that she didn't know if she could carry it out.

She defaulted to the mundane. "There's no reason we can't have a meal first."

"Oh aye," said Mick, and Rose's brows tightened. Together they headed back toward the cars. After a few paces he took her hand and she leaned her face briefly to his shoulder.

Maggie and Thomas fell in behind them. "The days of the end hasten to their completion," he said.

"You said that before you went back to Canterbury." Maggie stumbled. Thomas caught her arm. "Sorry, someone just walked over my grave."

"I should imagine someone just walked over *my* grave. Or perhaps David's grave in the crypt of the cathedral. The crypt dedicated to the Blessed Virgin Mary." His voice was warm, his hand steady. Whatever elation he'd felt, whatever fear, had ebbed into consent. . . . *I have consented,* said Eliot's Thomas as the knights raised their swords.

Something warm and fragile swelled inside Maggie's chest—grief, pain, love, blessedness, she didn't analyze it. Twining her arm with Thomas's, she walked with him down from the sacred place.

Chapter Twenty-four

A calendar by the door of the pub read November 5. According to Rose's watch, it was just past three. She hadn't been in Faerie for seven years.

Over the last couple of days she'd experienced seven years' worth of emotions and about a century's worth of ideas. She wasn't sure whether she was closest to a migraine, an upset stomach, or a screaming fit. She'd just met the mother goddess, the genuine article, up close and personal. *Be careful what you ask for,* Rose told herself. *You might get it.*

Across the booth sat Thomas Becket, a saint, an immortal being, drinking his tea like an ordinary man. Her teacher, Maggie, sat beside him, still as a mountain right before a landslide. Sex wasn't the issue with them, although honor was. Not only personal honor, but that of the Story.

Mick sat close beside Rose but was miles away, staring out of the window. Sunlight reflected off snow wavered across his face, reminding her of cold water wearing away stone. Revelation, the Lady had said. That was the issue, too. Rose asked, "You guard the Holy Grail, Thomas?"

"I guard the Cup of the Last Supper," he answered. "With it the Book and the Stone make the Holy Grail."

"Oh boy. So that's why there are legends saying the Stone of Scone is the Grail."

"Quite so," Thomas said, and to Mick, "Are you now convinced that the world has gone mad?"

"You know what you're about," he replied with half a smile. "Mere mortals like us have to take the evidence we're given and get on with it."

"I'm afraid that we must be getting on with it now," Thomas told him. "The days are short this time of year. In more ways than one."

"Yeah, and Robin's got the Book." From her pocket Maggie produced two index cards and a pen. "Time to co-ordinate phone numbers, y'all."

"This here's the phone number of the flat, this the office. I'll get me another mobile." Mick had the long, slender fingers of a musician, Rose noted.

Thomas's hands were large but deft, the hands of an artist and a warrior both. "The number of my mobile phone. Inspector Gupta. Temple Manor, although if you ring there, remember that Ellen Sparrow might be listening in."

"That I'll do." Tucking the card away, Mick looked tentatively at Rose.

"D.C.I. Mountjoy will be contacting you, I expect. Be very cautious. Whilst I believe in inclusion, I also believe in common sense, and I'm not sure but that Mountjoy has the wrong end of the stick in his investigation."

The bar maid turned on a television mounted above the shelves of bottles and glasses. An announcer described a battle between Moslems and Hindus in India, then went on, "Freedom of Faith Foundation rallies will be held tonight in Glastonbury, Hull, Manchester, and Dumfries. Coordinator Charles Mather says the Foundation's growth proves that all people of faith want a return to traditional morality."

"And what traditional morality is that?" Maggie asked as she slid out of the booth. "The one that degraded women, exploited people of color, and murdered anyone who was theologically incorrect?"

Thomas stood up beside her. "History is struggle of mankind to learn compassion. Or so I hope."

Rose followed Mick from the booth. She'd given up all hope of Maggie saying, "This is just a test." But it was a test. And she had only a few more minutes to get one section of it right. What she hoped was that Mick agreed with her. "How about a quick tour of the Abbey?"

"Oh aye," he said, with the other half of the smile.

Mick ushered Rose out the door and down the street, toward where the red sandstone shell of Melrose Abbey looked like dried blood against the snow. She waited until he took her hand, then squeezed his. "Everything that's happening is part of a pattern. Of a Story."

"It helps thinking it is," Mick said.

"You're one of the younger knights, like Galahad or Perceval. The ones who were still pure enough to see the Grail."

"I'm not so sure about purity, lass."

"Thomas is part Merlin, part Arthur, part Fisher King."

"Aye, that he is." Mick opened the gate in the low wall around the Abbey. They stepped onto a walk wet with melted snow.

"But Maggie's not really Guinevere, is she? Unless you take those stories where Guinevere was a queen in her own right."

Mick nodded agreement. "So who are you then, lass?"

"Dandrane, Perceval's sister, one of the Grail bearers?"

"You're not my sister." His eyes swept across her face, down to her toes and back up again.

"No, I'm not." That tiny pilot light in Rose's gut flickered and grew. *Appetite isn't shameful.*

"I owe my dad a proper funeral," Mick said. "And to see to the business. But I owe it to him to bring Robin down as well. You'll be seeing me again, whether you're wanting to or not."

"As long as you want to see me," she told him.

He squeezed her hand. She took that as a yes.

They walked past the arched arcades and the vaulted ceiling of the sanctuary. Each stone in the cemetery beyond cast a small shadow on the snow. Beyond the far wall creaked the bare branches of an orchard. There, by that wall, bathed in the light of the westering sun, Mick and Rose stopped and faced each other. She took the plunge first. "There at Holystone, Robin looked like you to begin with. Then he turned into himself, and—and damn it, he knows just what scab to pick."

"You didna see me with the illusion that looked like you."

Visualizing that scene sent a far from revolting quiver through Rose's stomach. "But you didn't actually, I mean . . ."

"Took me two minutes to see it wisna you. Two minutes you didna deserve of me. I'm sorry."

"So am I. I should've fought against Robin harder."

Mick's gray eyes were polished into silver by sun, snow, and emotion. "But this is what he's wanting, to keep us apart."

"Nothing can keep us apart." The heat of his breath made her shiver. Rose took a solid grip of his shoulders and turned her lips up to his. He bent toward her. And they turned awkwardly aside and stared off in opposite directions. *Nothing except ourselves.* "Mick," she said after a slow count of ten, "it's all right."

"Is it, then?" His eyes gleamed inches away from hers. Searching, but revealing as well.

It was only a kiss. They could handle it. She brushed her mouth gently across his. For a long moment they hung there, barely touching. Then Mick planted his mouth on hers. *Oh yes.* His lips and tongue were hot, supple, eager and yet delicate, working some alchemy of tenderness and passion that made her knees go weak. This was a hell of a lot more than a kiss. *Yes.*

Rose fell back the two inches to the wall. The sun-warmed stone was no less hard against her back than Mick's body against her chest and stomach. The miraculous medal purred on her suddenly sweaty skin. She could taste the salt-sweet of his tears on her lips. Unless they were her tears too. She embraced him all the tighter.

At last they separated and looked at each other, dazed. Beyond the mingled rhythms of their breaths and the sigh of the wind Rose could almost hear a voice very like the Lady's singing, *From the world, the flesh and the Devil make me anew.* "Yes," she said.

And Mick said, "Oh aye."

They left the Abbey and walked up the street to where Thomas and Maggie stood waiting. Mick's face was pink and his hair was tousled. By the heat in her own face Rose knew she was bright red. Fine. One of the things she'd wanted was Truth.

"Take care, Mick," said Maggie with a sympathetic smile. "Keep in touch."

"No fear," he told her.

Thomas made the sign of the cross, then touched Mick's head. "May the blessing of Almighty God, the Father, Son, and Holy Spirit, descend upon you and remain with you always. Amen."

"Thank you kindly." Mick released Rose's hand, leaving it cold. He looked at her, opened his mouth and closed it again. He climbed into the Fiesta and drove away toward the north.

Even as Rose waved, upper lip stiff as she could make it, she thought, *I might never see him again.* But the medal was warm beneath her sweater, her mouth tasted of his, and in her mind she could still hear the song, *Of one substance with the word, of one mind with the flesh, begotten not made by grace out of blood.*

The red car turned the corner and disappeared. A green one, not a Jaguar, pulled out of a parking place up the street and followed. Well no, it might not have followed, it might simply be going the same way.

Grimacing, Thomas opened the door of the van. Rose clambered in and sat on the back seat, alone.

She was scared. She was elated. She was heavy as stone. She was light as air. She'd disintegrated into fragments, each with its own flickering pulse. She felt the world and its history and every human belief centered in her own heart, whole. *The words made flesh in the world made true, and the Devil take his due from your hands.* "Amen," she whispered.

Maggie drove away toward the south, past the Eildon Hills making a smooth triple curve against the blue cloak of the sky.

Chapter Twenty-five

Slamming the door of the van, Maggie stared up at the walls and chimneys of Temple Manor. Just a few days ago she'd come here for the first time. If a few days could seem like years to her, what did years seem like to Thomas? She glanced at his sober face and answered, *purgatory*.

Rose retrieved her backpack and tramped off toward the house, her step firm, as though her center of gravity was lower now. The afternoon sun burnished her golden hair. The Virginia creeper waving against the ancient stone walls blazed a brilliant red. A strain of music in the distance announced that it was carnival night in Glastonbury.

Maggie hoisted her own bag and plodded beside Thomas through the archway and into the courtyard. "Have we just about worn you out with questions?"

"You've helped me collect my thoughts for the task ahead. We must find not only the Stone, but retrieve the Book."

"Easier said than done."

"Very much so." He opened the door.

Maggie stepped into the dim interior of the house. Her nose wrinkled. She'd been hoping for one of Bess Puckle's lavish spreads, but the only odor she detected was that of disinfectant. It was Alf who loomed in the kitchen doorway. "Welcome back! Fancy your tea?"

"Yes please," Maggie and Thomas said simultaneously.

"Rum bit of business with Calum Dewar, that," said Alf, turning back to the kitchen. "There are some filthy beggars about, make no mistake."

"I pray that I don't," Thomas said, half to himself.

From upstairs came Sean's voice. ". . . oh yeah right, like I'm supposed to believe nothing happened?"

"Even if anything did happen," Rose replied tartly, "it wouldn't be any of your business."

"Hey, we Americans have to hang together. Some of these foreigners are way the hell out in left field."

"We're the foreigners here, Sean."

"And your point is?" Sean appeared at the top of the stairs, saw Maggie at the bottom, and said, "Hi. Welcome back already."

"Thanks," Maggie said. "How are you doing?"

"Fine. Watched some movies. Did my reading. Went to a lecture. I'm heading up to town, the Carnival's starting." Sean galloped down the stairs and out the door. Through the panes of the lounge window, each image in the old glass warped from the next, Maggie saw him walking away with Ellen Sparrow.

Rose came down the stairs more sedately. "Yeah, I saw Ellen in Salisbury with Robin."

"Funny," said Maggie, "how her parents just happen to be here at Temple Manor."

"If she seduces Sean whilst spying on us," said Thomas, "so much the better for Robin's purposes."

"I hope you mean 'seduce' metaphorically."

"I do, but never underestimate a young man's libidinous drive."

"Give him a chance," Rose said.

"Your compassion does you credit," Thomas told her. "I shouldn't wonder but that your good example will help him find his path."

"Me? I'm the one who led y'all on a wild goose chase halfway up the U.K."

"In the Celtic tradition, the wild goose is a sign of the Holy Spirit."

Maggie shared a wry grin with Rose. "Why am I not surprised?"

Footsteps sounded from the upper hallway and Anna stepped down the staircase. "I'm glad you're back safely, Maggie, Thomas. Rose said you had quite an adventure."

"Yes," Maggie said, wondering whether Rose had edited the supernatural out of her travelogue. "I do intend to start teaching the course now."

"Did anything happen here?" asked Rose. "What about the Foundation rally?"

"Sean watched movie after violent and ugly movie, as though he were searching for some sort of validation. At the rally last night he seemed impatient and resentful. Ellen kept looking around, for Robin, I suppose, but stopped once she saw Inspector Gupta at the back of the room. She said something about police harassment. Neither she nor Sean has much imagination, I'm afraid, and that concerns me."

"Yes," said Thomas, "a literal mind does make one vulnerable . . ."

Maggie realized Bess Puckle was standing in the kitchen doorway, balancing a tray of dishes. A tremor in her body set the crockery to ringing. "Thomas? Do you think Ellen's all right? She had a rough time as a girl, with her dad leaving and all, but I tried to raise her right."

"She has opened herself to an unhealthy influence, but there is hope for her." Taking Bess's tray, Thomas carried it into the dining room and set it on the table.

Maggie had some sympathy for Ellen—she'd never known her own father. *There but for the grace of God and so forth,* she thought, and yet she knew only too well that God had nothing to do with the unhealthy influence of her mother's sexual guilt trip. Maybe she should be thankful for her instinctive skepticism, not irritated by it.

"Sit down, sit down." Alf sailed into the room waving the teapot. "Sorry, Thomas. I know you're in the religion business—we've had some grand talks haven't we, nice and polite—but this Foundation lot, they're over the top."

"Did you go to their meeting Friday?" asked Rose.

"No, but what with Ellen joining up Bess and I thought we'd better check them over, and we got us some newsletters. Load of codswallop." Alf distributed cups and saucers. "We have sandwiches and custard tarts from Safeway's. Bess didn't do the baking, another one of her headaches."

"The doctor gave me some tablets for my nerves. I'll bake a nice batch of scones tomorrow, see if I don't." Bess positioned the cream pitcher and sugar bowl just so. Maggie was shocked to see how drained the woman looked, her pallor accentuated by two red splotches of blusher.

Alf poured, and steam wafted upward. "Bess, let's let these folk have their tea in peace."

Thomas took Bess's hand as she turned to go. "I've been praying for Ellen. I'll say a prayer for you, too, shall I?"

"Thank you, Thomas, but there's no . . ." She glanced at Alf. He shrugged. "Thank you."

Why did he bother asking? Maggie thought. He was going to pray for Bess whether she wanted it or not. And Alf, too. If anyone had a direct link to the Almighty, it was Thomas. Maybe he even knew just what the Almighty was writing down in his book of the Story. She, though, she didn't have a clue.

Dunstan padded into the room and went from person to person, rubbing a welcome on each. Rose slipped him her last crust and pushed back her chair. "I think I'll call home. Not to spill my guts or anything, just to say hello."

"And," Maggie teased, "to tell your sisters about Mick."

"You think?" Rose vanished out the door and up the stairs.

Smiling, Thomas stood up. "The parade will be starting soon. We might as well walk, we shan't find a parking place."

"I'll go get ready." Maggie listened to his steady steps recede down the hall and out the door before she scooted back from the table.

"Are you all right?" asked Anna, perceptive as always.

"Tired. Tired and wired both. I'll be okay, thanks." Not that she was too sure of that. But as Maggie went on up the stairs she told herself to stop checking her emotional dipstick every few minutes. She was only slowing down the journey. The pilgrimage.

Bathing and washing her hair served psychology as much as hygiene, and by the time they all set out for town she was looking forward to the carnival. A cold crystalline dusk cast a blue sheen over the countryside. Along Bere Street cherry bombs crackled and a group of children ran away laughing. The truncated towers of the Abbey leaped in and out of passing headlights. The Tor still loomed above Glastonbury, Maggie assumed, but the lights of Chilkwell Street were so bright she could see nothing beyond the thicket of trees where the Tor path started upward.

People thronged the sidewalks, carrying fragrant bundles of fish and chips. Anna struck up a conversation with a woman and her toddlers. Thomas, Rose, and Maggie found a place at the curb. Another string of firecrackers erupted in the Chalice Well gardens behind them. "Remember, remember," intoned Thomas, "the fifth of November, gunpowder, treason, and plot."

"Guy Fawkes was caught piling up gunpowder in the basement of Parliament, right?" Rose asked. "Was it an anti-Catholic plot?"

"Fawkes and his companions were Catholic. King James—yes, he who sponsored that magnificent translation of the Bible—and his minister Cecil learned of the plot and used it to justify even more repression and more murders than were already taking place."

"Who was Robin encouraging?" Maggie asked. "Cecil or Fawkes?"

"Both."

"And you risked your life to celebrate Mass for frightened congregations in various hidey-holes."

"As Alf said, I'm in the business."

"I guess Guy Fawkes Day caught on because it was close to Samhain," Rose said. "You could still light bonfires, but to be patriotic . . . All right!"

A trumpet fanfare heralded the first float of the parade. The crowd surged forward. *All right,* Maggie repeated silently. Anybody who didn't enjoy a parade had an inner crab, not an inner child.

Thousands of tiny lights sparkled, outlining decorative curlicues, floral displays, castles and thrones. Some of the riders on the floats posed still as statues, others acted out scenes. Maggie cleverly detected a theme. Uther Pendragon leered at a simpering Igraine, ready, willing, and eager to beget Arthur. Merlin waved his magic staff. Arthur pulled the sword from the stone. Armored figures circled a round table. Lancelot bowed chivalrously to Guinevere in one scene, and in the next took her in a passionate embrace. Gawain battled the Green Knight.

The Arthurian legends, Maggie thought with a glance at Thomas's profile, a dark edge against the light, *were popular at Henry II's court.* During his century the Grail cycle merged with the Arthur cycle. And the other parts of the Story dating to the twelfth century? The identification of the Devil with the fallen angel Lucifer, and the veneration of the Blessed Virgin Mother. Talk about patterns in time and faith.

"Look," said Rose, "it's the actors I saw in Salisbury. They've got a papier mache dragon. St. George, I guess. Or is it St. Michael? Like Mick." She vanished into the crowd, following the strolling players.

"Rose . . ." The lights were hallucinogenic. So was the music, everything from madrigals to punk surging in waves through Maggie's head. The Lady of Shalott saw her fate come upon her and died of love. Galahad and Perceval beheld the Grail. Morgan le Fay and Mordred whispered not only lies in Arthur's ear, but also inconvenient truths. Three queens carried a dying Arthur to Avalon. Bedivere returned Excalibur to the Lady of the Lake.

The Story rooted, grew, and branched. But Maggie missed one blossom, a red-haired woman in a green cloak, the light in her eyes penetrating every defense, seeing all.

She looked around. Now Thomas had disappeared. But there was Rose, across the street in front of the Rifleman's Arms Pub talking to Sean and Ellen. All three looked like they were waiting outside the principal's office: Sean stiff, his hands on his hips, Ellen with her arms crossed truculently, Rose half-turned to the side, plotting her escape.

"Well hello, Maggie!" said a male voice. "Small world, isn't it?"

She spun around with a gasp. He was lean and sandy-haired, with shrewd brownish-green eyes. His voice was flat American, but the voice she heard in her head was Thomas's: *This is the worm that dieth not, the memory of things past.* "Anthony! Where did you come from?"

"I ran into Bart Conway at the British Museum. He said

you were here with a seminar group. I heard the Carnival was worth a look, so here I am."

Once she'd thought he was handsome. Now his face seemed a caricature, each feature, each expression overplayed. "What are you doing in England?" she asked, backing away a step.

Anthony came two steps closer. "Research. Same project I told you about in Boston. You remember the conference in Boston. Ironic that I'd run into you again at a carnival. You know, 'farewell to the flesh.' "

"I know the etymology of the word 'carnival.' "

"But with us it's 'hello to the flesh,' isn't it?"

Maggie's shoulders hit the garden wall. She stepped to the side, toward the woods. Another float was passing, drums beating and bagpipes blaring—Arthur in his Scottish avatar, no doubt.

She remembered the afternoon she found Danny with Melissa. She remembered the shouts, the hateful words, the slamming doors. She'd steeped her soul in anger, hurt, and fear for a month before that conference in Boston. There she'd encountered Anthony's handsome face. His purring voice. His deliberate charm, a dream then, now a nightmare.

He was smiling at her. His eyes glittered, but there was no humor in them. *Okay,* she thought, *if it really is Anthony he'll think I'm an idiot, but then, he already knows I'm a fool.* "Go away, Robin. There's nothing for you here." She raised her hand, but making the sign of the cross didn't come naturally to her.

Like the wind ruffling a reflection on the surface of a pool, Anthony's face dissolved into Robin's. "You're wrong," he said, his voice cutting through the music. "You're here. It's time we had a bit of a chin wag, you and me."

Even as Maggie told herself not to be afraid of him, she

took several more steps to the side and back. Her feet left the cement of the sidewalk and landed on dirt.

He followed her, his eyes glittering as brightly as the lights behind him even though his face was in shadow. "Don't bother making the sign of the cross. Or parroting Thomas's feeble buzz words. You know only too well that faith means hypocrisy, repression, and shame."

Her hand dropped back to her side and closed into a fist.

"You don't believe in Thomas. You feel contempt for him, for what he did that night in the cathedral. When he stood by and watched his young, innocent brother be hacked to death."

"You killed your brother on purpose," Maggie retorted. "Thomas is sorry for what he did. You're not."

Robin laughed. "Thomas is proud of his own guilt. You'll take him despite his crime? Well then, you must have your reasons. Playing at Guinevere, I expect, as he plays at Arthur, so noble, so sad."

"What?"

"Guinevere was a strong woman. Hungry for power. That's why she betrayed Arthur, isn't it, for power?"

"In some of the stories, yes. In others she betrayed him for love."

"Oh well, that's all right then. Love cancels out faith. That's how you're excusing your plans for Thomas, is it?" He cupped Maggie's face in his hand. His skin was cold, smooth, and dry.

She flinched away. "Plans?"

"To lure him into your bed. To show him all the ugly, degrading ways of the flesh that he's forgotten in his celibacy." In Robin's satiny voice the word was obscene. "Like Guinevere, you're jealous and you want to bring him down."

Maggie backed up again and collided with the trunk of a tree. "Jealous?"

"Of Her. Regina. Kyria. The Lady. Of what she means to him."

"Like I'm going to be jealous of a goddess? The Goddess?"

"You think he'll find your flesh sweet," Robin went on. "He'll take you, he's only mortal, after all, and what man passes up cheap meat? But once he realizes what you've done to him, how you've betrayed that perfect image he has of himself, then he'll hate you. And you'll not be part of his plots any more."

Quickly Maggie stepped to the side, intending to dodge around him, but he blocked her way. He was driving her deeper into the wood, deeper into the uncompromising dark. Already leaves fluttered across the lights of the parade and the music was muffled, oddly distant.

Seizing her arms, Robin pulled her against his chest. The night was cold but he was colder. His icy breath, invisible in the darkness, smelled of rotten flowers, cheap cigars, and mildewed basements. She gagged. "You want to drag him down with you into that monstrous wallow of flesh that is woman, and you'll call it love as you do it. But then, you've degraded yourself again and again. Men had only to tell you they loved you and they had free use of your flesh. A whore has more honor, more truth, than you do."

The last sentence was a chill explosion in her face, sending shivers down her back. "God, no!" she shouted, at Robin, at her own memories, and wrenched herself away from his grasp.

Maggie turned and stumbled into the trees, into a dark intensified by the brightness of the lights along the street. His voice followed her. "God can't help you. Thomas won't help you. They're powerless against your truth!"

Hot tears stinging her eyes, she blundered against one tree trunk and another. Maybe she could avoid him by paralleling the street—she glanced over her shoulder. The trees stood up like black bars against the lights but Robin was gone.

Robin Goodfellow. The King of the Wood. The Green Man, the spirit of the forest. Forests weren't always peaceful places for the environmentally-inclined to hold picnics. They used to be fearsome wildernesses, filled with wild beasts and monsters, like the dark places of the psyche . . . She stopped. She could hardly hear the music beyond the sound of the trees creaking, the wind sighing, and her own feet shifting among the leaves. Was that Robin, that shape in the darkness—no, just a low branch—a leafy face leering at her, skeletal hands reaching out for her, furtive footsteps closing in . . . "God help me," she whispered.

A man's voice, textured as velvet, called, "Maggie, where are you?"

The Green Man was also the symbol of re-birth, she told herself, and had been since time immemorial. Croaking, "Here," she blundered toward the light.

Thomas was standing on the sidewalk. His strong right hand took her elbow and buoyed her up. "What's wrong? What happened?"

"Robin." She stood for a long moment, catching her breath, then she pulled her arm away. Without Thomas's hand it was cold, but with his hand it was false.

He frowned down at her. "Whatever he said to you may have some basis in truth. But remember, I beg you, that it is in his best interests to separate us. He knows that I am incomplete without you, because you know the truth about me."

But you don't know the truth about me, Maggie returned silently. And she couldn't tell him.

The last floats passed by, Merlin shut up in a rock by Nimue and Guinevere ending her life as a penitent. Rose threaded her way through the crowd toward them. "I am

263

trying to set that good example, but Ellen isn't interested."

"She may well see you as a rival for Robin's affections," said Thomas.

"Oh yeah, right!" Rose exclaimed.

"What of Sean?"

"I think he sees her as a reclamation project. You know, a fixer-upper."

"It boosts his ego to help her," Maggie translated for Thomas.

"Ah," he said. "A benign aspect of the desire to control others."

Whatever blood had rushed to Maggie's face under Robin's taunting drained away, leaving her chilled. The last strain of music hung on the air and died. The crowd began to break up. "We ought to be getting back. It's late. Where's Anna?"

Thomas collected everyone and led them back toward Beckery, Ellen and Sean lagging behind. Now it was a parade of car lights that passed, strobing in Maggie's head. Only now did she realize how tired she was.

After the lights and the music the grounds of Temple Manor seemed unusually dark and quiet. A lamp beside the parking area and another beside the front door barely dispelled the night. The chapel was invisible. Thomas opened the door, courteously took his leave of the others, and shut the door before Maggie could slink inside behind them. "I have something for you." He reached into his pocket and handed her a small box.

She looked up at him. The face of one's age, she thought, owed less to genetics than to appetite. Lust accumulated in bags beneath the eyes. Gluttony padded the once clear-cut edge of the cheekbone. Anger deepened the crows feet at the edge of the eyes and despair cut lines between nostril and mouth. A face was the outer expression of the mind within. The unseen made tangible.

Except for Thomas. After so many centuries he should have had a face like a 3-D map of London. But he had the face of a fifty-year-old man, haughty, sensitive, strong, fragile. Faithful . . . He was looking at her every bit as intensely as she was looking at him. "Open it, Maggie."

The box was stamped, "Moon Childe Shoppe." That was where she'd stood talking to Gupta, the place advertising discounts to Bodhisattvas. She wondered whether Thomas had gotten his.

Inside the box lay a necklace, a pewter Celtic cross carved with simple interlace, no beginning, no end. She picked it up by the chain and it swung back and forth, gleaming in the lamplight. "For me?"

"Mick and Rose have their talismans. I wanted you to have one as well, as a token of my respect and affection."

No, she thought. She said, "I don't know what to say."

" 'Thank you' is generally considered appropriate."

One corner of her mouth turned up in a wry laugh. "Thank you."

He took the chain and lifted it over her head. The cross settled just where her sweater began to curve over her breasts.

Maggie said with a rush, "When I told Mick it didn't really matter whether he believed you or not, and implied I didn't, I didn't mean it as an insult."

"I know."

"It's not that I'm not with the program. I mean, with all the evidence the last few days . . . Well, my mother always said I was stubborn as hell. So did the Mother Goddess, I think."

"You can explain away the most inexplicable event or accept the most obvious hoax, but ultimately you believe because you choose to believe."

"Yes." She half-turned away from him. The courtyard of the house was like an Elizabethan theater, galleries, windows, doors encircling the actors on stage. "Did you ever want to marry?"

He tilted his head curiously, but he had to realize where that question came from. "There was Alice at the time of the Reformation, and Joan at the time of the Enlightenment. She stitched the samplers which are in my cottage. But no, whilst I felt a—personal attraction—I never seriously considered marrying. To petition to be released from my vows would have compounded the presumption of my ordination."

"Why bother to petition? No one knew who you were."

"I thought of that, yes, but I had already dishonored myself quite sufficiently without entertaining such a rationalization."

Yes, faith demanded honor. "Thomas, I'm not too good at keeping commitments."

"I've seen no evidence at all of that. Good night, Magdalena." With a smile that was either wistful or distant, he turned and strode away.

Holding the cross, Maggie watched him disappear into the darkness. Despite every wound she'd ever taken from the war between affection and desire, despite every sling and arrow in Robin's unctuous voice, still she wanted to pull Thomas's face down to hers, open his lips, and suckle the word from his eloquent tongue.

She was too old for a stupid schoolgirl crush, she told herself sternly. But she wasn't as old as Thomas. She wasn't a schoolgirl. It wasn't a crush. And while she'd had many stupid moments in her life, this wasn't one of them.

Chapter Twenty-six

A ray of sun pierced the clouds and winked out. But not before it illuminated Rose, standing in the garden talking into Thomas's mobile telephone. Appreciating the vision, he went on toward his cottage.

Intellectually he knew that he'd once been that young, but emotionally he had little memory of himself at twenty beyond a fleeting image of a bright arrogant boy, master of hawks and horses but not of his own ambition. Maggie now, Maggie was closer to his own age. At times Thomas wanted to shake her. More often he wanted to embrace her, no more so than last night, as she'd obstinately clutched the guilt with which Robin had hounded her. Not that he wasn't clutching his own guilt, he supposed, it being easier to see the mote in another's eye than the beam in one's own.

Inside the cottage he took off his coat, loosened his tie, and lit the fire. He warmed his hands in the heat of the yellow flames as he'd warmed his soul in the Lady's presence. She'd given him not only direction but blessing. Whilst he was properly grateful, still he couldn't help wishing she'd also provided him with a map, "x" marking the spots where Book and Stone were hidden.

Dunstan leapt down from the chair and rubbed against his thigh. Thomas stroked the cat's soft, warm back and went to put the kettle on.

It was whistling when Rose knocked at the door and returned his telephone. "Mick talked to Superintendent Mackenzie about the inquest, the funeral is Thursday, and a couple of his father's Foundation friends dropped by this morning. He said it was hard to be polite, considering."

"Most Foundation members are quite well-meaning," Thomas told her.

"Sure, but what's that line about the road to hell being paved with good intentions?" She sat down on the floor next to Dunstan.

The next knock was Maggie's. "Am I late?"

"Not a bit of it." When she took off her coat and sat down at the table Thomas saw she was wearing the necklace he'd given her. He hoped his gift had not been a blow upon her bruised heart.

He was pouring the water into the teapot when Jivan arrived. The rich mahogany of his cheeks seemed to be dusted with ash and the jet gleam of his eyes was dulled by fatigue. A rich, delectable odor hung over him. The detective smiled at Rose's furtive sniff. "It's the first day of Divali. Since I can't bathe in the Ganges, I purify myself with sesame oil."

Thomas steepled his hands in front of his chest and bowed. " 'Wipe away my ignorance, O Lord, and let my soul shine like a lamp.' Is that correct?"

"Word perfect, as always." Jivan returned the bow.

"Is this the festival with the lamps on the window sills?" asked Maggie.

"Yes, the lamps welcome Lakshmi, the goddess of abundance." Jivan sat down in the desk chair.

Opening the door to Anna's knock, Thomas offered her the large chair before the hearth. "Are you sure you want Ellen to participate?" she asked.

"We mustn't write her off—it would be arrogant to assume we can see all ends. Talking to her about the rally is a good place to start."

Rose waved her hand as though asking permission to

speak. "Sean's coming but Ellen flat refused. She says you're 'a crashing bore.' Sorry."

"There are none so blind as those who will not see," Thomas returned, not without a wry smile. He distributed cups of tea and handed round the milk and sugar. "Let us begin. Jivan, Vivian Morgan's death."

"The inquest brought in a verdict of murder."

"No one's going to faint in surprise at that," said Maggie.

"We learned very little from Ellen Sparrow," Jivan continued. "She hinted she was part of an elite within the Foundation, and was right chuffed about helping break up the Willow Band's ceremony last Sunday. Fitzroy went off with Vivian before the violence began. He was giving her an interview, Ellen said—with a good bit of jealousy."

Thomas sat down beside Maggie. "She said that Calum followed Robin and Vivian?"

"Yes. He probably witnessed the murder. That would put the wind up him good and proper, especially if he knew Fitzroy saw him watching. No wonder he took to his heels." Jivan tapped his cup on the desk. "Ellen says Calum must have murdered Vivian, upset she was having it off with Fitzroy, and Fitzroy went after him to bring him to justice. We can't prove her wrong, not yet."

"How does Ellen justify Robin's sexual behavior?" Anna asked.

"He had to humor Vivian, what with her being a journalist and all, the better to spread the word. Which is true as far as it goes, I'm thinking, moral considerations aside. Still, her flat in London has been turned over and all her files are gone, as though someone doesn't agree with the word she intended spreading."

"Robin may also have thought," Thomas said, "that Calum gave Vivian his *sgian dubh,* a Dewar family talisman.

Once Robin discovered that her knife was not the family one, he would have a second motive to chase Calum down."

"Was that the relic Calum was going on about, then?" asked Jivan.

"It's part of it, yes."

Rose asked, "What about Calum at Housesteads?"

"I expect he was murdered as well," Jivan answered. "By whom is another issue. By the by, Mountjoy in Hexham tells me that P.C. Armstrong is home from hospital."

"Thank God," said Thomas, amid a general sigh of relief.

"Mountjoy seemed more interested in you, Thomas, than in Fitzroy. Wanted to know the nature of your relationship with Calum and Mick, and wouldn't have it when I told him there was none at all. He wanted to know why you and Mick—and Maggie and Rose—went to Housesteads."

"Because Robin told Mick his father was there," said Maggie. "Alive."

"So I told Mountjoy. But still he asked me to take statements from the Puckles that all of you were here at the time of Calum's death."

Thomas envisioned Mountjoy's saturnine face. The man was innately suspicious, a useful trait for a policeman, yes, but only when his suspicions were directed the correct way. "Has he interviewed Robin?"

"He didn't say. He could be having as much of a problem laying Fitzroy by the heels as we are. Fitzroy didn't attend the rally last night, although the lecturer he sent was—a fine speaker." The edge of outrage in Jivan's eyes restored some of their luster.

A knock on the door was Sean. Sitting down on the floor beside Rose, he whispered, "I found an old broom. You want to play hockey with the ball?"

"Sure," Rose replied. "In a little while."

270

"Okay." Sean settled back against the brick of the fireplace.

"Tea?" Thomas asked, and upon Sean's, "No, thanks," turned to Anna. "Now, about the Foundation rally last night."

From her handbag Anna produced a small tape recorder. "I thought it would be easiest if I simply taped the speech."

It wasn't Robin's voice that filled the small room, but a woman's. Thomas allowed himself a moment to consider the dreadful hypocrisy of a woman promoting an organization that wished to limit women's activities, then turned his attention to the tape.

He had heard it all before, *ad nauseum,* with the words altered only slightly to fit each time and each place. Dehumanizing diatribes about those who were different, scapegoating, divisive rhetoric, prejudice—the poisonous sentiments pricked his skin into gooseflesh. "Moderation in defense of the faith is unforgivable . . . here in Glastonbury New Agers openly practice Satanism—God will punish us with fire and storm, he will give our enemies supremacy, if we allow such indecency . . . our work here is to save souls . . ."

Thomas's gaze moved from Rose's tight brows to Sean's rolled eyes to Maggie's scowl to Jivan's and Anna's grim faces. Even Dunstan's eyes were hard chips of amber.

". . . purchase copies of our videos, share the spiritual experience with your friends who are not saved . . . subscribe to our newsletter and we shall provide you with voting guides and news summaries . . . you need never again say 'I don't know.' " A burst of applause sounded like thunder. Anna switched off the recorder.

Thomas murmured, " 'Beware of false prophets, which come to you in sheep's clothing, but inwardly they are ravening wolves.' "

In the ensuing hush Sean's mutter to Rose was perfectly

audible. "That woman was two enchiladas shy of a combination platter. I mean, she was making sense there, about criminals and stuff, and then she started talking about how England is the best of the best when it's the U.S. that's on top. The Foundation should be glad Europe wants to take the U.K. on instead of bellyaching about the EU being out to get them. The U.K.'s a nice little country with all the history and everything, but they're like, podunk. Nothing important happens here any more . . ."

He realized every eye in the room was focused on him save for Rose's—she was hiding her face in her hand. "Oh," Sean said with a sickly smile. "Sorry, give me a minute to get my toes out of my tonsils."

"You're entitled to your opinion, Sean," Thomas said, as inwardly he rejoiced that Robin's tactics had backfired.

Jivan suppressed his own smile. "The Foundation is addressing legitimate issues. No one wants to tolerate wrongdoers. But their definition of wrongdoing needs re-thinking, and no mistake."

Unable to sit still, Thomas leaped up and paced across to the window. Outside the clouds were thickening. " 'If a man say I love God and hateth his brother, he is a liar, for he that loveth not his brother how can he love God?' "

"Which is why the Foundation re-defines 'brother,' " said Rose.

"What is the true Word?" Thomas asked. " 'Thou shalt love the Lord thy God with all thy heart and with all thy soul and with all thy mind. Thou shalt love thy neighbor as thyself. On these two commandments hangs all the law.' "

"To do justly, to love mercy, and to walk humbly with God," said Anna, in the words of her own story.

Jivan added, " 'O children of God, unite and love one another.' "

"Taking advantage of people's insecurities to make yourself powerful is the oldest ploy in history." Maggie sat back, arms crossed, lips tight.

"No surprise our friends and relations accept the modern myth that faith is incompatible with reason, when they believe that their only choice is between it and the religious totalitarianism that blackens human history." With a meaningful glance at Maggie, Thomas paced back to the fireplace. Beneath Rose's hand Dunstan was purring, a small but penetrating hum of serenity. *Introducing cats to the floor of Parliament,* he thought, *would greatly increase the civility of debate.*

"Robin has led the Foundation to make a mockery not only of Christianity but of religion itself. For it's through our shared stories—myths, legends, mythology, theology—that we build the bridge between the Seen and the Unseen that he wants to destroy."

Sean said, "Mythology and theology are two different things. Mythology is imaginary. Theology is real."

"They are metaphors of the same story," Thomas told him. "Robin and his ilk wish to corrupt the imagination of the heart, for how else to know God save through the imagination? What is the Golden Rule but imagining oneself in another's shoes? 'Judge not, that ye be not judged. With what measure ye mete, it shall be measured to you again.' "

" 'Forgive us our trespasses,' " added Rose, " 'as we forgive those who trespass against us.' "

Jivan sighed. "Buddhists teach compassion and reconciliation, but still there are Buddhist terrorists."

"Yeah, vindictive religious groups like the Foundation are nothing new. So far their violence is mostly verbal . . ." Maggie didn't need to finish her sentence.

"Robin has a legion of brethren. The Islamic world, for example, kept the light of knowledge burning whilst our ancestors stumbled through the Dark Ages, but is now bedeviled by . . ." Thomas hadn't intended to make a pun, but there it was. ". . . violent self-righteousness. Manipulating religious faith to gain temporal power undermines the integrity of faith itself."

Anna seemed small as a child against the high back of the chair. "The people who were applauding on Friday were ordinary people, like the people who watched passively as the boxcars left for Auschwitz."

"Not everybody was applauding," Sean pointed out.

"Very true," said Anna, "thank goodness."

"Still," he persisted, "that's just the way it is, bad things happen."

"I'm hopelessly helpless?" asked Maggie. "I'm helplessly hopeless?"

"Despair is one of evil's greatest temptations," said Thomas, "because if we despair then we do not act."

"Okay . . ." Sean's frown was a reflection, no doubt, of how painful it was to have one's mind stretched.

Sending a sympathetic smile in the lad's direction, Thomas went on, "Perhaps you would be good enough to share our thoughts with Ellen."

"Yeah, well . . ." Sean didn't seem entirely convinced. Looking at Rose, he jerked his head toward the outer door.

With a smile for Thomas, Rose stood up and brushed off her jeans. "Sure. Let's go. Thanks."

Sean held the door open for Rose, and shut it behind them, but not before a cold gust of wind swept the room. The fire leapt. Dunstan strolled over to the desk and allowed Jivan to scratch his ears. Anna looked at her clasped hands. Thomas's tea was lukewarm, but his impassioned—lecture? sermon? manifesto?—had left him dry. He sank into his chair and drank thirstily.

Maggie asked, "Feel better now?"

"Yes." He was quite aware that he'd been preaching to the choir.

"Moslems say that the Devil has no power over those who believe in God," said Jivan, "but only over those who befriend him. Now, the Devil may be an entity of Islam and Christianity, but we all understand evil. Robin Fitzroy is befriending evil."

Anna leaned forward. "You said he wanted to destroy the bridge between the Seen and the Unseen. How can he destroy a metaphor?"

"You might say," Thomas told her, "that manifestation of metaphor is the basis of faith. Christians, for example, believe that Our Lord was metaphor made man. When he died, the veil of the temple was torn from top to bottom—that is, the veil separating the Seen from the Unseen was opened, and he passed through. That veil will open again this New Year's Eve."

One of Jivan's dark brows arched upward. Anna cocked her head to the side. Maggie propped her elbow on the table and her chin on her fist. Her necklace swung forward and chimed against her cup.

"My task is to bring the three parts of the Holy Grail together at the New Year, to open the veil. Robin's goal is to destroy it, so that he can lead us into ignorance and darkness."

Anna's keen blue eyes moved from Thomas's face to Maggie's and thence to Jivan's, as though she suspected they were all playing a practical joke on her. "I have a hard time accepting that cult objects might have genuine supernatural powers."

"Supplication attracts deities to fill certain objects with holiness," Jivan told her.

"Ralph Waldo Emerson," offered Maggie, "said 'we are

symbols and we inhabit symbols.' Supposedly he once walked into a tree, saying he saw it but he didn't believe it. I've done that myself."

"Miracles don't happen in spite of natural law," Thomas concluded, "but in addition to what we know of natural law."

"Robin's a dangerous demagogue," said Anna, "but are you telling me he has supernatural powers?"

"Yes, I am," Thomas told her.

"Since the intelligence of the universe and the self is the same," Jivan added philosophically, "reality can be changed at the level of the self."

Dunstan directed an interrogative meow to the window. Thomas turned to see the white dove sitting on the wall beside the garden gate. Beyond it Rose and Sean hit the ball to and fro. Ellen stood in the shadow of the archway. When Rose hit the ball in her direction, she hesitated, then kicked it back. Sean laughed, as did Rose, and even Ellen smiled. There was hope yet.

Anna exhaled through pursed lips. "So it's no more important that I actually believe in the power of the relics than I believe Jesus Christ is the messiah? Just as long as I don't walk into Robin Fitzroy's perceptual tree?"

"It doesn't matter," Thomas said, "that you and Jivan are not Christians. In his pride and greed, Robin is no Christian. He squeezes the Unseen through the empty setting in Lucifer's crown, and the narrow aperture distorts it beyond all recognition."

"Ah, the consolation of metaphor," murmured Maggie.

"We must recover the Book," Thomas said, "and find the Stone. The Dewars guarded it for centuries—a chipping from it is in the handle of the *sgian dubh*—but Calum didn't know its location. Nor does Mick."

"What of the—ah—Grail?" asked Jivan.

276

"Until I myself bring the Cup from its hiding place, it is safe."

Anna sat back in the chair. "God is involved with the world, just not in the way we expect. And I certainly didn't expect this."

"This is just the sort of thing that would happen in Glastonbury," moaned Jivan. "Thomas, you've mucked up my murder investigation. I can't tell the chief constable our prime suspect has psychic powers, let alone that his motive is, well, Armageddon."

"I'm sorry, Jivan," Thomas said. "But I doubt you'll ever bring Robin to justice for Vivian's murder. Or for Calum's, although someone else could well have struck the actual blow at Housesteads."

"Robin isn't beyond God's justice," Anna said.

"He will be if I do not reveal the relics at the appointed time—or if he has them destroyed. Robin and his ilk want us to forget that we have a choice between good and evil."

"How can I help, then? By working with Ellen? I'd do that anyway."

"Everyone who accepts the grace of God rejects Robin and therefore weakens him," Thomas told her. "So, Jivan, Anna, show forth your own faiths, and the variety of God's creation."

"That doesn't seem like much," said Maggie.

Thomas could only say, "The best revenge is not to do as they do."

"Marcus Aurelius," Maggie returned. "Yeah, we're the good guys. By definition, the good guys don't shoot first."

Glancing at his watch, Jivan stood up and rolled his shoulders wearily. "I'll see to getting you copies of the police reports on the theft of the Book. But just now I'd better be taking Alf's and Bess's statements."

Anna, too, got to her feet. Thomas expected her to ask,

and just how do you know all of this? But she said, "Thank you for letting us know what's going on here, Thomas."

"Knowledge is strength," he returned.

Jivan paused. "Thomas, I . . . Well, I've no time for more metaphor just now. Cheers."

Thomas started to stand, but Maggie was ahead of him. She ushered Jivan and Anna out and waited until the cat trotted after them. Then she went round the room collecting the empty cups. Thomas levered himself to his feet by leaning on the table. He was quite fatigued. He must be getting old. "I'll clear away."

"No problem." Maggie piled the dishes in the sink, ran water into the kettle, and placed it on the electric ring. Her movements were stiff, sinews and nerves wound to their tightest, each plane and angle of her face cut like a facet of a gemstone. When she started washing up, Thomas hobbled to her side and picked up the tea towel.

She smiled wryly up at him. "Gee, you're handsome when you're mad."

"Mad angry or mad insane?" he returned with a smile of his own.

"I don't think you're crazy, not any more. You may be a card-carrying heretic, but you're not crazy. You simply have very broad horizons."

"Thank you." He turned a wet cup thoughtfully in his hand. "The Cathars of southern France were heretics. They believed that Our Lord had no human nature. They had the wrong end of the stick, but their beliefs could not possibly threaten God, only the power of the church."

Again memory carried him into reverie . . .

He saw not the ceramic cup but a thick glass drinking vessel. For the first time he felt that sound and heard that sensation which plucked every fiber of his being. "Thank you for this gift," he said.

A good Cathar, Esclarmonde de Perelha saw only a common Roman cup. "You are welcome to it."

"Don't give yourself up to the Inquisitors. They are too frightened to be merciful."

"My kingdom is not of this world. Now take your relic and go, before your friends find you here with me."

So be it. Bowing, Thomas took his relic into the torch-gutted night, leaving her to her fate in the meadow below Montsegur, where even now, centuries later, the winds of the mistral stirred the bitter ashes of the burning . . .

"Hello?" Maggie was holding a saucer toward him. "Flashback to the Albigensian Crusade?"

"Yes. Sorry." He took the dish.

"No, I'm sorry that you have such terrible memories. But I suppose that's why the broad horizons." He handed her the towel and she dried her hands. "So I guess what *I* do now is my job. You'll still lecture, won't you?"

"Of course. I shall follow the example of St. Dunstan and work and study. And pray for inspiration. 'In Thy will, our peace.' "

"Eliot?"

"Dante."

"So how do you know what His will—no, don't tell me. You base your decision on what's inclusive, compassionate, and will serve others."

"Very good," he told her.

She clasped the necklace tightly, her eyes large, dark, and deep. He was certain she was going to throw herself into his arms, and he wondered how he'd respond. But with a rueful laugh she turned toward the door, saying, "You've got me between the Devil and the deep blue sea, you know that?"

The door shut. Thomas gazed at its blank face. Was Maggie his last temptation? Not her body, pleasing as it was, but her wounded heart that called to his own? While Robin could never force him from his path, Maggie could lead him from it. *Caught between the Devil and the deep blue sea . . .*

Mary's cloak was the deep blue of the sea as well as of the sky. St. Andrew's bones had been brought across the sea to Scotland. St. Andrew was the first apostle called by Our Lord. The Stone was the oldest relic. The deep blue color of the flag of Scotland was emblazoned with a white *crux decussata,* a St. Andrew's cross. An X, which marks the spot.

Bruce, who fled westward from Methven, called upon St. Andrew, St. Fillan of Glendochart, and St. Cuthbert of Melrose. Melrose lay below the triple peaks of the Eildons. The triangular mountain Schiehallion rose above Glenlyon, which paralleled Glendochart. Fortingall guarded Glenlyon's eastern end. The eastern end of a church was where the altar stood. The Stone was originally an altar.

St. Bridget of Ireland was the Mary of the Gaels. The triad, the triplet, the trinity, was a metaphor bedded deep in the consciousness of men from Gaelic Ireland to Aryan India. Extending the edges of a triangle would make three St. Andrew's crosses, one at each corner: St. Fillan's shrine at Tyndrum in Glendochart, Bruce's battle at Methven, and Fortingall, where grew the oldest tree in Europe save for the tree of the Cross itself.

And in the center of this imaginary triangle? Inspired yet again by the quick tongue of Maggie Sinclair, Thomas reached for his Ordinance Survey map of central Scotland.

Chapter Twenty-seven

No day was a grand one for a funeral, Mick thought, but he supposed Remembrance Day was good as any. It used to be Armistice Day, when the Great War ended, the eleventh day of the eleventh month. But there had been a greater war since the Great War. And now he was about the greatest of them all, it seemed, because no armistice was possible.

Beyond the window the lights of the city smeared and ran in the mizzle. Traffic lights, Christmas lights, the windows of homes and pubs. Somewhere in the dark beyond the lights rose Arthur's Seat and Salisbury Crags.

This afternoon the sky had been gray, the buildings gray, the ground gray except for the black gash of the grave. After the funeral he'd put it about that Calum was robbed and murdered on his way home from a business trip. True, as far as it went. Dad had given his life for the Story. Now he and Mum were both cold in the clay, and the Story went on without them.

Wiping his eyes, Mick turned away from the glittering darkness. Calum's secretary Amy pushed through the kitchen door. "There you are, Mick, the food's cleared away. I'll bide a wee while if you like."

"No, no, Amy, get on home." He took her coat from the rack and helped her on with it. "Thank you for helping me put the flat to rights."

"Shocking, yobs breaking and entering during a man's funeral. Good job nothing was stolen save some loose coins."

Odd, Mick thought, *that nothing was stolen save some loose coins, when every cupboard and drawer in the place had been turned over.* But then, he knew what the yobs were after. He'd had the *sgian dubh* with him, humming gently in his sock as the hem of the kilt teased his cold knees.

"The solicitor is calling round to sort the will the morn." Amy's eyes brimmed with tears. "I'm so sorry, Mick. Calum was right lonely after your mum died. I thought that Foundation lot would help. He was right chuffed when the red-haired chap called in. But then he went—nervy."

"I dinna think the Foundation was what he expected," Mick told Amy, and saw her out. He'd see to repairing the broken lock tomorrow—just now, he dragged his mother's heavy kist against the door. Then he went into his parents' silent, empty bedroom.

His opening Maddy's jewelry box set "The Bluebells of Scotland" to jingling. She had preferred books to ornaments, but her engagement ring had a wee diamond . . . There it was. And below that lay a ceramic Celtic cross, glazed in a blue shading from royal to turquoise, like the sea about Iona.

Mick remembered the cool, fresh wind rattling the door to the Abbey gift shop, and the sunlight reflecting from the white-painted walls as Calum searched out a cross blue as Maddy's eyes. She'd worn it as her body wasted away and her eyes grew deep as the sea, her soul shining through the flesh. Mick thought she'd been buried wearing that cross, but here it was, a kiss in the palm of his hand. "Thank you, Mum," he whispered, not quite sure which mother he was thanking.

Mick changed into everyday clothes, fastened the necklace about his neck, and dropped it down inside his jumper to lie next his skin. When he settled the *sgian dubh* in the waistband of his jeans it plucked his skin the way the Lady had plucked his heart, part caress, part demand.

Closing the drapes above Calum's desk, Mick sat down

and booted up the computer. The hard drive held only business spread sheets and genealogical charts. He inserted the diskette marked "Personal," the one he'd found with the insurance forms, into the drive.

Slowly he scrolled down through the entries he'd already read. Calum's grief at Maddy's death, and his loneliness after his son went off to university—none of that surprised Mick. His father's deep affection for him had done. ". . . years to build up the business, years I could have spent with Maddy and Mick . . . he's a clever lad."

Mick scrolled down past Calum's economic worries. ". . . Inland Revenue their pounds of flesh, I may have to make some of the shop assistants and warehouse men redundant. So many lazy sods won't work, it's not right to sack the ones who will do . . . immigrants take the jobs that should go to our own . . . government regulations, the taxes—businessmen aren't criminals, a strong economy is to everyone's good."

And the social ones. "They've women ministers now, they're changing the old rites . . . parents are scared to discipline their weans. We took a firm hand with Mick and he's one to make any father proud." *A firm but fair hand,* Mick thought. Even when he saw his dad only at bedtime, their discussion of the day's events and the night's story had seen him into his own Dreamtime safe and secure.

". . . the first time since I joined up Fitzroy's visited here. He's a leader for troubled times . . . I never realized just what was going on in Whitehall and the EU, it's frightening . . . Fitzroy's taken a liking to me, says I can play an important role in the FFF. I'd like to make a difference."

"You did do," said Mick.

". . . a woman named Vivian Morgan. She's a New Age loony, joined up more out of curiosity than conviction, I reckon. We went to an Indian restaurant. It was like my face broke open, I'd forgotten how to laugh. She might like to be more than friends, but no, sex outside marriage is wrong, and I'll not re-marry."

Mick grimaced, thinking of a couple of casual encounters at university. Rose now, Rose was another matter.

". . . Ellen Sparrow not like Vivian, all smiles and daft notions. Ellen's scared. I offered her a job but she's wanting to live in London . . . gave her some books, hoping she'll make something of herself . . .

". . . Fitzroy is keen on genealogy, said my pedigree is impeccable, I'm just his sort of folk, gey respectable . . . going on at me about writing the Dewar family history. But beyond my grandfather it's not history, it's legend. Old Malise ran on for hours about fairies and magic stones and iron driving away evil spirits. When I told Vivian that last she took it dead serious. I gave her a knife from the shop and told her it was a valuable heirloom, taking the mickey out of her . . ."

The phone went. Mick snatched it up. "Hello."

"Michael Dewar?" asked a dry male voice. "D.C.I. Mountjoy here. We spoke on Monday."

Mick had taken himself to Edinburgh police headquarters and talked with several detectives. Mountjoy was the one who looked like he had a red hot poker up his arse. "Oh aye."

"D.S. Mackenzie tells me your flat was done over this afternoon."

That was fast. "Oh aye. They took a few pence is all."

"Do you have anything you'd like to add to your statement about your father's death?"

"I canna tell you any more today than I did do on Monday."

"Nothing more about Thomas London?"

"I just met the man last week."

"Your father was in Glastonbury. London was at

Housesteads. They knew each other, stands to reason."

"I'm the connection, Inspector. My dad never met the man at all."

"Are you sure? If you searched your father's office . . ."

"Mackenzie already has done."

"But he didn't know what to look for, did he?" said Mountjoy. "I could call round with a warrant, if necessary."

Mick gritted his teeth. "You'd be wasting your time, Inspector. If I were you I'd be looking out Robert Prince."

"Would you now?" A voice murmured in the background. "Very good then, Mr. Dewar. You have my number if you'd like to be a bit more cooperative."

Pulling a face, Mick put the phone down. When Thomas phoned Sunday he'd said Mountjoy was a real policeman, not like Robin playing at Robert Prince—no worry there. But being a policeman often meant having a poor opinion of human nature, and suspecting lies in the midst of truth. "Not," Thomas had added apologetically, "that we're being entirely truthful just now."

Needs must when the Devil drives, Mick thought, and turned back to the screen. ". . . Robin called in at the office and I gave him a tour . . . told him about my dad and Alex's dad and the old stone, the one they pretended was the Stone of Scone. I thought it was the sort of story Robin would dismiss as dangerous superstition but now he's going on at me about it . . . Robin is stinking rich, but when I asked him to help Ellen out he said a stupid cow like her deserved her lot . . . he goes on about self-reliance but seems to have inherited his brass."

Shouting at the computer will not help, Mick told himself.

". . . he asked if I had any family heirlooms about, saying the old errors need correcting and such old things should be destroyed for the good of the faith. I remembered a mathom—old Malise's *sgian dubh* . . ." Mathom, Mick repeated. When had Dad read Tolkien?

". . . but the way Robin went all over funny when I mentioned it put me off. In any event, I haven't seen it for donkey's years. I'd ask Mick's advice but he has his own life now, he wouldn't care. And Robin says we can't trust our families unless they're believers as well."

The *sgian dubh* pressed into Mick's ribs. "I'd have cared," he said. But he wondered if he would have done, with his classes, his friends, the pub crawls, and the girls. He swallowed what tasted like acid.

"Robin's always at me for reading, saying he'll tell me what I need to know. He's the power behind the scenes at the Foundation, I reckon . . . Vivian's only staying with the 'inner circle' so she can expose him in her newspaper. She thinks he's creaming off the donations even though he says giving money to the FFF is doing God's work." Mick's brows went up. Now that was a motive for murder even Mountjoy could credit.

The last entry was dated the day before Calum went away on his trip to the South. His last journey. ". . . Vivian's off to a pagan ceremony that night. But I'm worried about Reg and the others, Robin's been going on about witchcraft and the like . . . he's been at me again, wanting to see the *sgian dubh*. I found it in Maddy's kist amongst the blankets. They smelled of her. It was like she was standing at my back telling me there's no harm in the knife. And it's all I have of old Malise."

Thank God. Calum must have taken the knife, then decided when he stopped by the office not to give it to Robin after all.

The journal ended, ". . . Robin's flannel about FFF members being the only sort worth knowing. When I get back home I'll look out some old chums. I've neglected Mick as well. Maybe I'll break it off with the FFF, but Ellen is still there, and Vivian—if I stay, I can help them."

Mick minded all the times he'd neglected his dad, and again the tears welled in his eyes. This time he let them flow, searing his cheeks. If only Calum had confided in Mick. If only Mick had asked him questions.

If only. With a shaky exhalation Mick found Gupta's business card and forwarded the entire file to his e-mail address. Tomorrow he'd take a copy of the diskette to Superintendent Mackenzie.

He stared blankly at the window above the desk. In the slit between the drapes he saw a dagger-shaped reflection of his own face, dim and indistinct . . . Something slithered through his reflection, outside the window. A kite? Who'd be flying a kite on such a filthy night? A large bird, like the ravens at Housesteads? He switched off the lamp, pulled aside the curtain, and looked out. He saw nothing save the shapes of buildings and lights mirrored in the slick streets.

From the bedroom behind him came the tinkling notes of "The Bluebells of Scotland." He sprinted into the room. The box was closed.

The *sgian dubh* in his hand, he searched the flat, but he was well and truly on his own. The back door was locked tight. The front door was blocked by the kist . . . Someone knocked. "Who is it?"

He heard a soft laugh. Something slid across the outside of the door and shuddered gently against the hinges. Again, louder. And again, so that the thick wooden panels seemed to bow inward. From behind him came the crash of broken glass. Mick spun round. But the window above the computer wasn't broken. Nor were any of the others.

Again the front door rattled. A distinct tap-tap-tap came from the kitchen, like dripping water or bony fingers against the back door. The lights went out. Mick ripped the knife from its sheath and held it before him. It shone like a tiny flame, casting a rosy glow across the room. Shapes, distorted, twisted shapes, moved in the shadows. He smelled the stench of decaying flesh. In the distance a voice screamed and sobbed.

"Leave it, Robin! Your tatty wee tricks will not be scaring me now." Pulling his mother's necklace from his jumper Mick clasped it in his left hand. "I gird myself today with the power of heaven! With the faith of my fathers in all its themes and variations!"

The lights shone out. The shapes vanished. He heard the traffic passing below his window and the distant mutter of a telly. The air was scented with coffee and smoke. *Well then.* Catching his breath, he put Nevermas's CD into the player. The guitar solo at the beginning of "First Rites" filled the room. He'd spare his neighbors the full set of pipes—the chanter would do nicely.

Mick sat down and played along with the music, ". . . of one substance with the word, of one mind with the flesh, begotten not made by grace out of blood . . ." The music filled his head, overflowed his chest, trembled in his limbs. *The last shall be first and the first shall be meek when I open my heart to you.*

The iron had entered into his soul, right enough, and it wasn't the sort of iron tears could rust. No, he wasn't frightened, not any more.

Chapter Twenty-eight

Maggie parked the van at the south end of the village, beside the sign pointing to Camelot. "Everybody out. This is going to be a quick visit—those clouds are fixing to cut loose."

Rose and Anna climbed out and looked dubiously up at the overcast sky, followed by Sean and Ellen, who looked dubiously up at the massive hill of Cadbury Castle. "Yeah," Sean said. "And we'll be a mile away from the car when they do."

"Then we'd best carry on." Opening a gate, Thomas led the way onto a dirt track winding its way upward through stubbled fields.

Maggie fell in beside him, going around the muddy patches he simply stepped over. "Thanks for coming. I know you wanted to get some more work done on the chapel, what with it being—whose day?"

"November fourteenth is the feast of St. Dubricius. In his avatar as Merlin he's associated with Caerleon, but he might have come here as well."

The air was thick and damp. Sudden puffs of wind shook the trees encircling the hill, sending leaves scudding away to the northeast. "We could've left earlier if you and Rose hadn't gone to church," Maggie said.

"You went to St. John's with Bess."

She'd meant that as a joke. "You had their car, so she asked me to drive her. No big deal."

"No, I suppose not," Thomas said with studied neutrality. Ducking his scrutiny, she glanced back at the students.

Rose was using Sean's camcorder to videotape him and Ellen posing in front of several sheep. He was expounding, "Maybe Arthur was successful because he revived the old Roman cavalry—I mean, what did the Saxons have? Foot-soldiers. So today we think of Arthur and his knights. Ta da!"

"Old stories. Rubbish." Ellen grimaced at the camera, maybe thinking her expression was a smile.

"Thank goodness she's lost the hooker outfit," Maggie said as Anna walked up. "I've got to hand it to Sean, he doesn't seem to miss it. He's really protective of her these days."

"He says Ellen is dysfunctional," replied Anna, "but with the proper environmental conditioning maybe he can pull her through."

Maggie dared hope that Sean had absorbed something of her riposte to his "That's just the way it is" comment. By Thomas's approving nod, she supposed he did, too.

Just where the track bent upwards and disappeared into the trees, Thomas indicated a circle of brick clogged with dead leaves. "This has been called Arthur's Well since the fifteenth century, when the folk identification of Cadbury with Camelot was first recorded."

Maggie prodded them all into the gloom beneath the trees. After a steep but short climb over roots and around muddy spots, they emerged onto another high place, an expanse of grass that glowed bronze in the uncertain light. They jogged around the rampart, the strengthening wind blowing Thomas's lecture into sound bites. ". . . Neolithic, Late Bronze, and Early Iron Ages . . . the hill fort begun in the fifth century B.C. . . . Romans destroyed it during the first century A.D. . . . human remains . . . a large temple . . . defenses rebuilt at the end of the fifth century against Saxon invasion . . ."

"When it was Camelot," said Rose. "Sweet."

"Archaeologists found what they believe to be the foundations of a cruciform church," Thomas concluded.

To the northwest a forest covered the slopes, branches tossing and creaking. Brambles choked the depressions between the concentric embankments. Maggie squinted. Yes, barely discernible on the shadowed horizon rose Glastonbury Tor. At this distance the tower of St. Michael's was no larger than an apostrophe—a punctuation mark in the language of history. Even as she looked the sky darkened to charcoal and the Tor disappeared.

Ellen pulled the hood of her coat over her head. Sean checked the meters on his camera. A hint of sulfur on the wind made Maggie's nostrils close like gills. Thomas gestured toward the land below. "The ancient track running toward Glastonbury is King Arthur's Causeway. Tradition says he hunts there on winter nights. This ties his story to that of the Wild Hunt—Gwyn ap Nudd, king of Annwn, pursuing a stag with a pack of hounds."

"The hounds of hell," Rose said, "hunting for souls."

Maggie glanced around. The girl was looking off to the north, probably thinking of Calum Dewar chased down not by Gwyn ap Nudd's minions but by Robin's.

"Let us move on," Thomas said. They moved on, toward the south edge of the hill, where a gap in the trees revealed four great defensive walls of earth and a depression, the site of the fort's principal gateway. "This is one of Britain's many hollow hills. Like Glastonbury. Like the Eildons. Cadbury's fairy traditions no doubt pre-date the Arthurian."

Ellen was urging Sean toward the path down. Anna, Maggie, and Thomas turned to follow. Behind them Rose said quietly, "Look."

A horse stood where the ancient gateway had been, its

mane and tail floating in the wind, its chestnut coat glowing in the gloom.

"Where did that come from?" Anna asked.

Great, thought Maggie. *Think of the Devil . . .*

In the next instant Robin was sitting astride the horse, wearing a tunic, cloak, and malicious smile. The brass lilies of his crown gleamed dully. Four of them were set with green emeralds, ice-cold as his eyes. The fifth setting, above his brow, was empty. On his upraised wrist, fitted with a leather gauntlet, sat a falcon. It twitched, half opening its wings, jingling the bells on its hood. The horse shook its head, setting its bridle and bit to an echoing tinkle. The sound was not a joyful noise but the harsh clatter of swords drawn and lusting for blood. Or for souls.

"Oh my," Anna said. "I see what you mean by supernatural."

Thomas stood quietly, not reacting.

Lightning struck suddenly down from the clouds. Thunder rumbled. In one smooth movement Robin pulled the hood off the falcon's head and launched it into the air. It rose shrieking toward the clouds, wheeled, and dived. A mighty rush of wind threw Maggie against Thomas. Anna and Rose ducked. But the bird was gone. So were the horse and Robin.

"As much as I appreciate the natural world," Thomas shouted over the roar of the wind, "I think the time has come to flee from it."

Close together, they hurried to catch up with Sean and Ellen. Another bolt of lightning hissed down the sky. The eaves of the forest leaped into stark relief, steel etched on steel. So did the human figure standing at the head of the path, a man wearing a leather jacket and boots, hands thrust into his pockets, red head tilted to the side, green eyes glistening.

The light winked out, leaving the darkness tinted green. Ellen fell to her knees, gasping, "He's called down the wrath of the heavens because I've been going about with you unbelievers."

"Oh for God's sake," said Rose. "He told you to spy on us."

Maggie took one of Ellen's arms while Thomas took the other. They pulled her to her feet and dragged her along. The next lightning flash showed the path like a black tunnel beneath the thrashing limbs of the trees, empty. Maybe Robin was lurking in the underbrush, planning to jump out at them—fine, they could trample him.

The wind howled like a pack of dogs. Hailstones thudded into the ground like hoofbeats. Shapes rushed across the sky, wraiths mingling with and yet separate from the clouds, the flicker of lightning resembling spear points. Like a dense column of smoke a funnel cloud extended almost lazily down from churning sky and struck the farmland below, throwing up a bow wave of debris. "Oh, shit," Maggie said. A hailstone bounced off her head.

Sean raised his camcorder. Ellen was hyperventilating. Thomas handed her to Rose and Anna and shoved them toward the mouth of the path. Taking firm hold of Sean's collar, he spun the boy around and down. "Maggie!"

"Here I am." She slid into a drift of wet leaves and lay prone. Thomas threw himself down beside her. The noise of the storm made Maggie suspect a giant reaper was moving through the woods. She didn't look up. If a tree was going to fall on her she'd just as soon it was a surprise. "Let me guess," she shouted to Thomas. "November is tornado season here."

"That it is."

"You don't want to lecture us on how Neolithic people would interpret a tornado as a male fertility principle? You know, Sky Father, Earth Mother?"

He looked at her, his eyes pale gold. "Would you like me to do so?"

"Never mind." Maggie laid her face on her forearm and reminded herself to breathe, until at last the wind died down and the thunder faded. Creaks and rustles sounded from the woods. Feeling furtive, like a cockroach in God's kitchen, she stood up and took inventory. Did her eyes look as much like porcelain saucers as everyone else's?

A bit of leaf mold clung to Thomas's cheek. She wiped it away. Ellen's face was dirty, streaked with tears. Sean, wearing his best, "Shucks, tweren't nothing" expression, put his arm around her. Anna brushed leaves and dirt off her jacket while Rose brushed them off her jeans. "No," she said, her voice quavering, "he can't control the weather."

"Not a bit of it," said Thomas, "but he appreciates special effects as much as any film director. Shall we go?"

No one argued. They felt their way down the path and across the field, now scattered with debris that had probably been a barn. The sky was the color of tarnished silver. The wind blew raindrops into Maggie's face. She expected to see the sheep laid out with heart attacks, but no, they were huddled in a corner of the pasture, baaing their grievances.

Ellen babbled about Judgment Day, Armageddon, the four horsemen of the Apocalypse. Sean and Anna between them kept up a soothing commentary. Rose trudged through the puddles, her shoes muddy. "Rats. I thought we could deprogram her."

"Have faith," Thomas told her, and, to Maggie, "Before you ask, a natural disaster is not evil, but chaos."

Chaos, Maggie thought. The romantic poets used nature to reflect emotion. Her emotions had been chaotic—seven deadly sins and psychological dysfunctions and the story with its kaleidoscopic patterns—but the story wasn't chaos, just complicated . . . No, she couldn't control the weather either. "Right," she said, and opened the gate for the others.

A broken tree limb lay alongside the green, but only one hail ding blemished the van. Maggie was about to prescribe food and drink in the pub when a green Jaguar came down the street, swishing through the carpet of leaves like the death coach from a nightmare. The car passed so close beside the van she had to press herself against the door, but all she could see through the tinted windows was a dim shape in the driver's seat.

With a squeak of terror, Ellen scrambled into the van. Thomas stepped up beside Maggie and watched as the car turned a corner and disappeared. A few more raindrops fell, and thickened, and became a steady rain.

Right. "That's the lesson for the day," Maggie said. "Let's go home."

Chapter Twenty-nine

Ellen stopped at the top of the stairs and pressed her fingertips into her temples. She'd taken aspirin after lunch and pinched Bess's Xanax after dinner, but still her head beat like a bloody drum.

Time was running out. She'd seen the wrath of God on a sinful world, two days ago at the place called Camelot. She'd seen Robin standing there, all calm and quiet like, whilst the heavens went to pieces about him. That was just a hint of what was to come, soon, at the end of the year. At the end of the world. If she did what Robin told her, she'd be saved.

Hard as it was to go about with the unbelievers, she had to be strong. They were only pretending to be kind, they were laughing at her behind her back. But then, people of faith were always persecuted, weren't they?

Sean came out of his bedroom. "How's it going?"

She tried to shrug, but her shoulders were too stiff.

"Here." He started rubbing her back. "Just relax."

He was always going on at her about relaxing. She'd never get past her sexual issues, he said, until she learned to relax. He understood why she'd been coming on to him so strong at first. She was acting out, expressing the abused inner child.

Rubbish, all of it. Still, Sean wasn't a bad sort, considering the company he kept. Even considering what he'd said about Robin's speech. A pity, that he was condemned to hell.

"Maggie's watching TV," Sean whispered, his breath tickling her ear. "Let's get her laptop and go web-surfing. There's an awesome new interactive game. Or we could hit the Torrid Tales site again, remember that one?"

Ellen remembered. His probing fingertips made her tighten up all the further. She pulled away. "I've got a whacking great headache."

Once or twice he'd looked at her like she was having him on when she said that, but this time he said, "I'm sorry."

"Later, eh?" Ellen patted Sean's bum. Odd, how good her hand felt against the back pocket of his jeans.

"Okay. Hope you get to feeling better." He kissed her forehead and for half a tick her headache eased off. Maybe in time she'd learn to like this sex rubbish . . . That was just it. There was no time.

Ellen walked down the stairs, her boots thudding on each tread, her head throbbing at each thud. She found Bess sitting at the kitchen table, a glass of sherry close to hand. Her garden magazine was open to the same page as an hour ago, when Ellen had cried off drying the dinner dishes because of her headache, and Rose with her flowery perfume stepped in.

She pulled out a chair and sat down. "Where's Alf, Mum?"

"In town. Lodge meeting." Bess took Ellen's hand. "That plaster is filthy. And your skin's red—that cut's gone septic."

"Mum, don't fuss." Ellen pulled her hand away.

"I've only ever wanted what's best for you."

"I only want what's best for you. If you believe in Robin, he'll save you. Just as it says in Holy Scripture, he's the redeemer who's come in the last days."

"Have you actually read the Bible, Ellen?"

"I've one of the Foundation editions, haven't I, updated for the End Times. And Robin explains a passage in every newsletter . . ." Suddenly Ellen saw how to bring her mother round. She lowered her voice. "I'm not to tell anyone this, Mum, but you're not just anyone are you? I'm the chosen one. Me, of all women. I'm to be Robin's bride."

"Bride? You haven't gone and slept with him? And him always going on about morality?" Bess's face squashed up like an apple kept too long in the cupboard. "I never raised you this way. I did my best with you, but now—now you're scaring me to death." She hid her face in her hands.

Ellen stared at her mother's bowed head, the light glinting off the gray hairs amongst the brown. The stinks of sherry and disinfectant gummed her throat. At least she couldn't smell Rose's scent, not now. "Mum, please, you have to come round before it's too late. I don't want to lose you."

"I've already lost you," Bess said, her voice smothered.

Ellen's hand hurt. Her head hurt. Neither hurt as cruelly as her heart. She blundered away, leaving her mother, the unbeliever, behind.

Rose scurried through the rain toward Thomas's cottage, Maggie at her side. At least this Sunday it was only raining. "You know, we've only been here for three weeks."

"If we were cats, we'd be down several lives by now." Maggie pushed open the door of the chapel.

Thomas stood by the rood screen, haloed by his light bulb, his cell phone pressed to his ear. "*Merci beaucoup. A bientot,* Genevieve." The off button chirped. "Rose, Maggie, good evening!"

"My French doesn't go much farther than *hors-d'oeuvre,*" said Maggie, "but I gather by your tone of voice she couldn't help."

"Very few of my friends and fellow guardians can help with anything other than their prayers, but I have gleaned some important information."

"Which you'll tell us when you're good and ready," Maggie said.

"So I shall." Smiling inscrutably, Thomas picked up a brush.

The ancient chapel was a safe place, a sanctuary in a storm. Rose genuflected before the carved Jesus. His eyes were alive with wisdom and pity. The eyes of the saints in their niches below glowed with a serenity she envied. Had Bridget or the Virgin ever been tempted, not by the senses but by the brink of darkness just beyond? Or was that the story of Mary Magdalene? "You're working on the Blessed Mother today," she said.

"November twenty-first, the Presentation of the Virgin." Thomas applied another gold flake to the portrait's background. "To say Our Lord was born of a virgin is a symbolic way of saying he was born of compassion."

"He was born of the heart chakra," a voice added from the outer door. Closing his umbrella, Inspector Gupta picked his way past the extension cords and the space heater. "Am I late?"

"We're early," Rose told him, grateful to get the topic away from virginity. "Are you all right? Thomas told us last night someone painted racial stuff on your garden fence."

"I'm afraid so. Calling my daughter a 'mongrel' was over the top."

Maggie shared an outraged glare with Rose. Thomas put down his brush. "I'm sorry, Jivan."

"I'd rather have the threatening phone calls—they're directed at me personally. The last one called me a 'godless jack-booted thug.' "

"Because you want to question Robin?" asked Maggie.

"He's playing silly beggars with us. We've taken out warrants, searched Foundation offices . . . I can't explain to the chief constable why he keeps giving us the slip. And Mountjoy in Hexham keeps telling us to leave Fitzroy alone, he has important work to do."

"Perhaps he's visiting his co-workers in Russia," said Thomas, "where the Orthodox church is celebrating its liberation from Communist exclusion by warning their congregations off evildoers such as Jesuits, Baptists, and Seventh Day Adventists."

"Of course," Maggie said sarcastically.

Rose felt less sarcastic than sad. "Mick says the inquest on his father's death brought in a verdict of murder by persons unknown—Mountjoy kept going on and on about 'just the facts,' and they never even considered a Foundation connection."

"Now Mountjoy's asked me to take your finger and footprints to compare with those at the crime scene, Thomas. Sorry," Gupta apologized, although he sure wasn't Mountjoy's keeper.

"I did walk about the crime scene," said Thomas. "I'll stop by the station tomorrow."

"But what about Calum's journal?" Maggie asked. "All that with Robin and Vivian?"

"I take it as evidence against Fitzroy. Mountjoy takes it as evidence Calum was cracked. The Foundation's solicitors had most of the material disallowed as hearsay, but D.S. Mackenzie in Edinburgh is keeping an open mind."

Gupta eyed the paintings but didn't quite see them. "We've asked Inland Revenue for an audit of the Foundation's books—Fitzroy's pulling down a huge salary, for one thing. The governing board says he deserves that, for his contribution to the Foundation, and is threatening to sue the Somerset Constabulary for official repression."

"Tax evasion is better than nothing," said Maggie with a sigh, "but it's awfully small beans, considering."

"Ah, but even Goliath fell in the end to David's pebble," Thomas said.

Rose looked again at the figure on the cross. Calum and Vivian were sacrificed, in a way. Not that they'd volunteered, the way Jesus had. "There are parts of the Story that just don't seem fair."

"In the words of my fictional brother Cadfael," said Thomas, " 'every now and then I like to place a grain of doubt in the oyster of my faith.' "

"By now I have a string of pearls as tall as you are," Maggie returned.

Rose was up to at least a pair of earrings. She assured herself she just didn't have the big picture. Only God had the big picture.

"Do you have news of the Book?" Thomas asked Gupta.

"In a way, yes. The removal man who gave in his notice the day after it went missing, Stan Felton, is now working at a Newcastle warehouse owned by Reginald Soulis, a Foundation official. He was part of the Halloween pagan-bashing here in Glastonbury."

"Soulis." Maggie made the name a hiss. "Please tell me the Book wasn't at Holystone. Couldn't you have smelled it or something, Thomas?"

"Not a bit of it, sorry."

Rose crossed her arms over her chest, fending off memory. "Robin wouldn't leave the Book there, would he? That hateful old woman would burn it or something. Which is what he wants, but not yet."

"Fitzroy wants it close to hand, I expect. Mountjoy says there's no point to interviewing either Soulis or Felton, though." Gupta sighed heavily. "I must be off. Cheers."

"Bless you," Thomas said to his departing back. He picked up his brush and turned toward the Blessed Mother's tranquil face, even though his own face was more grim than tranquil. "I'm making inquiries where I can, but just now we seem to have no other options other than allowing the secular authorities to search for the Book."

The corners of Maggie's mouth were tucked into vertical creases that hadn't been there three weeks ago. "I think I'll stay here awhile," she said to Rose. "Go ahead and use my laptop. Send Mick a cyber-hello."

"And one from me as well," Thomas told her.

"Sure," Rose returned, without adding that a cyber-hello was cold comfort. She plunged back out into the rain.

In the gloom and wet, the house with its lighted windows looked like a huge submarine. Her head down, Rose went straight inside and up the stairs. From the third floor, the Puckles' private territory, came Bess's voice. "I might could understand if she was on drugs—she had a rough time of it—Alf, she's scaring me to death . . ." A door slammed.

Poor Bess. Since the tornado Ellen had relapsed into fanatic mode. Rose would have wanted to save her own mother from a terrible fate, yeah, but still . . . Shaking her head, she went into Maggie's room and plugged the laptop into the phone line.

She hadn't heard from Mick for a couple of days. He'd dropped his classes for the rest of the term, so he could work things out with the business, and God only knew the itinerary of the guilt trip he was on. Plus he'd e-mailed last week that someone was harassing him, knocking on his door in the middle of the night and stuff like that. Mackenzie was on the case, but wasn't getting anywhere. Go figure.

Rose decided she'd send him a note to let him know she was thinking of him. She booted up and accessed her e-mail account to find three new messages, one from Grace, one from a friend at SMU, one from Mick. *All right!* She opened his first.

"Jennie," it read. "Sorry I had to cancel our date. Next

time I'll bring you a tartan shawl—you'll look a treat wearing it, if you catch my meaning. Don't worry yourself, I'm well away from the Yanks. Nice enough lot, but not a patch on you. Soon, love—Mick."

Rose felt as though the floor had suddenly dropped away from beneath her. She stared at the phosphor-etched letters until the screen saver came on. She knew how easy it was to send a message to the wrong person—just last month she'd made a catty remark about Faith's new hairdo in a note to Grace and then sent it to Faith. But this . . . Tears stung her eyes and impatiently she brushed them away. Relationships started in a crisis didn't always work out—she'd known that from the get-go. Maybe that was why she'd never asked Mick if he had a girlfriend.

She had an adventure with him was all. So what if she'd thought those five minutes behind Melrose Abbey meant something. He'd never lied to her . . . Unless the e-mail itself was a lie. Lucifer was the Father of Lies. She could shoot back an e-mail demanding, "Is this legit?" But the last thing Mick needed was her in his face.

Rose clasped the miraculous medal, the net stopping her free-fall. Her biological mother couldn't be here for her. And it looked like Mick didn't want to be. But Our Lady was, and through her the Lady. She had to be, pearl earrings and all.

Chapter Thirty

Walking into the garden, Thomas inhaled deeply of the cold wind with its tang of the sea. Rays of sun broke through vast lumps of white and gray cloud. Maggie stood contemplating the statue of the Magdalene, her reddish-brown hair the same color as the *Spiraea betulifolia* banked below the gallery windows. He called, "A penny for your thoughts."

She grinned. "You've been getting them for free."

"I'm properly appreciative of the honor."

"Yeah, right," she said. "Thanks for lecturing on the trip to Winchester Monday. Not to mention the expedition to Caerleon last week. I know how busy you are."

"The students' questions are quite stimulating."

"A shame Ellen's refused to go out with us since the tornado."

"Ellen, bless her, thinks ignorance means safety."

"I wouldn't mind being a little more ignorant. Homeless children murdered in Brazil, a Turkish family bombed in Germany, Christians tortured and killed in Uganda and the Sudan, an evangelist railing about 'cults' such as Buddhism. It all makes that incredible election mess back home look tame. I can't see any of it as random noise that doesn't affect me, not any more."

"Good." Thomas told himself to feel no remorse for opening her eyes.

A human figure moved behind the gallery windows. Bess? No, it was Rose, hanging a Christmas garland. The green, gold, and red were reflected over and over again in the multiple panes of glass.

"Yesterday evening Alf told me Bess wasn't quite the ticket," said Thomas. "I found her lying in bed, in the dark. I sat with her a few moments, but she seemed unable to articulate what's troubling her."

"Like we haven't all heard Ellen badgering her."

"Bess blames herself for the unfortunate trajectory of Ellen's life. But there comes a point one must accept that what's done is done. The child has gone its own way. Brother David is dead." He looked toward the Magdalene statue, rising from a drift of saffron-yellow *Linera obtusiloba* like a martyr rising from the flames. "The Magdalene is the first apostle and the great whore, all in one. The bleeding heart of redemption."

Maggie's cheeks were pink. Her hair danced across her forehead. Her eyes evaded his, looking toward the gate. Beside it the *Euonymus europaeus* made a brave display, its leaves scarlet, its pink and red seed capsules breaking open to reveal the bright orange seeds inside. "My mother grows that. It's called 'hearts a-busting.' " Emitting a vaporous sigh, she turned the subject. "How's your research coming?"

Gravely Thomas replied, "Ian Graham at the Museum of Scotland has searched many an archaeological and geological survey on my behalf. His results, added to what I've gleaned from various texts, make me think my hypothesis about the location of the Stone is worth testing. Next Tuesday, November thirtieth, is St. Andrew's Day . . ."

Footsteps raced along the path. A wild-eyed Sean burst through the gate. "Thomas, Maggie, come quick." He spun back toward the house.

Thomas's heart plunged into a cold deeper than any winter day's. He didn't shorten his strides for Maggie, but still she kept at his heels past the archway, through the door, up the main staircase and then the small one.

Alf stood wringing his hands outside his and Bess's bedroom, his usually round face pinched and peaky, his eyes bulbous. "Thomas, 'twere an accident." One hand flapped helplessly toward the door.

Thomas walked into the small, dark, fetid room and switched on the bedside lamp. Beneath it sat two empty tablet containers, an almost empty bottle of sherry, and a glass tumbler. A frame held a photograph of a child with a ribbon in her hair and a wide if wary smile. Ellen, in her earlier life.

Bess lay curled on her side, her back turned to the picture, her ashen face half-buried in the pillow. Her eyes stared into nothingness. Thomas pressed his fingertips into the gelid flesh of her throat. She was long gone. She'd died alone with her distress, rejecting the hands and hearts which would gladly have helped her to carry it.

His voice caught as he spoke. "Blessed are those who mourn, for they shall be comforted. May the peace of God be with you always." He kissed her bloodless cheek, closed her staring eyes, and made the sign of the cross over her. Too little, too late.

He went back into the hall, shut the door, and faced the waiting people. Ellen stood next to Alf, mute, cold, brittle. Sean hovered ineffectually at her side. Anna, looking every year of her age, pressed Rose's shoulder. Rose stood with her hand against her mouth, her eyes huge. Maggie's face was no longer pink but stark white. "What happened?"

"Bess may have intended to alleviate her anxiety, and inadvertently mixed barbiturates with alcohol. Or she may have intended to die." Thomas forced himself to loosen his knotted fists and clenched jaw.

Alf turned on Ellen. "Here, you've been worrying her with that religious rubbish . . ."

"I was helping her," retorted Ellen, her voice thick. "I was trying to save her."

Thomas set his hand on Alf's trembling arm. "You'd best phone Inspector Gupta. The formalities must be observed."

Alf opened his mouth, shut it, and trudged toward the stairs, each floorboard creaking a protest.

With an almost audible crack of her shell, Ellen's face twisted and she charged Thomas. "You, Thomas London, Thomas Maudit, it's your fault, you took Mum down with you and now she'll burn in hell!"

He fended her off with an upraised arm. "She's not in hell, Ellen."

"You're a liar!" And she was crying, in huge, racking sobs.

Sean put his arm around her. "Come on, I'll—I'll fix you a cup of tea. In the kitchen. Downstairs. Okay?"

"There's a good lad," said Thomas. "Tea for all of us would go down a treat, thank you."

"Yeah, sure" Sean said dazedly. He led Ellen away.

Rose pulled away from Anna. "I'm okay, thanks. I'm just getting tired of people dying."

"As am I, Rose." The blank face of the door, stained with shadows, seemed to Thomas like an accusing glare. The silence of the room beyond condemned him. *Thomas Maudit.* "Here I am flattering myself I can open the kingdom of God whilst I cannot repair the evil in my own household."

"There are limits to what even you can do," Maggie stated. "One of your favorite themes is freedom of choice, remember?"

Trust Maggie's astringent manner to mitigate the stench of failure. Thomas raised his chin. "Yes, quite. We must . . ." He jerked at a sudden beeping noise, almost bashing his head on the slanting roof. Then, foolishly, he realized the sound was coming from the mobile telephone in his pocket. He fumbled for it. "Thomas London."

"Thomas, it's Mick. There's been a right turn-up and no mistake."

"Oh," Thomas said, wrenching his mind about. "Mick."

"Mick?" repeated Rose, oddly flat.

"One moment, Mick." Thomas led the three women down the smaller steps and peered over the railing of the large stairwell to the ground floor.

Maggie tiptoed on down the stairs and along the hall to the kitchen. In a moment she was back. "Alf and Ellen are glaring at each other across the table. Sean's making tea and muttering platitudes. I always hoped there was a sensitive New Age guy beneath that macho swagger."

"Very good." Thomas pressed the device to his ear. "Now then, Mick. What's happened?"

"I'm thinking," Mick said, "that I know where the Book is hidden."

Thomas wasn't sure what he'd been expecting, but that wasn't it. *The Lord taketh away, and the Lord giveth.*

"You've seen the entry in Dad's journal about Robin stopping by the office for a tour. Well then, I was having a wee plowter in Dad's files the day, and I found a receipt in his writing: 'One length MacNab tartan wool rec'd Reginald Soulis 13 May 00'. Dad mentioned a 'Reg' in his journal. Kin of that poisonous woman at Holystone, I'm thinking."

"I should think so, yes."

"And clan MacNab, they're kin of the Dewars."

"Yes. The MacNabs are descended from the Abbots of St. Fillan's shrine. When the Bruce was succored there by the Dewars, the MacNabs opposed him."

Mick went on, "I asked Dad's secretary, Amy Kirkpatrick, if she minded his visit. Oh aye, she says. He was thinking himself no small drink."

"Amy is a woman of great insight."

"That she is. But even so, she was thinking Robin a wool merchant, he was so keen on the work of the shop and the warehouse and all."

"He was, was he?" Rose, Anna, and Maggie stood in a half-circle before him, poised and eager. Thomas gestured patience.

"The next day, she says, a chap named Reginald Soulis stopped by, saying Robin was sending dad a sample of MacNab tartan."

"Did she see this sample, then?"

"No. She says it was a parcel wrapped in paper the size of a bolt of cloth. By the way Soulis was holding it she reckoned it was heavy. And a bolt of wool is heavy, right enough."

"So is a large book of 258 vellum leaves." Thomas closed his eyes. The Book, the third relic. He remembered the first time he'd come into its presence, on the long road south from Durham. The soldiers had wanted to add it to the fire that cold, bitter night. He'd taken it from them, concealed it in his cloak, and acknowledged one more time that supernal chord.

He could see the pages as though they lay open in front of him, the Word itself in black majuscule script, the Spirit symbolized by intricate decorations in colors that put the autumn garden to shame. The lapis lazuli had come from the foothills of the Himalayas. He liked to think of that lapis, the blue of the Virgin's cloak, passed from hand to hand until it reached Aidan and Cuthbert on their holy island off Britain. Like wisdom and faith passed from mind to mind in the pages of books.

He opened his eyes. Before him waited three women, old, middle-aged, and young. Three fates. Three graces. Three Queens escorting the mortally wounded Arthur to his last resting place in Avalon. He said into the telephone, "I don't suppose Amy knows where the MacNab parcel is now?"

"No," said Mick. "Dad didna say a word about it in his journal, but he'd not be thinking this sample was out of the ordinary."

"Nor should he. The question is whether Robin knows where your father put the parcel, and whether he's retrieved it by now."

"It's not in Dad's or Amy's offices, I'm telling you that. I'll have a shufti round the warehouse on the Sunday, when no one's about."

"Please do so. I'll speak with you again tomorrow, shall I, when my thoughts are more ordered. Good show, Mick. Very good show indeed. Here's Rose. I fear she has some bad news for you."

He offered Rose the telephone. With a strange, stiff reluctance, she took it and retreated down the corridor. "Hi."

From the lower floor issued the thud of the iron knocker. "I'll go." Anna started down the stairs.

Maggie's face was inexpressibly weary. "Vivian. Calum. Now Bess. I hear the Gabriel hounds baying . . ." Her voice broke.

Thomas opened his arms. In one swift movement she was embracing him, her grip so fierce his breath escaped in a gasp. Affection, yes, two grieving hearts attracted each to each. And yet he was very much aware how long it had been since he'd held a woman in his arms.

Jivan's voice echoed amongst several others downstairs. Quickly Thomas bent his face to the top of Maggie's head. "I beg you not to let your guilt rot your spirit as Bess allowed hers to do."

"Suicide isn't in my vocabulary," she said, half muffled in his coat. "Just doesn't seem sporting, somehow."

"There are many sorts of suicide."

"Yeah? Like martyrdom?"

"No. Martyrdom is a gift given freely."

"Sorry." She craned up at him. Her eyes were bright but she wasn't weeping. "That was a cheap shot. It's just that I don't know . . ."

Steps started up the staircase. Thomas broke from her embrace. "I don't know what's going to happen either, Maggie."

Her smile was cramped and cautious, but it was a smile. "Go on. Do your duty by Bess. She needs you more than I do. Right now, anyway."

"Thomas?" called Jivan's distressed voice.

Thomas turned toward him, his hands still holding the shape of Maggie's warm but unyielding flesh.

Ellen hadn't ever been to a funeral before. It was a right bugger to start out with her own mum's. She'd hear the sounds of the dirt clods hitting the coffin for the rest of her life.

She sat in the corner of the Great Hall, looking out of her own body like an animal out of a forest whilst people stood about noshing and nattering. Having themselves a rave-up, and Mum was dead.

By Robin's Word she was damned. Ellen had tried to save her, and failed. She scrubbed her hands on her skirt, scraping away the scab on her palm, uncovering the raw, red, hot skin beneath. It bled, but the blood didn't wash away the dirt of the grave.

Anna leaned over her chair. "I'll get you a fresh bandage."

Ellen had dialed up Robin's bleeper. She'd left messages on his answerphone. She'd e-mailed the Foundation offices in London. But he hadn't answered. He hadn't come to the funeral.

He was too righteous to hang about with these people,

wasn't he? He was too clever to stand by whilst the priest read off the corrupted rite. If he was here Gupta would harass him. It was best he wasn't here. Best by a long chalk he'd left her on her own. Even though she was his bride.

For the hundredth time tears welled up in her eye— *mustn't blub,* she ordered herself, *blubbing means weakness*— she clenched her teeth so tightly something crawled in her jaw.

Sean sat down on the arm of the chair and patted her shoulder. "Go ahead and cry, it relieves stress."

Alf stood by the fireplace, knocking back the hooch. It was all his fault, he should've watched Mum, he should've locked up the liquor, he should've seen to her pills. It was all his fault Mum wouldn't listen to reason, he'd polluted her mind with his prejudices.

The room was hot and close with the pong of winter coats, perfume, and coffee. The moggie, Dunstan, crouched in the shadow beneath a chair, only his white breast and gleaming eyes visible. Voices buzzed like insects inside the empty vault of Ellen's skull.

"Can I get you anything?" asked Maggie. "A cup of tea?"

"I'll get it," Sean said. "Be right back, Ellen. Hang in there."

And there was the traitor. He went down on one knee in front of her and took her hands. His hands were large and strong, not so soft as Mum's. His voice rasped against her senses. "Ellen, I must ask your forgiveness. I was unable to help Bess."

She frowned. Only the weak asked for forgiveness. Only the weak forgave.

"Sometimes we wish for strength so that others will admire us. But God makes us weak so we can learn wisdom. So we can know his grace. Do you know the root of 'grace?'"

It's *gratitas,* or thankfulness."

Thankful for bloody what? Mum was dead and Robin hadn't come and They were getting at her. She tried to pull her hands away but he held onto them. The brown eyes in the tired face were clear as windows. "You betrayed God," she muttered.

"Not quite, no, although I most certainly committed a grievous sin."

That wasn't what she'd expected him to say.

"Through such trials, Ellen, we become strong enough to be humbled and wise enough to surrender. Not submit, but surrender, in loving trust of God."

I trust Robin. Robin said it, I believe it, and that's that.

Thomas pressed her hands and released them. Maggie and Sean set a cuppa and a sandwich down beside her. Rose took the glass from Alf's fingers and handed him a cuppa of his own. Perfect Rose, who never doubted. Who knew nothing about darkness.

Anna wiped Ellen's hand with a cool bandage. The fresh smell of the salve made her giddy. "Monday I'm taking you to the doctor. That cut's infected."

Ellen should be telling them all to bugger off. But she was too knackered even to think. Nothing was sensible, not any more.

She lay her head back against the chair and closed her eyes. In the darkness she saw her mother's face and heard was her mother's voice. *You're scaring me to death.*

Chapter Thirty-one

Mick stepped into the warehouse and switched on the lights. The odor of wool and camphor filled his head and for a moment he was a child again, playing at Lancelot, Robin Hood, Aladdin, Luke Skywalker, Bilbo Baggins, hunting treasure and fighting battles amongst the shelves.

He leafed quickly through the pattern book hanging just inside the door. Nothing complicated about the MacNab tartan, green and red squares crossed by red and black lines. He'd recognize it straightaway.

The shelves ranged down the room were stacked with boxes and bundles. Bolts of tartan wool in glorious colors lay beside lengths of tweed in muted browns, grays, and heathers. The floor was swept, the shelves were dusted, the packing goods were stacked beside a table. Two step ladders stood like sentries in the corner. It was all familiar, and yet it was also strange, as though he was seeing it for the first time.

These last weeks the *sgian dubh* had worn a rut in Mick's side like "First Rites" had worn a rut in his mind. He felt naked when he set it aside to bathe or tucked it beneath his pillow when he tried to sleep. But the knife had only—spoken—the nights someone or something tried the doors of the flat, and the morning a car darted toward the curb as he walked to the grocer's, only to speed away when he jinked to the side. Now, though, at long bloody last, he had work to do. He had to find a real treasure the day.

There, "MacNab" and "MacNab Ancient." Mick un-furled each of three bolts of cloth, making a cascade of color and pattern but finding nothing inside save the cardboard stiffeners.

Something scrabbled in a distant corner. A mouse or rat, most likely. In his grandfather's day they'd kept cats, and sleek, well-fed beasties they'd been.

He folded the fabric back onto the shelf, then stepped off down the one row, and up the next, until he'd walked by each and every bolt of wool. None of them was marked with a label reading, "Holy Relic," more's the pity.

Beyond the stacks of cloth sat boxes of souvenirs, T-shirts, Loch Ness monsters, tins of shortbread. Jumpers, shawls, blankets, socks. The *sgian dubhs,* good quality knives. But no mysterious bolts of cloth. If needs must, Mick told himself, he'd have a look at every ell of wool in the place . . . Wait. On a shelf behind two broken teapots and a headless doll lay several paper-wrapped parcels and a large volume he recognized as another sample book. Was this Calum's catch-all corner?

He set a step ladder by the shelf, climbed up, and opened the parcels. Two Paisley shawls, fringes twisted into knots. A portion of heavy tweed. A bolt of MacNab tartan wool, stamped Soulis Estates Ltd. *All right!*

The parcel was gey heavy, and hard inside the give of the cloth. Mick hugged it to his chest and inched his way down the ladder. Standing at one end of the packing table, he unrolled the cloth.

Tartan wool. And a coarse bit of wool it was, too, reeking of dye. Calum had glanced at a foot of it, maybe two, and set it by as a bad job. But Mick kept unrolling. *Come on then, show yourself* . . . The ragged end of the cloth came away, revealing a length of plain cotton. And wrapped in that was the Lindisfarne Gospels. The Book.

Mick pumped his fist in the air, joy and triumph mingled. Then, gingerly, he turned a few vellum leaves. Vivid colors, decorated initial letters, fretwork, knotted interlace, birds and beasts—and the reason for it all, lines of meticulously formed letters, a translation by a less precise hand filling in the spaces. He'd expected to feel some sort of electric current transmitted to his fingertips. But the pages were just painted lambskin, cool and smooth. The current was in his own mind and in the *sgian dubh*, which chimed against his skin, feeling like a peal of bells sounded. Grinning, he reached into his jacket for his new mobile.

"Michael Dewar," said a man's voice from the doorway.

Mick spun round, his hand still inside his coat. Like water bouncing off a hot griddle his joy spattered and evaporated. He should've known. He bloody well should've known.

Inspector Mountjoy's thin smile had no humor in it, only satisfaction. Behind him stood a uniformed constable. In the doorway waited a red-haired man in a posh overcoat, whose smile showed every gleaming tooth. Robin hadn't heard a joke this good in ages, had he? He hadn't known where Calum put the parcel, not until Mick showed it him.

The trio walked toward the table, steps echoing hollowly. The *sgian dubh*. No. He mustn't let Robin know he had it on him. He moved his hand so that it pressed his mother's cross into his chest. "God help me," he whispered. "Lady help me."

Robin stopped dead, his eyes narrowing, the smile dashed from his face. He didn't disappear, more's the pity. But then, this time he had lackeys to give him strength.

Mountjoy and the constable kept right on. "Let's see both your hands, sir," said the younger man.

Swallowing a four-letter word that wasn't "amen," Mick raised his hands. "This here's my property. You canna just come walking in here."

"No fear, Mr. Dewar," said Mountjoy. "We have a warrant to confiscate any stolen art objects found on the premises, and to take you into custody for conspiring in their theft."

"Art objects?" But why should Robin think of a new bit of flannel, when the old worked so well?

The constable's clear blue eyes were apologetic, but his probing hands missed nothing. He pulled the cross from inside Mick's jumper and laid it on his chest. He took the mobile. He plucked the *sgian dubh* from Mick's waistband. "He's carrying a weapon, sir."

Mountjoy tucked the mobile into his own pocket and took the knife, slipping it in and out of its sheath curiously. His face grew even more dour. "Is that the book, Superintendent Prince?"

Robin circled the table, his hands folded behind his back. "I'll have it analyzed, of course. But it certainly fits the description of the book stolen from the British Library."

"Looks like the Book of Durrow or the Book of Kells," said the constable. "One of those old decorated Bibles."

"Never mind what it is, Constable. Use that paper to make a parcel of it." Mountjoy slapped the knife against his hand, sending echoes into the depths of the building. Again Mick heard what sounded like an animal scurrying. He shifted from foot to foot. Even if he could outrun the three of them, he couldn't leave the relics behind.

Mountjoy's sharp black eyes looked Mick up and down and found him wanting. "So you thought you could cosh P.C. Armstrong here and blame a Scotland Yard officer? Stupid, lad. Dead stupid. Only a fool would credit that, and I assure you I'm no fool. You wasted your time handing that diskette in to Mackenzie. It's easy enough to rewrite a computer file, isn't it? Spreading rumors and lies about the Freedom of Faith Foundation—well, you'll find yourself answering not only to a judge, but to God himself."

"Jesus Christ!" Mick exclaimed, and was chuffed to see Robin jink like he'd been skelped. "Next you'll be accusing me of murdering my own father!" And to the constable, "You're Armstrong, are you? If I'd known you were lying there at Housesteads, as God is my witness I'd have helped you."

Armstrong looked up from his task, his eyes moving inquisitively from face to face.

"Murdered your own father?" said Mountjoy. "Not quite. But you're protecting the man who did do, the head of your theft and slander ring, Thomas London. He bought off that detective in Glastonbury, I expect. Gupta. Some sort of foreigner. But then, Glastonbury attracts the inferior elements."

"You'll be banged up in prison, Mick," Robin added. "But we can bargain about the terms. All you have to do is shop Thomas London."

"The younger American woman will likely get by with deportation. The older—well, if you'd like to testify against her, too . . ." Mountjoy kept on slapping the knife across his palm.

The flat sound of leather against flesh, hinting of petty violence, would have been maddening had Mick not already been in a fine rage. He whispered Rose's words, "Blessed St. Bridget," to Robin's smug face.

Robin turned his back and paced off toward the door.

"Here it is, Sir." Armstrong had made a very neat parcel of the Book and the cloth, wrapping it in a length of paper and tying it up with twine.

"Put it in my car," said Robin over his shoulder. "I'll drive Mick to the station myself. I'm sure I can reason with him."

Mick saw the scenario in the cold green eyes. The car turning down some dark alley. An "escape attempt." His body turfed out like an empty paper bag. Even if he could hold the man off by faith or by force, Soulis or some other toady would be waiting.

Armstrong picked up the bundle. With the knife, Mountjoy gestured toward the door. Robin turned the knob. *Now!* Mick lunged. He tugged at the parcel, almost pulling it from Armstrong's hands. But Armstrong tugged it back again. It popped from Mick's grasp and Armstrong crashed against the table.

Damn! Mick's momentum carried him toward Mountjoy. He lowered his shoulder and hit the man in the chest, sending him sprawling. The knife spun away across the floor. In one fluid movement Mick snatched it up. Turn back and have another go at the parcel? No, three against one, they'd have him, then. He kept on as he was going, sprinting toward the back of the room. Footsteps scrambled behind.

Had Armstrong left the parcel on the table? Mick doubled back. The table was empty. The man was either sodding lucky or sodding clever.

The loading dock doors were locked. By the time Mick pulled out the keys, they'd be on him. He ducked down another aisle, heading for the fire door that opened from the inside. The footsteps pounded close behind him. There! He pushed at the step ladder as he ran by and it crashed onto its side. At the end of the aisle he dared a quick glance back.

Armstrong had tangled himself, parcel and all, in the ladder. Neither Mountjoy nor Robin could pass. They were swearing at him, vicious filthy words. Then Mick heard the ringing smash of the ladder falling against the shelving, and the footsteps coming on fast.

Something was standing in front of the door, a great rat-like creature, all teeth and claws. "I dinna have time for this!" With his teeth Mick pulled the sheath from the knife. He could hear his parents' voices, the hymn book shared between them, *Christ Jesus it is he, Lord Sabaoth his name, from age to age the same, and he must win the battle. . . .* He mouthed the words round the mildew and salt taste of the leather. His knife held like a lance before him, he ran straight through the beast. A reek of stale sweat and piss and dank dungeon depths filled his nostrils but his body met no resistance save that of the door.

Mick catapulted into an icy wind that cleared the stink from his nose. He pushed the door to, seized his keys, and threw the dead bolt just as a thud made the door shudder beneath his shoulder.

Frenzied blows rang against the door and shouts filtered through its metal panels. *I must look a treat,* Mick thought, *playing at Rambo.* He spat out the sheath, replaced the knife, and jammed both into his waistband. The shouts and blows stopped. They were coming round the other way.

A crumpled crisp packet skidded across the deserted car park. So did a flurry of snowflakes. Mick took the steps in one leap and raced toward his borrowed car, his cousin Rennie's Fiat, parked at the corner of the building. As he threw himself behind the wheel he saw a green Jaguar and something small and shabby parked in the visitor's spaces at the front.

The Fiat's engine wouldn't start. Here came Mountjoy out the front, followed by Armstrong's peculiar hirple beneath the weight of the parcel, and Robin trotting behind in his own good time.

Mick told himself to send Amy round to reset the alarms. And a word in Rennie's ear about automotive maintenance wouldn't go amiss . . . The engine roared. He threw the car into gear and screeched across the car park just ahead of Mountjoy's lunge.

The light at the street was against him. With a frantic look to both sides he turned anyway. A glance in the mirror. Here came the shabby wee car, and behind it the green Jaguar. Which of them had the parcel?

It didn't matter. What mattered was that he didn't have it. He'd led that smirking demon himself straight to it. All he could do now was protect the knife. If Robin got the knife, he'd have the Stone, too. Dad died for the Stone, he'd never known it was the Book actually in his hands.

God help me, Mick thought, *I put the boot in this time—I should've done something, anything different . . .* Snowflakes dotted the windscreen. The sky was low and leaden. The headlamps of the cars glinted in the mirror and Mick winced. But the Jaguar was falling behind. Robin had the Book. Why bother himself to chase down the knife? He'd won this round, why not the next as well? *God help us.*

There, a short one-way street led to the Queensferry Road. Mick went round the corner on two wheels, accelerated the wrong way up the street, turned again, and shot onto Queensferry well past the speed limit.

The dreich day, the thickening snow, the lights of the other cars—it was a grand time to be making an escape. Within minutes Mick lost himself in the flow of traffic and started breathing again. Now he'd have to own up to his failure, to Thomas, to Maggie, to Rose—not that Rose could be more than a friend, the e-mail she'd meant to send her sister proved that. Unless Robin . . .

All he could do the night was go where Thomas had told him to go. The flat was right out, and Mountjoy had likely taken the Fiat's number plate—though Robin might not stoop to calling out the Lothian constabulary . . . Mick sped on, towards the A9 and Schiehallion, the fairy hill that his father had remembered there, at the end.

Chapter Thirty-two

Rose peered out into the gathering darkness. Below the highway Loch Tay was the same dull metallic gray as the overcast sky. A thick fog veiled the hills. Back home SMU's red brick buildings glowed in the sunlight. Her friends were hanging out in the Starbucks or checking out the new videos at Blockbuster. They thought thirties-era Snider Plaza was old and quaint.

Dallas seemed long ago and far away, not quite real. Real was the cold, dark trip from Glastonbury. Real was Sunday night with Professor and Mrs. Llewellyn in Durham, where the great cathedral on its hill was as much fortress as church.

She could still hear Thomas's voice, resonant beneath the heavy Norman columns that tied heaven to earth and brooked no nonsense about it. "The Book rested in Durham's treasury until the Reformation, when it was looted and carried south. Unlike too many other relics, I was able to prevent it from being burned as an idolatrous object or melted down as treasure. I gave it into the hands of the Keeper of Records of the Tower of London. Some years later it went into the foundation collection of the British Museum."

Mick had called them at the Llewellyn's house. He'd found the Book, yes! And no! he'd lost it again, ambushed by Robin, Mountjoy, and P.C. Armstrong. He was crushed. *Well,* Rose told herself firmly, *he can still use a friend, can't he?*

A sign read, "Fortingall 1." Maggie glanced over her shoulder. "Rose, it's not my business, I know, but what's with you and Mick?"

"I got an e-mail he intended for a girlfriend in Glasgow. I

didn't know he already had a girlfriend."

"Are you sure it wasn't Robin, messing with your mind?"

"No, I'm not sure. I should have asked Mick the night Bess died, but it all seemed so petty then. I guess tonight's my chance to ask, even though I'm not sure I want to know."

"No relationship," said Thomas, "is without its moments of doubt."

"Yeah," Maggie said under her breath. Rose could make a pretty good guess what she was thinking, but her relationship with Thomas was her own.

Houses lined the road, their windows feeble gleams in the fog-thickened twilight. A huge yew tree stood beside a church, branches gnarled beyond all comprehension of time. Fortingall. Just past an Arts and Crafts style hotel, Thomas turned onto a gravel driveway. The house at its end was painted white. Each crow-stepped gable made a shelf of snow beside the slick black slate of the roof. Smoke curled from the chimney. The front door opened, light drove back the gloom, and Mick came down the walk looking like one of General Custer's scouts.

Fixing a smile on her face, Rose climbed out of the car. "Hi."

"Hello yourself." His smile didn't quite work.

"Hello, Mick," said Maggie.

"Thomas, Maggie, I'm sorry I dinna have better news for you. You trusted me, and I let you down. I made a right good show of running away is all."

"You didn't let us down," said Thomas.

"You did the right thing," Rose told him, imagining his body lying in a trench like his father's. "You saved the knife."

"Well then." Clearing his throat, Mick went on, "I was expecting the mini-bus."

"I thought we should have a vehicle with four-wheel

drive," explained Thomas, "so I hired this Range Rover. I don't suppose Fiona is preparing the tea?"

"That she is." Mick scooped up Thomas's satchel and Maggie's backpack, leaving Rose to shoulder her own.

Two people waited in the doorway of the house. "Come in, come in," said a man's voice. A woman's added, "It's cold as a witch's teat out there."

Rose shook hands with Stavros and Fiona Paleologos. He was short and stout, and most of his black hair had migrated downward to an amazing moustache. She was tall and thin, with a forelock of gray hair and prominent front teeth. "Mick," she said, "could you take the bags upstairs?"

Rose followed Mick while he dropped Thomas's bag in one room and Maggie's in another, decorated in flowery chintz. Throwing her backpack onto one of the beds, she gritted her teeth and turned to face him. Lines scored his forehead. His eyes glinted a hard steel-gray, like armor. He was wearing a blue Celtic cross. She tried, "Are you okay?"

He was looking her over, too. "Oh aye. Just. And you, with Bess and all? I reckon she was murdered, like Dad and Vivian, only not so direct."

"Ellen freaked out after the tornado and kept trying to convert her and she freaked out over Ellen . . ." Rose looked down at her feet, slightly pigeon-toed as though recoiling from Mick's feet a few inches away. "I'm trying to be compassionate, really I am, but it's not easy."

"What is?" Mick asked. "And the others—Anna and Sean?"

Rose looked back up, meeting his sober but non-judgmental eyes. "Sean decided to spend a couple of days with one of his buddies whose class is doing Boadicea's Rebellion. Anna's still at Temple Manor. She wanted to hear a concert at the Assembly Rooms, and she's taking Ellen to a doctor—

she's got an infected hand. Mind, too, I'd say."

"Robin, he's like a plague, spreading distrust instead of disease." Tentatively Mick brushed Rose's hair back from her face.

She leaned into the touch, suddenly hopeful, still afraid to come right out and ask. "Yesterday was the first Sunday of Advent. It's almost Christmas, New Year's, Armageddon, the Apocalypse, whatever. I have to go home the first week of January, assuming there's a home to go to, but right now home seems less real than—than Camelot."

"Real as e-mail?" he murmured, his hand retreating.

"E-mail, yeah." *Let's get this over with.* "Mick, I got a message you meant for a girl named Jennie."

"What? Bloody hell!" His eyes flashed from bewilderment to anger. "I got a message you meant for your sister, telling her I was a dead loss, that you'd rather have Sean."

Rose went dizzy with relief. She set her fingertips against Mick's necklace—like swearing on the Bible. "Sean was coming on to me at first. But nothing clicked, and then you came along."

"Jennie is a lass at university I'd have asked out if all this hadn't started up. If I'd not met you."

"So Robin *was* messing with our minds! Why couldn't I have trusted you?"

"And I you?" he asked with a grimace.

"Mick . . ." The name welled up from deep in Rose's chest.

From downstairs Maggie called, "Mick, Rose, food's on!"

Exchanging pained smiles, they walked side by side down the stairs. A calico cat greeted them with a meow. "Meet Ariadne," said Mick.

"Hello there. Got any balls of string to guide us through the maze?" Rose bent to stroke Ariadne's silky head. The cat purred.

Along the wall of the dining room were arranged several icons, the faces of Mary, Jesus, and various saints looking out from coronas of embossed silver and gold. Under the calm gaze of those eyes Rose sat down at the table and ate her tea, daring to hope that she'd find calm eventually.

Mick filled them in on his escape, concluding, "I wanted to help my dad by saving the Book."

"You are helping your father," Thomas told him.

Fiona and Stavros exchanged nods. Maybe they didn't know who Thomas or Robin really were, but they knew the Story, like the Llewellyns at Durham and the Shaws at Otterburn. Swallowing her last bite of toast, butter, and jam, Rose asked, "Can I help with the dishes?"

"Not at all. You have yourselves a rest," Fiona answered.

In the sitting room, Stavros poked the smoldering peats in the tiny grate until they flared into flame. Light danced across shelf after shelf, where photos of children and grandchildren nestled among stacks of books. Ariadne sauntered in and sat down on the hearth. Then Fiona clinked through the doorway with a bottle of whiskey, a pitcher of water, and six glasses. "Here's a wee doch and dorris to see you on your way the morn." She poured and passed. Rose held her glass to the light, admiring the whiskey's gold glints, like captured sunlight. The morning, yes.

Thomas offered the toast. "May Mick's courage of yesterday inspire us all in the days to come."

"Courage? Well then, thank you kindly." Mick drank deep.

Rose sipped. Her mouth filled with the sharp-sweet flavor of sunshine, grain, mist, and smoke. Her cheeks burned and her stomach glowed.

"We'll get on with the clearing up," said Stavros.

"Thank you," Maggie called after them, and the others echoed her words.

Rose sat on the couch, Mick beside her. The tingle reached her toes.

"I knew Robin wanted me to lead him to the Stone," Mick said, "but I never thought he wanted me to lead him to the Book."

"So confident was he of his hold over Calum he imagined he could have both Stone and Book conveniently together," said Thomas.

Maggie stretched her feet out to the fire. Ariadne sniffed at her toe. The firelight reflected off the glass in Thomas's hands and the glasses on his face, reminding Rose of the silver and gold decorations on the icons in the dining room. She asked, "Are you surprised about Mountjoy?"

"I was afraid some shadowed corner of the man's heart would lead him into Robin's hands. It's Armstrong who surprises me."

"I reckon Mountjoy told him I'd tried to kill him, and brought him along as muscle," said Mick. "But he didna seem at all hateful, not like the other two, and I'm not so sure he didna help me escape."

Thomas nodded. "Then we shall keep an open mind. As for Mountjoy, I got onto Kay Dunnet last night. She'll have a word with the chief constable of Northumbria, so that he can set Mountjoy straight. That should help us, but will do little to heal his fear and pride."

"Who?" Rose asked.

"Kay Dunnet is a judge. She is also the guardian of the Brecbennoch of St. Columba, the reliquary that was just given a place of honor in the new Museum of Scotland."

"Bruce had the Brecbennoch at Bannockburn," said Mick.

"It was carried into battle by the Abbot of Arbroath, an abbey that is important in the history of the Stone."

"I suppose," Maggie said, "it's no coincidence that Arbroath Abbey was founded by King William the Lion in your honor."

"Neither is it a coincidence that the English defeated William the same day Henry did penance for the murder at Canterbury."

"God having a sense of humor."

"I should distrust a deity without one," Thomas said with a smile.

Mick shifted uneasily. "Mountjoy'll not be doing me for assault?"

"Not unless he wants to be charged with aiding and abetting a criminal posing as a police officer."

With a long exhalation, Mick slumped toward Rose. Ariadne dozed, her eyes bits of ancient amber, exuding tranquility. Crockery jingled in the kitchen. A clock chimed seven. Thomas said, "We must make an early start tomorrow."

Maggie's eyes were half-closed, like the cat's. The cross resting on her sweater rose and fell, gleaming in the light. "Dawn patrol. Over the top."

"The calm before the storm. The eye of the hurricane."

Rose's mind surfed down the flames in the fireplace and the glow in her body. Tomorrow. Outside this house waited fog, death, and the Devil. She'd expected Thomas to deliver another of his sermons, lectures, whatever, steeling them to face their—no sense in mincing words—dangerous quest. Not that anyone thought it was safe. Thomas trusted their intelligence and their courage . . . She drained her whiskey, wondering if its courage was any more false than any other kind. But no. You just had to choose courage, didn't you?

Stavros looked in the door. "Anyone for Scrabble?"

"I'm on," said Thomas. "Maggie?"

"Sure. Just don't penalize me for American spelling. I take it y'all don't want to play?" she asked Mick and Rose.

"No, thank you," said Mick.

Rose waited until she heard the tiles clicking in the dining room and then turned to him. "I shouldn't have given Robin the satisfaction of doubting you for even one minute."

"Nor I," he returned. "If I can trust anyone, lass, it's you."

She saw the words leave his lips like bubbles of light. Trust was truth. It had to be chosen, like faith, even though it sometimes took a heck of a lot of courage to do it. "At least," she whispered, "if Robin keeps trying to break us up, then he keeps pushing us to make up, too."

"Then let's be making up," Mick whispered back.

Rose slipped as easily into his arms as though she'd been doing it for years. She rubbed her cheek from the muscle of his shoulder up to the angle of his jaw, inhaling his scent of shampoo and wool, and buried her face in his hair. Yes, he'd existed in her own personal Dreamtime for a very long time.

His mouth brushed her forehead. "I was scairt I'd not be seeing you again. And there's so much I'm wanting to see of you."

"Yes." And in blissful surrender she raised her mouth to his.

Chapter Thirty-three

Light streamed across a crystalline sky. The surface of Loch Tay looked like silvery blue glass. Nothing moved, not a branch, not a bird, not another car on the road besides the Range Rover. *A loud noise or a heavy breath,* Maggie thought, *would shatter the fragile peace and reveal*—what? Chaos? Or an even deeper tranquility? "Where are we going?" she asked in a whisper.

Even Thomas's baritone was quiet. "To the center point of a triangle whose corners are at Fortingall, Methven where the Bruce was defeated, and St. Fillan's shrine at Tyndrum. Between Killin, St. Fillan's cell at the southwestern end of Loch Tay, and the village actually named St. Fillans at the eastern end of Loch Earn, lies a place marked on an ancient map as *Tobar nan Bride,* St. Bride's Well."

"Another Bridget's Well," said Rose.

Mick said, "You're thinking Malise the *deoradh* hid the stone at one of those ancient shrines adopted by Christians?"

"I think so, yes."

At last they passed another car. A haze hung over the roofs of Aberfeldy where Thomas turned south. Not far past Amulree he said, "Look behind us, please, and tell me if that's a green Jaguar."

Snapping around, Maggie took a long, hard look. "It's a green car, but it just turned off." She tried to look every direction at once, but saw only the landscape, all Celtic curves, the road, the hills, leafless trees, a stream rimmed with ice, walls built stone upon stone and snaking away over the skyline. Vehicles of any color seemed anachronistic.

A mile past the town of Comrie, Thomas turned onto a road narrower than Maggie's driveway. A shabby red car passed, slowed as though for a look and then sped up.

Everyone pretended not to notice. The only reason Maggie couldn't hear teeth grinding in the back seat was because her own were making too much noise. Nobody needed to speculate what might have happened to Mick two days ago if he hadn't been as fleet of foot as of brain. Nobody needed to speculate just what might happen today.

As the road climbed above the trees the land opened out. The shining sheet of Loch Earn stretched away westward. Beyond it the mountains were waves of blue and purple shading into the blue of the sky.

Thomas pulled off the paved road onto a dirt track, and then after a few minutes went jouncing right out into a sheep pasture. Bundles of brownish wool with black faces stared as the car angled down the hillside into a hollow shaded by a Scots pine. Finding a level place, Thomas stopped.

They climbed out of the car and stood close together, their breaths rising into a sparkling cloud. "That knob of rock on the far side of the loch is an old Pictish fort, St. Fillan's seat," said Thomas. "Below it lies a well that pilgrims visited on the old Celtic holy days."

Maggie nudged a hump of heather with her toe. The snow-dusted ground was so lumpy with rocks and brush that anything up to and including a Volkswagen could be hidden here.

"One source mentions a hawthorn grove instead of this splendid pine . . . Ah, several stumps. And the ghost of a path leading up from the loch—see, where the snow outlines a furrow?"

Rose brushed the snow from a bit of broken stone. "Here are some carvings. Spirals and knotwork, really weathered."

"We're in the proper place, right enough." Mick hiked up his coat and pulled out his *sgian dubh*. "It's buzzing like a bee."

There was no wind. There was no noise at all besides their own hushed voices. Maggie couldn't think of any place she'd ever been—museums, churches—as still as this lonely place. Still, calm, peaceful—and alert.

"Earth to Maggie," Rose teased.

"Just appreciating the—the spirit of the place."

"The *anima loci*," Thomas said with a nod. "Mick, if you would be so good as to use your knife as a sensor."

Frowning in concentration, Mick held the knife by its sheath and turned in a circle. "It's like an electric current running up my arm, strongest there, by that ruined wall. It disna look like more than a sheep fank."

"A small oratory once stood here, built of flat rocks angled inward at the top to make a roof. I daresay its stones were re-used." Thomas stepped across the low wall and into what would have been the center of the building, assuming the building was the size of the Paleologos's dining room. He began picking up rocks. "We're committing archaeological vandalism here. Ian Graham has already offered absolution, but I think we should have a care not to create too much of a mess even so."

Mick set the *sgian dubh* on the larger stump. With Thomas, the alpha male, directing, they cleared the interior of the building down to a few brownish-gold lichens and ferns. Then with the trowels and shovels Thomas had borrowed from Stavros they scraped away the plants and several inches of what felt like soggy potting soil, revealing a slate floor.

The eastern end of the chapel was built into the slope of the hill. There the slate paving stopped at a rough slab of stone. Ordinary stone, Maggie saw, the same sparkly gray stuff she'd been heaving around. Scraping the mud off the slab revealed an incised Celtic cross. "Was this an altar? Don't you always put a relic of some sort inside the altar?"

"Here, I should think, the relic is below." Thomas brushed off his hands. "Very good. We've earned our luncheon."

"I could eat one of those sheep," said Rose, indicating the dozen or so animals which had meandered closer while they worked.

"We've attracted an audience," Thomas said bemusedly.

"A riff on the Good Shepherd theme," joked Maggie, but still she looked around to make sure only sheep were watching.

Mick was pulling Fiona's picnic basket from the car. "Oh good—flasks of tea, sandwiches, cake. Apples. Here you are, lass."

With a crunch Rose bit into the apple. *Eve and the tree of knowledge,* Maggie thought. *Comfort me with apples for I am sick of love* . . . Thomas handed her a sandwich. "Thanks."

The sun hung far to the south. A quarter moon flirted with the western horizon, just as it had done the day she stood with Gupta outside the youth hostel. Toy-like cars moved on the road far below and a boat etched the surface of the loch. The human race hadn't vanished, then.

"Listen!" Thomas said.

Water dripped. Icicles on the pine? No. The drips were coming closer together. Running water. Inside the semi-circle of stumps, the sacred precinct, the snow was melting. Some of the bushes broke out with bright yellow flowers. The ground smoothed into a green lawn dotted with more yellow blossoms. Thomas took off his glasses, mopped them with his handkerchief, and put them back on. "Dandelions, St. Bridget's flower."

"We're onto something," said Rose.

Thomas nodded. "Very much so."

The crisp air softened, a warm draft welling upward from the ground itself. A black lamb had appeared among the sheep, Maggie saw, an ambulatory stuffed toy who watched with bright beady eyes as they returned to the chapel and lifted the altar stone to one side.

The flat stone beneath was pierced by small holes. "Finger holes," Rose said. "It's a trap door. Sweet!"

Thomas used a trowel to clear the mud away from the square stone and ream out the holes. Together he and Mick heaved the slab up and, with an echoing thud, back. Beneath it opened a dark, circular hole. A thick musty odor wafted up from it, centuries of mud and decay. "This isn't a treasure room," Maggie said. "This is the well."

"So it is." Pulling a flashlight from his pocket, Thomas shone it into the darkness. Rose, Mick, and Maggie bumped heads trying to look. The light revealed a cylindrical, stone-lined passage, clogged about ten feet down with rubble. Pale root tendrils clung to the walls amid rivulets of water. "Rats," said Rose. Maggie had the feeling she'd almost said, *yecch*.

"We could clear it out," Mick said, without enthusiasm.

Thomas's jaw was set hard. Disappointment didn't describe it. He was doubting his own judgment. Averting her eyes, Maggie straightened and looked around. As though disappointment wasn't enough, she had the damndest itch between her shoulder blades . . . Well, everyone, especially Thomas, had looked over their shoulders as often as they'd looked at their work.

Except for the twenty or so sheep and a bird so high up it was almost microscopic, Maggie couldn't see one living creature. The lamb stood at the edge of the lawn, a dandelion hanging from its mouth.

Flowers didn't pop up out of frozen ground, she told herself. There was something here, they just had to find it. She looked at the engraved slab lying on its side by the wall. One corner was chipped. No big deal, it was an old stone . . . "Thomas?"

"Yes?" He tucked the flashlight back into his pocket.

"That stone there. Is it the same size as the capital-S stone?"

"The sources say the Stone is large enough for a man to sit upon without folding his knees to his chest. Taller than its sandstone copies. And larger than this. However . . ." Thomas knelt by the slab and traced the cross with his fingertip. Then he pulled out his handkerchief. "Mick, could you wet this in the rivulet, please? And fetch your *sgian dubh*."

"This stone's granite, isn't it?" Rose asked.

"It's schist, the common stone in this area, just as red sandstone is the common stone at Scone. Thank you, Mick." Thomas wiped the stone clean.

It was silvery gray, dusted with tiny quartz crystals that sparkled in the sunlight. Holding the *sgian dubh* by its sheath, Mick leaned over and touched the handle and its black marble chip to the carved cross. "Ow! It's gone and shocked me!"

A slow grin spread up Thomas's face. "Let's set this stone back in its place." The trap door thudded down. The slab fit back into its template in the mud. "It's not so heavy as you'd think, is it? Now take the knife from its sheath, if you would, Mick—the sheath is modern, the stone doesn't recognize it—and fit the chipping to that broken corner."

Kneeling, Mick held the knife close to the stone. The chip was the right shape, but the wrong texture and color . . . The *sgian dubh* flipped out of his hand and with a note like the ringing of a bell landed point first in the center of the circled cross. Landed, and sunk into the rock until the blade was completely hidden.

"I'll be damned," said Maggie.

"Oh no," Thomas said with a laugh, "I think not. There you are, Mick, the sword and the stone. Rose, look!"

The silver of the stone darkened. It grew larger. Each upper corner sprouted into a curved extension—the horns of the altar, described in the Bible and discovered by archaeologists from Rome to Crete to Israel. The stone was a deep, luminous black, like ripe berries or the pupil of an eye. Its surface was carved with sinuous figures that seemed to change as Maggie looked at them—animal, plants, clouds. She shook her head in amazement, magic not being something she was ever going to get used to.

"Here I have been expounding on the Unseen," said Thomas, "and yet I failed to recognize the Unseen laid before me. The Stone was incomplete. It was like a locked door that needed its key. Thank you, Maggie."

"No problem," she returned, with what was probably a dazed smile.

Mick reached toward the knife. "Should I pull it out?"

"I'd replace the chipping first."

"But it's glued on tight." With wary thumb and forefinger Mick tried the chip. It came right off. "Ah," he said, and set the chip into the broken corner. It attached itself to the stone and merged with it, the seam disappearing into the black marble whole. Mick removed his knife, effortlessly, and rock oozed back into the hole it had made, leaving the Stone unscarred.

"Glory be to God, by whom all things are made." Thomas stood up, laughing as free a peal of laughter as Maggie had ever heard from him.

Rose and Mick gave each other high-fives. Blowing out a

sigh, Maggie turned around and saw that fifty sheep stood ranged around the site. Where had they all come from? Their hooves were as silent as cats' paws.

A wavering cry cut the still air and then faded away. A closer one rose and fell like the wail of a soul treed by the Wild Hunt. The sheep twitched. Rose took a jerky step closer to Mick. Mick went pale, but still managed a jaunty, "There are no wolves left in Scotland. He'll not be scaring us away with illusions."

Two cars appeared on the hilltop. "They're no illusions," Maggie said, her elation icing over. "Here we go, folks."

Thomas's expression went stern and cold. With his knife Mick traced a circle on the pavement. All four of them stepped inside and stood shoulder to shoulder in front of the Stone.

A green Humvee lumbered down the hillside, squashing plants and sending more than one sheep jogging away. A decrepit red Nissan lunged and bounced and finally stopped just below the brow of the hill. A tall, gangly man climbed out and hurried down the path of destruction toward the Humvee.

From the Humvee stepped three men, led, of course, by Robin. He was wearing what Maggie assumed was his Robert Prince outfit—black overcoat, starched white shirt, striped tie, fancy leather gloves. One of the other men was a jowly individual with slicked-back hair—wait, she'd seen him on television in Glastonbury. Reginald Soulis. The third man looked like a Dallas Cowboys tackle, his shaved head smaller than his massive neck, which rose like a tree trunk from his even more massive body. And Mick thought Willie Armstrong was muscle.

The man from the Nissan *was* Willie Armstrong, dressed in jeans and a jacket. He took his place beside the others, his blue eyes darting so quickly from sky to loch to sheep to Stone that Maggie wondered if he was using some kind of X-ray vision. Unlike the close-set lead-lined eyes of the other two men, staring sullenly at Thomas and Maggie, Mick and Rose.

Robin's smile was the usual infuriating mixture of smug and malicious. He pulled off his gloves, slowly, aiming for maximum effect. "You've been having a busy day of it, haven't you? You look to have been digging sewers. I must thank you for sparing me and my men here the dirty work. At least, the dirty work of digging."

He strolled across the green grass. The black lamb hopped onto the ruined wall. A shudder went through Mick. Rose laid her hand on his arm.

Thomas raised his right hand. "In the name of the Father, the Son, and the Holy Ghost, begone." Robin stopped dead, grimacing. But he didn't disappear. Thomas dropped his hand to his side, where it closed to a fist. *On to Plan B,* Maggie thought, *whatever that is.*

"See there, Stan," said droopy-jowls to thick-neck, "he perverts the word of God. He needs stopping. In the old days he'd have been stopped, right and proper."

Stan—Felton, Maggie assumed—turned a disgusted look on his companion. "So Mr. Posh Toff Soulis is God's personal mouthpiece, eh?"

Armstrong looked down at his feet. Robin slapped at the lamb with his gloves, shooing it away, and advanced to the edge of the circle. "Stan, Reg, get this stone into the Humvee. Willie, you owe Mick here for bashing you. Come take his little pig-sticker. He'll not hand you any trouble, not if he wants to protect Rose."

All three men started forward, Stan and Reg kicking at the dandelions, Willie trudging along behind.

Robin's cold green eyes considered Rose. He ran his

tongue between his lips. "Your faith has come to naught, now, at the end."

"This isn't the end." Rose's voice was perfectly steady.

"Not for you, no." Robin looked Maggie up and down. "As for you, well, mutton can be as tasty as lamb. Especially well-seasoned mutton."

Maggie saved her breath. *Just goes to show you the banality of evil,* she thought, that a real live demon came across as a B-movie villain.

Robin stared narrow-eyed into Thomas's impassive face. "It will take only a moment for my friends here to drop you into that well. Burial alive in *her* cunt, isn't that appropriate? You'll have eternity to contemplate how terribly you've failed your trust."

Thomas's lips moved. *"Pater noster qui es in caelis . . ."*

Robin went on, relishing his moment, "I have two artifacts. They will summon the third from where you have hidden it. Winner take all."

"Mater noster qui es in terris . . ." Thomas murmured.

Reg jostled Mick and Rose aside and out of the circle. Stan leered at Rose but was recalled by Reg's muttered curse. They lifted the Stone and shuffled across the muddy flagstones, groaning and panting. Willie held out his hand to Mick. "Give me the knife, please, sir."

"Don't do this," said Rose. "He's not a Scotland Yard officer . . ."

Robin brushed her cheek with his gloves. "Close those delectable lips, Rose. Until I'm ready for them to open."

Mick stepped in front of her indignant glare, the knife at waist height, and pushed her back into the circle. "Leave off."

"Brigit daughter of Dugall the Brown," Thomas said, "son of Aodh son of Art son of Conn son of Criara son of Carbre son of Cas son of Cormac; I shall not be slain, I shall not be sworded, I shall not be put in a cell . . ."

Reg and Stan walked across the lawn. Sheep stood between them and the Humvee. "Naff off," Stan called to them.

Now would be a good time, Maggie thought, *for Thomas's prayer to be answered.* A little divine intervention. *Deus ex machina,* even . . . A breath of warm wind fanned her hair. She heard barking. Not the howling of wolves, but the barking of dogs. Over the hill ran two border collies, their black and white coats gleaming in the sun. The sheep, all ninety and nine of them, roused themselves. The dogs urged them into a run. The black lamb leaped up onto the hill above the eastern end of the chapel, his halo glowing.

"The Lord is my shepherd, I shall not want." Thomas gestured, and the gesture alone knocked Robin to the side.

Willie leaped out of the way as Robin stumbled toward him. Stan and Reg dropped the Stone, turned to run, and were submerged beneath a wave of wool.

Even Maggie knew the text Thomas was setting. "Yea, though I walk through the valley of the shadow of death, I will fear no evil, for You are with me."

Mick sprinted toward the Stone, sheep parting like the Red Sea before him. Taking one of the horns of the altar in his left hand, he brandished the knife in his right.

Robin's momentum brought him up against the ruined wall. His knees buckling, he sat down hard. His eyes flashed, his teeth ground, his mouth contorted into a sneer that was equally hatred and jealousy. "Get the Stone, Armstrong! Damn you, get the Stone!"

Stan and Reg reappeared, dirty and disheveled, as the flock stampeded past them. They staggered to their feet and toward the door of the Humvee. But the dogs were on them, snarling and snapping. Stan elbowed Reg aside. Reg kicked him. One dog leaped, got a mouthful of Stan's coat, and jerked him down. Reg leaped into the driver's seat and slammed the door not only on the second dog but on Stan.

Turning his back on Robin, Willie inched toward the Stone. Mick spun toward him. "Constable, you're needing to choose yourself a side. Now."

Willie stopped dead, raising his hands. "I only ever meant to be one of the good guys, and just now I reckon that's you lot."

Maggie and Rose lent their voices to Thomas's, the words spilling out in a musical cadence, "Surely goodness and mercy shall follow me all the days of my life, and I will dwell in the house of the Lord forever."

With a cry of rage, Robin vanished.

Reg started the engine. Stan threw himself at the Humvee. He opened the door just as Reg took off, spraying clods of dirt, and pulled himself inside. The car roared down the hill toward the highway, bouncing and heaving, Stan's feet flapping out the open door. It disappeared behind the shoulder of the hill and the noise of its engine faded and died.

The thunder of hooves and the protesting baa's dwindled into the distance. The sheep might never have been there, except the snow and the grass were churned by hooves. The lamb stood above the chapel, its dark eyes surveying the scene below with benign wisdom and no little humor. Maggie thought suddenly of what Gupta had said, about natural forces which are very much involved, intelligent, even ironic.

"Robin is powerless against the unblemished lamb," Thomas said with a deep genuflection.

The two dogs took up stances on either side of and just below the lamb, their mighty wings opening, their swords gleaming . . . Maggie blinked. Three ordinary animals were scampering away down the hillside.

"Wow," breathed Rose. Mick released the Stone and looked at his knife.

"What was all that in aid of?" Willie peered down the hill with a disgusted expression, no doubt thinking Robin had run after the Humvee. "Why were you staring at the dogs and the lamb?"

Thomas answered, out of breath, "We saw a vision."

"A hallucination, like as not," Willie corrected, "what with hyperventilating and all. I read about that in a science journal."

Thomas conceded the field to Willie's magazine. "Would you care for some food, Constable? There is a lovely picnic hamper in the back of the Rover."

"Don't mind if I do, it's a right cold day and Prince left me sitting in a layby for bloody hours." With a slightly snockered look at Rose, Willie marched over to the car.

Rose gave Mick a hug. "My hero!" she said with a grin.

"My heroine!" he returned, but his grin wobbled. He touched her cheek. "Are you all right, then, lass?"

"He didn't hurt me. He just made me mad."

Mick sheathed his *sgian dubh*. "It's still tingling."

"An object that comes in contact with a relic often takes on the virtue of that relic," Thomas told him.

Maggie's knees felt like jelly. She took Thomas's hand and he returned her grasp. Was that what the knife felt like to Mick? Except the thrumming of power she sensed was not in an artifact of steel and bone, but in a man. A man who was, at the moment, so white around the gills he was darn near green. "The Stone—it caused the sheep and the dogs and—and everything?"

"That was what we in the religion business call a miracle. A glimpse of the Invisible."

She wasn't going to argue. "You deliberately risked our

lives to get the Stone, didn't you?"

"Yes. Once again I apologize for my presumption."

"You just hoped we'd defeat him?" Maggie persisted.

"The relics perpetuate hope. If you needed any proof of that . . ."

". . . I got it. If there were an objective test of a miracle, then it wouldn't be one, right?" With a groan that was as much a laugh, she squeezed his hand and released it.

Willie came strolling back, half a sandwich in his hand. "Constable Armstrong," said Thomas. "I assume you're no longer working with Robin Fitzroy. Robert Prince."

"Robin Fitzroy? Well, he's lied about most everything else, why not his name?" Willie inhaled the rest of the sandwich. "He says you're some sort of master criminal, Mr. London. But I reckon if you'd killed Calum Dewar, then you'd just as soon have left me to die at Housesteads. I wasn't out cold the entire time, mind you, just muzzy. I heard voices. Prince's I placed when he was talking to Mountjoy, and Mick's I placed in Edinburgh."

"What did you overhear, then?" asked Mick.

"You asked Prince about the car I'd left in the car park. If you'd coshed me, you wouldn't be pointing out I'd gone missing, would you? He told you I was okay. Even if he didn't know I was lying there with my head bashed in, he had no call telling you I was okay. And why take you away to a safe house when Hexham police station was just up the road?"

Smart kid, Maggie thought.

"He and Mountjoy were going on about some religious foundation being under attack. Didn't sound at all sensible to me, but then, you wouldn't go wrong calling me an atheist. Each to his own."

Rose smiled indulgently.

"Prince was flannelling Mountjoy about promotions and

Scotland Yard and how everyone else was after bringing him down. Then, the way I hear it, the chief constable got onto Scotland Yard and they'd never heard of Prince. The chief was already unhappy with the way Mountjoy was handling the Dewar case, so had him in and dressed him down. Mountjoy resigned on the spot. When Prince rang me and told me I was still working for him, I came along to see what's what. And I saw it. He's some sort of master criminal himself, is he?"

"You could say that," said Thomas.

"Well, art theft can be as rum a business as drug-running. Anywhere there's brass there's crime." Willie made a face. "And I handed over that old book sweet as you please, didn't I? Prince said he'd take it to the evidence room in Edinburgh, but I reckon he still has it. Damn and blast!"

Thomas suggested, "You were only following orders."

"Ah, but there's more than orders to follow, if you take my meaning."

"I do." Smiling, Thomas pulled a scrap of paper and a pen from his pocket. "Here's my address and telephone number, Constable, and Mick's in Edinburgh. Superintendent Mackenzie will vouch for us, if need be."

"No need. I believe what I see." Willie took the paper. "Glastonbury, is it? Grand place."

"Please ring me if Robert Prince contacts you again," Thomas went on. "He'll have some explanation for what happened here today, never fear."

"If I acted as though I believed him, then I might could find the book. I need to be making up for backing the wrong horse, don't I?" He looked down at the Stone. "And what's this then?"

"It's an ancient Celtic inauguration stone," Thomas explained.

"Like the Stone of Scone," Willie said, and added confidingly, "My mates take the mickey out of me for reading history, but I reckon you need to know where you came from, eh?"

Thomas positively beamed on the young man. "You're welcome to join us in Fortingall tonight. I can promise you a feast in honor of St. Andrew."

"Thank you kindly, but I'd better be getting myself back to Hexham. I gave up my day off for that prat Prince."

"One more question," Mick said. "In the warehouse, did you fall over that step ladder of a purpose?"

"Well, now, I'll not be giving away police secrets." Willie grinned, a broad open grin that drew smiles from the others. "Would you like a hand shifting that stone? It looked right heavy."

"No thank you," said Thomas. "We can manage."

"Cheers, then." Willie shook hands all around, his grasp steady, and bounded up the hill toward the Nissan.

Maggie smiled. "Nothing like casting your bread upon P.C. Armstrong and having it returned a hundred-fold."

"Indeed." Making the sign of the cross, Thomas murmured a blessing toward the departing car and its occupant, then added to Maggie's quirked brow, "A blessing will not hurt him, will it? Mick, let us shift the Stone. Rose, if you'd be kind enough to open the boot of car."

Rose, Mick, and Thomas stowed the Stone in the back of the Rover while Maggie wearily gathered up the tools. She felt like she'd been riding a roller coaster all day. So did the kids, judging by Mick's drawn features and Rose's slightly bulging eyes, as though she was holding in a scream.

And Thomas? If the day's events had been a roller coaster ride for them, what had it felt like to him? He had to be profoundly moved. But he'd spent too many years constructing a rood screen before the altar of his soul to reveal himself even now, even to her . . . Maggie saw him lying on the floor of his chapel. *The shadow of death.*

A snowflake brushed her face and she looked up. A few fluffy pink clouds hung in the deep blue sky, their edges gilded by the sinking sun like the letters in an illuminated manuscript. They weren't snow clouds, and none of them were directly overhead, but the one snowflake turned into two, and twenty, and two thousand. Abandoning rationality, Maggie climbed into the car with the others.

In a few moments the lawn, the floor of the oratory, the scars left by sheep and heavy vehicles had disappeared beneath a cloak of snow tinted blue by the fleeting winter dusk. The snow fell behind the Range Rover as Thomas guided it over the hill, until its tracks, too, had been erased.

Maggie watched the stars appear in a sky as darkly polished as the Stone. Tomorrow was the first of December. She whispered into the darkness, "Surely goodness and mercy shall follow us."

Chapter Thirty-four

Thomas stood on the hollowed—and now hallowed—stone doorstep of his chapel, watching his friends walk across the lawn to the manor house. His hand still tingled from the touch of so many others.

The cold, fresh wind lifted the fabric of the chasuble like wings from his shoulders. It was the sort of day that lifted the heart itself, evidence of God's grace in bleak midwinter. A bright sun glinted off the windows of the house.

This day made a beginning. The beginning of the end. Of a good end. His chapel had been made whole again. He'd shown forth his faith. *How sweet are thy words upon my lips, O Lord . . .* He was as giddy as though he'd already drunk the champagne Alf had laid on. Although it was Bess who had begun organizing the festive buffet, last summer when Thomas first announced he planned to re-consecrate his chapel. Bess was here in spirit today, he was sure. Not the ghost at the feast, like Ellen, but a benign presence.

There was Ellen herself, looking out of an upper window, by her own choice left out. Even Sean had come to the consecration, his face, like Alf's, puzzled but polite. And Anna had reminded Thomas that today was the last day of Hanukkah, the story of the rededication of the temple in Jerusalem.

Thomas wondered how so many people had managed to pack themselves into the tiny chapel. Father Brian from St. Mary's, who lent the vestments and ritual vessels. George Shaw from Otterburn, Manuel and Cecily Llewellyn from Durham, Edith Howard from Salisbury, Ivan O'Connell from Canterbury, Genevieve de Bouillon from Chartres, Andrea Pellegrino from Turin. Teresa Gaunt from York, who assured Thomas that the Stone was safe in York Minster's treasury, close by the pavement of the Roman headquarters deep beneath the cathedral. Pavement trod by Constantine himself, who by tolerating and including the troublesome little sect of Christianity had assured its vitality.

Now Jivan, Maggie, and Rose emerged from the chapel. Jivan was saying, ". . . after your confrontation with Stan Felton in Scotland, the police had him in again. He confessed to stealing the Book from the removal van, and shopped Reginald Soulis very nicely indeed, saying he handed the Book off to him."

"So have you arrested Soulis?" Maggie asked.

"We can't find him. D.C.I. Swenholt, Mountjoy's replacement, swore out a warrant to search his offices and Holystone as well, but no joy."

Thomas forced himself to focus on the ongoing task. "And what of Mountjoy himself?"

"He's done a bunk. Even his family doesn't know where he is. P.C. Armstrong, now, says that he's heard from Fitzroy, and has told him he'd like to join up. He thinks he can trace the Book. That's a dangerous game . . ."

". . . but one he has chosen to play." Once again Thomas was grateful for Willie Armstrong.

Jivan held out his hand. "Sorry I can't stop. Thank you for having me in for the service. The old Latin mass is very impressive."

Thomas clasped Jivan's hand with both his own. "Thank you for coming."

"Cheers," Jivan said to the women, and strolled toward the car park.

"It was an awesome mass, Thomas. Thank you." Rose

stood up on her tiptoes to kiss his cheek, leaving a whiff of fresh flowers in his nostrils. "I'll go play sacristan and get Father Brian's things washed and packed," she concluded, and ducked back inside.

It was almost startling to see the young woman wearing a dress and nylon tights. And Maggie as well—she had, he noted, exquisite ankles . . . He might be elated to the point of drunkenness, but she stood looking out into the winter's day, her arms crossed, her shoulders bowed, as though she were despondent. That was puzzling—surely she shared his pleasure.

They'd had many fine moments together, not least the two trips to Scotland and the weekly trips to Salisbury. And they'd taken the students to Wells, to Exeter, to Portsmouth. To Caerleon and Winchester and Cadbury Castle, all identified as Camelot. To Tintagel in Cornwall, Arthur's birthplace. "You could have taken communion," he told her. "I should not have turned you away."

"I'm not Catholic," she said.

Nor confessed. Suddenly he saw who it was she was seeing—not the eccentric pedant in his blue jeans, her friend and companion, but the priest in the penitential violet chasuble and stole of Advent. Who knew better than he what it meant to be swollen with truth but too proud to speak it?

"Come inside." He led her back up the nave, their steps echoing. The faces in the rood screen seemed to turn toward them. The odor of hot wax mingled with that of incense, potent as perfume. From the door into the cottage came the splash of water and Rose's beautiful voice. She'd performed the *Te Deum* brilliantly for the congregation, but now she was singing Christmas carols.

Thomas removed the chasuble and set it aside. He replaced St. Bridget's bell in the cabinet. "Look here," he said, and Maggie stepped up beside him, her arms still crossed.

The reliquaries of Celtic and English saints—Bridget, Aidan, Ninian, Alban, Edmund, Dunstan—breathed blessedness into the room. Amongst them rested a box with enameled sides. "A reliquary of St. Thomas Becket."

"One of David's bones?" Maggie asked.

"Yes. This is truly a souvenir of death. Of sin and the search for redemption." He closed the cabinet and turned to face her.

Now she looked at him, perhaps finding the simplicity of the long white alb he wore beneath the chasuble less intimidating. "So now your chapel's ready for the big event on New Year's Eve. Rose and Mick and I ought to be here, but we're signed up for the concert at Canterbury that night—and it seems only right we should be in Canterbury the twenty-ninth . . ."

Something cold and hard as a steel blade punctured Thomas's heart, so that his elation gushed away like blood from an artery. Redemption. How could he have overlooked such an obvious point?

"What did I say?" Maggie asked. "Oh no, I reminded you that December twenty-ninth is your saint's day. The day David was murdered. And so close to the New Year, too."

Envisioning his own face, blasted blank and bare, he steadied himself. "Indeed, December twenty-ninth is approaching, but that isn't what gave me such a turn. I suddenly saw what an unwarranted assumption I've been making. Is this the place where I am to reveal the relics? It may not be, Maggie. It may not be at all."

She looked round, at the rood and the screen and the cabinet. At the sunlight spilling through the southern windows, promising spring to come. "Why not? This is your place."

"Yes, it is. I meant this chapel as evidence of my devotion.

What if it is evidence of my pride? How can I speak of redemption when I have not yet . . ." His ear caught the sound of a man's voice. "Who is Rose speaking with?"

Maggie frowned. "Let's go see."

Rose ran water into the kettle and set it on the electric ring. She lined the sacred vessels up on the cabinet. Gold didn't tarnish. That's why reliquaries were made of it, incorruptible gold for the incorruptible saints. "Lo how a rose e'er blooming . . ."

Dunstan had sat in the doorway during the service. She was sure he had genuflected along with the congregation. Now, though, he was curled on the seat of the large chair, picking his teeth with a claw. Well, she'd read that incense was a mind-altering drug.

Some water was left in one of the cruets. Rose poured it into the bowl holding the wine, the salt, and the ashes for the actual consecration. Thomas had looked like he stepped out of the rood screen, his pale skin radiant. That was what a saint did, after all—bring light into darkness. *"Gaudete, gaudete, Christus est natus ex Maria virgine, gaudete."*

Pouring the hot water in a second bowl, she added a squirt of detergent. The heavy gold vessels, the paten, the ciborium, the chalice, went into the suds and then onto a clean dishtowel.

Maggie had watched Thomas celebrate the mass with, for once, every emotion written clear as the sound of St. Bridget's bell across her face. She wanted him, and she wanted the healing he stood for, and she knew she couldn't have both. She'd been twenty, too, once, as eager for experience as Rose was, and yet something had gone terribly wrong.

Intellectually Rose understood that happy endings weren't guaranteed, but emotionally, darn it, she was rooting for one. For all of them. "O come O come Emmanuel, to ransom captive Israel."

She took both bowls outside and emptied them onto the grass. Was that someone standing in the garden gate? No, no one was there. She was jumpy. Big surprise.

Back inside, she dried the vessels and remembered the two nights in Fortingall, the supple curve of Mick's mouth, his musician's hands, his heart beating against her breast and the fire burning down to embers like a prologue to her fantasy. They'd chosen a relationship. If they worked at it nothing would go wrong. He'd be here in just a few more days . . . "God rest ye merry gentlemen let nothing you dismay . . ."

"Rose." She spun around.

Mick was standing behind her. She could see every seam in his jeans, every stitch in his sweater, every wave of his hair. No, thinking of Mick wouldn't make him appear. And this Mick, this image of Mick, wasn't wearing his mother's blue cross from Iona. His gray eyes were cold as iron. "You!" she exclaimed, and groped for words—"go to hell" wasn't going to cut it—"Mary, blessed among women, open my eyes."

Mick's face and body wavered sickeningly into Robin's. He was dressed in a classy suit and silk tie, like he'd dropped in on his way to an executive meeting. "How dare you," he said, "sing and smile whilst cleaning those dishes? The dishes that commemorate a vile blood sacrifice?"

No way she was going to argue theology with him. "I'm making a joyful noise unto the Lord."

"And all around you people are suffering." He clucked his tongue.

"Yeah right. Like you don't have anything to do with people suffering."

"I don't set impossible standards for *my* congregations, I make them happy by telling them what they want to hear."

"Just because you want to hear it doesn't mean it's right."

"Haven't you tired yet of your self-righteousness, Rose?"

"Me? Self-righteous?"

"Your all-too-conspicuous virtue is growing tiresome." Robin stepped closer, backing her against the cabinet. His voice dropped into a malicious purr. "I can have your body any time I wish, you know that. But why bother? Physical virginity is cheap. What I shall have off you is your faith."

Rose shivered. "No. I choose my faith, freely."

Dunstan's face peeked over the arm of the chair, ears back. The outside door opened. "Oh," said Ellen, like she'd just been punched in the stomach.

Robin's head snapped toward her.

"You told me to watch them and I'm watching, aren't I?" Ellen gabbled. "You don't need her!"

"Like I need *him?*" Rose demanded. "No, by St. Mary and St. Bridget and every holy relic, no, I reject him and everything he stands for. If that's self-righteousness then I'll do my penance for it."

Robin looked back at Rose. "Yes, you will," he said quietly. Brushing Ellen aside, he went out the door and slammed it behind him.

Whoa, Rose thought. A normal exit. But he wanted to keep Ellen ignorant, didn't he? She looked like death on toast. Worse. Death on a Belgian waffle. "No, you can't have him. He's mine. I'm his."

Among anger, revulsion, and pity, Rose chose pity. "He's just using you."

"I believe in Robin, the redeemer come in the last days."

"Sure," Rose said, "but does he believe in you?"

Ellen stared for a long count of five, then blundered from the cottage into the light of day.

There was Thomas, standing inside the inner door, in his

alb looking like a tall white candle. Beside him Maggie glared. "Beautifully done," he said, and Maggie added, "Class act, Rose."

"Thanks." *But,* she told herself, *something can always go wrong.*

Ellen had waited in the lobby of Safeway's for an hour now. Outside dark day was going on for darker night, the sky thick with clouds that were too tired to rain but simply pressed down, heavier and heavier. She remembered the candles in Anna's candlestick, the menorah, she called it, throwing a soft light against the dining room paneling. Right pretty, even if it was heathen rubbish. She remembered Rose singing three days ago, singing like it was possible to be happy, now, at the end of the world.

There! Shoving a woman aside, Ellen raced out the door and leaped into the green Jaguar. Save for that dreadful moment in Thomas's cottage, she hadn't seen Robin since the day of the tornado, over a month ago. She reached toward him.

He looked her up and down, his mouth a thin line, like the slit beneath a locked door. She dropped her arms, ashamed of acting needy.

He drove the car to a far corner of the car park, beside the dust bins, and stopped. There wasn't going to be any sex, then. They didn't do it in the car any more, not after she'd been so clumsy in that layby . . . If he didn't want sex from her, maybe he was getting it from someone else.

Robin's fingertips drummed the steering wheel. His eyes flashed through lowered lashes and his scowl was brutal. He wasn't half narked, was he? But she'd caught him out with Rose, not the other way round. He hadn't called in since Mum died.

"What's on at Temple Manor?" he asked.

"The traitor and the Americans came in from the north on the second."

"Did Thomas have the artifact with him?"

"The artifact?"

"A big black stone."

"The Stone? I thought we had that one, alongside the Book. Two for us, and one to go."

"Why trouble ourselves shifting it, when they can do the shifting for us? It's part of my plan to bring all three artifacts together. Do you know where he's put it?"

Ellen shrank away. Was it something she'd said? If everything was going along according to plan then it must've been something she said. "I'll look it out for you," she said quickly.

He nodded, and his scowl eased a bit.

Encouraged, she said, "My mum died. Took too much medicine, she did. 'Twas an accident. Mum took care of me. She brought me salves and such for my hand. It's healing up proper now." She raised her hand. The bandage was stained with blood. "She went to heaven, didn't she, Robin?"

"Haven't you learned by now that only members of the Foundation will enter heaven?"

"Yes, Robin." And viciously she squashed that echo of her mother's voice, *I only ever wanted what was best for you.* "You were talking to Rose in the traitor's cottage. She told Anna you'd been at her before, but . . ."

"If you believe anything that little bint says, then I feel sorry for you." His hand snaked out and grasped her arm, tight. But his look of utter contempt hurt worse. "All I'm hearing from you is questions and doubt. Do you deny my Word? Are you some sort of nutter like Vivian? Something's gone wrong with you, is that it?"

Tears of pain sprang to her eyes. She swallowed them

down. *Mustn't blub*. He wouldn't comfort her, not like Sean did do. Robin was strong.

"Are you after betraying me as Calum did do? Do you want to risk your immortal soul by defying my word?"

"No, no, never." Even his fury was cold. "I've been watching the traitor and the others, just as you said."

"When they have their days out, or just at the house?"

The last time she'd gone away with them she'd seen Robin himself drawing down the wrath of God . . . Oh no, hadn't she done right? "They're off to Bath Saturday, and Stonehenge Tuesday, I'll ride along, see if I don't."

"See that you do." His voice was satin-smooth. Dropping her arm, he ran his gloved fingertip down the side of her face. The leather was cold. The car was cold. The windows fogged over, so that the shoppers pushing their trolleys were only smears of color. In the orange light of the street lamps Robin's red hair was the color of dried blood.

Ellen's hand felt numb. So much fresh red blood was seeping through the bandage a drop fell onto her jeans. His lip curled in disgust and he pushed her away. "I have work for you to do, Ellen."

Oh, Ellen thought, sick with relief. He wanted her after all. If she could do this right, then Mum didn't die for nothing. Even though Mum was gone, and Calum was gone, Robin would be with her always. Save for funerals, that is. "Yes, yes, Robin. Tell me what needs doing."

He leaned so close the cool breeze of his breath tickled her cheeks and raised gooseflesh on the back of her neck.

Chapter Thirty-five

After three days of sullen clouds, stubborn winds, and several varieties of precipitation, frozen and otherwise, Maggie took Thursday's clear, quiet evening as an omen. This was it. Now or never.

She didn't ask herself what she was doing. She knew. Choosing truth and trust couldn't be any more painful than living a lie. If she'd learned nothing else from Thomas over the last six weeks or so, it was that. And that even stubbornness had its limits.

Carrying a plastic bag filled with warm cookies, she shut the door firmly behind her and strode off through the courtyard. Perfect timing—Thomas was emerging from the Puckles' station wagon. Maggie intercepted him outside the garden. "Lovely evening, isn't it?"

He smiled. " 'No thought, no action, no movement, total stillness; only thus can one at last become one with heaven and earth.' "

"One of the psalms?" Maggie hazarded.

"Lao Tzu." Thomas opened the door of the cottage for her.

She kept returning to the cottage, moving inward to the center of the labyrinth. Why shouldn't the center of the labyrinth be a cozy room filled with books and a cat dozing on the hearth? Maggie paid homage to Dunstan while Thomas poked the fire into a blaze.

"What do I smell?" he asked. "Ah, biscuits!"

"Cookies, please—biscuits are lumps of flour and lard, vehicles for honey or gravy. Rose's folks sent cookie cutters, and we didn't think Bess would mind our taking over her kitchen and laughing."

"She'd be delighted." Thomas chose a bell-shaped cookie and munched. "Ah, the blessings of cinnamon and vanilla upon the tongue."

The tongue that cannot lie? Maggie asked herself. "You should've seen Sean and Ellen inhaling cookies and milk like kindergartners."

"And how is Ellen faring?"

"Like an abused animal. You want to help, but she might bite."

Thomas shook his head sadly. "And Rose?"

"Thoroughly spooked. Afraid of Robin, afraid for Mick."

"Robin's emotional threat can be worse than his physical. Whiskey?"

"Ah, no, not tonight, thank you." Maggie's stomach was already uneasy. She wondered why the expression was, "get it off your chest," when "get it off your stomach" was anatomically correct. "So what saint's day is today?"

"On December sixteenth we celebrate Saint Sophia, Holy Wisdom. An aspect of the Lady."

"We could use some holy wisdom. Catholics bombed a Protestant church outside Belfast, so Protestants burned a Catholic church. Arabs and Jews got into it in Bethlehem—rocks, rubber bullets, you know the drill. And back home a skinhead tattooed with 'Jesus Saves' beat a homosexual to death."

"Robin's allies are formidable adversaries."

"And our score is tied, one to one. How about the tie-breaker?"

"The third relic? Next Tuesday, I think, we shall remove it from its hiding place. On the winter solstice, the shortest day of the year."

"That's your birthday."

"Yes." With his forefinger Thomas wiped away a smudge of flour on her cheek. Suddenly shy, she dropped her eyes. He turned away, and flipped through his tape collection. "Bach? Debussy? Hildegarde von Bingen?"

"Silence would be nice." Maggie plunked her pillow down on the floor.

"Very good then." Thomas lit a squat candle sitting in a dish on the table and turned off the light. "Excuse my indulgence in nostalgia."

"You've lived most of your life in world lit only by fire."

"Whilst I would be the last to scorn the virtues of electricity, I must admit that at times its light can be overly harsh. Even though we use the metaphor of darkness to describe evil, shadow can be very sympathetic."

He knows why I'm here, Maggie told herself. The odors of smoke and beeswax hung on the air, mingling with a suggestion of cinnamon, a scent so heady it should be a controlled substance. Like truth serum.

With a sigh, Thomas sat down in the chair. "Once I thought the Scottish Highlands to be a fearsome wilderness. Now they're picturesque. Once I thought the crossbow to be the most dreadful invention of mankind. Now I should like to arm the soldiers of the world with nothing but crossbows. History is a very uneven stumble, but I do think we are inching closer to enlightenment."

"So far." Maggie stroked Dunstan, eliciting a rumbling purr, and kept herself from leaning against Thomas's leg as she usually did.

"What I was about to tell you on Sunday, before we heard Robin speaking with Rose, is that in all these long years I've never returned to Canterbury. I think now that I shall not be redeemed until I do, and there accept at last the full measure of absolution."

"Come with us, if that would help."

"Thank you." His hand squeezed her shoulder and retreated. "You're wearing your red jumper."

"Oh." She glanced down. The sweater glinted blood red beneath the shadow-pattern cast by the interlace of the cross.

"Red is the color of martyrs. Of passion. Of Christ's Passion. Of the Magdalene, the original 'scarlet woman.' It takes courage to eat of the tree of knowledge, but we are not fully human until we do."

She leaned gingerly back against the corner of the chair. "And then we get Christianity. Judgmentalism. Guilt."

"No, no." Again his hand fell firmly upon her shoulder, and this time it stayed. "Christianity is the resolution of guilt. The contrition that leads one to confession, penance, redemption, and joy. Even the *Dies Irae*, the Wrath of God, is at heart a plea for mercy. It is God's role to judge. Not yours. Not mine."

Pressing her lips together, Maggie watched the flames dance in that alchemy of light and dark that created shadows. The light sparked in her eyes. Damn it, she'd known his compassion would make her cry. "It's stupid, but all I want is to love and be loved."

"There's nothing stupid about loving." His hand caressed her hair. "I love you, Maggie."

She knew her face was as red as her sweater. The tears bloated her chest to bursting. "You love everyone, Thomas. It's your job."

"It's my choice. And I choose to love you more than on principle."

"You wouldn't, not if you knew me."

"If I knew why Robin was taunting you the night of the Guy Fawkes Festival? But how could I not guess?"

Robin told her faith wouldn't save her. But how many

360

leaps of faith had she already made, with her heart if not her mind? Didn't she know better than to listen to Robin?

"Like you, my pride keeps me from surrendering," Thomas said. "My pride murdered a man. It led me to spend many lifetimes, if not lying about the murder, at least concealing its truth. Being unfaithful to my own identity. I pray that soon I can at last make atonement not only for my crime, but for my pridefulness. At-one-ment, the wholeness that comes from accepting your own imperfect humanity."

The words, the tears, squirmed in her chest.

Thomas's fingertips stroked her cheek. " 'For out of the abundance of the heart the mouth speaks.' "

As if drawn by that touch the tears burst from her chest and flowed down her face. Like mud, like sludge, like lava from the deep earth's core, thick and hot. "It hurts," she said, her voice trembling.

"Lancing a wound always hurts. But pain comes before healing."

"Yes." The tears clogged her throat and she sobbed. Thomas's hand appeared in her peripheral vision, offering his handkerchief. A square of crisp, clean linen, like a priest's robe. Priests conducted rituals of connection. She mopped her face. "I never thought that marriage and an intellectual life would be mutually exclusive. I mean, Danny was very supportive—you go ahead and get that advanced degree, you can make a bigger salary that way."

"He didn't match you intellectually?"

"No, but it's really petty to say so. And there was more to it, like the never-ending snide remarks because I kept my maiden name."

"How long were you married?"

"Fifteen years."

"One can hardly accuse you of not trying to make it work."

Dunstan stretched. Maggie blinked—gauzy wings made slow figure eights above his sleek fur and then settled, disappearing. The tears caught in her lashes making prisms, no doubt. "We just didn't speak the same language. For a while we fought all the time. Then we stopped even trying. I came home one afternoon because I felt horrible—a cold, a nervous breakdown, whatever—and there was Danny with Melissa, one of my students."

The tears ran again. She sponged and sniffed. "I lost it. I screamed, I swore, I threw things. Melissa dropped out of school rather than face me. Danny said it was my fault for turning frigid on him—like I wasn't burning up inside. Then I went off to a conference in Boston. Anthony was there. One of those guys who looks like a Ken doll, too handsome to be real."

"Aware that his smile makes him look good?"

"Not like your smile, which makes me feel good." Maggie squirmed. "I'd known Anthony for ages. We'd flirted. Big deal. But that night we had sex. We didn't make love, we had sex. You think if I was going to break a Commandment I'd do it out of love instead of spite. But no.

"Then Anthony commented that he always went off to conventions hoping to get lucky. Did that make me feel like a worm or what? He's married, too, by the way. Just to double the felony. The sin. Not that chastity was my strong point before marriage—estrogen overload, low self-esteem, weak morals, acting out—take your pick. But I could at least have honored my marriage vows."

She took another deep breath. Funny, how empty her chest felt. Her head lolled heavily back against Thomas's leg. Instead of slapping her silly he caressed her hair again. "I was so ashamed I thought, okay, Danny and I have both made mistakes, we'll forgive each other and go on. So I confessed to him. He looked at me like I had leprosy, moved out, and filed for divorce. It became final last Sunday."

"Ah," Thomas said. "I see."

Her tear ducts should've been drained, but no, here came a fresh spate. She was going to subside into a puddle there on the hearth, boneless, gutless, leaving Thomas to get a mop and bucket and wash her away. "That's my Story, and a tacky one it is, too. I can't even sin with distinction."

"I have too much respect for you to scorn even your sin. I know very well that mankind has a deplorable tendency to lead with the genitalia rather than the heart."

"Yeah, well, celibacy is an unattainable ideal for most of us."

"Celibacy means giving the gift of sexuality back to God, thereby centering oneself on the Holy Spirit. For we are made in His image, Maggie. The lure of the flesh is powerful but it isn't evil, not when it's tempered with the heart's affection. It was the breaking of your vow that was the sin, and your damaging the integrity of your soul."

The heart's affection. The integrity of your soul. She liked those ideas. She like his hand on her head, his fingers laced in her hair.

"Now. You have admitted you did wrong, and you have resolved never to do so again. But not until you ask for forgiveness, and forgive, can you be restored to the grace of God which you have been trying your hardest to reject, and yet which is there for you even so."

That subtle crackle was either the fire or the ramparts of her ego crumbling into dust. *Holy Spirit strong when my flesh is weak—from the world, the flesh and the Devil make me anew—when I open my heart to you* . . . Heedless of her smudged and swollen face Maggie looked up at him. "I forgive Danny. I forgive Anthony. I forgive my poor pathetic self. God help me and take me back, yes."

Thomas extended his hand. "Come here."

She crawled to her feet. By turning sideways and folding her legs over his she managed to fit into the chair beside him. She worked her left arm behind his back and laid her head on his shoulder. Like a child with a parent. Like lover with lover.

On the hearth Dunstan stirred, stretched, and began to bathe himself. Each lick of his pink tongue sounded like a drop of water—the quality of mercy dropping as a gentle rain from heaven. Again tears welled from Maggie's eyes, not grief but gratitude. Thomas's thumb touched her cheeks, collecting the tears, and with them made the sign of the cross on her forehead. The dampness glowed hot and cold.

"In the Greek, the word 'baptism' means catharsis," he told her.

"It would."

"*Ego te absolvo.* If you'll accept absolution from such as me."

"Oh, yes."

"*Pax domini sit semper tecum.*"

The peace of God be with you always—in his first life the peace of God not only meant an actual kiss, it guaranteed a contract—when he'd come out of his vision at Old Sarum he'd given her the kiss of peace. She looked into his face, each eye lit by a tiny flame, the curve of his mouth no longer haughty as a Norman arch but soft as a Celtic hillside. *He's not going to . . .*

Thomas kissed her mouth. Firmly, with a passion even more stirring for being controlled. Her breath stopped, then started again. She'd wanted to suckle the truth from his eloquent tongue. She'd needed to. And now she did, reveling in vanilla and cinnamon, incense and smoke. His lips and tongue were gentle, delicate, subtle. She kissed him back, giving him fervor for delicacy, and soaked pore by pore into his being.

When they at last separated she lay back against his shoulder in utter contentment. *I've been going about physical intimacy all wrong,* she thought, *throwing my body into the ring first and leaving mind, heart, and soul to play catch-up.* And now, past hope, she'd fallen in love so deeply she wondered if she'd ever known the meaning of the word. Fallen for not only a priest, but a saint—which might be safer than falling for an ordinary man, but which also proved God wrote divine comedy.

Thomas murmured, "Her lips suck forth my soul."

"Shakespeare?"

"Marlowe. Dr. Faustus, inappropriately."

She smiled. "The love you take is equal to the love you make."

"Eliot?"

"The Beatles."

With a chuckle, Thomas pulled off his glasses and squinted at them. Maggie could see the smudges made by her skin on the glass. She offered him the wet, crumpled ball of his handkerchief, grimaced, took it back again. He shrugged and set the glasses down by the chair.

Dunstan scrutinized their intertwined limbs. Maybe he was sending an alarm through the Pearly Gates—got a back-slider here, mobilize the seraphim. "You're not going to go off on a guilt trip?" she asked. "You know, put on a hair shirt and moan about Lancelot betraying his king for a woman?"

"For a queen," Thomas corrected. "I cannot believe that acknowledging the power and mystery of the physical world with one kiss is a betrayal of any sort."

"Not like this it's not, no."

His smile deflated into a sigh. "I must confess myself to

you as well, Maggie. I implied that I wanted to die. But now—now I want to live. Even if I were never to see you again, I would want to know that somewhere in this world you lived, joyful in the presence of God. For to me, Maggie, you are a pearl beyond price."

Maggie watched his lips forming the words she'd been dreading.

"But loving my life may well make its sacrifice all the more necessary. Because giving up something that has little value is no sacrifice . . ." His voice caught and broke.

She snugged her arms around him, willing her heart to beat in the same rhythm as his. "I love you. That's my penance, isn't it? Knowing that I might lose you just as I've found you."

"I'm sorry," he returned, his breath tickling her temple, "that your love might bring you pain as well as redemption. Might. I don't know."

"I think we're going to have to pray not for a happy ending but for the right ending. As Eliot's Becket said . . ."

". . . I have consented." He cupped her face in his strong, capable, kind hand. He leaned forward so that his forehead touched hers. His lips moved an inch from her own, making Word and Flesh and Spirit into one. "Set me as a seal upon thy heart, for love is as strong as death."

"Yes," Maggie said.

Dunstan slept. The flames died. Beyond the Word, the Lady had said, beyond the Blood, lay silence. But Maggie had never heard silence before. A rock thrown into the silence of this room would take a full minute to hit bottom. A minute in which eternities rose and flourished and passed away. A minute of infinite grace.

This is now. Maggie lay back in Thomas's arms, secure in the peace of God which passed all understanding. *This is forever.*

Chapter Thirty-six

Considering the long night of his own soul, Thomas thought, December twenty-first made an apt day of birth. He might have owed his name to that day being the feast day of St. Thomas, but the fact that this apostle was called Doubting Thomas was perhaps less than chance.

Rose contemplated the last morsel of her steak pie and pushed it away. "So Robin sent Ellen back into the ring with us, huh?"

"I wonder what else he's been up to recently?" Maggie emptied the teapot.

"Taking advantage of the season," said Thomas. "A priest molesting the children of his parish, evangelist fund-raisers brought up on charges of embezzlement . . . Well, one understands why even such intelligent individuals as Willie Armstrong choose atheism."

"Mick never called back to say what Willie wanted," Rose said, "just that he'd left a message telling Mick to call him ASAP. Something about the Book, I guess, but I was hoping Mick would be here with us tonight."

"He'll be with us tomorrow," Thomas told her. "For now, we must leave the lads to their own resources and God's help. Shall we go?"

The two women donned their coats, hats, gloves, and scarves like knights girding themselves for battle. Leaving the warmth of The Rifleman's Arms, they walked with Thomas into the foggy night.

The longest, darkest night of the year, he thought, a New

Year's of a sort. He remembered spring lambs, midsummer poppies, a kingfisher above the Brue, deer on the stubble and curlews on the marsh. Now the Earth had once again completed its journey round the heavens, meting out the stages of existence. Of eternity. Of his life.

Once away from the orange glow of the street lamps, like candles guttering for lack of air, Thomas switched on his torch. The diffused light made the surrounding trees look like charcoal sketches on a gray background. The mud of the path muffled their footsteps. Another gate, and the trees ended. The path led gently upward, across an open field now concealed by the fog. At its far side they crossed a stile. "Here we are at the base of the Tor," Thomas said.

"Weird," said Rose. "You can feel it even though you can't see it."

Yes, the great conical upwelling of earth, a high place where earth and sky wed, loomed over them. "Like the Eildon Hills, the Tor is *locus terribilis*. As long as the relics are safe, Robin cannot tread this ground. But even at night his spies might could see us here, so this fog is an unexpected blessing."

"You specialize in following paths into obscurity," said Maggie.

"I always find light at the end. Note the marker stone behind the bench." Thomas climbed onto the first steep incline of the Tor proper. "The labyrinth may have been here since long before the birth of Our Lord, shaped from a hill by the same religious impulse that constructed such sacred sites as Avebury and Stonehenge. Then, like so many such things, it was forgotten until believers cared to search for it."

Rose's voice was muffled by her scarf. "Like the Zodiac?"

"The Glastonbury Zodiac is a product of recent wishful thinking rather than of ancient topographical features."

"Faith is a product of wishful thinking," Maggie commented.

Thank God, Thomas thought, *that the rebirth of her faith hasn't stilled her well-honed tongue*—whose felicities were of the flesh as well as the word.

"So when did *you* first figure out that the Tor is a three-dimensional labyrinth?" asked Rose.

"Soon after I bought Temple Manor. I'd viewed the hints in the Old Church in my original life, when rumor had it that the stone pavement contained some holy secret. Romano-British work, I thought, but parts of it could have been much older. It certainly suggested a pre-Christian geometrical awareness, even to my unenlightened mind." Thomas paused. The fog distorted his perceptions, making the familiar path seem strange.

Ah, yes. "This way." They moved off again. "A sixth century Greek, Hecataeus, wrote of a spiral temple here—perhaps to Apollo and his mother. And the Celtic myth of *Caer Sidi* tells of a spiral castle that guards the entrance to the Underworld."

"So after you met the Lady," Maggie said, "you suspected there was an entrance to—well, to another dimension—here, too."

"To *Annwn,* the Welsh Underworld. Or *Tir nan Og,* the Otherworld, an island, as the Tor has often been during times of flood. When I arrived here during the latter part of the fourteenth century, I was obliged to conceal the Cup. Since the Story of the Grail is rooted in Celtic myth, where better than in Annwn?" Thomas's torch picked out the second marker stone. "Now we turn along the terrace. Slowly, the way can be both narrow and vertiginous."

The light of the torch picked out snowy patches, muddy spots, and broken and weathered grass. To the left the slope fell precipitously into nothingness. To the right the embankment rose just as precipitously upward into a darkly gleaming mist.

Here, at the precipitous east end of the Tor, the path kinked. Thomas was obliged to cast to and fro until he picked up the terrace again. They stepped carefully along the northern side of the hill and found themselves a short distance above the marker stone where they'd started. "First circuit."

"You haven't been back inside in six hundred years?" Maggie asked.

"I've threaded the labyrinth many times—some prayer is a laying on of hands, this is a laying on of feet—but I've never gone back inside, no." Thomas led them down and then along the terrace immediately below the one they'd just traversed.

"Whoa!" Rose exclaimed. Maggie grabbed her hand, steadying her until she regained her footing.

"The path is uncertain here," said Thomas. "We must stay inside the fence, even though the terrace is actually outside it. Have a care."

After a good twenty minutes of picking their way, they came out just above the bench and the lower marker stone. "Second circuit." Thomas set a slow pace along the path at the very bottom of the slope, beside the fringe of the woods, at the perimeter of the labyrinth. At one point they had to divert back to the second path, the lower one disappearing into the surrounding fields, but before long they were back at the ascending route not far above the bench and the stone.

"That's three circuits." Nothing like taking brisk exercise on a cold night—he could hear the breathing of the women mingled with his own. Beyond that the silence was profound, as though the town, the countryside, the world itself had disappeared behind the curtain of fog, not a wrack left behind. A faint scent of smoke hung on the air, but from what fires he couldn't say. "Shall we press on?"

He led the way upwards, past another stone and onto a path that meandered off to the right. The fog seemed a bit thinner here, less a curtain than a veil. That suggestion of rectangular solidity in the darkness above must be the tower at the peak of the Tor. "Excavations have shown a succession of forts atop the Tor, the last dating from Saxon times."

"Where else," said Rose, "would you build . . . Watch it!"

Maggie scrambled and grasped Thomas's coat. "Sorry."

"Feel free," he told her, pulling her up by her arm. "Just a few more yards and we'll find another terrace . . . Here we are."

Twice more he had to pause and consider his path. But still he felt his way onward. In due course they returned to the ascending route at the upper marker stone. "Four circuits," he declared.

"Look," Maggie said.

Through the mist appeared the softly glowing orb of the full moon. A hush lay over earth and heaven alike. The air itself seemed solid as glass. *Caer Sidi,* thought Thomas. *Caer Wydr,* the glass castle, yet another portal. *Ynys Witrin,* the Isle of Glass. The Isle of Avalon.

"The world in solemn stillness lay, to hear the angels sing," Rose murmured.

Thomas smiled. "The circuits are shorter this high up. Come along."

They climbed the ascending route onto the shoulder of the hill and emerged from the last clinging tendrils of mist. Now the moon-circle appeared hard and bright, a window cut in the obsidian of night and adorned with a scattering of jewel-like stars. Billows of fog glistened in its light, shrouding house, street, automobile. Shrouding the twentieth and twenty-first centuries. The top of the Tor was an island in time and space.

"Wow," Rose said.

"It's magic," said Maggie.

The tower loomed close above, a dark masculine vertical rising from the glistening feminine curve of the hill. "Mind your step," Thomas said softly. They passed another bench, and turned left along a ridge not far below the tower. Behind it, at the most precipitous part of the hill, Thomas took first Maggie's and then Rose's hand and guided them onto a lower terrace. A flight of steps and a circular track just below the flat ground where the tower stood brought them back to the main path. "Fifth circuit."

"Isn't this where the last abbot of Glastonbury was judicially murdered by Henry VIII?" asked Maggie.

"Richard Whiting, an aged and gentle man, was done to death with two of his monks—one of whom was named Arthur. The gallows was set up just there, where tomorrow that cresset will hold a solstice bonfire." Thomas's gesture toward the black shape of the fire-basket on a pole retracted into the sign of the Cross. "It was a cold November day, the wind sobbing through the doors of the church. The lands below lay hazy and gray, like repudiated legend. The commissioner who watched as the head was struck from Whiting's body and mounted above the Abbey gates had red hair."

For a long moment Rose and Maggie stood silent. Then Thomas said, "A cautionary tale, yes, but this place is haunted less by it than by echoes of life ever-blooming. Lift up your hearts—we're almost there."

In silence the women followed him back down the main path to the brink of a sharp slope and then around to the left, just above an exposed area of rock and sandy soil. Once again

Thomas helped them climb the kink. Back at the ascending path he announced, "Sixth circuit. One more," and led them down and to the right. Past the kink they went, and a row of trees and a muddy spot covered with nettles. They found themselves standing at the bottom of the exposed area, upon a patch of snow.

Save it wasn't snow. They stood amongst white flowers growing thickly together. Flowers which glowed. The face of the Tor shimmered and thinned into a curtain that parted before them.

"Very good," Thomas breathed. "Shall we go in?"

He had to prod Maggie forward with his torch, and grasp Rose's sleeve to hold her back, but inside they went, to a staircase of hewn stones. The air was cool, but warmer than the icy night outside, and smelled not only of the deep earth but of spices. Voices ebbed and swelled like the murmur of the sea. Thomas switched off his torch. "Down."

They walked down the spiral staircase. The walls were of closely set stones like the pavement of the Old Church, save these stones glowed like parchment lit from behind. At the foot of the stair the pavement crossed a stone bridge above a stream of dark green water. Beyond the bridge a bronze mist filled some vast but undefined space . . . The mist parted. A man and a woman walked along hand in hand, smiling over a private joke. "Calum and Maddy Dewar," whispered Rose. "Mick showed me pictures."

Behind them came Bess Puckle, talking animatedly with Vivian Morgan. "My God," said Maggie, "they're . . ."

". . . reflections," Thomas told her.

A horse trotted through the gauzy light. Its rider's armor was dented but his face was bright and eager. He closed his visor, set his lance, and spurred the massive horse onward in a drumroll of hoofbeats. A dragon stirred and woke, its scales gleaming in jasper, lapis, sapphire, carnelian. Then knight, rider, dragon—all were gone.

Another knight, this one older, dragged a woman across the pavement. Her long flaxen braid swung back and forth as she struggled. Melwas, king of Somerset, abducting Guinevere to his palace on the Tor . . . Arthur stepped from the mist, an Arthur with Thomas's own face. Excalibur gleamed in one hand, his other extended toward a Guinevere who looked suddenly like Maggie—and they, too, were gone.

A man in a monk's robe emerged from the shadows, clutching an earthenware flask. Before him the mist rolled up and vanished, exposing a hall lined with stone pillars. Brightly-clad men and women sat at long tables, laughing and feasting and throwing tidbits to several cats and dogs. On a dais sat a powerfully-built red-bearded man wearing a crown. Thomas felt both Maggie and Rose tense. He said, "That is Gwyn ap Nudd, King of Faerie, Lord of the Underworld. The monk is St. Collen, a hermit who had a cell on the slopes of the Tor."

Each luminous face—for good reason were they called "the Fair Folk"—turned toward Collen. Gwyn stood, raising a cautious hand.

"Demons!" Collen scattered water from his flask.

For just a moment the voices stopped. Then Gwyn threw back his head and laughed, a rich bass laugh that had in it thunder and deep waters and solid rock. Collen shrank into the mist filling the spaces between the pillars.

"Oh," said Maggie. "If Gwyn and his court weren't demons then holy water wouldn't have much effect, would it?" Musicians began playing a subtle melody on flute and harp. "I know that music."

"That's the tune Mick heard at the Eildons," said Rose.

The deep note of a bell vibrated in the stone itself. From

the dais a wisp of vapor spiraled upward and became the Lady, a red-haired Lady wearing a gold torc and a plaid caught by a jeweled brooch. She turned toward Thomas, Maggie, and Rose, opening her arms.

At her feet appeared a steaming cauldron. Nine young women walked from the glistening shadows and paced solemnly around it. Every face reflected Rose's, bright, clear, radiant with intelligence. The original Rose gasped. "It's Ceridwen."

Or perhaps it was an image of Mary in her blue cloak, light shining from her brow. She picked up the cauldron and it contracted to a small shape, so bright Thomas winced to look at it. A knight with Mick's face knelt before it, his head thrown back, his gray eyes reflecting the light of the woman's halo and of the Grail itself. Galahad, who saw the Grail at a Mass of the Glorious Mother of God.

Suddenly the hall went silent, empty save for the Lady. Gwyn, his court, the maidens, the tables and the foodstuffs—all had vanished as utterly as last winter's snow. A cold wind blew away the fragrances of flowers and food. With one last keen look from her earth-deep brown eyes, the Lady set the shining object down and faded into the darkening mist.

Curls of vapor crept across the floor and down from the ceiling. A box sat upon the stone pavement of the dais, gleaming faintly, like a moon rather than a sun. Thomas walked forward and picked it up. It was the olivewood box he himself had fashioned long years past.

Maggie and Rose waited by the bridge whilst he returned back down the hall, the mist closing in at his heels. "We should be going."

"Yeah," said Maggie dazedly.

Rose was grinning from ear to ear. "Awesome! Totally awesome!"

They climbed the spiral staircase, darkness following at their heels. In a small, damp, stone-lined chamber at the top of the stairs Thomas pushed open a stone slab and one by one they stepped out into night. "Where?" Maggie began, and then saw the empty archways to either side. "Oh. The room at the base of the tower."

Moonlight silvered the fog below and the heavens above, illuminating the carving of St. Bridget in the side of the tower. To the north rose the black bulwark of the Mendip Hills. To the southwest the mount of Chalice Hill resembled a whale, a hint of substance beneath the surface of a misty sea.

Thomas looked from Maggie's face to Rose's, and smiled tenderly at each. A glance at his watch showed that it had gone midnight. The witching hour. The cusp of a new day. Of a new year.

"Now what?" Rose asked at last.

"We go from the center out, although I should suggest instead of threading the labyrinth again we simply go straight down and home."

"Just like a man," teased Maggie.

"How do we know home is still down there?" Rose asked. "What if we come out in 1256 or 1702 or 2138, for that matter?"

Thomas tucked the box under one arm and switched on the torch. "I should think it is still the threshold year of 2000, otherwise there would have been no point to our retrieving the Cup."

Leaving the silent radiance of the moon behind, they entered the fog, walked down the slope, and returned to the world. Streetlights still glowed orange. A few cars traversed the streets. The mini-bus sat in the Chalice Well car park where Maggie had left it. They piled inside and sat shivering whilst she switched on the engine.

Chapter Thirty-seven

Thomas's fingertips quivered with the faint but unmistakable chord that emanated from the box he held. Here it was, again in his hands, exposed to the world and its dangers. He was elated. He was grateful for his companions. He was bone-weary of his everlasting task.

"How did you get the Cup to begin with?" Rose asked.

Maggie switched on the heater. A breath of warm air touched Thomas's face. "From people who never perceived it as a sacred relic."

"The Cathars," Maggie said, "who denied Christ's humanity."

"They led relatively ascetic lives, and did not go about torturing their neighbors over points of doctrine. There is something to be said, I suppose, about refusing the symbolism of the blood."

The lights of the town streamed by the windows of the car like sparks thrown from a bonfire. "The Inquisition was started," said Rose, "to root out the Cathar—well, they said it was heresy."

"The Templars refused to join in the Albigensian Crusade. Our refusal tainted us with heresy as well. In 1244 many Cathar leaders were besieged in their fortress at Montsegur. I volunteered to act as mediator but failed to bring about a compromise. The night before the Cathars surrendered, their leader—a woman—gave me the cup, as thanks for treating her and hers with respect. Or as thanks for speeding their entry into the next life, however unintentionally."

"So she died?" Rose asked.

"The defenders of Montsegur walked down the mountain singing, and were, to a man—and to a woman and to a child—burned to death in the field below. Robin stood amongst the Inquisitors that day, truly powerful, as two hundred twenty souls were butchered in the name of the Prince of Peace."

"That didn't wipe out the Cathars, though," said Maggie, turning onto the Beckery roundabout. "Or the Inquisition, which is still with us in many different forms."

Thomas shook his head. "The Cathars, steeled by violence and injustice, survived. That they eventually faded away is due partly to St. Francis's example. Through his love of birds and animals, of the sun and moon, he demonstrated the goodness and joy of God's material world." The mini-bus turned through the gates of Temple Manor. "Speaking of the goodness of the material world, would you care for a nightcap?"

The main house was dark. He had left one small light burning in his cottage, where they found Dunstan having a wash and brush-up in the chair. "And what've you been up to?" Rose asked, tickling his ears.

A note lay on the table. "D.C.I. Swenholt called about the B. He'll call back tomorrow. Anna."

"I hope that means Mick and Willie pulled it off." Maggie reached for the bottle of whiskey and set out three glasses.

"You didn't have your cell phone with you?" Rose asked Thomas. "What if Mick tried to call?"

Reverently Thomas set the box on the table. It was like removing an iron filing from a magnet to take his hands away from it. But it was not his alone.

He retrieved his mobile from the desk. "I didn't think it appropriate to carry something so relentlessly contemporary on the evening's quest, Rose."

"I guess not," she said. "Can I call Mick now? Just to see if he's okay, and on his way."

"By all means." Thomas handed over the mobile and accepted a glass of whiskey from Maggie.

The small electronic instrument chirped as Rose played its buttons. She put it to her ear. She frowned. She replayed the same melody and held it again to her ear. "He's turned off his phone," she announced.

"Trying to get a good night's sleep?" suggested Maggie, her slightly forced smile refusing to admit any other conclusion.

Her brow furrowed, Rose put away the mobile and accepted a glass of whiskey. The three glasses clinked lightly together. "To the solstice," Thomas said, "the re-birth of the sun and the hope of the future. May Christ, the light of the world, illuminate our path, and Mick's, and Willie's. In the name of the Father . . ."

Dunstan leapt from the chair, raced to the window, and bounded onto the sill. His bottle brush of a tail swished back and forth. Thomas peered out between the drapes. He saw nothing, but he could imagine any number of things.

The fur settled down on Dunstan's back and tail. "He could've seen a dog," offered Rose.

"Yeah, right," Maggie said.

Firmly Thomas tugged the drapes closed and turned back into the room. "In the name of the Father, the Son, and the Holy Ghost."

"Amen." Rose sipped at her whiskey. Her cheeks, already burnished pink by the cold, flushed a glorious crimson. Maggie drank, and the fault lines in her face eased.

Thomas let the bright, hot liquid warm his mouth before he swallowed. How could anyone, he thought, reject the felicities of the material world? And yet love of the material world could lead terribly astray.

Putting aside his glass, he said, "Well then. A preliminary revelation is in order." He opened the box. Inside, nestled in rich red velvet, sat the gold reliquary in the shape of a chalice he himself had fashioned long ago.

"You made that, didn't you?" Maggie said. "It's beautiful."

Even in the dim light the gold glowed, and the filigree knotwork with its morsels of color on handles and base seemed to ripple gently, like a flowing stream or leaves shifting in a spring breeze. "It looks like the Ardagh Chalice in Dublin," said Rose.

Thomas lifted the chalice from the box, and the upper half of the chalice from its base. Inside gleamed a common Roman drinking vessel, a flat cup made of thick glass.

Rose genuflected. Even Maggie was speechless for a long moment. At last she asked, "May I?" She set her fingertips against the rim of the glass. "Should I be feeling something?"

"I sense a harmony emanating from it. From each of the relics. But then, I'm not exactly of this world myself. Rose?"

First wiping her hand on the tea towel, Rose ran a forefinger round the rim of the glass. "Maybe there's a sort of vibration, like a bell after it's been struck."

Dunstan leapt down from the windowsill and onto a chair, so that he, too, could see. For a long, silent moment they watched the play of light along the uneven surface of the glass, so that the Cup seemed to be filled with a palpable radiance.

Then Thomas closed the chalice, replaced it in the box, and fitted the lid in place. "Tomorrow, Maggie, I'd like to borrow the mini-bus and take this to Edith Howard in Salisbury. We've removed the Cup from the most secure hiding place possible, which is what the Lady instructed us to do, but we have also done what Robin wants us to do."

"He said if he had two of the three relics," said Rose, "then they would call to the third. Maybe we were supposed to get the Stone and the Cup to rescue the Book."

Thomas could only say, "All will be revealed in time."

"We're almost out of time," Maggie pointed out.

"In your patience is your soul."

"The devil's in the details."

"Okay, okay," Rose told them both. "What about to-night?"

"Tonight, I shall keep vigil." Emptying the largest desk drawer, Thomas put the box away. "I shall go so far as to lock the doors of the cottage. Dunstan may indeed have seen a dog. He may not."

"I'm staying, too," Maggie said, with that stubborn a set of her mouth Thomas knew he'd be wasting his breath trying to dissuade her. "After I walk Rose back to the house."

Yawning, Rose pulled her hat and gloves back on. Dunstan was already sitting by the door. "Good night," she said, and went out into the darkness, both cat and teacher at her side.

Thomas shut the door behind them and turned to the fire. Flame licked at the tinder, casting light and warmth into the room. Maggie opened the door, shut it, and locked it. "Funny how quickly I've come to accept the raving supernatural as perfectly normal."

"You were searching for it."

"Yes." She set her hands on his chest and turned her face up to his. The cross he'd given her dangled between them, a bond and a barrier both. "Happy birthday, Thomas."

"Thank you." He kissed her, lightly and quickly. How better to end a year of endings than by loving, even if that love had a razor's edge of regret?

Smiling ruefully, she turned away to take up her own vigil.

Chapter Thirty-eight

The headlamps of the car raked the sides of Holystone Priory like a searchlight raking a prison wall. Mick had never seen the place in broad daylight. But even a braw summer's day wouldn't make the place look couthy, it was that heavy-handed and dark.

"Get down," Willie said.

Mick crammed himself as best he could into the footwell of the Nissan. He glanced at his watch. Half past ten. Again he cursed himself for not phoning Rose before he came away from Edinburgh. When he'd tried the number of Thomas's mobile from Hexham no one answered, and the line at Temple Manor was engaged. But Willie had told him to come quick if he wanted to help rescue the Book, so he'd gone quick as he could.

Now Willie peered up at the house. "So Prince brought you here, did he?"

"Oh aye. Rose and me, some six weeks ago now."

"The same day he was going about coshing the odd muggins of a constable." The car bounced across rutted mud and gravel and stopped.

When the headlamps went dark Mick lifted his head. Holystone Priory's turrets and towers cut black angles from the charcoal gray of the overcast sky. The two windows either side of the *porte-cochere* were faint lighted squares, one ice-blue, the other little warmer.

"Prince said there'd be two others to shift the artifact," Willie went on. "But he wasn't after telling me where we'd be taking it."

"If he was an open and honest sort he mightn't have believed you when you told him you lied to us," Mick said. "You chap at the door and I'll slip round the back."

"Have your mobile, do you? Though I'm not signaling Swenholt till I have the Book in hand. No good charging Prince with thievery and not recovering what he thieved."

Mick knew that no one would be charging Robin with anything. But recovering the Book would put his wind up, and no mistake—especially with Thomas, Maggie, and Rose fetching the Cup this very night.

Willie strode purposefully into the *porte-cochere*. Mick heard the thud of the knocker, the grate of the opening door, and a mutter of voices. When the door slammed he slipped out of the car. The frosty air prickled his scalp. From the darkness came the sough of the sea. The snow seemed gray and tired. When his foot went through the surface with a crisp crack, he stood off-balance, waiting. No one came.

Round the corner he went, and saw two more lighted windows. Steps and a porch signaled the kitchen door. Beyond them rose a wall gashed by spear points of sickly light—the windows of the chapel. A clear light blinking on the horizon was St. Mary's Lighthouse.

Mick peeked through the window. Dirty dishes were piled in the sink, the dustbin needed emptying, and the floor hadn't felt a mop for a wee while. All the posh appliances and ornaments looked to be tarnished and dusty. At the table sat Mountjoy, his face sullen, his eyes hard between narrowed lids.

The kitchen door swung open. Reg Soulis's thickset body filled the opening. "He's here."

With an obvious effort, Mountjoy pulled himself up and followed Soulis into the dining room. Mick tiptoed along the wall and tried the door. The knob was so cold it almost took the skin off his palm, but it wouldn't turn. So then, a bit of housebreaking wouldn't go amiss.

With the heel of his mobile he rapped smartly at a pane of glass in the door. Shards rattled down. Again he waited, and again no one came. Protecting his hand with his sleeve, he reached through the broken window and turned the dead bolt.

Easing inside, Mick shut the door behind him. The chilly air smelled of mildew and old fry-ups. He tiptoed across to the door, listened, and pushed slowly through.

The dining room was lit only by the light leaking round the closed gallery doors. Empty cups and plates sat on the table, next to a tea cozy . . . The cozy sat up and opened golden eyes. Mick almost jinked back into the kitchen, then recognized the gray cat. He extended his hand. The moggie sniffed at his fingertips, yawned, leapt down, and vanished beneath the tablecloth.

Mick put his ear against the gallery doors. Save for a distant television laugh track he heard nothing. No, there was Willie's voice, pitched loud, coming up the hallway behind him. "We can take my Nissan, I reckon."

"We've got the boss's Humvee," Soulis retorted. "Just goes to show how important our mission is."

Footsteps approached. Mick dived behind the table, ready to join the cat beneath the cloth if needs must. But the men walked through the room without putting on the lights. Willie was lumbered with a large parcel, tawdry red and green tartan peeking through rips in the paper.

The gallery doors slid shut behind the men. All they had to do was keep walking straight on to the car park. Mick reached for his mobile.

"Well now," said a soft, silky voice from the gallery. "I see we're all getting on famously."

Damn. Robin was here. If you could trust him at all it was to be the spanner in the works. Mick wrapped the mobile in one corner of the tablecloth, muffling the chirps of the buttons. "Swenholt," said the surprisingly mild voice in his ear.

"Willie has the parcel. He's in the gallery with Prince."

"How many others?"

"Two. I reckon the woman's in the television room off the entry. I've unlocked the kitchen door."

"We're moving in."

Mick glanced at his watch. It had gone midnight. The witching hour, eh? He crept to the gallery doors and put his eye to the crack between them. Robin stood casually, one hand in the pocket of his khakis, saying ". . . the Tyne tunnel and then the A1 south . . ." Mountjoy, Soulis, and Willie nodded.

Light burst in Mick's eyes—no, it was only the yellowish glow of the chandelier. Lydia Soulis stood in the far doorway, permed white curls and all. *Damn and blast.* She'd popped out for quick stir at her cauldron—must be time to add the eye of newt. "You!" she exclaimed.

With a crash the door slid open. "Mick," said Robin. "Incapable of leaving well enough alone, are you?"

Behind Robin's back, behind Soulis's staring face, Willie clutched the parcel to his chest and took silent steps toward the front door. Mountjoy looked round. Fast as an adder his fist struck Willie's jaw, making a nasty crack of bone against flesh. Willie's eyes rolled up and he crumpled to the floor, Mountjoy pulling the parcel from his hands as he fell. "So they've corrupted you, lad. Pity."

Soulis went for the parcel as well. Snarling, he and Mountjoy tugged it back and forth. Robin shouted, "Leave it, the both of you!" Mick leapt for the kitchen doorway, reaching for the *sgian dubh* at his waist.

With a ghastly simper, Lydia Soulis pushed a chair into him. He jinked to the side, but Robin was on him. An arm like a cold steel bar pressed into his throat. The smell of moldering gardenias choked him. The satiny voice murmured, "Like father like son, stubborn to the end. Save I'll have to do this job myself, I see. Goodbye, Mick."

Mick tried to wrench free. Robin bent him back so that his feet slipped out from under him. With both hands Mick tore at that rigid forearm. He might just as well have tried to shift the entire house.

Christ behind me and before me . . . The words sieved through his mind and vanished. His lungs burned. Robin's free hand pulled the necklace, Maddy's necklace, from inside his jumper and ripped it away.

Stars spun behind his eyes. In each one Mick saw a wee bittie picture: Calum lying hurt and scairt amidst a tumble of cold stone—Thomas cut down by four knights with long swords, his brains spilling out—Maggie tormented by demons—Rose kneeling before Robin, eyes downcast.

Through the gathering blackness Mick felt Robin pull the mobile from his coat and the *sgian dubh* from his waistband. His last trace of consciousness convulsed into the sound of his mother's voice, and he sang along with her, *Oh God, our help in ages past, our hope for years to come . . . sufficient is thine arm alone, and our defense is sure.* With a shriek of pain and rage Robin dropped the knife. The arm across Mick's throat loosened. He drew one deep shuddering breath and the darkness ebbed.

Mick's feet found purchase. He heaved himself backward, but Robin was gone. He crashed to the floor, landing so hard on his right elbow pain shot up his arm and out his ears. Voices were shouting. Policemen. Blessed be the policemen, who came when called.

He lay on the gritty carpet, filling his lungs and emptying them again. Before his eyes feet ran to and fro. A pair of lop-eared slippers was caught between two pairs of shiny black shoes. They had Lydia, then. Two muddy boots were spread against the wall. In the next room Willie was sitting up, rotating his jaw experimentally. A constable knelt beside him.

The *sgian dubh* lay on the floor. A hand picked it up. A trench coat folded itself into Mick's vision. Swenholt's voice said, "Mountjoy's away with the artifact. Are you up to showing us about the house?"

Mick sat up. The walls danced a reel, then settled. His neck stung—Robin had jerked the cross away so violently the cord skinned his neck—well then, let him have it, let it sap his strength . . .

Swenholt was waiting, his rabbity moustache drooping. Mick croaked, "Oh aye."

"Prince was here," the detective went on, "and then he was gone. Slipped away in the confusion, I expect. Here you are."

Mick took the *sgian dubh* from Swenholt's hand and clasped it tightly. Robin had taken Mum's cross, but the knife had—what? Burned him? It was a relic itself, Thomas had said. Or was it the hymn that hurt him? From beneath the edge of the tablecloth Mick caught the clear amber gaze of the cat, the cat that had led him to Rose. *Oh. Thank you kindly.* The cat blinked and disappeared.

Mick slipped the knife from its sheath. The wee blade was glimmering and humming, like when it had led them to the Stone. His watch read half past twelve.

With Swenholt's aid, he stood up. Several constables were taking the Soulises away, the man glowering, the woman screeching about official repression. In the next room Willie was standing as well. "Mountjoy legged it," he said thickly, "towards the back of the house."

"The chapel," said Mick. "I reckon there's an outside door."

"You and you, round the side," Swenholt ordered.

"This way." Mick led Swenholt, Willie, and two constables to the chapel. The place hadn't grown any couthier. Thick pillars cast even thicker shadows in the colorless light of the lamp. A cobweb dangled listlessly from the cross on the slab of rock. Shards of history and myth lay scattered across the floor like petrified tears.

Something scrambled in the shadow of a pillar, and a human form ran down the aisle. The constables ran after, Swenholt and Willie just behind. A door slammed, then slammed again. Shouts filtered through the windows.

Hang on . . . Mick considered the song of the *sgian dubh*, rising and falling as though it were trading song and refrain with another voice. The Book was still here.

Skirting the stone debris, he knelt in the dense shadow behind the altar. His fingertips touched a parcel wrapped in paper. He sheathed the knife, tucked it away, and gathered the Book into his arms. It wasn't at all heavy, just solid. Weighty, with all the symbols inside. Relief flooded his body. *Thank you.*

Willie and Swenholt returned up the aisle, their faces going from disappointment to surprise to pleasure when they saw Mick. "I reckon he hid it," Mick told them, "aiming to come back for it."

"Clever guess, Dewar." Swenholt's almost invisible brows arched up his forehead. "I'm told that Prince is using the art and antiquities trade to finance the Freedom of Faith Foundation. There's a bit of hypocrisy, and no mistake. But then, I reckon the Foundation has as much to do with faith as Godzilla with paleontology."

Mick grinned. Willie chuckled.

"A Canon O'Connell rang and asked if you'd take the Book to a chap named London in Glastonbury. Quite the scholar, O'Connell says. He'll check it over, see that it's the genuine article."

"No problem," said Mick, his grin broadening.

"I'll give you a lift into Hexham. Let the doctor have a look at those bruises on your neck and you'll be on your way." Swenholt headed toward the outside door without waiting for an answer.

Between the anemic light of the lamp and the dank smell, not to mention his own uneven breath, Mick's head went spinning and his stomach quivering. He supposed the place needed tearing down, and the land spread with salt after, but he also supposed no place was beyond hope.

Willie's face was pale, light or no light. The bruise on his jaw promised a proper Technicolor display. *Like the bruise on my throat,* Mick thought. Good job he still had a throat.

Side by side, he and Willie walked out of the chapel and into the house. In the kitchen, in the cold fresh draft from the broken window, Willie said, "All's well that ends well."

It hadn't ended, not by a long chalk, but Willie's part had done. Clutching the parcel in one arm, Mick shook the man's hand. "Thank you. Above and beyond the call of duty and all that."

"It was the right thing to be doing," Willie said with a shrug, as though doing right was the most ordinary motivation in the world.

"Armstrong!" shouted Swenholt from outside.

"Merry Christmas," Willie said, and was gone.

Even the atheists celebrated Christmas, Mick thought, *the stories were that inviting.*

He'd phone Thomas or Rose from Hexham—no, they'd

be in their beds. He'd ask Swenholt to tell them he was on his way. If he stopped only for petrol he'd be in Glastonbury in the morning—he wasn't at all tired, just nervy, like—the drive would be long and dark at first but if he pressed on he'd soon find Rose and the dawn waiting for him.

Chapter Thirty-nine

Rose stood in the door of Thomas's chapel, tracking the rising sun as it ducked and dodged behind lumps of cloud—there, the sunlight warmed her face—nope, dark again.

They were three for three. Mick was on his way. Rose told herself she should be dancing with joy, but no, her chest was tight and her nerves squirmed. Calum Dewar had disappeared on the road, hadn't he?

Going back into the chapel, she sat down on one of Thomas's chairs and hoped that he and Maggie would hurry—they were changing clothes and eating breakfast after their long night sitting up. But it was Anna who walked in the door and gazed quietly up at the rood screen.

A ray of sun picked out the vivid colors of the row of saints. Above them the carved faces of John and Mary Magdalene looked up at Our Lord, asking for reassurance and receiving it . . . Somebody was talking loudly outside. Rose stood up. Anna turned around.

Sean blasted in the door. "Who the hell does that guy think he is? Ellen and I were minding our own business and a car pulls up and two people get out—I saw them at the Foundation rally—then here he comes himself in that Jaguar and takes her arm, like," Sean used a prissy accent, " 'Come along, we've work to do, you and I.' "

No. No! Every neuron in Rose's body fired at once. She started toward the cottage. Anna started toward the door. Sean exclaimed, "What's up with . . ."

"Rose," said Robin's voice, slick as grease.

She stopped, braced herself, and made an about-face.

Holding Ellen's upper arm in his left hand, Robin brushed past a red-faced Sean and a tight-lipped Anna. His glittering eyes grazed the rood and the cabinet of relics. He spat on the flagstones Rose herself had swept clean. "Idols," he said. "You should be ashamed, going against God."

He wasn't forcing Ellen along. She was smiling, smug, like she was on a date with her favorite rock star. Rose wished she could have had hope enough for Ellen that she was surprised, but she didn't and she wasn't . . . Robin threw something down at Rose's feet. Her throat clamped itself shut and her eyes bugged out. It was Maddy Dewar's Celtic cross. Mick's necklace. The catch was broken, like it had been torn off his neck. Rose snatched it up. It was ice-cold. *No.*

When she looked up Robin was holding a *sgian dubh*. "Do you recognize this? No matter. If you say one word, if you make one gesture, I will kill her." He pressed the point of the knife against Ellen's throat.

"Hey!" Sean started forward, then stopped.

The color drained from Ellen's face. Hadn't she expected that? She was on Robin's side, it was all just pretend. Rose said, "In the names of all the saints gathered here . . ."

The knife pricked. Ellen gasped. Blood trickled down her throat. Robin's smile was curled at one edge, like a leaf with blight. "Mick tried and failed to take back the Book, Rose. He'll not annoy me ever again."

He was just yanking her chain, Rose told herself. When Swenholt called Thomas this morning he said the Book was safe. The cross, already warm in Rose's hand, didn't have any identifying marks. Maybe it was Mick's. Maybe it wasn't. That sure wasn't Mick's *sgian dubh*—his was a relic, too, so how could Robin even hold it? That one was Vivian's. Robin took it from her body.

Ellen had not only not blinked, Rose didn't think she'd breathed. Ellen didn't believe it was all pretend.

Sean looked from face to face, obviously hoping for either a clue or a cue. Anna edged toward the door. "Stop just there," Robin said. "Your sort causes quite enough trouble as it is. Now, Rose. Go into Thomas's cottage and fetch the Cup. Don't tell me it isn't there. I have a witness." Again the knife pricked. Ellen squeaked.

Pocketing the necklace, reminding herself to breathe, Rose stumbled toward the door. Robin was clever, all right. If he held a knife on her she'd grit her teeth and tell him to get it over with before she chickened out, but to threaten somebody else, even Ellen—especially Ellen . . . Prayers whirled through her mind and winked out before she could grasp one.

Dunstan was sitting just inside the cottage, the hair on his spine making a serrated edge. Rose skirted around him and opened the desk drawer. Maybe she could take out the Cup and only give him the box—no, either he'd just know it was gone or he'd make her show him. Maybe she could lock the door and sit tight . . . "Rose!" shouted Robin, and Ellen emitted a cry of terror.

Trembling, nauseated, Rose carried the box into the chapel.

Again Robin smiled. This time his eyes glinted with amusement. "You, boy, give this to my disciples waiting in the car park."

Sean grabbed the box from Rose's hands, stamped past Anna's set face, and went outside. Robin angled himself and Ellen so he could watch through the open door as Sean made the delivery. Rose watched the blood run down Ellen's throat and onto her sweatshirt. Her hand was bleeding too, and her skin was a nasty shade of green.

A car started up and sped away. Robin gave Ellen a little

shake, reminding everyone who was boss. "Now, Rose, kneel before me. Admit that your faith is false. That I would not be here if God hadn't sent me to punish you for the errors in your belief. And whilst you're about it, anticipate what Thomas and Maggie will feel when they hear what you've just done. They trusted you, didn't they? But now you've betrayed them. You've failed. You can't rationalize it all away, saying that God will forgive you, for he hates a hypocrite like you, with your all-too-conspicuous virtue."

Rose gulped down something between a sob and a scream. She had betrayed Thomas and Maggie, that was the truth. She had failed. And Robin was here, in spite of all Thomas's prayers.

"Kneel before me," Robin repeated. "Show forth your shame."

A sour taste filling her mouth, Rose dropped onto one knee. Footsteps raced across the lawn and Thomas catapulted through the doorway, Maggie and Sean at his heels. Painfully Rose stood up again, horrifyingly not sure if she was glad to see Thomas or not.

"Thank you, lad," Robin said. "You saved me the effort of looking out Thomas myself."

Sean flushed an ugly purple. Anna set her hand on his arm.

Robin tightened his hold on Ellen. "Her life is in your hands, Thomas."

Thomas's eyes burned, but he said nothing.

"I have the Cup," Robin said. "I have the Book. I've sent Mick Dewar to join his father."

Maggie's eyes widened and then narrowed cautiously.

"In nine more days, Thomas, I shall win. You and yours cannot withstand my strength, just as you could not withstand your own weakness. But this time your failure will be for all time." He twisted the knife and Ellen whimpered. "William de Tracy. Reginald Fitzurse. Hugo de Morville. Richard le Bret. You know those names."

Becket's murderers, Rose thought. Robin was talking about . . .

"Canterbury. The holy blissful martyr for to seek. Except he isn't holy, he isn't blissful, and he certainly isn't a martyr."

Thomas's expression hinted of thunder and lightning. Of the storm the night Arthur was born. Of the comet the night Caesar died.

"Forty-eight hours after your feast day, Thomas. After the day you celebrate your fraud. New Year's Eve, when the people of the world will be open to signs and wonders. The passing of the last millennium and the end of time." Robin threw one last sneer at the rood and started dragging Ellen toward the door. She stumbled. He jerked her up again, forced her across the lawn, and piled her into the Jaguar like a bundle of laundry. The car took off in a spatter of gravel and vanished down the road.

Rose's knees gave way and she sat down hard on the nearest chair. Tears gushed from her eyes, scalding her face. "I gave him the Cup and if he does have the Book we're road kill—maybe he didn't really murder Mick but I betrayed you just like he said. And he came in here, I thought it was safe here, but it's not. Wasn't I praying hard enough?"

"You did not betray us," Thomas said through his teeth. "So long as Robin has friends, no place is safe from him but your own heart."

Swearing under her breath, Maggie sat down and put a shaky arm around Rose's shoulders.

Sean flapped his mouth open. "What the hell was all that about?"

Thomas asked Anna, "Would you be so good as to ring Inspector Gupta yet again? And you'd best explain the importance of the relics to Sean, I see he's a bit bewildered."

"No shit." With several skeptical backward glances, Sean walked off toward the house with Anna.

"I gave away the Cup," sobbed Rose. "I betrayed the faith."

"Don't allow Robin to lead you into pride. To lead you into assuming what happened here is on your head and yours alone." Thomas laid his hand on Rose's shoulder. The firm clasp steadied her, mind and body. "God made us many promises, but never that His path would be an easy one."

Maggie bounded to her feet and paced toward the door. "I hope Robin was meant to have the Cup. And yes, I know hope is the point, but damn it, Thomas . . ."

"Rose did the right thing in giving it up. If she had let Robin kill Ellen—and have no doubt he would have done, and taken the Cup in any event—*that* would have betrayed the faith."

That made sense. Rose looked up at the face of Our Lord, filled with compassion and wisdom, and down at the face of Our Lady with her serene smile. Neither of them had changed, no matter what Robin said, no matter what he did, even here. "Yes," she said with a sniff.

Maggie peered out into the sunshine, the set of her shoulders saying *make my day*. "So it all comes down to a duel. A pitched . . ." She stopped, stared, and waved her hands like a traffic cop. "M—M—Mick—Mick just pulled into the driveway!"

Mick! Rose jumped up and ran, wobbly knees and all. Behind her came two sets of footsteps. Thomas called, "Have a care, this might be another illusion, intended to turn the knife in the wound."

Mick was opening the trunk of the car. His grin went lopsided when Thomas, Maggie, and Rose galloped up to him and stopped dead a few feet away. Thomas raised his hand and sketched a cross six inches from Mick's face. *"In nomine patris et filii et spiritu sancti, ite."*

"What's happened?" Mick said hoarsely.

She threw her arms around him. It was him. Crumpled and frayed, but him. How could she ever have doubted God's mercy? *Thank you.* "I tried to call you!" she said into his shoulder.

"Ah, that sod Robin's had three mobiles off me now."

Thomas and Maggie joined in the affection frenzy, banging Mick on the back and hugging him from the side. "You saw Robin?" Thomas asked.

"Saw him? He came within a gnat's eyelash of murdering me." Mick pulled at the neck of his sweater, baring an expanse of purple and puffy skin that made Rose wince. "And he stole my mum's necklace to boot."

"Oh!" Rose fumbled in her pocket. "Here. I bet Thomas can fix the clasp."

Mick clutched at the necklace. "He was here, then. He told you he'd murdered me and taken back the Book. Is that it?"

"That's it," said Maggie. "Except for the part where he stole the Cup."

"Where I gave him the Cup," Rose confessed.

"He threatened to kill Ellen," explained Thomas, "unless Rose brought out the Cup and gave it to him."

"Filthy sod," Mick said, and instead of shoving her away he snugged her even more tightly against his side. "Still messing with your mind, is he? And here I was thinking we were three for three."

"Every solstice celebration must have its Lord of Misrule," Thomas stated firmly. "Is P.C. Armstrong all right?"

"Oh aye, just. Mountjoy slipped clean away, I thought Swenholt was after chewing off his moustache." Mick's disappointed expression softened. "Still, when Robin had me round the throat he said, 'Like father like son, stubborn to the end, save I'll have to do this job myself.' "

"Ah," said Thomas. "Someone else struck the blow that killed your father."

"So I'm thinking. I told Swenholt, and he'll have another go at Stan Fenton."

"Good. Let us hope, Mick, that Fenton will give the secular authorities something to go on."

"Oh aye." Mick considered Rose, then the house and the surrounding hills, like he was afraid they were the illusion. "I'm knackered, and no mistake. But the Book's in the boot."

"Well done, Mick. Superbly done." Thomas hoisted a paper-wrapped parcel out of the trunk of the car. "Let's have a look."

They moved off toward the cottage, Rose hanging on to Mick for dear life, not that he was shoving her away. Dunstan was waiting on the doorstep, and escorted them inside. There Thomas untied strings, unwrapped paper, and unrolled a red and green tartan cloth. Gently, he laid the Book on the table.

Rose leaned closer. Parchment glowed. Colors danced. Patterns changed subtly from abstract shapes into living images—the intricate patterns through which she and the others were walking, and the knotwork of flesh that bound their spirits to the world. Through them all wound the exquisitely written letters of the Word. The cramp in her throat finally eased. "Oh yes."

Dunstan stretched, his chin brushing the floor. The deep lines in Thomas's face eased in the glow of the vellum and its rainbow hues. "Robin held the Book for much too long, but he was not yet, thank God, moved to defile it."

Maggie touched the Book and then looked at her fingertips, as if that Otherworldly glow was paint she could rub off. "Is this why Mick didn't get the Book back at the end of November? So he could show up with it now, when we needed a jolt of hope?"

"I should believe so," Thomas told her.

"We have two of the three," Rose said.

"And I still have my own wee relic." Mick lifted his sweater to show his *sgian dubh* safe at his waist. "But Robin's won a round."

"He succeeded only in setting the place for the revelation of the relics," Thomas told him.

"Only?" Maggie made a face. "We've been playing musical relics. Now it's time for the tug of war, winner take the future."

"A pitched battle," said Thomas, "on New Year's Eve, at Canterbury. Robin thinks my guilty conscience will weaken me there, and so it might."

"No," Maggie told him. "By the time New Year's Eve gets here you won't have a guilty conscience, not any more."

Thomas's eyebrows tightened into doubt and then so obviously threw that doubt away Rose could hear it shatter on the floor.

"Taking the Book and the Stone to Canterbury will be delivering them straight into Robin's hands," Mick protested.

"Since we do not have the Cup, we must take the other relics to it," answered Thomas. "Robin is taking as great a chance."

"Can he waltz right into Canterbury, the holy of British holies?" Rose asked.

"Robin can venture even there if his true believers carry him in their hearts. For the cathedral, like my chapel—like your necklace, Mick, and yours, Rose—is but a symbol of the faith we hold in our own hearts. It is when we show that faith from our hearts, passionately, in word and deed, that he is repelled. For our words, our stories, are the greatest relics of all." Thomas's stern face cracked into a smile. "Let us remember that Robin's stories, his lies, are more likely to divide his forces than our own."

"Yeah," said Maggie, "may the Force be with us."

"It is." Thomas's long, elegant fingers began folding the Book into its tartan wrapper. "Maggie, we must carry this to Salisbury straightaway."

The door opened. "Thomas?" asked Gupta. "You've had a spot of bother? Oh, hello Mick, Rose, Maggie."

Rose almost laughed. A spot of bother? Yeah, right. "Tell you what, I'm going to get Mick over to the house."

"An admirable plan," Thomas told her. "Would you please ask Sean to step across so Jivan can interview him?"

"Oh aye." Tucking the necklace into his pocket, Mick took Rose's hand in his. Together they retrieved his backpack and a tartan carrying case from the car, then went into the house, where they met Alf lumbering down the staircase. "What's this about Ellen getting herself kidnapped?"

"Inspector Gupta's in Thomas's cottage . . ." Rose began.

Alf clomped on past. "The lass needs help. Oh, hello there, Mick." The door slammed behind him.

Mick and Rose went on up the stairs. Anna and Sean were sitting in the gallery beside the Christmas tree, Sean shaking his head. "Hi, Mick, we saw you from the window. I figured Fitzroy was lying about you. You wouldn't believe, he actually had a knife on Ellen."

"I believe it," said Mick. "No problem."

"Thomas wants you to tell Inspector Gupta about it," Rose said.

"Let's get that bastard Fitzroy behind bars—going after

Ellen with all this woo-woo crap like she didn't have issues already." Sean stalked off.

"He'll never fully understand, but I told him enough to satisfy him for the moment. Not that I'll ever understand it all, either." Briskly Anna stood up. "I'll get lunch started. No, Rose, stay with Mick."

No problem. The piney smell of the tree reminded Rose of the hillside where they'd found the Stone. Where a miracle had happened. She wasn't sure what had happened today—a test of faith, probably. Mick was the miracle.

He sank onto the loveseat, Rose beside him, and leaned his head against her shoulder. She heard his breath whistling in his bruised throat and felt his heart beating in his chest, steady as a drumbeat. Her own heart finally stopped fluttering and fell into the same rhythm. She told him about the Tor maze, Annwn, and Maddy and Calum together.

"Oh aye." A tear rolled down his cheek, in the Christmas lights a tiny rainbow. A moment later his breath lengthened and his head went heavy against her. He'd dozed off, drained, wrung out, and permapressed, bless him.

Sean's footsteps marched up the stairs. The sound of "First Rites" echoed through the house, first the rock and reel, then the quiet Gaelic blessing: "Deep peace of the running wave to you, deep peace of the flowing air to you, deep peace of the quiet earth to you, deep peace of the shining stars to you, deep peace of the gentle night to you, moon and stars pour their healing light upon you, deep peace of Christ the light of the world to you, deep peace of Mary the vessel who bore him to you."

The words trailed away on a sigh that was both passionate and peaceful. Then the pipes swelled again, dancing with fiddle and guitar and drum, until the song ended in a crescendo of thought and feeling intertwined.

In that completion, Rose saw clearly that no one, human or otherwise, could deny her the presence of God so long as she chose it, freely and honestly. She kissed her fingertips and touched them to Mick's bruised flesh. *This is now,* she thought. *This is forever.*

Chapter Forty

Ellen crouched in the Jaguar, watching Robin lean in the window of the other car parked in the layby. The thin wintry sunlight glinted on his hair and his teeth. He was right chuffed, wasn't he?

She pressed her scarf to her neck, trying to stop the bleeding. He'd put a knife to her. He'd cut her. He'd said he'd kill her. She'd have gone along, if only he'd asked.

Rose gave up the artifact. The artifact They thought was more important than anyone's life, Rose gave it up for her.

"Ellen!" shouted Robin.

She opened the door, stumbled across the gravel, took the box handed out the window and carried it back to the Jaguar. She sat down, the box on her lap. Something inside chimed. Her muscles cramped. Mustn't hurt it. It was more important than her life. To Robin. But not to Them . . . *I believe!*

Robin climbed into the Jaguar and switched on the engine. He was still grinning, tight-like. "Fasten your seat belt. If we stopped suddenly you'd crush the box."

She fastened her belt. Robin pulled onto the road. In the wing mirror Glastonbury Tor grew smaller and disappeared behind the trees and hedgerows. Ellen opened her dry mouth and said, "You scared me, there."

"Scared Rose, too, didn't I? I humbled her, as I promised."

"Good job I was there for you, with the house and all. Part of the divine plan, wasn't it?"

The green eyes flashed at her. "Yes. Of course."

A chill like the point of a knife traced Ellen's spine. He hadn't ever chosen her just because of the house, had he? He wanted her for herself, not Alf's stupid sodding house.

"You'd like to stop at a posh hotel, wouldn't you?" Robin asked.

She didn't answer. She felt the knife at her throat—he was always stabbing her, with the knife, with his body, with his words. He told her it was Them who'd hurt her. But even too-sodding-pretty-by-half Rose and too-sodding-clever-by-half Maggie didn't stab her. Anna was kind to her, even if she was heathen. And Sean sat with her in front of the telly, rubbing her neck and shoulders. She couldn't ever go back to him, not now.

If she couldn't trust Robin who could she trust? If he wasn't the truth and the light then who was? Or was there any truth, any light at all?

"I want you in Canterbury December thirty-first," he said. "For the final battle."

"And then?" she asked.

"Why then," he said, not half sarkey, "I'll prove my devotion to you."

Like fun you will, she thought, and took the thought back, forcing it down until it choked her. *I believe.*

The mobile chirped. Robin reached inside his coat and pulled out the knife, the knife Calum gave Vivian long since, as a joke, like, but the stupid cow thought it was an artifact. Chucking it on the floor at Ellen's feet, Robin pulled out the mobile. "Fitzroy. Oh, Mountjoy."

He scowled. The car swerved. Ellen shut her eyes and clutched the box in both hands. The lid went loose. The chime was loud, insistent, but Robin didn't seem to be hearing it.

"So some prat at the station told you Dewar took it away

with him, is that supposed to excuse your losing it! May your soul scream forever in the darkness!" His voice burned like acid. "What? Yes, perhaps you can redeem yourself . . ."

Forever in the darkness. By Robin's word, that's where Mum was now.

". . . December thirty-first," Robin concluded, switched off, and thrust the mobile into his coat. He overtook one car, then another, whipping back and forth, faster and faster.

The lid fell from the box. Inside Ellen saw a gold dish like a tureen. She'd never seen anything so brilliant, tiny gold beads on the handles and the base arranged in patterns that had no beginning and no end. The colors filled the swirls clear and bright. The gold gleamed.

Robin swerved again. With a peal like a bell the gold lid slipped aside, revealing a flattish glass bowl. Ordinary glass, not especially pretty, thick and uneven. That was never Jesus' cup, holding his wine, holding his blood. It was nothing but an idolatrous artifact.

The glass was clear, and yet light welled from it and into it like a spring morning in the midst of winter. Robin shuddered. The car veered across the road, jounced against the far curb, veered back again. "Cover that up, you gormless bint! Now!"

Ellen covered the box. But her eyes were still dazzled. Her ears still rang with that soft chime. If the artifact had no power why wouldn't Robin let her look at it? If he was the truth and the light, why was it that the Cup was filled with light and he was . . . It was like he was afraid of it, Robin was. Who'd never shed any blood for her. It was her who was always bleeding for him.

Robin said he'd take her up to heaven with him. What if there was no heaven? What if death was the end and there was nothing more, no joy but no pain, either? Was that why Mum

Lillian Stewart Carl

died, so she wouldn't be frightened, so she wouldn't doubt, not any more?

Robin's hands were clenched on the steering wheel, face flat white. The sun dipped behind a cloud and the landscape darkened. A thin rim of gold light showed beneath the lid of the box. Robin said it was a lie. *I believe Robin.*

In the back of her mind, Ellen heard Rose's voice asking, *But does he believe in you?* And she answered, *No.*

Here it was, December twenty-third, Maggie thought. Probably the most important two months in her life, and they were nearly gone.

She and Thomas walked past Beckett's Pub—"no relation," he said—and on down Silver Street. The shop windows, filled with New Age tchotchkes, were decorated with tinsel and holly. In the cold sunlight the shadow of St. John's steeple pointed to the northwest. Tomorrow morning Maggie and the students were heading east.

"I hate to leave Glastonbury," she said, trying to keep her voice relaxed. "Not all the New Age stuff makes it past the you've-got-to-be-kidding threshold, but loonies, theologians, whatever, they're still trying to solve the mystery of the nature of God."

"Most solutions are positive ones," Thomas said.

"The ones that aren't stand out because they're unusual. Yeah, I get it." Maggie walked beside Thomas through the Abbey gateway.

He pointed upward. Two contrails crossed in the blue sky above the broken towers of the Abbey church. *"In hoc vinces."*

"In this sign conquer. Constantine." Their game of literary/historical line-and-response would be the least of a hundred things she'd miss once they were separated. However they would be separated. Having him as a pen pal would

406

be better than having him—gone.

Maggie took his arm, lightly, knowing that clutching at him would do neither of them any good. Placing his warm, strong hand over hers, Thomas led her on toward the transept that had once been his chapel.

Rose and Mick were standing at the spot where Vivian Morgan died. In the almost two months since then the scuffed and muddy patch of grass had healed into a thick greenish-gold carpet. Rose gestured. Mick put his arm around her. This morning they'd been working out the logistics of her transferring to Glasgow or Edinburgh for her senior year. *More power to them,* Maggie thought. At least *they* could plan a normal relationship, although whether they actually got to have one was another matter.

Anna, Sean, and his camcorder came across the lawn from the Lady Chapel, Anna saying, "Poetic justice, perhaps, for Celt-descended Henry VIII to eject the Roman church from Britain. A shame he did it so violently."

Sean shrugged. "Sometimes violence is the only way to make your point."

"The question," Maggie said, "is whether your point is a valid one." Was it nature or nurture that squeezed some people's imaginations into such small holes? The business with the Cup had left Sean bewildered, and resentful at his bewilderment. And yet he'd done well in the seminar, his literal mind grasping military tactics faster than her own often chaotic one.

"Elizabeth I's alchemist, John Dee," said Thomas, "supposedly found a book written by St. Dunstan in the ruins of the Abbey. And in his day they were ruins, not this manicured park."

"A book telling how to turn base metal to gold," Maggie added, "using the philosopher's stone. In some stories that's the stone that broke off Lucifer's crown when he fell from heaven."

"I thought that was the Holy Grail," said Rose.

"Both are symbols of what Lucifer lost when he rebelled—wholeness."

"So did Dee turn metal into gold?" Sean asked.

"He died poor in material wealth," said Thomas.

"Go figure." Sean focused his camcorder and moved off toward the signpost marking the site of Arthur's medieval shrine.

"Jivan!" Thomas waved.

Inspector Gupta came striding toward them. "I hear you're going up to London tomorrow, Maggie."

"Yes, it's time for us to rejoin the other groups. Mick's coming with us." *Not,* she thought with a glance at his arm wrapped securely around Rose's shoulders, *that I'd even try to unglue those two.* They'd have to separate soon enough.

"Thomas? You usually spend Christmas in London."

"I'll be helping out at the homeless shelter as usual."

In his first life, he'd washed the feet of the beggars gathered at his door. Ostentatious humility? Maggie met Thomas's wry glance with a smile.

"We've turned up the couple who carried away the Cup on Wednesday," Gupta reported. "They handed it over to Fitzroy and Ellen Sparrow, no surprise there. We'll charge them with aiding a theft."

"What's their version?" Maggie asked wearily.

"God told them to destroy objects of superstition and heresy, the Somerset Constabulary is conspiring to restrain their free expression of religion, and their solicitor will be phoning. He'll need to wait in the queue, we've already three suits pending."

"I see." Rose rolled her eyes. "Freedom of religion for

themselves but not for anybody else."

"Swenholt released both the Soulises," Jivan went on. "They'll also have to answer charges of aiding a theft. But just now . . ."

". . . they're free to make more trouble," concluded Mick.

"Mountjoy was seen in Hexham on the Wednesday. If Swenholt can lay him by the heels he can charge him with assaulting Armstrong as well as theft."

"And my dad?" asked Mick. "And Vivian?"

Gupta looked around the grounds of the Abbey as though seeking inspiration. A cloud passed over the sun and over his face as well. "The inquiry into Vivian Morgan's death will run on for a time, I expect, and be shelved, and at the end of the day be filed under unsolved cases. I'm every bit as certain as you are that Fitzroy murdered her. But the only witness was your father, Mick. If it's any consolation, now that Mountjoy's out of the picture, no one's likely to conclude that Calum killed Vivian himself and tried to shop Fitzroy."

Mick looked down at his feet, lips taut. Rose wrapped her arm around his waist.

The sun shone out again, making Gupta's eyes into gleaming jet—*if jet*, Maggie thought, *could ever be intelligent.* "However, Swenholt tells me that when Stanley Felton heard Reg Soulis had been released from custody, he turned Queen's evidence. He admits to helping Soulis kidnap Calum from the phone box in Carlisle and drive him to Housesteads, where they met Fitzroy. But when Fitzroy and Soulis told Felton to wait in the car park whilst they went up to the ruins with Calum, he followed, thinking they were after cutting him out of some moneymaking plot. As they'd done before."

"He saw what happened?" prompted Mick.

"He overheard a violent argument, Fitzroy tearing strips off Calum. Then he heard a blow, and a body falling. And

Fitzroy, very cold and tight, ticking Soulis off for acting without orders but for doing what needed doing even so. Now Swenholt's people are reassessing the crime scene evidence."

"Soulis killed my dad," said Mick, a catch in his voice, whether of anger or sorrow Maggie couldn't tell.

"We'll charge him as soon as we find him," Gupta said. "But Fitzroy himself—well, Thomas, you said that he's beyond human justice."

Mick's face was pale but his chin was high. "Oh, we'll bring him to justice, right enough. On Hogmanay. New Year's Eve."

God help us, Maggie added to herself.

"I'll be there," Gupta went on. "I don't suppose I'll be providing much more than moral support, but . . ."

Thomas smiled. "Why, Jivan. How very good of you. Moral support is just what we'll be needing."

"You can count on me, too," said Anna with a firm nod.

Sean came cruising back again, taped the entire group standing against the walls of the chapel, and asked, "Inspector, have you heard anything about Ellen?"

"No, lad, we haven't."

"Anna and I talked to Alf and made a case for her, you know. It wasn't her fault Bess died, and Alf's pissed off at Fitzroy more than he is at her. He says he'll take her back in."

"If we find her," Gupta said, "we'll tell her."

"She'll need psychiatric help," said Rose.

Maggie added, "Not to mention exorcism."

"No kidding." Sean moved on, the camcorder whirring.

"Was talking to Alf your idea or Sean's?" Maggie asked Anna.

"His," Anna answered. "He wants to see her again before we go back home. As much to tell her 'I told you so' about

Robin, I think, but even so, there's hope for him yet. If only there's hope for her."

Thomas stated, "There's hope."

"Hey," Sean called from the Lady Chapel. "I need some bodies in this shot."

"Bad choice of words," Rose said, but still she tugged at Mick's hand. His sober face cracked into a thin smile and they walked away with Anna.

It isn't hard, Maggie told herself, *to figure out why Ellen had fallen for Robin.* Because she was weak and he appeared strong.

Gupta tilted his head to the side. "Thomas, I'm thinking you're one of the old monks who can remember his past life. No," he said as Thomas started to speak, "let my imagination enjoy itself. The next time we play chess, we can discuss it. Merry Christmas, Thomas, Maggie."

"The blessings of the season upon you," Thomas told him.

"Thank you," added Maggie, and Gupta walked off toward the gate.

Thomas raised his face to watch a dove land on the shattered top of the tower, a white ideogram on the gray stone. "St. Columba. Mary Magdalene. The brotherhood of the Grail. The Holy Spirit." He looked back down at Maggie. "Sorry. I find myself continually looking out signs and portents."

Maggie looked for her own signs and portents in his face—the face of a man who didn't just appear strong, but who was. "What are you seeing? The Old Church? The medieval Abbey? The ruins Dee saw?"

"The ruins," he replied. "Do you remember the sixteenth-century poem written about the destruction of another great Marian shrine, Walsingham? 'Bitter, bitter, O, to behold the grass to grow where the walls of Walsingham so stately did show. Walsingham, O, farewell.' "

The dove took wing again, spiraling above the broken walls. "Walsingham's been renewed," said Maggie. "Catholic and Anglican shrines share the site. It's as big a deal for pilgrims as it was in the Middle Ages."

"Time brings renewal and reawakening, doesn't it? If we can preserve the power of the Grail so that there will be time to forgive and be forgiven . . ." His voice broke. "Magdalena, I shall miss you dreadfully."

She bit her lip, hard, and touched his face, memorizing the high places of his cheekbones, the wells of his eyes, the landscape of his brow and mouth and jaw. His gestures, the timbre of his voice, every word he'd ever uttered to her and every touch he'd ever bestowed on her. His soul, that old soul on whom time had worked its will as it had on the trees and stones of the ancient shrine itself.

Glastonbury, O farewell.

Mick wrapped the elastic round his tail of hair and buttoned the top button of his shirt. *Ow.* Quickly he unbuttoned it. But despite the bruises he felt himself again. The new himself, not the himself he'd been two months ago, not a bit of it.

Rose sat on the bed holding his chanter to her lips. She blew. It squawked. She looked up with a laugh. Yesterday he'd seen tears in her eyes. Now she was laughing. That was amazing grace, right enough. How sweet both the word and the woman.

Putting the chanter aside, he scooped her back onto the bed. She wrapped his body with hers and said with a wicked grin, "Open thou my lips, and my mouth shall show forth thy praise."

He opened her lips. Her mouth tasted of honey. *This is*

now, he thought. Her willowy body flexed to his touch and her scent filled his head, making him giddy. *This is now.* Her bones were fine and strong beneath her skin, and her skin smooth beneath her jumper, straining toward his hands and mouth—in a moment both their jumpers would be gone and they could lie skin to skin—and their jeans, with their buttons and zips, no trouble at all . . .

"Oh, Mick," she said in his ear, a warm breath trembling with delight. And with caution.

He blinked into Rose's bright blue eyes.

"Mick," she said again, a wee bit steadier. "Not like this."

He wrenched himself away, sat up on the edge of the bed, and re-seated his jeans. The wallpaper seemed to pulse in time with his heart. The *sgian dubh* made a hard exclamation point against his ribs. "I'm thinking we have a choice. We can be getting on with it. Or we can be proper guardians of the Grail and possess ourselves in patience, as my Dad used to say."

"I like the idea of possessing myself. You know, honor and all that." Rose sat up and re-seated her bra. "Have you ever gotten on with it?"

"Oh aye. It didna mean overmuch. I was a gowk to settle for cheap."

"Robin said physical virginity was cheap. But I won't let mine be cheap. I won't let it be casual. You know, okay, so much for that, what do you want to do now? Watch a video?"

Had she told him she was a virgin? He wasn't surprised.

"I don't want to fumble around in some corner and then pretend nothing happened. I want to do it with knowledge and intention and consent. With affection aforethought. I want to shout out, 'I love this man. I worship him with my body because there's no shame in the flesh.' Of course," she added, "I do want to do it with you."

He smiled, tentatively. "Is it love, then?"

"Feels like it from here."

"And from here." Mick raised her hands to his lips. "I dinna suppose we're gey important with Armageddon and all. But then, if it is Armageddon, would you not hate to miss out worshipping the flesh?"

"Oh, ye of little faith," she said with a grin. "We're going to prevent Armageddon, aren't we? Because we're just what's important. And because we possess ourselves like proper guardians of the Grail."

Mick grinned back. She was a canny one. She knew no matter how complex the labyrinth he'd been treading, no matter how long and dark its path, he'd come at last to the center. Whatever tasks lay along the path out—the university, the business, a trial—he would have her heart and soul, body and spirit, with him. "Well then, we should be asking Thomas to marry us."

Her eyes glowed. "Let's ask him for a nuptial blessing when we're at Canterbury. Then in God's eyes we'll be engaged, and sex will be okay."

"Oh no, lass. It'll be grand."

Footsteps thundered up the stairs and blows hammered on the door. "Hey!" shouted Sean. "Do we have to throw a bucket of water on you two? Rose, you came up here to get Mick to play for us!"

Rose laughed. "Yeah, I did, didn't I?"

Mick opened the door. Sean looked past him, saw a fully-clothed Rose standing innocently by the basin, and shrugged.

Mick clapped Sean on the shoulder. "I'll be down in a tic, Sunshine." And to Rose, "You go on, lass, blowing in the pipes is no treat for the ear."

"We'll be in the courtyard," said Sean. "Thomas says there's a reason they're called the Great War Pipes."

"The yard it is, then."

Blowing him a kiss, Rose walked away. Mick set about inflating and tuning, until the bass note of the drones sounded loud and clear and the bag was tight, straining beneath his arm. If fondling the pipes wasn't as fine as fondling Rose, well, they had their glamour.

Down the stairs he went, and out into the lamp-lit yard. They were all waiting, Alf, Thomas and Maggie, Sean and Anna, Rose. Even Dunstan, who was sitting inside the lounge window like a deity enthroned.

Rose smiled and Mick thought, *This is forever.* He cut loose with "Scotland the Brave." The skirl of the pipes filled the courtyard with sound and glory. Alf covered his ears. Everyone else cheered.

So then, the music was enough to wake the dead. Let it. Let Robin Fitzroy know this was the wappenshaw, the muster of the warriors. Let him know they were ready to take him on, and win.

Chapter Forty-one

Ellen sat down next to a niche holding a statue of a woman and a baby. Three candles burned in front of it. Superstitious rubbish, those images.

Mary didn't die. It was Jesus who died. Maybe he scared his mum as well. *I never meant it. I never.*

Ellen didn't know where in London's maze of streets she'd found the church that housed this shelter. She'd walked since daybreak, when the cheap hotel turfed her out, Christmas Day or not. The gits driving by in their posh cars didn't so much as see her, save for the pillock who ran through a puddle, splashed her, and laughed. That's what Christmas meant, brass for the toffs, and the likes of her left out in the cold and the rain.

Even if Temple Manor wasn't half Alf's rubbish, Christmas went down a treat there, lights shining in the glass, roasted goose, pudding, crackers and funny hats. Mum only ever wanted what was best . . . Mum was dead. Alf hated her. Anna and the others, they wouldn't be good to her ever again. And Sean—she missed Sean.

The good smells that had lured Ellen in from the street now made her feel sick. Even in the warm room she was perishing cold. Cold as bonking Robin. But Wednesday he'd taken no for an answer. Snarling about Canterbury, he'd shoved a few notes at her and left her at St. Pancras station. He never saw her pinch the knife, did he? Now it was a rigid outline in her pocket. Now it was hers.

She glanced over her shoulder. Shabby folk like her were

scoffing down lashings of food. Toffs stood by with cups of tea and cakes—*they're falling about at the sight of us,* Ellen thought.

They weren't laughing. One tall man was even kneeling in front of a child, slipping new shoes onto her little feet. It was the traitor, burned brown eyes, nose like a bird's beak.

Robin said Thomas betrayed God. She didn't know what he'd done any more than she knew what Calum had done. Robin said he'd tell her everything she needed to know. But he hadn't done, had he?

The bloody wound on her hand hurt, the bloody cut on her neck hurt, and something bloody well hurt in her chest, like her heart had been pulled right out. *I believe* . . . She didn't believe in anything, not any more.

Someone switched on a radio. "First Rites," again, she'd gone off "First Rites," the pipes squealing and the drums beating. A man sat down beside her. The traitor, Thomas, holding a first-aid kit. She was too knackered to move away. "I don't know where it is," she mumbled.

"I know," he said. "Are you all right?"

That was too complicated a question. "Yeh."

"Alf wants you to come back to Temple Manor."

"Alf hates me."

"He was distressed when Bess died. But he's always cared for you. Temple Manor is a place for you to go, and work to be going on with."

Ellen said, "I have a place to go. Canterbury."

"You'll be going on the thirty-first, I expect." Opening the kit, Thomas dabbled at her neck with something that burned. Tears filled her eyes and she blinked them away.

Robin told her Thomas was a traitor and a liar. But Thomas had the Book and the Stone off Robin, hadn't he? What did that make of him? Of Robin?

417

". . . the light of the world to you, Deep peace of Mary the vessel who bore him to you," ended the song. Thomas's hands were as gentle as Mum's. He bandaged her neck and took her hand. Shaking his head—her hand was a dog's breakfast, wasn't it, all puffed and purple—he wiped it off. Again the sting brought tears to her eyes and this time they ran hotly down her cheeks.

The image of Mary and her baby swam before her. The three candles blurred into one streak of light. A choir on the radio sang, "Silent night, Holy night, son of God, love's pure light . . ." The Child looked into that hole which had been Ellen's heart. She'd seen light filling his Cup, beautiful light. But that was probably a lie, too. The knife wasn't a lie. It lay cold, hard, and smooth against her ribs.

Thomas closed the kit. He touched her head, murmuring something in another language, heathen Latin, most like. He was praying over her. She wasn't strong enough to turn away. "God loves you," he finished.

The man was daft. No one loved her.

"I'll bring you some food," he said, and walked away.

Canterbury, Ellen thought. Robin was after cleaning out the artifacts, wasn't he, and the traitor was after stopping him, and neither of them would so much as notice if she was there or not. Unless she made them take notice. One more week, and she'd go to Canterbury. And then, if it was blood that mattered—well, the edge of the knife was razor-sharp.

She no longer gave a toss about the new world coming on. She just wanted the old one to end and be done.

The towers of Canterbury Cathedral rose above the rooftops. Gray towers against a mottled gray December sky, Thomas thought, remembering other towers and another December sky. But his cathedral was long gone. This new one had been built to the glory of God and His martyr as well.

In the west hung a quarter moon, like a cryptic smile. He'd seen such a moon the day God's merciful hand brought Maggie and the students to Temple Manor. He'd seen such a moon the day they found the Stone and were delivered by that same omnipotent hand. He wondered what he would be feeling if he saw next month's last quarter moon—relief, or disappointment?

Setting his jaw, he turned toward the group of American students queuing outside the Burger King. "Makes me feel old just to look at them," said Maggie at his elbow. "I can't imagine how they make you feel."

"Pleased to be alive. And to see you again." He took her hands and found that he was still capable of a broad smile.

"I need to thank Canon O'Connell for putting in a good word for me at the hotel. I've got the best room in the house, canopy bed, fireplace, and the cathedral right outside the window. You should have seen Rose's face when she looked in, like Cinderella watching her pumpkin turn into a coach."

"Good man, Ivan," Thomas told her. "Did you enjoy your Christmas?"

"Yes, thank you. Comparing notes with the other instructors was a heck of a reality check. They were talking about flat tires and sore throats like they were hair-raising adventures."

"You and the students downplayed your own adventures, I take it."

"We were inadvertently caught up in a murder investigation is all—I passed the treks north off as field trips." Maggie took his arm and they walked off. "Do you recognize anything?"

Thomas considered the medieval facades modernized by shop windows and advertising signs, now decorated for the season. "Even the oldest of these buildings is younger than I am."

"Especially that brick shopping center over there."

"During the last war the Luftwaffe dropped incendiary bombs onto the cathedral, but a wind—the breath of God, I daresay—blew them onto the medieval town. The destruction proved a boon to archaeologists."

Maggie shook her head. "Thomas, if you bit into an apple and found half a worm you'd give thanks for the protein."

This is the worm that dieth not. "I should hope so."

"And your Christmas at the homeless shelter?" she went on.

"Ellen Sparrow was there."

"She was? There's a—no, it wasn't a coincidence, was it?"

"No. She's fearfully depressed, and, it seemed to me, fey. She intends to be here on the thirty-first . . . Look!" Above the street rose Christ Church gate, decorated with crenellations, gilded shields, and the benign stone faces of angels. "Built in 1517 under Henry VIII."

"And twenty-five years later Henry was looting your—the shrine. A century after that the Puritans were happily breaking and burning. And now . . ." Maggie was not obliged to finish her sentence.

Together they walked through the gate and into the spacious grounds of the cathedral. What had been a chill breeze in the streets of the town here became a raw wind scouring Thomas's face. He had seen drawings and photographs, but the grandeur of the actual building, the towers, buttresses, windows, arches a symphony in stone, took his breath away.

"Do you want to walk around outside first?" Maggie asked gently.

"Yes." Pressing her hand, he let her guide him alongside the south facade. There, the stair tower tucked into the angle

420

of the southeast transept—he remembered Prior Wibert adding its arcades. Biting his lip—*lancing a wound always hurts*—he walked on.

A striped cat prowled past the base of the Corona Chapel at the far eastern end of the cathedral, a miniature tiger at its hunt. Thomas and Maggie went round into the network of blank walls, empty windows, and passageways which lay against the northern side of the cathedral. The water tower with the conical roof, that was Wibert's as well.

The cloister wasn't the one he remembered, and yet still it smelled of mold and damp and time. Those uneven stone flags might as well be the ones he'd once walked, and the door into the northwest transept, a wooden slab with an iron latch, the one he had entered that fateful night.

A burst of sunlight cast the shadows of the pillars black across the walkway, like prison bars. Then the sun went out. He was walking toward the door, the shouts of the knights ringing in his ears, his bowels churning and his heart beating in his throat—his martyrdom was upon him, and yet mixed with his exaltation was a leaden fear that made his feet slow to rise and fall—David, Edward, the others told him it was no time to be standing on his dignity. They pulled at him, urging him to run, to hide, to lock the doors. "No," he whispered. "It is the hour of vespers."

He blinked. It wasn't night, but a gray noon. The faces round him coalesced to one face, that of a woman, her dark eyes touched with incorruptible gold. "Are you sure you want to do this?"

"How can I confront Robin, if I fear to confront myself?" His voice broke and he swallowed fiercely.

She offered no tawdry affirmations. "Let's go in the main door, then, not this one."

Not this one. Unresisting, he walked beside her round the

far end of the building and into the nave. Two rows of tall, graceful columns marched eastward, joined far overhead by interlaced stone branches. Just beyond the base of the main tower and its decorative braces, an arched doorway in the choir screen opened onto a gleam of light.

The scent of incense hung in the air. That night the scent of incense had mingled with wool and beans. Sweat trickled cold down Thomas's back, but Maggie's hand was warm on his arm. She led him not to the north but to the south side of the choir. A second circuit, then, one closer to the center. He tried to breathe deeply, but his chest felt as though it were packed with lint.

The southwest transept held a souvenir stand and the St. Michael Chapel, hung with regimental flags. Up a flight of steps, and the southeast transept was illuminated by two very recent stained-glass windows. Thomas said, "Many of the original windows were broken out by the Puritans—'rattling down proud Becket's glassy bones,' they said. I was indeed proud, and needed bringing down. But aren't the reformers and purifiers who resort to destruction and murder guilty of even greater pride?"

"You don't have to convince me," said Maggie.

Opposite the transept sat the high altar and the austere stone chair of St. Augustine, the archbishop's seat. Thomas felt the miter on his head, heard the voices singing a *Gloria*, saw the blaze of candles that sent the shadows fleeing—his heart leapt in the presence of God—he was chosen not by an earthly king but by the King of Kings . . . Whose teachings he betrayed eight years later. *Thomas Maudit.*

Maggie drew him on up another flight of steps, their stone worn into curves. Between the columns circling the Trinity Chapel sat tombs with carved and gilded canopies and effigies, all focused on an eloquent emptiness. There, where the mosaic zodiac gave way to stone flags still hollowed by the knees of pilgrims, there Thomas Becket's shrine had once stood.

In a way the site has always been empty, Thomas London told himself. *Were those laid to rest in the surrounding tombs disappointed to discover whose bones they actually companioned?* Surely they were honored to encounter David, whose courage in life was matched only by his humility in death.

"You know," said Maggie, "the focal point of this entire— magnificent, glorious, gorgeous, take your pick—structure is the Unseen. Right there, in that empty spot."

"Yes," Thomas said, pleased yet again by her perception, "you're quite right. Yes."

Past the Trinity Chapel opened the Corona Chapel, where once the crown of David's skull had rested. Its windows told tales of his miraculous healings, mis-attributed though they were. Thomas knelt to light a votive candle. His hand trembled but Maggie helped him guide the candle to the flame.

They walked on down the ancient steps past the northeastern transept, along the north choir aisle to another stairway. There, in the northwestern transept, the floor remained at its twelfth-century level. Thomas recognized those drab stones, the stones spattered by David's blood. There, just inside the wooden door into the cloister—a pillar had stood there, against which David had fallen . . . *Lord have mercy.*

He turned toward the Altar of the Sword's Point, an austere modern altar like a table tomb set against the wall. Above it hung a contemporary sculpture, a cross formed of jagged sword blades. At its feet the word "Thomas" was etched deep into the floor.

Several Japanese tourists strolled past, chatting softly. What Thomas heard was shouting and the ring of swords. He knelt with a thump on the kneeler set before the altar. Clasping his hands to still their shaking, he bowed his head. This then, had been his Camlann, early in his story rather than at the end. In two days he must circle back to his Mount Badon. *Lady have mercy.*

With a quivering exhalation Thomas lifted his face to the sculpture. A murmur of voices and footsteps might be angel's wings fluttering amongst the columns. Far above, muffled by stone, the bells in the great tower began to ring. Each stroke reverberated in his living bones as they no doubt reverberated in the dried bones upon which this building rose.

"It's time for the service," Maggie said. "Come on. You can do it."

"Yes." He would have expected his limbs to be numb, but no, whilst shaky they were warm, as though a ray of sun penetrated the shadows not only of the cathedral but of his heart.

He and Maggie walked up to the choir. Mick and Rose were saving seats for them amongst the superb carved stalls and as he sat down he smiled dazedly upon them. Still his chest seemed full, straining like the seed pods of the *Euonymus europeaus* in the garden at Temple Manor.

Above him the mellow stone pillars spread into soaring vaults that made the stone itself into an airy substance. The multitude of colored windows brightened. Rose whispered, "It's beautiful."

"Brilliant," Mick agreed.

Maggie interlaced her fingers with Thomas's, blessing him with her flesh, and he hung on for his life. For his death.

The bells ceased. His Anglican brethren in their robes—red for a martyr's feast—filed in, the shapes and colors of their faces showing their homes in Uganda and Indonesia and Farleigh Wallop. One intoned the prayer specific for this day, the day honoring England's greatest saint. "Almighty God, who didst suffer thy martyr to be cruelly slain by the swords of men and yet madest him in his death to become a sword of witness to the might of things unseen . . ."

Amen, Thomas thought.

The high clear voices of the boy's choir were finer than any he had ever heard, the words bits of light raining down upon his upturned face. "You have placed over his head, Lord, a crown of precious stone. You have given him the desires of his heart . . ." The crown of precious stone rose above him here and now. As for the desires of his heart . . . *Lamb of God, have mercy on me.*

Thomas met Maggie's anxious glance with a thin smile. Beyond her Mick and Rose sat close together, their faces enrapt, cleansed of every doubt. They'd asked him for a nuptial blessing before the battle to come—that much he could do, joyously.

The voices died away, leaving subtle resonances amongst the wraiths of incense. Another priest walked forward and made the sign of the Cross. "The grace of our Lord Jesus Christ, and the love of God, and the fellowship of the Holy Spirit, be with us all evermore."

Amen, thought Thomas. *Amen.*

Maggie, Mick, and Rose stayed with him until the congregation had dispersed. Then the young people, with sympathetic glances at his no doubt pale and fissured face, slipped away. "Come on," Maggie said, with a tug at Thomas's hand.

They walked past the place of martyrdom and down into the crypt, the oldest part of the cathedral. Massive pillars lifted their carved capitals to the low ceiling just as they had the night Thomas had cowered beneath them, the hounds of hell howling for his soul. But now the subterranean chamber was lit by electric lights and high windows.

They walked from the treasury with its glass doors along

the south ambulatory of the Lady Chapel, past the closed door of the Huguenots' Chapel to where, amidst a semi-circle of pillars, David's shrine had first been set and Henry II knelt to do penance. Then, circling back along the north ambulatory past St. Gabriel's chapel, they returned to Our Lady's altar in the center of the crypt.

And yet to Thomas the heart of the crypt, of the labyrinth, was beside and below the place of the martyrdom. Before the chapel of St. Mary Magdalene lay a grave, a cement slab topped by the bas-relief of a Celtic cross and encircled by an iron chain.

"When Henry VIII's commissioners came here," Thomas told Maggie, his voice husky, "the monks supposedly gave up the bones from the shrine. In reality, I am told, they disinterred one of their brethren and consigned his bones to the flames of the fanatics. Here is where David's relics lie, anonymously and modestly, as he lived. As he died."

"And now you're here to give him his due," Maggie murmured.

This building has known violence, Thomas thought, *and yet it is a place of supernal peace.* The silence of the crypt was broken only by the occasional footstep or murmur, like his own conscience walking quietly through the isolation of his soul. Chill welled from stone floor and a shiver wracked his body from crown to toe. He knelt before Mary Magdalene's altar, but his tongue stuck to the roof of his mouth.

Kneeling beside him, Maggie echoed his words to her, setting an example for him to follow. "Your pride is preventing you from surrendering to the grace of God which you have been trying your hardest to reject, and yet which is there for you even so."

The red light of the sanctuary lamp blurred and ran. The tears that puddled the frames of his eyeglasses and wet his cheeks were warm as spring rain. What was the song the young people sang, *From the world, the flesh, and the Devil make me anew . . .*

This, then, was God's plan for him, to live to return to this place and to beg for forgiveness, not with his now silent tongue but with his heart, so that he might at last put aside his pride and be reborn. The red light, the color of blood, of passion, of Mary Magdalene, the beloved of Christ, filled him to overflowing. His breath stopped. His heart stopped. Time stopped and the air itself crystallized. His chest cracked open and from it rose a bubble of joy that, bursting, carried away fear, regret, and the last rags of pride. Like a lark ascending, his soul soared up the columns and into the sky.

The beauty and joy of God's creation filled him, gardens and wildernesses, mountains and shore, beasts of field and forest, faces of humankind—he glimpsed circles of blessed souls unfolding in the rose of heaven—Joan, Alice, Esclarmonde—David, who had died so Thomas could live and come to this moment.

"You're glowing like a lamp." Maggie's voice was filled with both awe and love.

Yes, the vessel that was Thomas London brimmed with the fullness of time and the peace of God, whose plan, with its ironies of fate and fortune, had worked itself out. Enfolding Maggie's hand in his own, he nodded toward the cross. "God has absolved me. And at last, at long bitter last, I consent."

Chapter Forty-two

This is it, Maggie thought. *God help us.*

The night was cold and still, as though the world was holding its breath. Assuming the world had a breath to hold, and the awareness to hold it, an assumption Maggie was fully prepared to make, now. Now that they were eyeball to eyeball with Armageddon.

The floodlit towers of the cathedral were silhouetted against a sky like the polished marble of the Stone, broken only by stars as hard and bright as diamonds. The windows of the nave glowed in subtle traceries of color. Maggie walked on past, threading her way through the crowd that was headed toward the New Year's Eve concert. When she came to a gate in the wall east of the cathedral, she tapped her gloved knuckles on the wood. Creaking, the gate opened. In the dim light Mick's gray eyes looked like burnished steel. The willowy figure beside him was Rose. "Did Sean make it to the concert?" she asked.

"He's not about to commit himself to a concert until he's scoped out the party at the hotel," Maggie answered, "but I think he can find his way to the biggest building in town."

"I hope he comes," Rose said. "I mean, he's part of the Story."

Yes, he was part of the Story. Maggie looked past Rose into the walled garden. Flashlights gleamed. Several people were clustered around a bench. She recognized Ivan O'Connell, in his black cassock looking like a particularly debonair crow. "Ah, Maggie," he called. "Good to see you again."

In the far corner a second gate opened and shut behind two men carrying a crate. Manuel Llewellyn and Stavros Paleologos, with, presumably, the Stone, concealed in a tidy wooden box fitted out with brass handles. A similar box sitting on the bench was somewhat smaller, and no doubt held the Book. Thomas materialized from the darkness, his pale face gleaming like fine bone china. "Are we going in with all these people?" Maggie asked him.

"Their presence nearby is what matters. Moral support, as Jivan said." Thomas marshaled his troops, and within moments everyone was strolling onto the cathedral grounds. Thomas and Mick carried the Stone, Maggie and Rose the Book. They headed around to the north while everyone else took the route to the south, to the main door and the concert.

As they plunged into the dimly lit passageways Rose hesitated, forcing Maggie to stumble. "Sorry," the girl said, "but the shadows and the ruined arches remind me of the morning I found Vivian's body."

"When my dad phoned me," said Mick. "We've come a long way since then."

And yet, Maggie thought, *we've also returned to the beginning, several circuits closer to the center.*

"Here we are." Thomas stopped beside another massive door, and, balancing his load, opened it. They eased their burdens through. Maggie realized they were in the north transept of the crypt, beside Mary Magdalene's chapel and David's grave.

Setting the crates before Our Lady's altar, they took off their hats and gloves, but not their coats. Cold oozed from the stone floor and the deep British earth beneath. The murmur of voices from above rose and fell like the rhythm of the sea. Maggie felt as though she were standing on the shore of an island, between earth and water, air and fire. This, too, was *locus terribilis*. . . . No. Robin could tread here easily, for the relics were under threat. But as yet they were whole. As yet, she told herself, there was hope.

The occasional light bulb leaked only a few lumens. Mary Magdalene's red lamp glowed. From the two stairwells leading to the upper transepts spilled a warm but faint candle-glow. Only the votives burning in the Lady Chapel seemed bright, making a small but brilliant corona of white light against the surrounding shadow.

"Ivan took the precaution of reserving the front seats along the aisles, whence you can just see the steps, for our friends," Thomas said.

"At least no one's selling T-shirts," said Rose. "You know, 'I survived the Apocalypse.' "

"We've not survived it yet," Mick told her.

"Thanks," said Maggie. Was that a furtive scramble in the shadows? Church mice, maybe. Or cathedral mice, correspondingly huge. No wonder they'd seen a cat.

Thomas glanced over his shoulder. "Maggie, let's have a recce, shall we?" Without waiting for her reply he walked across the south ambulatory and tried the door of the Huguenot Chapel. It opened.

"That has an outside door, doesn't it?" she asked, catching up with him.

"Yes." He disappeared into the black nothingness of the room.

Maggie heard a second door open and shut. She called, "Why aren't you locking these doors?"

"Because," said Thomas, reappearing with a sardonic smile, "it is the hour of vespers."

Oh. Yes. He led the way eastward, peering into corners and behind screens, while Maggie kept as close as she could without tripping him up. The shadows that had been soft and evocative during the day were now opaque, filling aisle and alcove with sinister darkness. She kept expecting Robin or one of his bogeymen to leap out at them, but nothing moved except their own tenuous shades.

Beside the Jesus Chapel, Thomas stopped and looked down at her. She'd seen his face in daylight and darkness, in firelight and shadow. She'd seen him laughing and frowning. She'd seen him cold as marble and warm as wool. Now he was lit from within, like a candle burning down into its own wax and yet at the end throwing out the brightest, clearest light of all. He was fey—he was facing doom and destiny both. He wasn't hurried along by forces outside himself but was walking calmly and consciously forward.

He set his hand on her head. His voice plumbed the silence like a deep pool. "Your faith has made you whole, Magdalena. *Pax domini sic semper tecum.* Go with God, and with my love."

She felt tears starting in her eyes and blinked them away—that was the last thing he needed now, a weepy woman. His hand slipped down the side of her face and his mouth pressed hers, firm and warm. Then he was gone, and the dampness on her lips turned to ice. But the bargain was sealed. She was here, for God's sake. She was here for God's sake and Thomas's. Her nervous system felt like the fur on a startled cat's back looked, every fiber on the alert, scared, angry, elated.

Side by side they walked along the north ambulatory and around the corner into the Lady Chapel, where Mick and Rose were sitting in the front row of chairs. ". . . Hogmanay," he was saying. "Used to be I'd call round the neighbors just past midnight, playing the first foot."

"What?" Rose asked.

"A man with dark hair first across your doorstep in the

New Year brings good luck. Some old pagan custom, Thomas will be saying."

"I'm sure that it is," Thomas replied. "Rose, Mick—you asked for my blessing."

"A nuptial blessing," Rose explained to Maggie's elevated brows, "announcing our engagement." She took Mick's hand and together they knelt in front of Our Lady's altar.

Thomas stepped up. "Maggie? You are their witness."

"Rose . . ." The words clogged her throat—*what will your parents say—don't rush into anything—if you just want to sleep together why* . . . She smiled. *The right thing for the right reason.* "Go for it."

Thomas lifted his hand above the two bowed heads, light and dark. "Look O Lord, we beseech Thee, upon these Thy servants, that they who are joined together by Thy authority may be preserved by Thy Help. And may the blessing of Almighty God, the Father, Son, and Holy Spirit, descend upon you and remain with you always, amen."

"Amen," Maggie whispered.

"Amen," Rose and Mick said together. Sharing a look that was partly shy, partly triumphant, they got to their feet and traded necklaces, his mother's Celtic cross for her mother's miraculous medal.

A breath of fresh air rippled the flames of the votive candles, as though Our Lady herself sighed. Then Thomas said quietly, "We should be opening the boxes. It's gone eleven."

He swung back the hinged lids. With Mick, he lifted out the Stone and placed it on the gray carpet runner several feet from the altar. Maggie and Rose laid the Book on top, just contained by the Stone's four horns. The creamy suppleness of the vellum contrasted with the hard black stone. The colored patterns of the pages repeated the embroidered fruits and flowers of the altar cloth and the carving of the stone screen behind.

The Stone was the past, Maggie thought. The Book was the future. All they needed was the Cup, the present, because you always lived in the present, after all . . . Upstairs the audience fell silent. An organist began to play "Jesu, Joy of Man's Desiring."

Rose sang along, "Come with us, thou blessed Jesus." Her clear voice rose like a bubble of light. *If she was only the second soprano in her choir,* Maggie thought, *who was first? Beverly Sills?*

Mick looked at her like a pilgrim would look at a long-desired shrine. Thomas gazed into space. Much as she'd rather pace back and forth, Maggie sat down. The song ended and Rose's voice slipped away into breath and heartbeat. Then the organ began another melody and the voices of a full choir rose to heaven, ". . . when you look down on Magdalena, the flames of love you wake in her, make soft a heart once frozen." *Yes,* thought Maggie, even as she heard another scrape in the shadows.

Thomas said, "I was born and baptized on a Tuesday. I left Northampton after defying Henry on a Tuesday. My exile from England began and ended on Tuesdays. David accepted martyrdom on a Tuesday and his remains were translated to the new shrine on a Tuesday. It was a Tuesday when we found the Stone and dealt Robin a defeat. And my birthday, the solstice, fell this year on a Tuesday. The day named for the Norse Tiw, god of swords. I expected this day to be a Tuesday as well. But then I discovered that today would be—is—a Friday. Named for the goddess Freya, an avatar of the Lady. For when swords have gone at last to rust, she waits with Our Lady, at the center . . . What's that?"

All four of them swung around. With a soft pad of paws the

tiger cat ambled around the corner and rubbed its cheek against the Stone. Mick's eyes narrowed. "You've kin in Northumberland, have you? Friends amongst the sheep in Perthshire?"

The relics anointed, the cat sat down to wash her face. Rose extended her hand. "She might be a cat, you know. Kitty, kitty?" The cat graciously allowed herself to be petted.

Maggie blinked. The air was hazy. She smelled smoke. Is that what she kept hearing, a tourist's smoldering cigarette butt growing into a fire? Thomas's nostrils flared. Rose and the cat looked up. Mick said, "He'd not set the place on fire, would he? To flush us out, like?"

"I think not." Thomas turned in a slow circle. "Stop playing games, Robin. Show yourself!"

As though to his command, both doors, north and south, opened. From one side came Reginald Soulis and a white-haired lady—his mother, Maggie realized. The anti-Madonna, who'd taught her child very well indeed. From the other came ex-Inspector Mountjoy and Ellen Sparrow.

Maggie jerked to her feet. She, Mick, and Rose ditched their coats and formed a line beside Thomas. The cat dived beneath a chair.

Now what? Maggie waited to see a hundred more people walk in. She could have listed the ones she expected, religious leaders, politicians, terrorists. But Robin had summoned only four of his followers. Four of the people who mirrored his own lack of completion. Four people to carry him onto hallowed ground. *That was pride,* Maggie thought, *to think so few . . .* She glanced at Thomas's taut white face. Four knights had been more than enough to murder David's body and wound Thomas's soul. There were, after all, only four horsemen of the Apocalypse.

"The lions entering the arena," Mick muttered. Rose elbowed him.

Like schoolchildren the Soulises and Mountjoy jostled for precedence. Ellen hung back, shoulders hunched, hands hidden in the pockets of her coat. Her eyes were the huge, dark, hollow holes of an Oxfam poster child's.

The other three made Maggie feel underdressed. Reg was wearing a yellow power tie with his pin-striped suit. He might have been on his way to a business conference, except for the sledgehammer in his hand. Lydia wore a maroon suit and ruffled white blouse decorated with a gaudy emerald-green brooch. She held the olive wood box in her white-gloved hands, pinkie extended just so. Mother and son's eyes were cold, their noses raised as though they smelled something bad, their smiles thin slits of self-righteousness.

Mountjoy wore his dark police inspector's suit, right down to the spit-polished shoes. His eyes were narrowed as suspiciously as they had been the day Thomas and Maggie first met him, but his chin and cheekbones were sharper, as though he'd been sucked dry of everything but that fear of fear that was malice.

Upstairs the choir sang on, waves of words and music flowing across the hostile faces. *Vergine madre, figlia del tuo Figlia . . ."*

Lydia snorted. "Can't even sing properly in English, can they?"

And by those words of arrogant prejudice, Robin was called from the darkness at the far end of the crypt. He strolled down the aisle, dressed to kill in a three-piece suit and paisley tie. Had he been there all along, Maggie wondered, laughing as Thomas blessed them all? Or had he materialized out of sight of his true believers?

Mick eased his *sgian dubh* from beneath his sweater and

held it beside the seam of his jeans. The medal gleamed as his chest rose and fell. So did the blue cross against the gentle curve of Rose's breast. Maggie glanced down to make sure her knotwork cross was front and center on her red sweater. Time for the faithful to choose their faiths freely, with passion . . . Suddenly she was chilled to the bone with fear, wondering what hope they had.

Reg began, "You lot are heretics, you are. You need sorting out."

"It's folk like you, with your secret agendas, who cause all our problems," said Mountjoy.

Ellen stared at Robin. Robin's hooded eyes stared at Thomas. His pink tongue passed between his lips and they parted into a smug smile.

Thomas stood straight and tall. *All he needed,* Maggie thought, was the dented armor, the long sword held upright between his hands, the white tunic with the splayed red cross of the Templars. "Let him who is without sin cast the first stone."

"We're proper moral people," Lydia retorted. "It's our right to express our beliefs."

The music stopped. In the sudden silence the shifting of Mountjoy's and Reg's feet echoed against the low ceiling like the tread of a marching army. The cat resembled a hedgehog, all spiky fur and bright green eyes. The air was thick with the stench of overripe gardenias, expensive cologne, and no doubt equally expensive alcohol—so they'd started partying in advance. *Pride goeth before a fall,* Maggie thought wishfully.

"Blessed are the poor in spirit," sang the choir, "for the kingdom of heaven is theirs. Blessed are the gentle, for they shall inherit the land."

Reg considered the altar, the votive candles, the relics.

"Idolatry and superstition."

"Blessed are those who mourn, for they shall be consoled. Blessed are those who hunger and thirst for justice, for the justice of God shall be theirs. Blessed are the merciful, for mercy shall be shown unto them."

"It's up to us to restore public morality," Mountjoy said.

"Blessed are those who bring peace," sang the choir, "for they shall be called children of God."

Ellen swayed, caught herself, braced herself upright. She was clutching something in her pocket, Maggie saw. If Reg was carrying a sledgehammer to deal with the Stone and the Cup, Ellen probably had a butane lighter for the Book. And then Lydia would come out with broom and dustpan and sweep all the shards, all the ashes, into a bleak future.

Robin raised his arms, palms up. His voice was satin-cold. "Thomas, by your treachery you condemned yourself to my hands. I have held you for many years now, despite your occasional wriggle like a fish on a hook. Like that day at Sarum, when I let you think you had released yourself, the better to take you back tonight."

Rose and Mick stepped closer together, so that they were shoulder to shoulder. As much as Maggie wanted to throw herself in front of Thomas and shield him—sticks and stones may break my bones, but words can break my heart—she knew she couldn't protect him.

"Tonight," Robin went on, "your soul shall at last be damned."

"I think not," said Thomas. "My soul belongs to God."

"Does it? That's rich, when you betrayed him in this very place."

"You twist theology, as always," Thomas replied. "I never rejected my faith. I chose to ignore its teachings. I sinned in this very place, yes. I have done penance for it."

"Oh well, that's all right then. David's come back to life, has he?"

Thomas's jaw tightened.

"All these years you've buried your head in your faith, thinking God has forgiven your faithlessness. Thinking you know His will. And you accuse me of pride! Has it never occurred to you, Thomas, that God's judgment is betrayal in return?"

Thomas seemed to shrink. Maggie frowned, the persuasive voice sucking the strength from her body.

"If you had ever had the courage of your own worst nature you would have realized that your Lord was setting you up. But no. You went on, sweeping others along in your folly, until now. Now, at the cusp of time, the moment of destiny. Thomas, your pride has led you into the greatest folly of all, and your piety has brought you naught."

Robin made a sweeping gesture over the relics. Our Lady's candles guttered. "It's you who brought the Stone and the Cup from their hiding places. It's you who brought the Stone and the Book here. Why? Because you trusted what *she* told you? This is your penance, Thomas. The knowledge that God has betrayed you and delivered you and yours into my hands. I now have the three parts of the Grail. When the door opens on the hinge of eternity I shall destroy them. You have betrayed your Lord again, this time for all time. I have won. Thanks to you and your faith, that like you is utterly false." Robin's voice hissed the last word, and it slithered like a snake down Maggie's spine. That actually made sense, that Thomas was the one with the wrong end of the stick. With the blind faith.

The glow in Thomas's eyes, in his skin, guttered like the candlelight. Rose bent her head against Mick's shoulder. He sagged, the knife dangling uselessly at his side. The Soulises shared a self-satisfied nod with Mountjoy. Ellen looked hungry and yet nauseated.

"Submit to me now, so that your friends may survive to know my power. Accept that I and mine are your superiors, and you'll have peace. Place your hands in mine. Through me pay homage to my master, and he will care for you. You need never make choices again, for I shall lead you in the paths of righteousness for his name's sake."

Maggie choked on her despair. After Robin destroyed the relics the sun wouldn't die, or the moon fail, nothing so conspicuous. No, the world would go on, unsupported by stories, without hope. The proud and the greedy were the stronger after all, and their vindictiveness was rewarded.

"Thy will be done," Thomas whispered.

It was over. Maggie bowed down, beaten.

Chapter Forty-three

"*Thy* will." Slowly, painfully, Thomas gestured toward the statue of Mary and her son. He straightened. His face hardened and his eyes flashed. "If I risk everything here tonight, so do you," he said to Robin. "Your greatest power is in deceit. Your lies are all the more effective for being cunning perversions of the truth. But they are still lies."

Robin's expression curdled from smug to spiteful.

With a start, Maggie awoke from her evil dream, and followed Thomas's gesture toward the calm face of Our Lady. Of her statue, a symbol of faith. *Be it unto me according to thy word,* she repeated silently, and her heart swelled with emotion. She turned on Robin. "You're lying. You're really good at it, but you're still lying."

Rose and Mick shook themselves. "Yeah," said Rose. "You've told us enough lies already."

"We're not listening to you, not any more," Mick added.

Reg muttered, "Been brainwashed, I expect."

A shimmer began to gather in the air above the relics. Ellen slouched against a pillar, rubbing her hand across her face as though she could wipe it off. *Change a few words in Robin's little speech,* Maggie thought, *and it could have been her own confession, all her piety brought to nothing. Come on, Ellen, don't do this to yourself.*

The voices of the choir stirred the heavy air like a cool breeze. ". . . spare us, good Lord, spare thy people whom thou hast redeemed with thy most precious blood."

Maggie did a double-take. Sean stood at the foot of the

stairs, his hands hanging at his sides, his mouth gaping open. She thought of racing past him and grabbing Ivan or Stavros or someone. But more bodies wouldn't help. Beneath the chair, the cat's tail switched back and forth.

Reg hoisted his sledgehammer and Sean retreated partway up the steps. Ellen looked at Robin, her face utterly blank, inhuman. Robin circled the relics, each footfall echoing. "Do you have the time, Thomas?"

"It's getting on for midnight," Thomas answered.

This time Robin's smile was fierce and bright. A wave of his hand, and two of the votive candles winked out, trailing ghosts of smoke. Turning to his people, he ordered, "Get on with it."

Mountjoy started forward. Reg fell in beside him. Lydia followed, smiling. She probably would have thought an execution jolly good fun. Ellen, too, began to walk toward the relics. The others looked at her like they'd look at toilet paper stuck to their shoes. She didn't seem to see them. She moved like a zombie, her right hand deep in her pocket.

"Have a care," said Mountjoy, "this is a church."

"Not my church, it isn't," Reg retorted. Lydia shook the box tauntingly. The chalice rang.

Time to put my body and blood where my words are, Maggie thought, and braced herself. Mick raised his knife. Rose whispered, "Blessed Mother conceived without sin pray for us." The air itself shone, as though sunlight leaked into a dark room around a partly opened door.

"Move aside," Mountjoy ordered Thomas. "You're alone."

"We're not alone," said Thomas. "We are here with our friends, in the company of saints."

"I gird myself with the might of heaven," Mick said. "I gird myself with the power of God . . ."

"In all his names and all her forms throughout the history of human thought," Rose concluded.

All Maggie could think of was, "Now I lay me down to sleep."

Robin waved Lydia and the Cup to the side. Mountjoy seized Thomas's wrist and he pulled it away. Reg grabbed at Mick, only to fall back when he saw the knife. *If both men attacked Mick,* thought Maggie, *they wouldn't get nicked too badly before they wrestled him down—assuming he'd actually cut anyone . . .* Ellen screamed. The harsh, shrill cry echoed through the vaults and disappeared into the thunder of organ and choir. Robin turned, eyes glittering. "How dare you interrupt!"

She had a knife, a *sgian dubh*—probably the one Robin had used on her in Thomas's chapel. Calum's replica. The one Vivian had been holding as she died.

Sean ran back down the stairs. "Ellen, don't!"

"Lies! Every bleeding one of them, lies!" She lunged. The knife sliced Robin's sleeve. His face contorted into rage. She struck again. Sparks flew from the Stone. Mountjoy stepped toward her. She stabbed at him and missed.

Rose and Mick went after Ellen, Maggie close behind, her mind moving a heck of a lot faster than her body. What was the girl trying to do? Get revenge on Robin? She couldn't hurt him, could she? Was she trying to earn points by killing Thomas? Could she hurt him?

Now she could.

Ellen stabbed at Rose. Mick grabbed her arm. She wrenched herself away. She was striking out at everyone who had hurt her, Maggie realized. That was Robin's Story, wasn't it? Your inadequacy was always someone else's fault.

Ellen stabbed at herself and the knife blade bounced off her belt buckle. Maggie grabbed for her arm. She struck again at Robin. Again Mountjoy clutched at her. She shook him off. He sat down hard in the chair sheltering the cat. It scraped. The cat bristled and hissed.

Reg brandished the sledgehammer but didn't seem to know what to do with it—this wasn't what Robin told him would happen. Lydia edged around behind Robin, clutching the box to her bosom, her red mouth still smiling. Maggie and Thomas reached toward Ellen but only managed to shove each other aside.

Again Ellen turned the knife on herself. Okay, so she was blaming the right person this time. She ripped her jacket—there was blood on her shirt—no, it was the cut on her neck opened up—Mick, Rose, and Maggie closed in but she threatened them all, the knife flashing in every direction. Tears glistened on her sallow cheeks.

"Ellen," said Thomas, opening his arms, "the grace of God is with you. He wants you to live, and heal."

Sean danced back and forth like a prizefighter. "Ellen, let me help!"

"How touching," snarled Robin. "But all the likes of her can understand is strength." Stepping forward, he seized Ellen's forearm. She jerked and then dangled from his grasp like a rag doll, her breath sobbing.

Time stopped. Mick, Rose, and Sean stood petrified in attitudes of alarm. Thomas offered his embrace. The air shone in faint whorls of light. Maggie imagined Michelangelo's white-bearded God leaning forward, fingertip extended, ready to intervene in history, but His door was locked because the gatekeepers were scuffling.

Robin was turning Ellen's hand, the hand that held the knife so tightly its knuckles stood out hard and white. He was turning the knife back toward her chest—she'd already tried to stab herself, he was only helping her out—funny, she seemed to have changed her mind and was pushing him away.

Thomas extended his hand, trying to deflect the knife. *Don't,* Maggie screamed silently, but her body wouldn't move.

The infernal green glow of Robin's eyes swerved toward her. In them Maggie saw the future, how her warning, her push, saved Thomas from the descending knife. So what if it condemned Ellen to death, that was like putting a dumb animal to sleep, no great loss.

Together she and Thomas walked out of the cathedral. The events in the crypt faded into memory and vanished, because they'd made new memories to take their place. The world might be hopelessly dark, but they had each other, soul-mates. Nothing and no one else mattered.

Maggie's entire body spasmed. Thomas loved her, yes. It was a measure of his integrity that he'd told her the truth. But the larger truth was that he'd chosen God. The only way she could be unfaithful to him was by taking away his choice, now, at this moment.

She looked up into Thomas's face as she'd looked into it the night of her confession. She surrendered her love to his radiant true self, and stopped even trying to move. *God help me!*

Robin's gaze released her. He pushed the knife in Ellen's hand toward her own chest. She struggled, but he was strong. Thomas leaped forward, arms spread, his embrace encompassing not only Ellen, pitiful sinful humanity, but Robert the Devil himself, who was, after all, a poor excuse for a man.

Robin's hand holding Ellen's drove the blade into Thomas's chest. He gasped, his face going stark white. Maggie heard her own voice cry out in pain.

Rose emitted a strangled scream. Robin dropped Ellen. Ellen dropped the knife. Picking it up, Maggie seized

Thomas's arm. He touched the wound and looked at the blood smearing his fingertips, for once at a loss for words.

Someone was swearing. Mick? No, he was struck dumb. It was Reg or maybe Mountjoy, who still sat in the chair above the bundle of irate cat . . . No. It was Robin, his voice tearing into ragged ribbons. "You stupid cow! You've gone and done the one thing he wanted!"

"I never," Ellen wheezed, "I never . . ."

Sean waded in, pulling her back against his chest. "Fitzroy, you're full of crap. You did it, not her. We all saw you."

Maggie held the hot, hard little blade in her free hand. Beneath her other hand Thomas's arm, his mortal flesh, was perfectly steady. He stood straight and tall as ever despite the rip in his sweater and the blood spreading outward from it. She balanced on her own knife blade between hope and horror, telling herself that the knife was a little one, that it had bounced off one of his ribs and caused only a flesh wound. That maybe the shedding of his blood would be enough.

The choir fell silent. Thomas raised his hand with its red fingertips. Making the sign of the Cross over Ellen's head he said, "May the blessing of Almighty God, the Father, Son, and Holy Spirit, descend upon you and bring you peace."

Sniffing hideously, Ellen looked up. Something flickered in her eyes, some reflection of the light in Thomas's face, of the light winking and glimmering in the chapel. Far, far above, one ancient bell began to toll the passing of the old millennium and the beginning of the new. With a baleful backwards glare, Sean dragged Ellen several paces away.

Thomas tucked his handkerchief into his sweater as a makeshift bandage. He squeezed Maggie's hand and removed it from his arm. He nodded reassuringly at Mick and Rose and their taut faces eased. He turned toward Lydia.

"It's gone midnight. I'll have the Cup now, Mrs. Soulis."

She clutched the box to her chest. The bell tolled. Each note trembled in the air, in the stone vaults, in the earth beneath.

"You, Mountjoy," said Robin, his voice dripping contempt. "Reg, Lydia, stop your gawping, get a move on."

Rose and Mick started forward. Mountjoy leaped up to face them. His foot crushed the cat's tail. Yowling, she catapulted from beneath the chair, made a warp-speed figure eight between Lydia's pumps and her son's wingtips and disappeared into the depths of the crypt.

Lydia lost her balance and fell. Reg dropped the sledgehammer, which rang against the stone floor in leaden echo of the tolling bell, and grabbed for the box. So did Rose. The lid clattered to the floor.

Rose had it! Mountjoy jumped toward her and stopped, staring cross-eyed at Mick's *sgian dubh* a foot from his face.

Each stroke of the great bell drove the old millennium deeper into the past. Maggie felt each note in her skull, in her spine, in Thomas's body beside her. He was praying, his hands raised, his lips moving, Latin cadences and Gaelic measures repeating the rhythm of the bell.

If Robin had shouted, "Why am I surrounded by incompetent fools?" Maggie would have answered. But he saved his breath. His lips cramping into a scowl, he started forward, Reg at his heels. Lydia struggled to her feet.

Maggie looked from the self-righteous frowns closing in on them to the knife in her hand, sticky with Thomas's blood. Mick swung toward Robin, his knife raised. Robin raised his arm, shielding himself from the relic that had burned him at Holystone.

Mountjoy dived to the side, trying to outflank Mick. Reg moved at the same instant, around the other way. Maggie

446

jumped forward—too late, they'd knocked the box from Rose's hands—Mountjoy and Reg, Maggie and Rose juggled the box until it clattered to the floor and Rose was left holding the reliquary, a dazzling glow shining through her slender fingers.

Vicious, obscene words spewing from his lips, Robin struck. The crack of his open hand against Rose's face was shockingly loud. She stumbled sideways. The reliquary opened and the Cup flew from her hands.

"Amen," Thomas said.

No one moved as the Cup flew into the air, weightlessly, a feather on the breath of God. It hung, trembling to the repeated notes of the bell, and began to fall. *How art thou fallen from heaven, O Lucifer, son of the morning star* . . . No, the Cup was the brightest star of all time, the star of Bethlehem, shedding a glorious radiance across every upturned face, just and unjust alike.

The lid of the reliquary descended one way, and the base another, each lighting against an opposite horn of the Stone. And the Cup itself, a shallow clear glass vessel, landed gently as a dove in Thomas's outstretched, bloodstained hand.

Gracefully he went to his knees and placed the Cup on the Book. Its light penetrated vellum and stone both. The glimmer in the air coalesced around the three relics, so that they began to glow in colors that made the rainbow look drab.

Robin was shaking his hand—his palm was a nasty red. "Damn you all! Are there none amongst you who will rid me of this troublesome priest?"

No takers. If anything, Mountjoy and the Soulises were shrinking back. *Oh you of little faith,* Maggie thought. But then, fanaticism wasn't faith.

The bell stopped tolling and the last note hung shivering in mid air, sending waves of sound forward into the future.

Maggie wasn't breathing. No one was breathing. They were caught between one breath and the next, between one second and the next, between one millennium and the next. The millennium, which meant everything because they chose it to mean everything. She knelt beside Thomas, beside the Holy Grail and its supernal glow. Mick and Rose, too, went to their knees.

Robin shuddered in paroxysms of fury, cursing Thomas, cursing Mary, cursing Christ, cursing God himself, his voice harsh and ugly. Suddenly he was wearing a Norman tunic and his master's crown. It was too big for him, tilting lopsidedly across his forehead. Tiny flames licked along its rim, illuminating the empty setting.

Mountjoy's face registered nothing. Reg's eyes bulged. Lydia slumped down on chair and hid her face with her hands. Thomas reached out. "Kneel beside me, Robin. Kneel before your Creator, and together we'll confess our faults. Accept the infinite variety of his creation, and be healed."

"No!" Robin snarled. "Never!"

"Then, by your own words, you choose oblivion."

"No!" But Robin's cry unraveled, thinner and thinner, and broke on a growl of unrepentant rage. He fell. Crouching on all fours, his body was engulfed by the folds of the tunic, which flickered green and gold and then faded to gray.

All three relics were one. They glowed from within, brighter and brighter, so that Thomas's shadow, and Rose's and Mick's and her own, Maggie supposed, stretched across the floor.

Sean and Ellen were watching, their eyes shining in the multi-colored glow flowing out from the Grail and along the floor, so that each flagstone was outlined in light. It flowed up the pillars like the warmth of spring rising up the veins and leaves of trees.

The great bells of Canterbury began to peal, cascades of notes pouring down like spring rain. The voices of the choir were lifted in joy. *"Magnificat anima mea Dominum, et exultavit spiritus meus in Deo salutari meo . . ."* Maggie heard the words, the music, with her heart rather than her ears. "My soul doth magnify the Lord, and my spirit hath rejoiced in God my savior."

Beside her Thomas murmured, "He hath scattered the proud in the imagination of their hearts, he hath put down the mighty from their seat and exalted the humble and meek. He hath filled the hungry with good things, and the rich he hath sent empty away."

The floor, the columns, the arches of the ceiling were made of light, bright transparent gauze, not stone. All shadows were gone. All light and dark were as one. For all Maggie knew the brilliance was shooting out of the tops of the three towers like Roman candles, and yet the choir kept singing and the organ kept playing. But the victory didn't have to be proclaimed from the rooftops.

Robin's crouching shape bulged and twisted and was suddenly swept into the air, caught up by another shape formed of nothing but light. Maggie gasped—an archangel, ancient of days, so bright and beautiful she shaded her eyes with her hand. Michael? Gabriel? Or Lucifer, in the image of what he lost when he refused the grace of God?

The shape that was Robin shrank, twisted, and darkened. Above him the great wings shriveled and the hands withered away. He fell from the heights of heaven. When his body hit the glowing stones of the floor it shattered into bits of ash and charcoal, emitting a sulfurous stink.

Each burned bit winked out with a tiny snap and a curl of smoke. Only the crown remained, rolling across the floor until it clanged against the base of Our Lady's altar. Maggie's eyes were watering—from the brilliance, the emotion, both—but she swore Mary and child moved, looking down sorrowfully at the loss beyond redemption of a human soul.

"Did you see that?" whispered Rose.

"Oh aye," Mick returned. "That I did."

Mountjoy sank down onto his haunches. Reg collapsed at his mother's feet, his stunned face sagging to his chest. Still Lydia refused to look.

Thomas knelt quietly, one tear, a drop of light, hanging on his cheek. The crown spun on the floor before him, its empty setting upward. Maggie stared as it, too, glowed white-hot. It sagged out of shape, melted, and as liquid light flowed in between the stones of the floor and disappeared.

She blinked. The light was gone. The floor and the pillars and the vaulted ceiling were returned to—well, no, not ordinary stone. The Stone and the Cup, too, had disappeared. Back to Tobar nan Bride, probably, and Glastonbury Tor. Or perhaps they'd been drawn back into the Dreamtime, there to be made new for a new age, so that the Story could go on.

Maggie looked around. She and Thomas, Mick and Rose knelt in front of Our Lady's altar, the Lindisfarne Gospels sitting on the floor before them. A quick breeze turned its heavy pages and then stilled. The future was still before them, as it had been since the depths of time.

Maggie was holding Ellen's—Calum's—little knife. Mick was tucking his, the original, into its sheath. The olive wood box lay crushed beside the empty crates. Reg Soulis was a pile of misery on the floor. Mountjoy moaned softly. Lydia Soulis rocked slowly back and forth, her hands fists against her face. "It was all a trick. It didn't happen. Robin said it, I believe it, and that's that." Ellen clutched Sean. He looked like he'd been hit by a truck, but he held onto her.

The choir ended the hymn but the organ kept on playing

and the bells kept on pealing. How many more of Robin's followers had seen the light and rejected it? Maggie wondered. How many would go on gnawing the dry bones of their prejudices, afraid to look beyond their own egos?

Mick and Rose levered each other up. With a wary glance at Ellen he returned his *sgian dubh* to his waistband.

Maggie, too, stood up. But Thomas stayed on his knees, his eyes fixed on the altar and the statue above it. He'd survived. He needed to work through that. The best thing she could do was leave him alone—maybe, just maybe, she'd done the right thing and was going to be rewarded for it.

Chapter Forty-four

Ivan O'Connell walked down the stairs from the nave, followed by Anna Stern and Inspector Gupta. All three shared the same expression, curiosity edging into caution and then, seeing Thomas on his knees, alarm.

Maggie looked down at the top of his head. He still hadn't moved. She touched his shoulder. "Thomas?"

He whispered, "Into thy hands, O Lord, I commend my spirit," and slumped forward onto the floor.

He lay in the same pose, face down, arms outspread, as he'd lain the night Maggie had peeped into his chapel. The day she'd discovered who he was. The day she'd begun loving him. *Oh God!* She dropped the knife. With the help of the others she turned him over and lifted his head into her lap. *Oh God!*

His sweater was soaked in blood. His glasses were bent, one lens scratched. Gently Maggie pulled them from his face. Barely two weeks ago they'd been smudged by her own warm skin. And she'd stood here flattering herself she'd done the right thing while he bled to death at her feet.

Each inhalation was long and rasping, drawn from far beyond his mortal body. His burned-over eyes were a dark amber-gold, rich and rare. Maggie bent over him, trying to dive into his gaze, but its depths eluded her.

She'd dreaded this moment, she'd had nightmares about it, she'd thought it wasn't going to happen after all and yet here it was. Her heart melted like the brass crown and trickled hotly through her body. "Thomas, no."

He smiled. His right hand twitched, as though in his own extremity he blessed her again, and fell heavily so that his fingertips just touched the Book. "Yes," he said. A shudder ran through his body and his eyes dulled, emptied of his spirit, of his soul, of his long mortal life.

Tears spilled down Maggie's face. Thomas's head was heavy in her lap, a dead weight. She set her trembling fingertips on his eyes and closed their lids so he could rest at last. A sob burst from her chest. She was going crazy. She couldn't handle this.

She thought, " 'Yet some men say in many parts of England that King Arthur is not dead, but had by the will of our Lord Jesu into another place.' " But Thomas wasn't going to come back with, "Thomas Malory."

Someone was holding her—oh, it was Mick on one side and Anna on the other. Gupta was crouching beside her, his black eyes brimming. Beyond him Rose was crying, too. Mick reached out with his other hand and took hers. O'Connell picked up the Book and held it against his chest like a shield.

Maggie's hands were covered in blood. His precious blood, the blood of the martyr. Of St. Thomas Becket, not England's but Britain's greatest saint. Although she couldn't see the crown of gold shining on his brow, she knew it was there. It wasn't her reward that mattered, but his.

His face was as serene as the face of the Lady, who had been queen of heaven for millennia before Arthur rode to battle with Our Lady's image on his shield. Beyond the Word, She had said, beyond the Blood, lay silence.

The music of the organ stopped. The bells stopped pealing. In the hollow hush one soprano voice sang, "The Lord bless you and keep you, the Lord make his face to shine upon you and be gracious unto you, the Lord lift up the light of his countenance upon you and give you peace."

"Amen," said many voices. The vaults echoed with the whispered word.

"What happened?" O'Connell asked shakily.

"Robin Fitzroy was trying to stab Ellen and Thomas intervened." Maggie didn't have to add that by corrupting Ellen, Robin had defeated himself. Thomas was no doubt fully appreciative of the irony.

"Fitzroy's legged it, has he?" asked Gupta.

"We won't be seeing him around any more, no," Maggie answered.

Mick said, "But his power's been broken."

"Robin's power has been broken. I have the awful feeling, though, that what we've won tonight is the chance to keep on struggling against his relatives. To choose to set a good example . . ." Maggie's voice broke.

Anna's intelligent eyes met hers. "It isn't incumbent on you to finish the task, but you are not free from beginning it."

"Oh yes," she agreed in a whisper. "Yes."

Ellen crept up, leaning heavily on Sean. Her face looked like a nuclear wasteland. And yet the light of the relics lingered, a furtive reflection in her eyes. "I never meant it."

"Yes you did," Maggie told her. "When you gave yourself to Robin you chose to mean it."

"I don't mean it any more, do I?"

Maggie pulled Thomas's blood-soaked handkerchief from inside his sweater. She looked from it to the bloody wound on Ellen's neck, and the one on her hand that lay open and helpless in Sean's, and could only say, "Get help, Ellen."

"Counselors," said Sean. "Prozac."

Gulping down something between a scream and a hysterical laugh, Maggie laid Thomas's head upon the stone floor and folded his hands on his chest. Between them she placed the tiny knife—now it was a relic too. Beside it she left the bundled handkerchief, looking like a full-blown red rose.

She wondered whether his body would disintegrate into dust or be assumed into heaven or glow with light as the relics had glowed . . . No, he'd remain as modest in death as he was in life, and return quietly to the earth whence he came so many years ago. Her nostrils filled with a fresh, clean scent. Frankincense, myrrh, spring flowers and the earth after a rain. The odor of sanctity. She breathed in deeply, and the pain began to ebb from her limbs. *Set me as a seal upon thy heart, for love is as strong as death.*

O'Connell inhaled. His already shocked eyes widened even further. "Who was he? What was he?"

"A saint," Maggie said, "leading us by example. A light so powerful it lifted all our souls."

Anna pressed her shoulder. "You go on, I'll take care of Ellen and Sean."

Mick helped Maggie to stand up. Rose got her coat and held it for her. She slipped her rust-red hands through the sleeves.

Clearing his throat, Gupta turned to the deflated balloon that was Reg. "Reginald Soulis, I charge you with the murder of Calum Dewar."

"Eh?" asked Mick.

"Amongst the crime scene evidence Mountjoy here collected was a bit of polished stone with your father's blood on one end and Reg's fingerprints on the other. Taken with Felton's testimony . . ."

Dully Reg looked up at Gupta's mahogany complexion, which made his own doughy pallor look defective. "I was just standing up for my beliefs."

Mick leaned his face against Rose's hair. Gupta began to caution Reg. Lydia stared blankly while Mountjoy sank his face into his hands. O'Connell considered Thomas's body, abandoned like the chrysalis of a butterfly, and shook his head. "There'll be an inquiry, I expect."

Let the police investigate, Maggie thought. Let the church come to whatever conclusion it wished. Faith had nothing to fear from rational thought.

The bells began to peal again, joyful and triumphant, notes cascading from heaven to earth while the angels sang— no, it was the choir, their voices flourished in the *Te Deum*. The cat sat before Mary Magdalene's altar, paws primly together, head cocked to the side, eyes glowing green. Maggie nodded her thanks and, by placing one foot before the other, walked away.

With Mick and Rose on either side, she went up the stairs into the northwest transept, past the Altar of the Sword's Point, out the heavy wooden door, and into the cloister. Here the peal of the bells was louder, each rich, full note falling into the night and spreading outward like ripples in a pool.

They went on around to the lawn, where the air was crystal cold and clean. People stood in knots, upturned eyes shining . . . *Oh!*

The sky was no longer black. It shimmered with light, rays, screens, crowns, the colors flowing with the pealing of the bells. *The light of the relics really had shot up into the sky,* Maggie thought. The Aurora Borealis was pouring its luminescence down the northern skies just as it had in December of 1170, when the body of another saint lay before the altar of Canterbury.

Now it was January of 2001. "Well then," Mick said huskily, "heaven will be having good luck for a thousand years to come—the first man past the pearly gates the morn had dark hair."

No, Maggie thought, *I'm not going crazy.* She'd never felt more sane. Drained, shaky, grief-stricken, joyful, but sane.

The last two months hadn't been a dream. She'd been asleep all her life and now was awake.

Robin was gone, the relics were gone, Thomas was—no, he wasn't gone, he was with her always. "So is the Story," she said aloud.

"A romance," said Rose.

"An epic," Mick offered.

"Tragedy."

"Myth."

"All of it," said Maggie, "true if not real. All of it real, if not true. Written small and personal, affecting all existence."

"You sound just like him," Rose said.

Maggie smiled even as the tears ran down her face like warm kisses. The aurora filled the sky with light. The bells pealed. And she knew that while it might be hours yet before the dawn, the dawn would come.

About the Author

Lillian Stewart Carl has published multiple novels and multiple short stories in multiple genres. Her novels blend mystery, romance, and fantasy, have plots based on history and archaeology, and often feature paranormal themes. She enjoys exploring the way the past lingers on in the present, especially in the British Isles, where she's visited many times.

Lucifer's Crown is her eleventh novel. All the others are in print, and one is available in audio. Many of her novels and short stories are available in electronic form from www.fictionwise.com.

Lillian has lived for many years in North Texas, in a book-lined cloister cleverly disguised as a tract house. She is a member of The Author's Guild, Novelists Inc., Science Fiction Writers of America, and Sisters in Crime. Her web site is http://www.lillianstewartcarl.com.